Praise for *Digging to Indochina*

"An always interesting, authentic story about the next generation, the children of Vietnam veterans—children who dig, not to China, but to Indochina. A good solid read."

—Grace Paley, author of *The Little Disturbances of Man,*
Enormous Changes at the Last Minute, and *Later the Same Day*

"Digging is an apt metaphor for Connie Biewald's writing, which probes and sifts the buried storage vaults of family relationships with an archaeologist's precision. Her work will appeal to those readers who love the fiction of Anne Tyler and Carol Shields."

—Lois Lowry, author of Newbery Medal Award-winning books,
Number the Stars and *The Giver*

"This is realism at its finest—sharp, poignant, with plenty of redemptive moments but no magical solutions. Biewald's characters have to scrape and struggle for every scrap of luck. They dangle love in front of each other and then snatch it away …. The characters move and grow and, ultimately, show us the kind of people they could have been long ago, if grief hadn't buried them. A finely crafted novel."

—Chris Abouzeid, author of *Anatopsis*

DIGGING TO INDOCHINA

Also by Connie Biewald

Bread and Salt

Roses Take Practice

DIGGING TO INDOCHINA

A Novel

Connie Biewald

iUniverse Star
New York Lincoln Shanghai

Digging to Indochina
A Novel

iUniverse Star
an iUniverse, Inc. imprint

iUniverse books may be ordered through booksellers or by contacting:

iUniverse
2021 Pine Lake Road, Suite 100
Lincoln, NE 68512
www.iuniverse.com
1-800-Authors (1-800-288-4677)

ISBN-13: 978-1-58348-546-0 (pbk)
ISBN-13: 978-0-595-67728-3 (cloth)
ISBN-13: 978-0-595-83959-9 (ebk)
ISBN-10: 1-58348-546-5 (pbk)
ISBN-10: 0-595-67728-2 (cloth)
ISBN-10: 0-595-83959-2 (ebk)

Printed in the United States of America

All of us are better when we are loved.

Alistair MacLeod

CHAPTER 1

Bryan's sister, Ivy, ran off the day after their father's birthday.

John MacKenzie would have been forty-six years old. Every year since his death, at Ivy's command, because their mother had stopped baking, Bryan made a birthday cake from their grandmother's famous marble pound cake recipe. He had no memory of eating the cake when John MacKenzie was alive, but Ivy assured him it was their father's favorite and they'd all loved it. She showed Bryan photographic proof—their mother, Carol, fork poised above her slice; Ivy herself pushing a generous chunk toward their father's laughing mouth; Bryan in his high chair, fists full of soggy crumbs, chin and cheeks plastered with chocolate.

Bryan would always wonder how his cake measured up. He never minded Ivy telling him to make it. But always, after breaking the third or fourth egg (the recipe called for a dozen), he'd feel the beginning of a sharp tightening in his stomach, and the crack of eggshell merged with the sound of the first eggs he'd learned to crack, his mother's hands over his, the satisfying slip of clean egg into the bowl, two broken pieces of shell whole in his small hands, his mother's body warm against his back as he stood on a kitchen chair, dishtowel an impromptu apron clothespinned at his neck, proud little boy unaware of what the fifteen-year-old Bryan knew came next—his father, swooping down, yanking at the towel; the snap of the clothespin shooting across the kitchen; the crunch of eggshell in suddenly clenched fists; the clatter of the overturned chair; the sputtering of a small heart as Johnny laughed a scary laugh and tossed him too high in the air.

Bryan didn't remember eating the cake, but he remembered trying to make sense of his father's words: "No son of mine wears an apron. You turning him into a pussy? Get Ivy in here to help with the cooking."

Carol had shouted back, reached for their son, picked up the chair. She must have won the argument because Bryan kept on in the kitchen. He could break an egg with one hand and knew his dead grandmother's recipe by heart.

All the old photos showed happy people. The only record of the raging fights between their parents was the mutable one of memory. Ivy and Bryan carried their own versions of those short years as a family of four, more distinct than mere variations on a recipe, more like the difference between chocolate and vanilla.

This year, when Ivy demanded cake their mother said, "Enough is enough! Your father's been dead ten years."

"Not to me!" Ivy yelled back before slamming out of the house.

"She makes him out to be a saint," Carol had muttered. Bryan wanted to say something, but put the flour away instead. Ivy and his mother weren't fighting about cake, but about Carol's date with Neal Richards. For weeks Carol had been raving over the flowers Neal sent her at work. Then the excited twitter when the phone rang. You'd think she was talking about Robert Redford, her favorite movie star, not a middle-aged high school shop teacher with a fringe of hair, a big belly, and glasses thicker than Bryan's. Anyway, his mother could have saved her breath—Ivy didn't understand "enough." Add her loud mouth and you've got it, the recipe for his sister. Ivy. Poison Ivy, the neighborhood kids used to tease.

A day later Ivy was gone with Gil Thompson, a guy with rotten teeth and a worse temper. She'd talked about getting out of Rivertown for so long no one heard her anymore, like you get used to the sound of traffic on a busy street and don't notice until it stops. She left behind a quiet so heavy it pressed Carol's head to her folded arms on the kitchen table, beside the untouched macaroni and cheese Bryan had made. From scratch, he never used a mix.

The police said they couldn't do anything—Ivy hadn't been gone long enough and besides, did Carol have any idea how many seventeen-year-old girls were out there not wanting to be found? Bryan, glad to hear about those other girls, glad Ivy wasn't alone as she wandered through vast country searching for who knew what with a creep she just met, looked at his mother slumped in her chair and felt the kitchen walls tighten around him.

"We don't have any idea who this guy is? Do we?" His mother's eyes begged.

Bryan had only seen Gil once, at the mall, arm around Ivy like he owned her, Ivy leaning into him like there was nowhere else she'd rather be. He was tall with big shoulders, beaklike nose, a dark tooth in front, tattoos across his knuckles—letters Bryan couldn't make out, and piercing blue eyes so bright it hurt when he looked at you.

"Why did I ever let her hang around that pool hall?" Carol moaned. Bryan knew trying to keep Ivy from Rivertown Billiards would be like trying to keep bread dough on a radiator from rising.

Ivy's note lay on the edge of the table. "Don't look for me," it said. "I've got to get out of here before I go crazy. Gil left his stuff in the basement. Don't worry, Mom. It's all neatly packed in one small box. I know exactly what I'm doing. I'll be fine. I'll send a postcard." No signature.

She'd wanted to leave since she was seven, that summer the concrete slab fell on their dad. He'd been working on the new high school, the one Bryan went to now. Ivy hated every minute she spent inside those cement walls. "How can any asshole expect me to learn in the building that killed my father?" She yelled at Bryan for liking school, for not being as mad as she was.

That terrible summer their dad lay in a coma, Grandma Harrington came from Pennsylvania and wedged herself in a lawn chair, her feet in the plastic pool Bryan had outgrown, peering at Ivy and him over *The Weekly World News* as Ivy told Bryan to dig faster, work harder, on their tunnel to Indochina. Other kids dug to China, but Ivy wanted to dig to Vietnam. She said Indochina was another word for it. She wanted to see where their father had fought in the war before they were even born, before he even knew their mother. Johnny had told Ivy he couldn't talk about it. You had to have been there. So, of course, she wanted to go. Bryan didn't, but he was the lion to her lion tamer, student to her teacher, customer to her waitress, patient to her doctor, slave to her master. She said dig, he dug. He knew the core of the earth burned with molten rock. He didn't want to go anywhere, but he was more afraid of Ivy's temper than of burning or being miles away from home. After the funeral, when Grandma left and the ground finally froze, Ivy gave up. Bryan was glad.

That summer would have been different if Grandma MacKenzie, the supposedly kinder grandmother, the one with the cake recipe, the one whose house they lived in, had been alive to take care of them instead. When neighbors murmured what a blessing it was she hadn't lived to see her only child die so young, seven-year-old Ivy narrowed her eyes at them and hissed words that made them flinch. Bryan couldn't remember the words exactly, but he could picture the ladies' shocked expressions and just thinking about their gentle powdered faces, felt his stomach clutch the way it did whenever his sister used her power on a grown up. She'd probably made some caustic remark about Grandma IJ MacKenzie dying just before she was born and never knowing Bryan or Ivy either.

The refrigerator hummed. His mother whimpered. He had to get out of the house full of Ivy's absence, but he couldn't leave his mother alone, waiting for the phone to ring. He slapped his harmonica against his thigh like he did whenever he was nervous, paced the kitchen, the hallway, ending up with no jacket or gloves outside on the cold front porch. The houses along both sides of the deserted street glowed in the early winter dark. Families would be sitting together around tables eating dinner or in their living rooms watching TV, or maybe they were scattered throughout their houses—someone in the bedroom doing homework, someone loading the dishwasher, someone else chatting on the phone. They could yell a sister's name, and if she didn't answer it only meant her music was on too loud or the bath water was running.

"I've got to get warm, Bryan," Ivy had said, days before she actually left. "I want to see some things, manatees, flamingos. Coconuts and oranges growing on trees." She'd squeezed his shoulder. "Besides, I'm sick of that bitch trying to run my life." Bryan continued grating cheese, not looking at her.

He watched the father across the street carry a bag of groceries into the house. Bryan blew on his fingers and stomped his feet wondering if he could have, should have, done something to stop his sister. He didn't blame her for wanting to leave. If he had the chance, he'd go to Hollywood. He'd have a cooking show. He'd teach people how to make meals in one pot out of whatever they had in their cupboards and refrigerators. "Kitchen Alchemy," he'd call it. He'd show up at people's houses with his camera crew. "Hi, I'm Bryan MacKenzie, kitchen alchemist. I'm here to make dinner for YOU." He'd push past the astonished homeowner. The camera would follow him into the kitchen and focus on the inside of the refrigerator. He'd make gourmet meals out of limp celery, eggs, parmesan cheese. People would beg him to knock on their doors.

As the battered green Plymouth sped along I-95, Ivy glimpsed the official sign "Welcome to Virginia." Only three rides from Rivertown, Connecticut, and already in the south. They'd be in Florida sooner than she'd expected—palm trees, flamingos, white sand beaches, Disneyworld. Gil had told her with his luck and her looks hitchhiking would be as fast as driving a car of their own and a lot cheaper. She leaned away from the stranger at the wheel into lucky Gil. He handed her the fifth of Jack Daniels. She took a slug, shivered, and wiped her mouth with the back of her hand.

"So then I tell him, get your hands off my old lady …" Gil squeezed Ivy's shoulder, staring at the driver, gauging his audience. Rides lasted longer if the driver shared the bourbon and laughed at Gil's stories. This one, Rich he'd said his name was—had refused a drink at first. At the end of Gil's long tale of handing out the peanut butter cups and cans of tuna he and his brother had stolen from an open delivery truck in the Stop and Shop parking lot, and a "Watsa matter, you too good to drink with me, man?" Rich had changed his mind.

Rich lifted the bottle from Ivy's hands, his fingers skimming hers. Licking his mustache, he winked. She rubbed Gil's thigh and stared out the window. Glaring signs announced fast food places, motels, gas stations near the exits. Between them stretched darkness that streetlights and neon couldn't penetrate.

"So this silver cigarette lighter, monogrammed, looked like it belonged to a fucking duke or lord or something, don't know what the hell it was doing under a bench on the New Haven green, waiting for me I guess. People don't notice things, rushing around the way they do. Not me. I take my time. I know what's important, don't I baby? I sit on benches. I notice things."

Ivy had heard this story more than a few times. She could tell it herself with all of Gil's inflections and dramatic pauses and bluster—how the lighter hadn't worked and Gil opened it to see if it needed fluid or what, and found two tabs of acid and a hundred dollar bill hidden inside. Rich chuckled as Gil boasted about his luck. Most of the stories she'd heard in the days since she'd gone with him to his room over the Capital Theater, after beating him three games straight at Curly's pool hall, had Gil's luck as a main theme. The sadder, poignant stories interested her more, the ones about his mother leaving him and his brother alone in the house for days with only a box of Cheerios to eat while she did who knows what, his string of foster homes, the art teacher he had in junior high who gave him lunch money and told him he had talent, the list of cats he adopted wherever he settled long enough—Fluffy, Serena, Bill, Flatface. Those stories he whispered in the dark and only told once.

"You know," Gil finished the story with one of his favorite lines and a satisfied chuckle. "Some people say the body is a temple, but they've got it all wrong. I call it nature's own amusement park."

"Look," said Rich. "I'll take you further tomorrow. Let's stop for tonight. I'm shitfaced. The road's wobblin' like a son of a bitch. I'll spring for the room."

"I can drive." Gil banged the dashboard.

Rich laughed. "You're in worse shape than I am."

"Yeah, but you said before you don't usually drink. I can hold my liquor. What you don't realize," Gil leaned across Ivy, "is that I drive better when I'm loaded."

Rich snorted. "That's what we all think but some of us know better."

"Ask her!" Gil waved the bottle. Ivy pulled her head into her shoulders like a turtle. "Honey, you know, I drive better when I'm drunk. Tell him."

Curly had tried to stop her, offered to close the pool hall early, give her a ride. She'd ignored him and followed Gil into the deserted parking lot. "Where's your car?" she'd asked.

"We're walking," he said. "It's not far." His hand burned hot as he stroked the length of her finger with his thumb. He brought it to his lips, took it between his teeth, staring into her eyes. She stopped laughing and swallowed. Something was finally happening to her. Car or no car, she'd found a way to go somewhere.

"Tell the man what a good driver I am." Gil tickled her ear with his tongue. "Tell him, baby."

Why not? It could be true.

"You should see him." Ivy shrugged. "He's something."

Rich laughed. "Nah, you all want to keep going, you can. I gotta stop." He pulled into the deserted parking lot of the Rainbow's End Motel. The headlights shone on crumbling blue stucco and the trunk of a scraggly tree.

"If you're still out here in the mornin', I'll pick you up. Or you're welcome to share the room. Don't cost much more for two beds." Rich turned the key, silencing the engine. Gil's ragged, steady breathing filled the car. He might be sleeping. Ivy hoped he wasn't passed out, wasn't sure she knew the difference. Tendons in his neck quivered as he snored. Love bites she'd given him in the windy back of a pickup truck outside of Philadelphia marked his throat. She wanted to hide them from Rich.

"I don't think you're going much further tonight unless you ditch this guy," Rich leaned back against his door, folded his arms, and grinned at Ivy. "Or carry him."

If it hadn't been so cold, Bryan would've sat on the porch until a light went on in his mother's bedroom window. He began to worry about frostbite, his toes rotting and falling off. He could see the doctor asking how it happened and answering, "My sister ran away and I was afraid to go into my house."

His fingers refused to grip the door knob. He had to use both hands, then push with his shoulder. Light still shone from the kitchen. Dishes rattled.

His mother turned at the squeak of his shoes on the linoleum. Flour streaked the front of the skirt she'd put on that morning for work, one of the straight, dark ones Ivy made fun of but Bryan liked. Morning was a lifetime ago.

She stared, her eyes too wide, too bright. "Good, you're back. Just in time. Where do you keep the shortening? It's been so long since I've cooked. My own kitchen and I don't know." She'd rolled up the sleeves of her white blouse, her hands and arms dusty with flour.

"Shortening's down there." He pointed to the corner cupboard. She squatted to peer into it. A run near the heel of her nylons zipped up her calf like a live thing. Carol MacKenzie did not wear ruined stockings, even at home, even for a moment. She hugged the Crisco can and laughed.

"What's the matter? You look like you've seen a ghost. It's not that strange, is it? Your mother in the kitchen, cooking?" Bryan shook his head. "Good." She faced the counter, humming a song he didn't recognize, measuring shortening.

"What are you making?" he asked. She didn't answer. He stepped closer. "I said, what are you making?"

"Oh." Everything stopped, her humming, her hands. She studied the bowl. "A pie, Bryan. I'm making an apple pie. Won't that be nice? A pie."

He nodded. His fingers and feet stung as they warmed.

She began to cut the shortening into the flour. "Your father, he never liked apple pie, why ruin a good apple, he'd say, but he's not here, is he? Your sister wouldn't eat it either, copying him, like everything else. Daddy, Daddy, Daddy, that's how it always is with her. He lived at the pool hall. She lives at the pool hall. Makes sense, really. What he does, she does. They leave." She spun around waving the knife with clumps of greasy flour stuck to it. "When are you leaving?"

"Mom." He stared at the phone on the far wall of the kitchen, praying it would ring. If he thought hard enough he could reach Ivy telepathically, she'd call collect, he'd accept the charges, she'd tell him what to do.

"He leaves. Ivy leaves. Surprised it took her this long."

"Mom," Bryan said, "he didn't leave. He died."

Her eyes narrowed. "What's the difference?"

He started shouting. "What are you talking about? There's a huge difference. He's dead. He didn't die on purpose. And he can't come back. Ivy's alive. We'll see her again."

"Don't kid yourself." Carol squeezed her head between her hands. The knife clattered to the floor. "She's gone. What are we going to do?" Her body shook.

Bryan wished he had the nerve to call Neal Richards, but he'd only met him for the first time the day before.

"It's okay. It's okay. She's coming back. You know Ivy." The more he said, the greater his chances of hitting on the right words. "She wouldn't leave us. She wanted a vacation is all."

Carol bent and picked up the knife. "I'm okay," she said, standing up.

He wanted to believe her.

"No, really." She held her hand, like a police officer stopping traffic. "I'm sorry Bryan," she said. "I'm okay. It's just …" She forced a smile, her face streaked with flour and tears. "I am about to make an apple pie. Are you going to help or just stand there?"

He swallowed. "I'll help." The words squeezed past the tight place in his throat. Standing beside his mother at the counter he could see the line of pale scalp where the part ran through her light hair.

She cut the shortening with the knife. Bryan's mother didn't do that, use silverware off the floor. His stomach began to ache.

She mixed the dough with her hands, squeezing it like it was hard clay. Pie crust toughens the more it's handled. She'd taught him that. He wanted to shout, "Stop!" Instead he went to the refrigerator and got the plastic bag of apples. Carol took one to work each day in her lunch. He pulled a paring knife from the rack.

She held the lump of pie crust in her hands. They stared into it, as if it were a crystal ball. "We have everything we need," she said. "Apples, cinnamon, sugar. We'll bake it. And then we'll eat it, warm." She slid the rolling pin from a drawer.

Bryan peeled the first apple, round and round, one long curling strip of red. He held it for a moment, dangling it like a loose spring, before dropping it into the sink. She glanced at him, almost smiled, then laid a rounded piece of crust in the pie plate. She flattened the second ball of dough under the rolling pin. Bryan peeled another apple. He remembered standing on a stool with her behind him, hands over his, one on the knife handle, one rotating the apple, over and over until he could do it himself.

When he finished slicing apples into the pie, sprinkling them with cinnamon and sugar, she tucked the top crust over them like babies under a quilt.

"There." She gave the edge of the crust one last pinch and stepped back, admiring their work. "I guess I haven't lost my touch." She seemed calm, as if all her craziness had seeped through her fingertips and was trapped in the pie.

"Making a perfect pie crust must be one of those things." She sighed. "You know, like riding a bicycle. Once you learn, you never forget."

"I'll put it in the oven." He slipped his hand under the pie plate.

Bryan wiped the counter. She washed the dishes. "I'm going upstairs," she said. "Call me when it's ready, when it's cooled." She poured herself a shot from a dusty, brown bottle she found under the sink. With the glass in one hand and the bottle in the other, she stepped carefully across the kitchen, like a tightrope walker performing for the first time without a net.

Cinnamon and apple smells filled the kitchen. Bryan thought of the apple slices softening in the oven, melting into each other. Shortening and flour baking, becoming something completely different from what they'd been before. The chemistry—that's what he loved about cooking—that and making people happy.

He started to play a tune to pass the time and remembered Gil's box. He could open it, go through his things. No one would know. If Bryan left the door open he could hear the oven timer from the basement.

Ivy and Gil had crammed the small cardboard box into a spot on the shelf over the washing machine, next to a box of their father's that Bryan opened from time to time to read the letters Johnny had sent to Grandma MacKenzie from Vietnam. They didn't say much—talked mostly about the heat and mud and how he missed Grandma's cooking, but Bryan knew them by heart and handled them like sacred relics. Gil's things shouldn't be rubbing up against them. It wasn't right.

Bryan hoisted himself onto the washing machine and wiggled the box toward him. It slid into his chest, heavier than he expected. Hugging it, he jumped backward neatly to the floor and set it down. It wasn't even taped shut. He unfolded the flaps, surprised to find it so well packed—full of small containers, and along the side, a sketch pad and some paintings. Sliding out the paintings Bryan recognized the landscapes, flower arrangements, "The Last Supper"—paint by number sets. Gil hadn't followed the color scheme. He'd mixed his own—magenta barns in bright blue fields, yellow clouds in silver and black skies, Jesus had a turquoise face. Bryan couldn't look at them for long.

He flipped through the sketch pad. Penciled pigeons, cats, cars, self-portraits, seven of them. He examined each one, trying to know the man his sister ran away with. Gil drew well, his eyes as disturbed and disturbing as Bryan remembered. He'd included every pock mark, every scar. Bryan would have been tempted to make himself look better than real life. The last sketch was of Ivy, half naked on a bed. When could he have drawn it? They'd only just met. But that was Ivy—as fast as she was loud. Her hair fell over her shoulders. She was laughing. Her breasts looked great. Bryan closed the pad, embarrassed, and unpacked the rest of the box, arranging everything on the floor—a plastic cream cheese container of pennies, small boxes of brushes and tubes of paint, an envelope of photographs, mostly cats, a few people, none looked like Gil, a bunched up gray sweater with something wrapped inside. Bryan unrolled the sweater and a tee shirt inside that.

A dagger with a gleaming, six-inch blade. It looked like something you'd see in a museum, shining sharp and silver with a handle made of shell or pearl or bone, some startlingly luminous substance, that changed from white, to pink to yellow depending on how the light fell. Bryan turned it over and over in first his right hand, then his left. He stood, tensing his shoulders and stabbed the air with short, sharp thrusts. He stretched his head back, clutched his neck with one hand and touched the tip of the knife to his Adam's apple; for a quivering moment, both attacker and attacked. He reexamined the knife at arm's length. Bryan couldn't figure where someone, anyone, would get something like it. It must be worth a lot of money. Why hadn't Gil taken it with him? Bryan repacked the box, smuggling the dagger and its wrappings to his room. It changed everything. His posters of Little Walter and Sonny Boy Williamson. His harmonica collection. The shelf of cookbooks that wouldn't fit in the kitchen. The backpack he carried to school every day. Even the pile of change and his inhaler on the top of his dresser. Everything—different. He was a man with a weapon, a real one. He turned the blade over and over. Beautiful, simple, the shine and smoothness of it. It could hurt somebody. The timer rang. The pie. He wrapped the dagger and shoved it under his mattress.

Carol, not about to muss a neatly made up bed by flopping across it no matter how distraught and tipsy she might be, folded back the covers, stepped out of her black pumps and fit them into their places on her wire shoe rack before slipping between her sheets. She covered her face and with sharp gasps, almost sobs, breathed in the smell of winter sunshine. Dryers were useful, but she believed in hanging sheets on the line. Today she would have had to hang them in the basement or they'd be frozen, but luckily she'd washed all the linens the day before, when the sun warmed the air, melting the icicles lining the eaves of the house, the morning of her dead husband's birthday when she woke full of optimism; for heavens sake—time to make a new life, enough regret. Ivy might have ruined everything, but the fresh smell lingered in Carol's bedclothes, a testimony to the fact there was a right way to do things and Carol's ability to adhere to it.

She wanted to call Neal, but it seemed too early in their relationship to burden him with serious family matters. He made her laugh in that out of control, liquid through the nose, forget everything else way that was better than sex, better than anything, the way she laughed with girlfriends, only one of the basic joys that ended when Johnny came into her life, or more accurately, when Johnny's mother died, or maybe even more accurately, when Ivy was born. One of those things that you did for the last time without realizing it, that you were too busy to miss until so much time had passed you had no idea how to make it happen again. You'd forgotten your friends' telephone numbers you used to know by heart and you were too miserable to be seen in public anyway.

Baby Ivy, Johnny's mother's death, the headaches that seized whole chunks of her brain and pinched the backs of her eyes—they all began at the same time. But Johnny MacKenzie, Vietnam vet, knew about headaches and the drugs to cure them. He massaged the back of her skull and gave her a pill case made of a translucent shell, a pinky-yellow-white color that seemed to collect light. It snapped together with a gold clasp, fit cool and smooth in her palm, pills nestled inside like pearls. Pills that worked, not the useless ones prescribed by the doctor. Somehow, during the summer Johnny died, she'd misplaced the pill case. She hadn't thought of it in years. Why was she thinking of it now when, knock on wood, she didn't even have a headache? She needed something to help her cope with her ruined life, her selfish daughter, her failure as a mother: a man, a pill, a piece of pie.

Car lights from the interstate passed over the Plymouth like searchlights in a prison yard. Ivy shoved Gil with her elbow, his body impossibly large, heavy. His snores continued uninterrupted. The scar near his eye from a belt buckle, he'd said he couldn't remember who had held the end of the belt, gleamed puffy and white every time the lights swung through the car. Her mother had slapped her a few times when she 'mouthed off' but she'd never been hit with anything. She couldn't imagine it. The yelling her mother did was bad enough.

"I know it's none of my business," Rich whispered. "What are you going to do in Florida anyway? Are you running away? How old are you?"

Her age was the only question she had an answer to. She remembered Gil's raised eyebrows when she'd accepted his invitation to his room if he'd promise to take her to Florida for a vacation. She remembered Curly's anxious face as she left the pool hall—Curly, who'd known her father and taught her everything she knew about playing pool. She remembered her brother's confused stare when she announced she was leaving. Gil shifted beside her.

"We live in Connecticut," she said. "This is a vacation. A change of scenery. Change of climate. A change. Just a change."

"How long you been with our friend here?"

"Awhile."

"And how old are you?"

"Eighteen."

"Right, and I'm a hundred. How old are you really?"

"Okay, seventeen." Why lie?

"I have a sister about your age. If she was hitchhiking across the country with a loser like …"

Gil groaned. Rich swallowed the end of his sentence.

Loser? Misunderstood, maybe. A survivor of a tough life. Gil approached her for the first time right after she'd beat Leo Leveaux, the best player in Rivertown after Curly and her, and handed her a napkin. "Love the way you hold that pool cue," he'd whispered. Before she could react, he took back the napkin, held it up in front of her and there she was leaning over a pool table, in sure, quick pencil strokes. He'd been watching her. The drawing made her look good. Better than good. He leaned close, his breath tickling her ear. "Wham. Crack. Balls scattering across the felt, just where you want them to. How do you do that?" She kept the napkin folded in her inside jacket pocket.

"Listen," Rich took her hand. "Let's get the room. We'll come back and drag him in. You don't have anything to worry about with me. Cross my heart." He held his fingers in a boy scout salute, brushed them across his chest and opened the car door. He ushered her out with a smile. His eyes were a red-brown, tea color, like the pond behind Ivy's house where she skated and swam with her family, until the town declared it too polluted. She imagined, for a moment, that Rich was her boyfriend, she was driving to Florida and tonight was just one of a long string of nights in clean motels, with shiny bathtubs and comfortable beds.

Rich paid for the room and handed her the key. "I never stayed in a motel before," she said. Her family never traveled. When she was small they'd camped at the state park, but that was it. Rich opened the door, switched on the light. Ivy bounced on the edge of one of the beds. "Do you think they really have those little bars of soap?"

Rich smiled. "Bathroom's right there. Go check."

"They do!" Ivy called. The bathroom down the hall in Gil's rooming house had smelled so bad she'd held her breath and avoided sitting down. "And a strip of paper around the toilet seat too." She tore it off, peed, and spun back into the room twirling the paper streamer around her head. Rich faced the mirror, slugging from Gil's bottle. He wiped his mouth with the back of a hand and grinned. Ivy's reflection grinned back. Rich peeled tissue paper from a glass and poured. She watched his face in the mirror. In slow motion, he winked, before turning to offer her the drink. Their fingers touched.

"Wait," Rich said, raising his glass, Jack Daniels sloshing up the sides. "A toast. We need a toast. Yes. The occasion demands a toast. A beautiful girl. A bottle half-full."

Ivy flushed, glancing at the mirror, trying to decide if she might be beautiful or was he up to something. What about Gil passed out in the car? What was she doing here? Anything could happen. Anything could happen any time. She'd never thought about that before. Desiring, needing, the exactly perfect, meaningful toast, she stood silent, her drink held high.

Rich shrugged, "What the fuck?" and emptied his glass with one long swallow.

Ivy sipped hers. Her glass—half-full or half-empty, however you looked at it. When it was gone, she'd have to find something else to fill the long hours until morning.

"So ..." Rich stretched out on one of the beds, arms crossed behind his head, the sharp toes of his worn cowboy boots pointing toward the ceiling. "Feels good to lie down after all that driving. You should try it." He patted the bedspread beside him, yawning.

Ivy perched on the other bed, not looking at Rich. She didn't know a thing about him except that he had a car, drank Jack Daniels when persuaded, and said he had a sister.

"Where are you going?" she asked.

"That depends." Rich balanced the heel of one boot on the toe of the other, grinning at her. In the glow of the bedside lamp, his eyes matched the bourbon in her glass.

She walked to the window and lifted the stiff curtain. Squinting, she could barely see Gil's slumped form.

"Look." She dropped the curtain. "I can't sleep with you." She thought of the door to Gil's building, the shattered glass he'd admitted to kicking in when he'd been angry and drunk. "Even if I wanted to. I'm with him. It wouldn't be right."

Rich smirked. "Don't tell me you're a good girl?"

Ivy raised her eyebrows, smiled, feeling shy and pleased. She'd left her mother and brother and taken off for Florida with her father's army duffel bag and a tattooed man she'd met shooting pool. Good girls didn't do that. Good girls didn't sneak out to the pool hall when their mother had strictly forbidden it, make their mother and brother miserable by talking about dead fathers every chance they got, storm around the house when their mother had a date. Good girls had friends and parties and their own date for the prom. She wasn't good, not at all.

"Shit." Rich took another pull from the bottle. "Guess you are. Got any cards?"

Ivy shook her head.

"Scrabble? Dominoes? This shitbox doesn't even have a TV."

"We could sleep," Ivy said, tugging at the bedspread. "I'm really tired. Then we can get up early in the morning and drive … where are you going anyway?"

Rich lurched toward the bathroom. "I could rape you, you know." Ivy froze. He pissed loud and long. Back in the room, zipping up his fly he continued, "But I wouldn't. Remember, I promised. Scout's honor. Even if I wanted to, I wouldn't."

Ivy folded back the thin orange bedcover. The phone, the lamps were all bolted down. The only potential weapons appeared to be pillows, the bourbon bottle he'd just picked up again, or a small, glass ashtray. Her aim was good enough. If she could get him to lie down, maybe he'd fall asleep, then she'd fall asleep and in the morning they'd be on their way.

"You look exhausted," she said. "All that driving."

He yawned.

"Lie down." She pointed to his bed. "We'll talk. With Gil around it's hard to get a word in. I don't know anything about you."

Rich grinned. "Okay. A pajama party. You lie down too."

"Over here." Ivy put the pillows on top of each other, centering them.

He nodded. "Over there. My sister and I used to do this," he said. "We had bunkbeds. We'd turn out the light and talk until we drifted off."

She and Bryan had separate rooms. The summer their father died they slept together every night without Grandma Harrington finding out. Bryan came sneaking into her room but when he didn't, she'd sneak into his. They didn't talk much, just lay beside each other in the dark. One night they stopped. No special reason. Nothing different. A wave of sadness swelled inside her.

A shower would feel good, long and hot. Maybe in the morning when Gil was up and everyone was sober. She crossed her arms tight over her breasts and waited for Rich to say something.

"What do you want to talk about?" He clicked off the light. "Religion? Politics? Love?"

"You still haven't said where you're going." Ivy hoped he'd fall asleep soon.

"Jacksonville."

"Do you live there?"

"My daughter does."

"Your daughter?" He didn't look old enough to have a daughter living on her own.

"Amanda. She's three. Cutest little thing. I haven't seen her in a year and a half. Her mother took off with her. Bitch."

Passing the time became a field of hidden mines. Ivy dug her nails into her palms. Better to be still than chance triggering one.

"Send her money every month. She gets my kid and my money. Figure that one out."

Ivy's ribcage rose and fell. Such a little thing, breathing. Something she did all the time and never even knew it. What if she just stopped? She exhaled and waited.

"Bitches. They get the kids and the money. Equal rights? Men need equal rights. The world today the goddamned homosexuals got more rights than a regular, decent, working guy who wants a smoke."

Two weeks and two days ago Ivy had never slept with a man. The past four years she'd done most of her homework and spent the rest of her time shooting pool, practicing bridges, open and closed, follow, draw, and English, thinking of nothing except the stick, the balls, the table. On her thirteenth birthday, she'd hovered in the doorway of the pool hall, hugging her father's cue, and Curly, the bald guy in a Hawaiian shirt, noticed the monogram on the cue case. "Don't tell me you're Ivy MacKenzie all grown up?" He ushered her in as if he'd been waiting for her. Rivertown Billiards became her world. Even as it closed around her until she knew she had to break out or hurt someone, she hadn't imagined Rich or this motel. Or Gil.

"You all right?" Rich went on without waiting for an answer. "I'm telling you. All these people bellyaching about this right and that right. You hear that joke about the dog, doesn't want to be called a dog anymore? Wants to be called a Canine-American."

Rich sounded like Gil after a few drinks. She pressed the pillow against her ears until his voice just droned. When the sound ended abruptly, she loosened her hold on the pillow.

Rich's breathing, loud and regular, filled the room, surrounding her. She unclenched her fingers and toes and picked at the grit under her fingernails. Her hair felt stiff and smelled of wind and car exhaust. Dried sweat coated her underarms. She wanted a shower, more than anything, more than she'd wanted to leave Rivertown, more than she'd wanted Rich to fall asleep. Maybe that's all life was, wanting. When one desire was satisfied, another popped up to take its place. After a shower, what would she long for?

Bryan and her mother would be asleep at home, her own bed empty. Maybe they weren't sleeping. Maybe they were awake and worrying about her. If they weren't, they should be. Anything could happen.

They worried the night she'd met Gil and stayed out until morning. Her mother, who nagged and yelled at her daily for the last ten years, since her father had died, about everything from leaving the cap off the toothpaste to eating too much to not joining the Future Homemakers of America or any other club, to hanging around Rivertown Billiards, sat silent at the table, dressed for work.

"Mom," Ivy wanted to say. "I have a boyfriend. I made love for the first time and it was great." She'd wanted to tell somebody. In the middle of the table sat a bouquet of tulips so purple they looked black, a present from Neal Richards. He'd had them sent to Carol at the bank.

"Where in hell were you?" Carol had asked.

"None of your business!" Ivy shouted.

"I'm your mother. Unfortunately, it damn well is my business."

Bryan stood in the doorway, watching, saying nothing, as usual.

"Unfortunately!" Ivy hollered. "It is unfortunate. For me. The parent who cared about me died."

Her mother didn't answer. She sat, mouth tight, shared a look with Bryan. Ivy stormed off without her school books or money for lunch. Then, on her father's birthday, when Carol forbade Bryan to make the usual cake, Ivy went straight from school to Gil's. She crawled into bed with him until noon the next day, today—was it still today—when they picked up his check, dropped a box of his stuff off at her house, and left.

Maybe her mother was out having fun, on a date with that Neal Richards guy. Ivy pushed back the covers, slipping her arms from her sleeves as she tiptoed over the worn carpet to the bathroom. She locked the door and turned on the shower.

Her face appeared in the foggy mirror. Ivy MacKenzie, eyes so dark the only way to see her pupils was to look real close and even then, in dim light, like in the pool hall, they barely showed: dark, matted hair, windburned skin, chapped lips. Wild, tough, the kind of girl who rode horses into canyons. She was afraid of horses. Motorcycles, maybe. Her mother told stories about the motorcycle her father had when they'd first married. He'd gotten rid of it when Ivy was born. Her mother never said whose idea that was, but Ivy could guess.

She tilted her face toward the shower's spray as hot water spilled over her. Layers of dirt from standing on roadsides, stiffness from sitting in cars and the freezing back of a pickup truck swirled down the drain. Ivy laughed, swallowing the urge to sing. She didn't want to wake Rich. Fuck him. Rich, Gil, a long day on the road, sweaty armpits, Rivertown, all of it led to this warmth, this cleansing. If it hadn't happened, if any of it hadn't been, she wouldn't be here now. And now was worth it.

Ivy rubbed the tiny bar of soap over her arms and shoulders. When she reached her breasts it slipped through her fingers. She cupped her breasts in her hands, feeling their weight. Water ran like small rivers over their rounded surface, cascading to the shining floor like waterfalls.

Ivy closed her eyes, thought of Gil with her nipple held gently between his teeth, Rich, calling her gorgeous. She felt a pleasant ache between her legs. Feet firmly planted on the skidproof surface of the bathtub in room seventeen of the Rainbow's End Motel, Ivy understood she was finally a woman, a traveling woman on her way. She liked her body. She washed her hair the best she could with no shampoo and turned off the shower, whistling softly.

She wrapped one skimpy towel around her hair, dried herself with the other. Foot resting on the lid of the toilet, Ivy dried each toe as thoroughly as she chalked her cue before a difficult shot. A banging outside.

She pulled on her dirty jeans and sweater and rushed to unlock the door. Rich lay unmoving, a shadowy mound of covers. Fumbling with the chain lock, then the knob, she pulled the door open.

Gil stumbled to keep from falling forward into the room. Steadying himself he looked Ivy up and down, wiping a hand across his mouth. In the neon glow of the motel's sign, his skin had a greenish tinge.

"You slut," he whispered. A muscle in his cheek twitched. Her stomach lurched. She stepped back. "I'll kill you. I'll kill that mother fucker for messing with you."

He lunged before she could put the door between them. His fingers dug into her cheeks like a trap into the leg of an animal. "Slut," he hissed. "You fucking slut."

He twisted her jaw. Her knees buckled. When he let go she fell to the floor. From far above she heard him. "What's the matter? Can't get enough. I can't satisfy you?" She curled into herself, shivering, knees and arms protecting her breasts, her stomach, her pounding heart.

"What the fuck?" At the sound of Rich's voice, Ivy lifted her head. He would help her. They'd tell Gil nothing had happened. He'd apologize. They'd all go to sleep.

"I'm the one saying 'what the fuck?'" Gil shouted. He moved away from her, toward Rich. "I'm the one. Do I look like an asshole to you? My old lady shacked up with you, in a motel room, with the door locked."

"The door locks when you close it," Rich said. "The chain, I just used out of habit. I wasn't thinking too clearly."

"Yeah, what else did you do out of habit? 'What the fuck?'" The bed groaned as Gil grabbed Rich by the throat. "Yeah, I'm the one saying it. And I'm the one saying you better get the fuck out of here before I kill you."

Ivy inched along the floor toward the bathroom. She'd lock herself in until Gil passed out. Rich, in a strangled voice offered him a drink, swore he hadn't touched Ivy.

Keep talking, Ivy thought.

"What are you up to, bitch?" Gil pinned her to the floor with his foot on her back. The carpet scratched her cheek and smelled bad.

"Rich!" she hollered. "Please!"

"You want Rich?" Gil's voice chilly and unfamiliar. Where was the man who had covered her with kisses, promised her love and adventure, fed her M&M's in bed, and warmed her body with big, gentle hands?

A door slammed. A car started. She knew not to call Rich's name again.

"Lover boy is gone," Gil sneered. "You're stuck with me again." He prodded her with his foot. "Get up."

"Hey, I …"

"Don't talk. You're gonna give me what you gave to him and then some." He grabbed her hair, pulled her to her feet, and threw her against the wall.

She should hate him. She should feel afraid. She thought of her mother hanging onto her arm to keep her from the pool hall. All that fighting, screaming, worrying, for nothing. She'd been improving her game, nothing dangerous, nothing bad. Now her mother had something to worry about. So do you, said the knot in her stomach, but she ignored it. Curly, her mother, Bryan, they'd all be thinking about her, frantic maybe. She'd wanted Rich to touch her. Gil knew. She awaited his next move.

Rage twisted his face. He raised a fist. Ivy ran into the bathroom, leaned against the door with all her strength. He pushed. His bellow began in a dark and hollow place Ivy recognized, a hole that demanded filling with something, anything. The air left her lungs. He charged. She squeezed into the small space between the sink and the bathtub.

"Gil, Gil, please, you don't know what you're doing. I didn't do anything with him. I took a shower, that's all. I was going to wake you up." Her hips and elbows bumped the sink.

"Shut up." He ripped the shower curtain rod from the wall. She raised her arms to protect her face as he smashed the shower rod against her skull, her shoulders, her back. She shrunk herself into a tight ball. She thought she should know how to stop him.

"You make a pie, you eat it," Carol said later, when their plates were empty. Her first words since Bryan called her back to the kitchen. "You raise a kid. She leaves. In the end, you're left with, what?" She looked at her hands. "Nothing."

"I'm still here," Bryan said, washing each plate for a long time.

"Bryan." His mother touched his cheek. His glasses had fogged up. He didn't want her to see him crying. She lifted them from his face, polishing them on the wide sash of her bathrobe. She set them on the counter, ignoring his reaching hand. Her breath smelled of cinnamon and whiskey. He wanted her to hug him.

"Mom," he said. She stiffened. Her hand on his shoulder held them together. He turned off the water. She dried his cheeks with the end of her sash, and set his glasses on his nose. He stared hard at her through his clean lenses while she studied the linoleum, the ceiling, the telephone, finally settling on the remains of the pie. "There's a lot left," she said. "We'll have it tomorrow." She looked at him then, mouth smiling, eyes sad.

He hated eyes and mouths telling different stories. Like on his seventh birthday. Mom, smiled all day, the same smile as now. He hadn't wanted a party, didn't want to run relays, but these festive, invite-the-whole-neighborhood, old-fashioned birthday parties for her children were her twice-a-year way of showing the town she was fine on her own, a more-than-competent single mother, so for her sake, he did it. He tied his leg to his friend, Everett's, and ran. He sweat, hopping along in a sack. He ran the egg race against Ivy, a step ahead of her, close to the finish line, egg perfectly balanced in his spoon. Ivy stepped on the heel of his sneaker, so quick he thought he'd imagined it. Blades of grass poked through the broken yolk of his egg as his sister ran across the finish line, shoulders high, head tilted back, people cheering for her. He leaped on her like a monkey, knocking her down, punching her face until her nose bled. "You cheated!" he screamed. "You shouldn't have cheated."

Still wearing the smile, their mother pulled them apart, sent Ivy inside, ordered the kids to the picnic table with a cheerful voice. That morning Ivy had given Bryan a venus fly trap, bought with her own money. No matter how much they'd begged, Carol wouldn't let them have pets, she said she had too much to take care of already. Before the party Bryan watched Ivy feed the fly trap raw hamburger from the end of a toothpick. They'd named it Rex and stood side by side, staring as the fringed mouth closed over the meat. He flexed his fists, Ivy's blood already dry on his knuckles. He'd wanted to wash his hands but his mother had lit the candles and kids were singing.

"We can eat the rest of this pie tomorrow," Mom said again, sighing. "Neal might like a piece. Should we put it in the refrigerator?"

"Sure." Bryan's fingers tensed on the sticky edge of the pie plate. He knew he'd always wanted to throw a pie in someone's face. He wished he'd realized it sooner, when Ivy was still around. He liked to think that if he'd only realized it, he would have done it. Imagine Ivy peeking out through a mask of whipped cream or cooked fruit and shards of crust, the pie tin clattering to the floor. Imagine being the kind of person who could smash someone with a pie and walk away, leaving the whole mess behind.

"Honey, baby, I brought you some coffee." Ivy heard the words from beyond the constant shriek of pain in her head. She opened her mouth to speak. Her teeth ached. She licked her lips. They were sticky, more than twice their normal size.

"I'm so sorry, sweetie." He hovered over her, tucking the sheets around her shoulders, holding the coffee toward her lips. "It's ten. We have to be out by eleven. Drink up."

Breathing hurt. Swallowing hurt. Everything hurt. Someone who couldn't walk to the bathroom couldn't walk to the road, couldn't climb in and out of cars and trucks, sleep on the ground.

"Have to pee," she whispered. Arm around her shoulders, Gil half carried her to the bathroom. Towels hung neatly from the shower curtain rod. The next people to use the room would never know what had happened. She didn't look in the mirror. She sat on the toilet.

"Do you need any help or should I leave you alone?" He knelt beside her holding her hand.

"Go." Ivy whispered.

"All right." He stroked her knuckles with his thumb. "You call me if you need anything. Listen, Ivy, honey, I'm really sorry. Last night. That was the bottle talking. Not me. I know you wouldn't fuck around. I'll never drink again. I promise. I swear on a stack of Bibles."

"Go," she said again.

"You believe me, don't you?" Gil seemed unable to release her hand until she gave him what he wanted.

"I believe you."

"You love me, don't you?" Gil's forehead wrinkled like a baby's.

"I love you."

"Really?"

She pulled her hand back. He tightened his grip.

"Yes."

"I'll never hit you again. I'd do anything for you. I'll never drink again."

"Go."

"Fuckin' Rich, took off with all our stuff. Want something to eat?" Gil went for his coffee, leaving the bathroom door open.

He loved her. Ivy stayed on the toilet, hurting too much to form a plan, afraid to face herself in the mirror. Her father's duffel bag and all her clothes, gone. How many states lay between her and home? Gil was good. Bourbon was bad.

Gil hollered. "Want a twinkie? I bought three packs."

Ivy had no voice to holler back.

Zipping her jeans she noticed a crack halved the mirror, split her swollen mask of a face. She traced the line with her finger. The next occupants would know something had happened. She leaned over the toilet and vomited.

"Everything all right?" he called around a mouthful of twinkie. Cellophane crackled as he tore open another pack. "You need me, baby?"

Ivy leaned against the sink and forced herself to look again. Need him? The man whose fingerprints matched the bruises on her cheeks and neck. She should tell him to look, to draw her now. She stared, memorizing the face she'd take with her to the next mirror and the next and probably the one after that until her crushed and broken capillaries healed and her blood flowed steadily through her body the way it was supposed to.

"Come on, baby." Gil's voice, from the next room, gentle, rough at the edges, wrapped around her and drew her to him. "Let's hit the road."

CHAPTER 2

Bryan and Everett, the only two guys in food lab, washed their dishes two sinks over from Martine Leveaux and Casey McLaughlin. The meringues the boys just baked sat perfectly browned on the counter. Ms. Walker complimented them. Instead of moving on, she paused. "Bryan?" He rinsed sugar and egg white from a beater. She was going to ask about Ivy. His bad sister. He'd learned to sense it. Something about the way they breathed deep, looked at the floor, then at him, oozing concern. He braced himself. "Have you heard from Ivy yet?"

Everett stiffened. He'd been Bryan's best friend since second grade when, instead of joining the rest of the boys in ferocious and blood thirsty dodge ball games, the two of them wandered the edges of the playground in complicated adventures involving jeweled swords, poisonous insects the size of small dogs, volcanoes, and quicksand. He knew Bryan didn't want to talk about Ivy. Martine shut the water off at her sink. The whole room waited.

"No one's heard anything," Bryan said. Ms. Walker made sympathetic noises with her tongue, waiting for him to go on. He walked out with his faucet running. Carrying the beater with him. He chucked it in a drinking fountain then ran for his locker. He grabbed his coat and pack and fled school hating Ivy for continuing to ruin his life.

"Bryan! Wait up!" Everett hollered.

Bryan stopped. "You'll get detention. Skipping class."

"Ms. Walker told me to go find you." Everett frowned.

Bryan shifted his pack. Here on the pavement in front of Rivertown High nothing moved, everybody inside where they were supposed to be. Bright noon sun blanked out the windows. The building could have been empty.

"I think Walker felt bad," Ev said.

They started down the hill toward Main Street, their steps matching. All the snow had melted leaving everything bare and muddy. They passed Rivertown Trust. "Hope my mother's not looking out the window," Bryan said. He didn't walk faster or hide behind Ev. "But maybe it wouldn't matter. People don't even see me, you know that?"

Ev raised his eyebrow and Bryan realized he'd spoken aloud. Words spun around in Bryan's head. Words he wouldn't even say to Ev. *All they see is my sister. Or the kid whose sister ran away with the tattooed creep. Used to be the poor kid whose dad got killed. They're all wondering why my mother hasn't found her. I don't know! I don't know why she hasn't tried harder. My mother's afraid of Ivy. I'm afraid of her. Everyone's afraid of her.*

He stopped suddenly in the middle of the sidewalk. Ivy left with Gil Thompson because she finally found someone who wasn't afraid of her.

"What's the matter?" Ev asked.

Bryan couldn't tell him. He couldn't tell him how during the first couple weeks his mother called the police all the time. Then it was like she gave up. She started seeing more of Neal. Bryan wondered if Neal had told her to stop.

Everett stood ready to listen.

"See you later," Bryan said.

Everett looked confused, hurt even. Bryan owed him an explanation, wanted to give one, and couldn't. At least Ev got to escape school early, some reward for his trouble.

Bryan turned back toward the bank before he knew he was headed there—Rivertown Trust, one of the oldest and fanciest buildings on Main Street, with a polished marble floor, a high domed ceiling, and lots of brass and wood. His mother's nameplate gleamed on the counter. Carol MacKenzie. Sometimes when Bryan wrote his name, it looked wrong and he'd check the spelling. Mom's looked weird now. She didn't notice him waiting in line.

Everyone said his mother was beautiful. For awhile after Ivy left she'd looked too thin, deep, dark circles under her eyes. Whenever she wasn't working, out with Neal, or in her bedroom with the door shut, she sat at the kitchen table with an untouched cup of tea. Here, at the bank, out in the world, forced to function, she chatted with her customer, her honey colored hair just cut and dyed, her fingernails red against the dull green money; she didn't look like a woman whose husband had been killed, whose daughter had run away.

She looked up and smiled, "Next? Bryan?" She checked her watch. "What are you doing here? Shouldn't you be in school?" His mother's face mildly questioning, floated in front of him.

Someone behind Bryan cleared his throat. *Go use the machines if you're in so much of a hurry,* he wanted to tell him and everyone else in line.

"Bryan?" His mother tapped the counter with her fingernail. His head buzzed with words that wouldn't come out.

"Nothing ... sorry ... I was walking by. Will you be home for dinner?"

"I left you a note at home. I'm going out with Neal. I won't be late. You could get pizza at the mall. Want some money?"

He wanted someone to cook for. The pizza he made was always better than what they sold at the Italian Pavilion. She said so herself.

"Are you okay?" Carol asked.

"Ms. Walker wants to know where Ivy is," Bryan blurted. It seemed to echo through the bank. He turned and ran like he'd set a bomb. First Ev, then his mother. Let her worry about him. He wanted to talk about Ivy. And Neal Richards. And his father. Ivy talked. Too loud and too much but at least she talked. Since she'd been gone Bryan and his mother lived their life; Neal pushed at the edges. They never said anything. He missed his dad. Or Ivy's memories of their father. He didn't miss the fighting, the slamming doors, but without Ivy no one said anything.

Ivy dragged herself onto the crumbling balcony of the Sand Dollar motel to watch the sky turn light. She hung her head over the rusty railing and threw up, just missing the empty swimming pool. Early mornings, when the cement and asphalt held their night time coolness, before the harsh sun sucked the colors from the world, she could almost remember feeling happy, the month and a half of long, lazy days in Daytona Beach before this sickness began, when she and Gil were enough for each other, when Florida appeared to be all she'd hoped for. Late at night, they'd swim naked in the pool at the Beachfront Motel where they worked four hours a day, cleaning in exchange for their white, breeze-filled room with striped yellow curtains. Gil stayed funny and careful, sober and kind. In the dark, cool water, while everyone else slept, they'd twine around each other, swim without splashing. An orange tree grew outside their window. Then Gil met a guy on the beach, bought some pills, drank again, put a hole in the wall, got them fired and evicted. On to Ocala. Then Gainesville. Finally, Tampa. And the Sand Dollar with its rusty patio furniture, dry pool full of cracks and weeds, and cheap rooms they couldn't afford. Three cities in two weeks.

Gil slept. He'd drunk a six pack before bed. He'd persuaded her that beer didn't count; only hard liquor made him crazy. She fell asleep early and woke early, craving the stillness, the time to herself, before he woke needing coffee and cigarettes. On the patio below, a sea gull pecked at her puddle of vomit. Gil's snores filtered through the open window. Since leaving Rivertown, they'd had four jobs, three of them in the two weeks after leaving the Beach-front—distributing leaflets, sorting used clothes, and the worst, picking oranges. Their bodies still ached from five days of bending and stretching and they'd only managed to fill three bins. Not enough to cover the cost of beer, a loaf of bread, package of baloney, and Gil's cigarettes. Never mind the room. Except for the twenty she kept in her shoe, folded and stuck together with sweat, all the money they'd brought from home was gone.

Home, as in running away from. She'd just begun to understand that was exactly what she'd done—run away from. The Florida she'd imagined didn't exist, not for a teenage girl with one twenty dollar bill saved for an emergency. Disneyworld cost forty dollars just to get in.

If she felt better, she could figure out what to do. If they had some friends who lived nearby, knew the area. The only people they spent time with were guys passing through, guys with things to sell, drugs, watches, socks, CD's. She'd had no idea there were so many of them. Her shoulders shook with dry heaves, a bitter taste stung the back of her throat.

"Baby," Gil mumbled. "You all right? Where are you?"

He grinned as she appeared in the doorway. "You look like an angel," he said. "All that light around your hair, like a fuckin' halo."

She squinted in the dimness. He sat up in bed, held out his arms. "Let's get married today," he said.

"Tomorrow," Ivy replied, as she always did. When he'd said it the first time, in Daytona Beach, she'd laughed, thinking he was joking.

"What's so funny?" he'd demanded.

"I'm too young to get married," she'd said, flattered, careful of his feelings. Marriage and a man like Gil didn't go together. She wondered where he got the idea.

"Tomorrow, tomorrow," Gil laughed, imitating her. "Haven't you heard the saying, Ivy, baby, tomorrow never comes?"

She slid the door closed and crawled in beside him. No one had ever mentioned love to her as much as he did. He'd do anything for her. He said so. With his arms around her he told her how beautiful she was, how sexy, how good. He only lost his temper badly enough to hurt her twice, and only when he was really drunk on hard liquor, not beer—the night with Rich and the other time when he'd conned a rich college student into buying him shots and her pina coladas, the sweetest things she'd ever tasted, like a dessert. She couldn't believe they had alcohol in them.

He loved her too much, he said. He couldn't help being jealous. "Three strikes," he'd begged. "Even in baseball a guy gets three strikes. Be fair, baby, give me one more chance."

Gil lifted her hair. "I love you," he said. "I fucking love you." He pulled her on top of him. Her sickness subsided and she lost herself in the pure pleasure of bodies connecting.

"I love you." In the romantic gloom of the River Restaurant Neal Richards grinned at Carol over the table littered with greasy dishes. When Carol had waitressed at this very restaurant, before she landed the job at the bank, standards were higher. She would have had the table cleared by now, the coffee and spumoni delivered. Carol squinted at her watch.

"Did you hear me?" Neal asked.

"I'm worried about Bryan," Carol said. "He stopped at the bank today … when he should have been in school. All upset. I shouldn't stay out too late. I can't even see the time; it's so dark in here." She held her wrist out toward him. "Can you?"

He held her hand and bent his head as if to peer at the watch, then ran his lips across her knuckles instead. His beard still startled her. Johnny had never grown a beard or a mustache. He hated them. Even in the photos she'd seen of him and his buddies in Vietnam, he was always clean shaven. Everyone else had a mustache or at least stubble—not Johnny. She'd never been with a hairy man before. She wouldn't have said she remembered how Johnny smelled, not exactly, but on some level she did remember, because Neal's sharp clean scent of freshly cut wood surprised her even more than his facial hair did. Touch and smell—memories stored so deep in her cells she couldn't erase them if she tried. She could avoid Johnny's photographs, the music they'd listened to, Rivertown Billiards and Curly, but every time she moved close to Neal Richards and he smelled wrong, Johnny was there. Carol wondered if Neal's back and shoulders were hairy too. She hadn't slept with a man since Johnny. Her daughter had run away. Her son was miserable. What kind of a mother was she to think about sex at a time like this?

"It's not even seven thirty," Neal said.

"I should get home."

"I'll take you."

"My car's just across the street in the bank lot." She pulled her hand back.

"I know, but I'm not ready to leave you yet."

"I guess I could walk to work in the morning."

"I'll drive you."

"Neal, that's silly."

"I don't mind. I'll swing by and get you on my way to the shop. Or ..." He hesitated. "I could stay at your house."

To lie in bed and touch someone. To have someone hold her. Not someone. Neal. If she woke rigid with terror, imagining Ivy dead, blaming herself for everything, he would be there breathing beside her. She could slow her panicked breath by matching it to his, feel the warm bulk of him with the length of her body.

"Okay," she said.

Bryan headed home in the dark, to the empty, silent house. He felt his harmonica in his pocket but didn't feel like playing. He practiced questions for his mother: Do you think Ivy will come home? Why don't we hire a private eye? Do you love Neal Richards? Did my father love me? He knew that when he had the chance to ask them, they'd stick in his throat.

He unlocked the door wishing he'd gone to the mall with Ev. Martine and Casey would've showed up eventually. Even full of braces Martine's smile gave him shivers and she had a laugh better than any music he ever heard. They could've shared a lousy pizza and he would've played music right there in the mall until the security guard stopped him and then they could've gone back to the arcade. Martine hated video games but she liked skiball. She was saving up tickets for a plastic goose lamp. Maybe he loved her.

He went to his room and unwrapped Gil's dagger. Some people could say what they wanted to say. Some people could do what they wanted to do. Even things they knew were wrong. Like running away or stabbing someone. He rolled the knife up and pushed it way under his bed.

Early in the summer of his father's accident, the family had gone camping. Ivy told Bryan the woods were full of bears and wolves. He stayed up all night listening. The second night she ate flaming marshmallows. She cried and screamed. They had to go home and Bryan was glad. The next morning Ivy peeled blisters from the roof of her mouth and bragged she'd eaten fire. They had photos of that trip, a whole album of photos, the last pictures of their father alive.

Bryan went downstairs to look for the album. Around the time of Dad's accident, Ivy had stolen a bunch of photos leaving gaps in Mom's careful chronological sequence, but there were plenty left. Bryan wanted to see one shot of that camping trip, Dad, Mom, Ivy, and he crouching in front of the tent. Dad had set the timer, placed the camera on the splintery picnic table and raced back, tripping over a tent stake, but still in time to wrap his arms around all of them. When the camera clicked, it caught them all laughing.

The album wasn't in the bookcase or the cabinet under the TV or anywhere else Bryan looked. Maybe Ivy had taken it with her. Could be the album was pushed under her bed or in her closet.

Ivy had left her room a mess. He'd go in occasionally and sit on her bed, thumb through her spiral notebook, but never learned anything from it. "In my opinion, *Romeo and Juliet* is unrealistic and gives the wrong idea about teenagers. No one I know would run away with someone she'd known for less than a fortnight, never mind kill herself over that person. Even bearing in mind that this takes place in an earlier time period, I find it ridiculous ..." Doodles, curvy, bubble letters, diagrams of what might be pool tables covered with dotted lines and circles, sentence fragments. "I wish ..." "If only ..." Since the last time he'd visited, her pen had bled onto the rumpled sheet. How did a ball point pen spontaneously begin to leak? Their mother had never come in to clean. Strange, when their mother hated messes so much, that she had pulled the door closed on this one.

Clothes and papers cluttered the floor. Rubber bands twisted with snarls of her hair littered her dresser top. He picked one up, pulling free a dark strand. A part of his sister. He could make a voodoo doll, burn it to cast a spell forcing her return. He rolled the hair between his fingers, then dropped it. No photo album in sight. The closet door hung open, clothes and shoes spilling out. He checked her closet shelves for the photo album. The name plate on her pool cue case, their father's pool cue case, winked at him. So she hadn't taken that. He didn't touch it. He squatted to check the floor. Old games in their boxes—Monopoly, Sorry, Stratego. She always won. If she started to lose, if he built hotels, or got three of his men into home, or came close to her flag, she'd quit, leaving him full of silent rage. He'd swear he'd never play with her again, but he always did, hating himself as he set up his pieces, hating himself for believing even for one second this time would be different. He'd hate her too, but only for a minute when she won or quit. Sorting the colored money, putting the deeds in order, lining up the pieces in the box, he'd hate himself for being such a sucker.

He dug deeper in the closet. Camping equipment, a blow drier, old magazines. Something weird on the back wall. He pulled a lamp over from the dresser and switched it on. He pushed the clothes to the side. On the back wall of the closet, Ivy had made a mosaic of broken glass and torn photographs, mostly of Dad, one of Dad in his army uniform, his arm around Grandma MacKenzie, a few of Ivy, herself. That's where the photos had gone. The summer they'd dug the hole she'd been collecting glass. She took all they found, even the pieces Bryan wanted to keep. Everett had a collection of sea glass, worn smooth and cloudy by the sand and water. Ivy's glass gleamed bright and sharp. If you touched that wall you'd bleed. He wondered if his mother knew it was there. She'd noticed the missing pictures. Bryan didn't remember Ivy being punished, but there was so much he'd forgotten. He'd only been five years old. The weight of all he didn't know about the people he lived with, the house he lived in, pushed down on him. Ivy had knelt, right where he was kneeling, applying glue to glass, hour after hour.

He heard the front door open and voices, Neal Richards' braying laugh. He wound one of his sister's skirts around his head to block the sound.

"Problem with sex is that it has to end," Gil said, standing naked, searching through the pockets of his clothes for cigarettes. "Come to think of it, that's the same problem with cigarettes—smoke them, they're gone. Food—eat it, what do you have? Money ... That sucks. Nothing lasts." He sat on the edge of the bed, threw his jeans against the wall, held his head in his hands. "I got to go buy cigarettes," he said.

"We've got to find jobs," said Ivy. She piled crumpled bills and coins on the blanket. "This is all the money we have left." Except the twenty he knew nothing about. She felt it when she walked, not just under her foot but all around her.

He slid into his pants. He never wore underwear. Smoothing and stacking the dollar bills she liked the idea of him, naked under his jeans but maybe he wasn't so unusual in that. She had no way of knowing.

"So how much we got?"

"Thirty-seven dollars and sixty-three cents." Ivy held the bills in one hand and jangled the coins in the other.

He reached for the money. Ivy gave it to him. "Get me a plain yogurt," she said.

The bed creaked as he leaned over her, kissing her breasts. They seemed swollen and achey—maybe from so much sex. "I could look at you and touch you all day long," Gil said. "Back in a minute. Soon as I get cigarettes. I'll get a paper too—we can go through the want ads." Sunlight flooded the room during the moment the door opened. Then, it closed.

He adores me, Ivy whispered, loving the sound of it. She brushed her teeth and felt better. She decided not to bother dressing; she wrapped a sheet around herself instead, noticing how creamy white her stomach looked against her brown arms. They hadn't swum in the Gulf of Mexico yet.

At home Mom would be slaving away at the bank, Bryan at school, the sidewalks edged with shrinking piles of dirty snow. She thought of calling but what would they say? More yelling. Come home. She couldn't go back. Not yet. People thought she was trouble before, the girl who hangs out at the pool hall. They'd have more to say now and she didn't want to hear it. Curly, Leo Leveaux, all the regulars at Rivertown Billiards—she wouldn't mind seeing them. Curly and all the sentences he dropped here and there about her father, like pictures she grabbed and hoarded and looked at as if she'd pasted them in an album. Curly's sentences glued together into some kind of story. Her father, smiling, perfectly relaxed even with a hundred dollars at stake. "He knew he'd win," Curly said. "When you know you're gonna win, you usually do." Her father wailing on his harmonica surrounded by clapping, stomping, people. "He took his game seriously, but he knew how to have fun. Everybody wanted to buy him a drink.

"Your Dad, he could've been a pro, before …" Curly always stopped there, squinted at the cue ball, then at Ivy. Before he went to Vietnam? Before marrying their mother? Before kids? Before he died? She always felt Curly would stop telling her anything if she seemed too eager to know more.

"He'd bring you in here in one of them little seats, set you on the table. Ruined the felt but I never said anything. Good for business, John's happy little baby drooling on a billiard ball. You never cried in here, not once."

Gil came back without the newspaper, a cigarette dangling from his lips. He dropped a bag of chips and a giant container of yogurt on the bed and popped open a beer. Foam spilled over his hand. At the smell Ivy raced for the bathroom, shoulders heaving, nothing to throw up. She wiped cold sweat from her forehead.

"What's the matter?" He stood in the doorway, swigging from the can.

Ivy sat back on her heels in front of the toilet, shaking her head.

"Maybe you just better rest today." Gil flicked his ashes into the toilet. "I'll go out and look for a job. Guy at the store said he'd heard they were hiring at the carwash. Think you've got a flu?"

"Don't know."

"Maybe you're pregnant."

"No way!" Ivy said suddenly worried she was. She wanted to ask him why he hadn't bought a paper but she didn't want to make him mad. If he had any sense, he would have bought a small container of yogurt. They had no way to keep anything cold. He always overdid it. More wasn't always better. She didn't feel like eating anyway.

Pregnant! She remembered Bryan's Sunday morning breakfasts, waffles with strawberries and whipped cream. Or oatmeal with raisins and brown sugar. She could eat oatmeal, warm and bland, settling her shaky stomach. She lay on the bathroom floor and closed her eyes. She heard Gil open another beer and tear open the chips.

"Bet you didn't know beer is loaded with B vitamins," he said, standing over her. "And potatoes … the most perfect food. If you could only pick one thing to eat for the rest of your life, you'd survive longest on potatoes. Come on, honey, I'll help you to bed. You rest. I'll take care of you. You know I will. You're my baby."

Baby. Baby. Sick in the morning. Full breasts. When was the last time she had a period? She'd remember spending money on tampons. She hadn't, not once since leaving home. Two months. And condoms. They'd used the ones they had by the time they reached Daytona and hadn't wanted to spend money on more. Gil said he'd be careful, pull out. How could she be so stupid? She pressed a hand to her abdomen. Gil's voice splashed over her. She couldn't make out the words. He crouched next to her, lifted her, his baby. Carried her, head cradled against his shoulder, legs dangling, tucked her into bed.

Gil slipped off his clothes in one fluid motion and lay beside her. He rubbed her forehead, her cheeks; his fingers moved along her body with love and something else. He desired her. He needed her.

"I'll always love you," he murmured. When they lay still and satisfied, his cigarette smoke curling to the ceiling, he told her again his version of their happily ever after. "We'll get a little house with a porch. And a couple kids—not too many. And cats, at least three. You sure you're not pregnant?" He kissed her ear. "And we'll help the kids with their homework and make sure they do good in school. They could even go to cub scouts and swimming lessons, summer camp, shit like that."

Ivy forced a laugh.

"What?" Gil grinned. "You had all that stuff."

"Some of it," Ivy said. "The swimming lessons and the homework." All she'd wanted was adventure, not a baby or a partner for life. "I don't want kids. Not for a long time."

"Well, you call it. You're the mother. Whenever you're ready." He opened another beer. "I'll finish this and go see about that job."

Ivy wondered why it took her so long to realize she was pregnant. It wouldn't take long for Gil, who knew every inch of her body, to know the truth. He didn't believe in abortion, said he'd kill her if she ever had one. When she tried to envision the house he talked about, all she could see was the house she'd grown up in and her mother's face when Ivy told her she was pregnant. What would her father have said?

"Did you say Daddy?" Gil asked. "Are you okay?" Without waiting for an answer he dressed again. "You know," he said, putting the last beer in a bag to bring along. "I've figured it out. You might think I'm an alcoholic. Lots of people are. Not me. I'm an alcoholist. One who knows alcohol. Good word, huh? Who do you call to get words added to the dictionary? Wonder if they pay you anything." He brought her a glass of water. "You take it easy. This is how it'll be when we're married. You can lie in bed all day if you want while I work to bring home the bacon. A lady of leisure ... alcoholist ... that should be worth at least a thousand dollars. No, two. A two-thousand-dollar word." He kissed her hard leaving a sour taste of beer in her mouth.

"Bryan?" Carol called up the stairs. No answer.

"The lights are on." Neal unzipped his coat and threw it over the banister.

With a cluck of annoyance Carol picked it up and hung it in the hall closet, before taking off her own. She didn't know if she could go through with this. Once they were in her room, in her bed, with the door closed, it would be all right, but how would they get there?

"Bryan, are you home?" She called again, poking her head into the living room on her way toward the kitchen. Neal followed her. No smells of garlic or onion frying. The four chairs pushed in against the edge of the table, undisturbed. She circled the table, looking for a drop of sauce, a crumb, anything to indicate he'd been here. No unwashed dishes in the sink. The dishrag hung dry. "He's not here," she said, her throat suddenly parched. "It's late. No sign he even came home after school." For a moment her legs wobbled. She leaned against the counter to keep herself upright. "Now he's gone too."

"The lights are on," Neal said again, crossing the kitchen with comforting arms open wide. In the moment it took him to charge across the small stretch of linoleum Carol's mind raced back and forth through the thirty-six years of her life. How stupid she was as a child, thinking parents have all the power. If a daughter could just take it into her head to run away, then the parent had no power at all. None. Now, she'd lost her son. Neal held her. Bryan, Ivy, Johnny all gone. If she had tears or the capacity to make them, she'd cry. A good mother would.

"Hey." Neal's voice rumbled in his chest, a hearty tone he wouldn't use with her, and without looking, she knew Bryan had appeared. Neal relaxed his hold on her and stepped back. Feeling suddenly exposed, she hugged herself, shoulders hunched.

Bryan waved an old photo album, the one with the yellow smiley faces dotting the cover. The browning pages had lost their stickiness. Pictures slipped around under plastic sheets, corners protruding from the closed book. "Give that to me," Carol said. "I'll fix it."

Bryan hung on to the album, face twisted in wordless accusation. She hoped he wouldn't yell the way he had in the bank. She'd tried to raise her children with good manners. "Can't you even say hello to Neal?"

"What's that you have there?" Neal asked.

"Old pictures," said Carol. "From ten years ago at least. You should see my hair back then!" Her attempt at an airy laugh sounded strangled.

"Let me see." Neal reached for the book.

Bryan yanked it out of reach, then clutched it to his chest. Two photos fluttered to the floor.

"No need to be rude," Carol succeeded in making her tone mild. Neal was great with teenagers. He was one of the most popular teachers at the high school. If Bryan, like a regular boy, chose shop instead of food lab, he'd know from personal experience what a good man Neal was. She rescued the pictures. Johnny in his uniform, taken just after basic training when he looked tan, tough and gorgeous, and so young. The other showed him and her together sitting in the lifeguard chair at the pond. His friend, Larry, posed them there and insisted on taking the photo "… so when you're old and ugly you'll remember how in love you are today."

Neal breathed at her shoulder. In front of her Bryan hugged the album and seethed. "They used to let you swim at Long Pond," she said. "Before it got too polluted."

Neal cleared his throat and she knew he'd changed his mind about staying.

"I can make some tea or coffee," she said hoping she didn't sound desperate. "Or, Bryan, you can make some hot chocolate. He makes the best cocoa in Rivertown. I always tell him he should set up a stand at the football games."

Bryan scowled.

"Not tonight, Carol. Another time." Neal patted her arm. "I'll talk to you tomorrow. See you, Bryan."

Carol followed Neal out of the kitchen. "My car," she said. She would go with him, get away from this house and her son, at least for a few minutes.

"I'll pick you up in the morning," he said. "Both of you. We'll drop you off on the way to school."

"Neal." She squeaked out his name.

Bryan stood, silent in the kitchen doorway, watching. One quick, friendly hug and Neal was gone.

Carol curled into herself, slumped on the bottom stair.

"I found this album in Ivy's closet," Bryan said, voice tentative and thin.

Carol didn't answer, afraid of what she'd say.

"You should see what else is in there," he went on.

"I don't want to talk about your sister right now," Carol said. "She's the last thing I want to talk about right now. Or even think about. I'm tired." If he knew how tired, how close to giving up, how his adolescent selfishness had destroyed the fragile sprout of happiness Neal had coaxed into being, he wouldn't be standing there so smugly.

"She glued pictures of Dad …"

"I don't want to hear it!" Carol yelled. She covered her ears. "Just shut up."

Bryan darted past her; the photo album clipped her cheek. The door to his room slammed.

Ivy listened to the quiet Gil left behind—the stillness of a summer evening at home after the power mowers had been put away in garages and basements. She loved her neighborhood then, lightning bugs against the bushes, low talk on porches, sound of television laughter through screen doors.

"I'm not pregnant," she said aloud. She was homesick. Sick. Sick. Homesick. Bryan. Mom. She missed them. She missed the pool hall. "What the hell am I doing? What am I going to do?" She couldn't go back there—to school. She hated it. Every day the same. Everyone hating her. The troubled girl with no friends whose Dad got killed. The girl who plays pool in a pathetic attempt to be like him. "Which is not why at all." She bit her lip to keep from wailing, hugged herself, arms against her tender breasts. "I can't go back. Everybody talking. I won't go back. I don't want a baby."

"I'll find a job." She pulled on a tank top and jeans. She'd earn money for the abortion, set a little aside each week, tips maybe, from waitressing. She already had the twenty. Gil would never have to know.

A key turned in the lock. She needed more time. He couldn't be back so soon. She folded her hands over her belly, the zipper of her jeans, and drew into an alcove under the empty clothesbar.

A clanking accompanied by a whistled rendition of "When Irish Eyes are Smiling." The cleaning man, bald and cheerful like Curly, opened the dented venetian blinds.

Ivy coughed.

He spun around. "Ah, saw the fella leave, thought you'd both gone out, excuse me, Miss." He stared at her with eyes as electric blue as Gil's. He studied her face, made no offer to come back later, no move to leave the room. His forehead wrinkled in concern.

"I'm on my way out," she said.

"Heard some noise the other night," he continued, staring at her. "Been in the business long enough, I know the sounds of love and ..."

"You don't know anything about me," Ivy said, the muscles in her face beginning to twitch.

"Nothing wrong with a little nooky," the man grinned. "But that's not what's happening here."

"Mind your own business," Ivy whispered. "I mean it. Please."

"This is my business, my motel, not much to look at but as the proprietor, what goes on in these here rooms matters to me. Don't want anybody getting hurt." He hefted a vacuum cleaner from the cart.

"Nobody's getting hurt," Ivy snapped, heart racing. Gil hadn't hurt her, hadn't hit her or anything, only pushed her against the wall, not hard, and yelled a little. They'd leave as soon as he came back, before this guy said anything to Gil or the cops.

"Listen," the man said, plugging in the vacuum cleaner. "Guys like him ... nothing but trouble. You think he'll stop banging you around. He won't. Don't you watch the news? Talk shows?" He switched on the vacuum and shouted over the noise. "You made a mistake with him. Happens all the time, people making mistakes. Get away before you get killed. Or pregnant."

"Too late," Ivy muttered, rubbing her eyes. The small, round man spouting unasked for advice as he vacuumed the rug couldn't be real. No one cleaned while the guests stood in the closet. Strangers didn't take an interest in someone else's life unless they expected to get something out of it. Maybe he'd offer her money in exchange for … what was it? Nooky? She'd do it. She'd fuck him if he'd give her enough for the abortion. If he'd pay for that, she'd do whatever he asked.

He unplugged the vacuum cleaner and wound up the cord. "You seem like a good girl," he said. "Go home."

"How do you know I even have a home?" Ivy asked, stretching out on the bed. He ignored her body by staring into her eyes.

"I can tell."

"What else can you tell?" She cocked her head, licked her top lip.

"I can tell that if you stay with this guy he'll make you miserable for the rest of your life." He put the vacuum cleaner back on the cart.

"What do you want from me?" Ivy asked, sitting up.

"Here's some clean towels." He set them on the dresser. "I'll leave you alone. You can make the bed when you're done lying in it."

He bumped the cart over the door jamb and rattled away. Ivy stifled her sobs in the pillow. She didn't want to be pregnant. She didn't want to be two thousand miles from home with twenty dollars and a boyfriend who hurt her. She remembered her note, "I know exactly what I'm doing."

When Gil found out, he'd never let her go. He might have been laughing when he'd said he'd kill her if she ever had an abortion. But he meant it. If she had his kid and he knew about it, their lives would be tangled forever. She'd never meant for that to happen.

"You're a good girl," she said aloud. After Rich had driven off with all their stuff, Gil had sweet talked a clerk at a Goodwill into giving them another duffel bag and some clothes. Ivy emptied it on the bed. How much belonged to her? How much to Gil? How much did they share?

She sorted through the clothing, burying her face in his Aerosmith tee shirt. She breathed his sweet and sour smell, then dropped it on the pile she'd take with her.

With his persuasive tongue and hypnotic blue eyes, Gil got what he wanted, short of love and money. For some reason, he said, money kept its distance and love … well, until Ivy he'd never had any. So his story went. But when it came to trinkets, Gil was a magnetic force. People gave him things, a silver roach clip with a secret compartment from the driver of a cement mixer outside of Philadelphia, a confederate cap from a cabby in Richmond, a rhinestone studded St. Christopher from the dashboard of a soft-spoken lady in Jacksonville. All Gil's. She needed the bag. He could use a pillow case. She left the handful of stubby pencils, his ragged drawings on backs of placemats and flyers. She still had the one he'd given her the night they met.

Ivy scooped her pile in one arm. A rolled paper napkin fell onto the rug. She dropped the clothes to the bottom of the bag and clipped it shut. She might write a note if she could find a pen and think of something to say. She picked up the paper napkin and felt something wrapped inside, a miniature pink parasol.

It had decorated her pina colada the night they'd left Daytona. The college guy in a BMW picked them up, took them to the fanciest restaurant Ivy had ever seen. They sat at the bar, a Plexiglas fishtank. She laughed, watching goldfish swim under their drinks. The student bought round after round of shots for Gil and sweet fruity concoctions for Ivy and himself. Ivy kept the pink paper umbrella, her favorite, as proof she hadn't dreamed the whole evening.

She'd watched the BMW cruise out of sight, then stumbled after Gil down an embankment, under a bridge. Out of sight of traffic, Gil began yelling, "I saw the way you smiled at him."

She started to say, "I don't know who ..." when he slapped her mouth, then grabbed her by the ears, shaking her, fuming.

Holding the tiny umbrella between her fingers, Ivy touched her tender earlobe. He'd yanked her earring out that night. If the cheap catch hadn't opened it would've torn right through her ear. He'd stopped yelling to stare at the blood running down her neck and the small, silver hoop in his hand. He'd thrown up, then passed out.

She moved the paper cylinder up the umbrella's toothpick shaft. It had been in her pocket when Gil knocked her to the ground, picked her up, shoved her down again, yet the paper and toothpicks hadn't torn or splintered. It still worked. She held it toward the light. The pink glowed. She tossed it onto the bed next to the unopened yogurt, lifted the duffel bag to her shoulder and forced herself out the door.

CHAPTER 3

"It's his baseball caps," Bryan said to Ev on their way home from school. "Middle-aged men in baseball caps. Why? To hide their bald heads. To make themselves look younger." He shook his head. "And every time he takes it off one clump of that fringe sticks out, like Bozo the clown. I never know whether to say anything or not."

Everett sneezed and wiped his runny eyes. "I don't know what's so great about spring," he said. "Everything in my head itches, the roof my mouth, deep in my ears, everything. I should leave every April. Just get the hell out."

Trees budded. The magnolia at the corner exploded with heavy pink and white blossoms. "It's not so bad here," Bryan said.

"Not for you, maybe." Everett blew his nose on a shredded tissue.

They clomped up the porch steps. Bryan reached a hand into the mailbox, while jiggling the door handle with the other. He pulled out a handful of postcards. Ivy! "Key's under the mat," he told Everett before turning his back and hunching over the cards. He checked the handwriting. Yes. But why two, three, four, five, six, postcards in one day, after so long with nothing? Why today? Thursday. Tomorrow was the last day of school before April vacation. Why on such a nondescript day, the day before the day before vacation, when Everett was standing there expecting to hang out in his room and listen to music like they always did, why now? Why hadn't he sensed it all day long? For months now he'd focused his psychic energy on his sister. He checked the post-marks—Miami. He checked the dates, to put them in order before reading them—all mailed at the same time.

Ev pushed the door open and the key back under the mat. "What's the matter?"

Bryan shuffled through the cards again. No dates written on them either. *I'm fine. Warm here. Haven't seen any manatees. You wouldn't believe how every-*

one speaks Spanish. He flipped the card over to see a gray blob of an animal in turquoise water. The next card pictured an orange grove. *When you drink your juice think of me. Maybe I picked one of the oranges they squashed to make it. If I didn't, someone did and believe me, it is hard work. We did it for five days. Would have done it longer but on the fifth day, neither of us could move anymore. Had to lie on the beach to recover. I still ache. For filling a huge bin, the size of two bathtubs, they paid us five dollars. In a whole day we were only able to fill three. The people who were used to it did a lot more than that.*

"Postcards?" Ev asked.

"Yeah." Bryan fanned them out like a poker hand. "From Ivy. Finally." He kept his voice even.

"Really!" Ev slapped him on the back. "She's okay, then? What does she say?"

Bryan passed him the two he'd read and went on with the others. *The sun is hot. The ocean's warm. I wish I could send you a Cuban sandwich or even tell you how they make them, Bryan. They're really good. I found a perfect sanddollar, as small as a dime.*

"Great! So she's okay!" Ev gave Bryan a celebratory shove.

Great. She wasn't dead—they finally knew it. Bryan hated her again. Fun in the sun while he coaxed his mother, their mother, to keep going, living her days. Never mind the convincing he had to do on himself. And now he was crying. "This pollen's bothering me too now. Fuckin spring."

"Hey." Ev peeled a paint chip from the porch rail. "Listen, it must be a shock."

Bryan nodded, concentrating on the peeling paint.

"Your mother'll be happy."

Bryan sat on the railing, wiped his eyes, and looked at the house. Everett stood beside him facing the street.

"It's not fair," Bryan said sounding like a whiny baby. He stopped himself from adding, "the way some people rush through life thinking only about what they want and other people try so hard."

"Weird how she went with Gil," Ev said. "Girls don't like nice guys. They say they do, then they pick scum." He sneezed hard three times.

"Yeah." Relieved his tears had dried up and his throat felt back to normal, Bryan led the way into the house. Parents were the same. The bad kid mattered most, even when she wasn't there.

In the kitchen Everett helped himself to a banana while across the refrigerator door Bryan arranged a colorful display of Ivy's postcards: the orange grove, the manatee, a cartoonish map of Florida with a smiling sun instead of an o, Florida's gators, and a shot of neon trimmed, art deco hotels along Miami Beach.

Ivy cleaned rooms at the Paradise Gardens guesthouse in Miami Beach to save money for her abortion. She slept at the Salvation Army. The woman at the traveler's aid counter in the bus station told her about both. Celine, a small white girl with dreadlocks, and her only friend, slept in the next bed. "We have to stick together," Celine told her. "Us white girls from the cold north. Not knowing no Spanish or Creole. We need each other."

Sometimes Ivy felt she'd gone farther from home than she'd meant to. The only English heard in the women's dorm was the slurred music of the deep south, strange as a foreign language. Other times, looking at her joyless face in the cloudy mirrors over the row of sinks, she felt that for all her pains, she hadn't gone anywhere.

She took three buses to get to the guest house on Collins Avenue. When she finished work in the late afternoon she walked the block and a half to the beach and lay on the white sand, listening to the waves lap or crash, wondering if Gil tried to find her, hoping and fearing he would. She wondered why they called it morning sickness. She felt sick all day. Sometimes she'd have just cleaned a toilet and she'd go and mess it up with her pitiful puking. On the beach she scratched out holes to spit into, then filled them in. Planes approaching the airport flew low overhead, full of people on vacation or people coming home.

Ivy brushed sand from her shorts and squinted up and down the beach, looking for Celine. Most days, by sunset, they were back at the Salvation Army, eating soup and stale donuts. Ivy knew they were missing curfew, they'd be locked out for the night, but it was Saturday and warm and Celine had decided they deserved some fun. "Besides, we'll miss that lousy church service tomorrow morning—them in their stupid army of the lord uniforms and that ridiculous music," she'd said. "Maybe we'll meet some rich guys. Don't you want to meet a rich guy, Ivy? This town is full of multimillionaires. Why shouldn't we meet them?"

Along Ocean Drive car horns blared, the tasteful neon signs glowed against the pink streaked sky. The silhouetted palm trees at sunset reminded her of an old viewmaster slide—Barbie and Ken in Hawaii.

A roll of bills, her week's pay, bulged in her front pocket. In the shadow of the outdoor shower Ivy split it, a hundred dollars in her left pocket for the abortion, twenty in her right for spending. She rinsed her mouth at the drinking fountain, chewed a piece of peppermint gum to take away the taste of vomit and tepid water, and steeled herself for a night of fun. She'd rather be sleeping on her cot. She sat on a low wall to wait and in her head, composed another postcard to Bryan. *Miami Beach has the most small, perfectly groomed dogs in the world. Surprisingly, they always belong to big, perfectly groomed men. In Rivertown, if you even saw a dog that fancy, it would belong to an old lady who lived alone in one of those big houses over by the library. Tonight I saw eleven of them walk by in just the fifteen minutes I spent waiting for my friend. You'd like her. She's from Michigan. She has dreadlocks to her waist and a tattoo of Bob Marley on her back and a ring in her belly button and a jewel in her nose. I'm sure it's a rhinestone, but it could be a diamond. You never know.*

"Sorry, sorry, I'm late." Breathless, Celine rushed across the strip of well tended grass where dogs did their business and owners followed with plastic bags. "Listen, I got you a job if you want it. No more cleaning toilets. One of the waitresses quit and I told the boss I knew someone who could start Monday. He said just come in. You'll get tips on top of minimum wage. And you'll get to work with me at least sometimes, when our shifts overlap."

Celine worked at the diner on Washington Avenue. "I know it's not the most glamorous place, but with restaurant experience, in a month or two we can get jobs in fancier places and really bring in the bucks."

Ivy hesitated. She wondered if she could stand to be around food.

"What?" Celine boosted herself onto the wall next to Ivy. "It's a better job, I'm telling you. The boss is a creep, but the tips are good. We'll have enough for an apartment in a month, maybe sooner."

A tall white bird, looking like it belonged at the edges of a lake, landed on the grass and stood regally until a poodle yapped, and it flapped away, long legs dangling. Two young guys slouched toward their wall. Ivy wondered for the thousandth time why Gil hadn't found her yet and why she wasn't more relieved. And what about her mother and Bryan? Were they just glad to be rid of her? No one knew her in Miami Beach except Celine. The boys approached, jostling each other, laughing. Celine laughed back and waved.

"Destin and George," she said.

"What?" Ivy whispered.

"You do know what a good time is, don't you? Don't ruin this. They'll take us out, spend money. They're nice. Come on, smile."

"Hey, chicas!" George, the taller of the two, called out. "Celine, introduce your friend, why don't you?"

"Ivy." Celine scooted off the wall and posed, hand on hip, chest out, tight tee shirt rising just enough to expose a strip of belly flesh and glittering navel ring. "Destin and George. From New York City. Came into the diner and asked where they could find a good time. I said we'd show them."

Destin, dark and compact, had the body of wrestler and a huge, gleaming smile. He nodded at Ivy. Somehow it had already been decided he was with her.

Celine cocked her head at George. "Do you like Mexican food? Margaritas? We know a place off Lincoln Road, right Ivy? It won't cost you much."

"Whatever you say, baby," George draped an arm over Celine's shoulder. Ivy willed herself to her feet. Palm trees, sunset, soft night air, salsa music, a friend, cute boys with money to spend—just what she had in mind when she first imagined Florida, long before Gil.

"How long you been living in Miami?" Destin asked. They fell into step behind Celine and George. "You like it?"

Was this living? "Awhile," said Ivy.

They walked in silence through the Lincoln Road Mall with its crowded stores, trees encrusted with tiny white lights, and restaurants with outdoor seating, lacy wrought iron, candlelit tables, and chalkboards advertising specials—food Ivy had never heard of. Bryan would know what it all was, even if he'd never tried it.

Celine paused in front of a menu and pointed. Ivy and Destin stopped short behind her. He used their near collision as a chance to touch Ivy's arm. Steadied by him she didn't mind.

"Stone crab," pronounced Celine. "Best thing I ever tasted."

"Twenty-seven dollars for five claws." Ivy read the board. "How could it be worth that?"

"It is," said Celine. She waited for George to say they'd splurge for it. Ivy touched her roll of money, wondering what George and Destin did to earn theirs. She'd rather pay than owe them anything. The moment stretched long, Ivy's embarrassment grew as Celine wheedled silently just by widening her eyes. George and Destin exchanged glances. Destin tipped his head, the slightest of shrugs.

"They're good?" George asked.

Ivy swallowed a combination of puke and panic. What if trapped around a table, George and Destin didn't like the crabs? What if she had to get up and be sick?

Celine showed no doubt or hesitation. She herded them closer to the door of the restaurant. "They're about the only meat you can eat without killing the animal," she said. "Besides the taste that's what I like about them. The claws grow back."

She spoke to the hostess. Ivy sat on the edge of a giant pot full of spiky plants. Destin and George swapped quick whispers.

"Outside or in?" Celine asked them.

Ivy waited for George or Destin to answer, but when they didn't, she suggested outside. She'd never sat in an outdoor restaurant. The only time people ate outdoors in Rivertown was in a neighbor's backyard.

Ivy tried to enjoy herself. Girls who slept at the Salvation Army didn't often sit in Lincoln Mall restaurants ordering stone crab. Then she remembered they wouldn't be sleeping at the Salvation Army tonight. She took a roll from a napkin covered basket to keep from resting her head on the table. Hope for the evening grew when the warm bread actually felt good in her mouth. She gulped water flavored with a lemon slice, her sickness subsiding.

"Thirsty?" Destin pushed his water glass toward her.

"I'm okay," she said. "So you're from New York?"

"Staten Island."

Celine and George, heads bent over the wine list, paid no attention to them.

"I don't … didn't … live too far from there," Ivy said. "But I only went once. They took our eighth-grade class on a bus, a nice one, not a school bus, and we went to the Statue of Liberty and Ellis Island. I wanted to go to the Empire State Building and Greenwich Village. Felt like we missed the city just taking that boat away from it."

"Staten Island ferry passes right by the Statue of Liberty," Destin said. "No waiting in line. A lot cheaper! You ever come back north, give me a call, I'll show you some things."

Back north. The waiter poured red wine in Celine's glass. She tasted it and nodded, impressing Ivy. How did she know to do that? He poured glasses for everyone.

"A toast," Celine said. "To new friends and fun in Miami Beach!"

"I'll drink to that," said George.

Glasses clinked together over the table. Ivy brought hers to her lips, afraid the smell would make her sick, but it didn't. She sipped and swallowed, drank some more. A soothing warmth filled her chest, a blurring of worries. Fun in Miami Beach seemed possible. Destin refilled her glass.

"Might as well order another bottle right now," Celine observed, bouncing a little in her chair.

George beckoned the waiter.

Carol stared at the postcard display on the refrigerator. In the past twenty-four hours, since Bryan called her at the bank, she'd studied the screaming colors from the safe distance of the kitchen table. Bryan seemed to view the cards as permission slips. Now he could leave her alone in the house. He'd been careful for so long, good boy that he was, not to do anything to make her feel more alone, more of a maternal failure. She'd been careful too. Three months into her relationship with Neal and they still hadn't managed to sleep together. This Saturday, the start of April vacation, with Bryan gone with Everett's family to their cottage on Plymouth Lake, Neal, his week off stretching pleasantly before him, was coming over to spend the night. She should shower, put on some fancy lingerie. She had some somewhere.

She tried to imagine Ivy and couldn't. All those stories about parents having psychic connections to their kids, but since Ivy disappeared, Carol hadn't once felt anything other than anger and sadness and despair, nothing supernatural about any of it. Even after reading Ivy's scrawled messages she had no sense of what her daughter was doing. She'd chosen some postcards, written and mailed them—the only things Carol knew for sure, the only concrete evidence.

Neal knocked at the door—a perky pattern of taps that irritated, more than cheered her.

"Don't get up!" he called, letting himself in. He sprang through the door of the kitchen with a bouquet of freesia in one hand, a bag from Jimmy's Barbecue in the other and a bottle under his arm. Dropping everything on the table he swooped down on her with a kiss.

She barely kissed him back.

"Bryan's not here, is he?" Neal asked.

"He's gone," she said.

"What's wrong then?" He took off his steamed up glasses, laid them on the table, and cupped her chin.

"Nothing." Carol shifted her gaze to the side to avoid looking into his watery blue eyes. They were tired and blood shot and old looking.

Neal waited, and when she wouldn't say more, picked up the champagne bottle. "I'll put this in the freezer. Just let's not forget about it. Whoa! So these are the postcards!" He stepped back and squinted at them. "That's a relief, huh?"

"Not really," said Carol.

He fit the bottle into the freezer.

"They don't say much."

"At least you know she's alive." Neal pulled up a chair close beside her. The flowers and food sat where he'd put them. Carol stared past him.

She couldn't stop looking at the postcards. They shouted at her, as loud as Ivy herself. Her face ached around her eyes.

Neal sighed and moved his chair behind hers. He began to rub her scalp, fingers buried in her hair at the crown of her head, thumbs circling over the two bony lumps at the base of her skull. She let her head fall forward and loved him for knowing not to talk.

Strange noises escaped her throat. The increased pressure of his fingers told her to go ahead and moan, sob, wail, whatever she wanted. He moved to her forehead, temples, eyes, cheeks. His hands held the heavy weight of her head. Her edges softened. She felt like broken glass, melted, shaped into something new, something that could hold water.

Knees aching, underwear twisted around her ankle, staring up at the bottom side of her kitchen chair, Carol laughed. Neal joined in.

She rubbed his beard and laughed harder. "Who would ever believe I have Neal Richards, Rivertown High School technical arts teacher, naked on my kitchen floor?"

"Who would ever believe Carol MacKenzie, uptight bank teller was naked beside him?"

"Uptight? Maybe. I am thinking this floor isn't exactly comfortable and I am worrying someone's going to walk in and find us here." Carol struggled to her feet. "Shall we reconvene in the bedroom?"

"I don't want to let go of you." Neal stood behind her. She felt his hard round belly against her back.

"Don't then." She placed his palm against her left breast and covered his hand with both of hers. Bodies joined, in step, they climbed the stairs.

There hadn't been a man in her bed since Johnny. She'd only recently moved toward the middle in her sleep.

Now there was Neal. Together they filled the bed. She pressed her nose to his neck, just under his ear.

"You smell like wood," she whispered, lips against his skin.

"What kind?"

"Just wood, I don't know. Saw dust."

"There are lots of kinds of wood, Carol," he said. "There's oak—that smells like clean water and maple smells more like toast and cherry has a spicy smell.

Or do you mean the vinegary smell of mahogany?" He stroked her hair. "Or do I smell like a hamster cage? That would be cedar. Or—"

"Don't make it so complicated!" She laughed. He knew worlds she didn't. He understood wood and teenagers and he knew how to build things.

They made love again slowly.

Neal wrapped a tissue around the used condom before setting it on the bedside table. Carol got up and threw it in the trash.

"I could've done that," he said.

"It wasn't bothering you." She crawled back between the sheets, fitting the cold soles of her feet against his calves.

"Do you ever think about having another baby?"

She answered quickly. "No." His question hung over the bed, solid inside a bubble, like words in comic book. The next frame. Him: Why not? Her: Why?

"This is nice," Neal said. He ran his hand along her hip.

"Yes."

The music pounded through the wall, a muffled throb, swelling sharply when someone opened the restroom door. Locked in a stall Ivy sat on a toilet with her shorts on, head in her hands, sweaty from dancing, sick from drinking, too full of regret to move.

Images of the evening cartwheeled through her alcohol soaked brain, her pickled brain. Her pickled baby. Her drunk baby. She tried to count the drinks. Two glasses of wine with dinner, two mojitos at the bar, that wasn't so much. Enough to brain damage a baby the size of a pinto bean, maybe, but did it matter if the baby had just days to live? She felt her roll of money, still whole in her pocket. Destin and George paid for everything. She'd offered to pay the tip, but they wouldn't let her.

On the crowded dance floor at the Lizard Lounge the four of them danced in a clump, twisting, shaking, wriggling around and against each other. When the music slowed they paired off, Ivy tight in Destin's arms, her head tucked against his shoulder, shirts damp and sticking to their bodies. She pretended this part Haitian boy with the quick smile and gentle questions, a beautiful boy her own age from New York City was her boyfriend. She imagined kissing him on the Staten Island ferry with the buildings of New York in the background, glittering over his shoulder like Oz. Dancing she was happy, but eventually, you always have to stop and pee.

"Ivy?" Celine called out. "You okay?"

"Yes." Not the truest answer, but certainly the easiest.

"Listen," Celine spoke through the crack in the stall door. "They've asked us back to their hotel. One room, two beds. I think we should go for it."

Ivy thought longingly of a bath. They probably had a tub.

"So, should I tell them we'll go? Ivy?" Celine's eye appeared at the crack. She jiggled the door. "What are you doing in there?"

"I drank too much," Ivy said. "I'm drunk."

"So what? We're all drunk. It's fun especially when someone else is buying. Are you puking? Driving the porcelain bus?" She laughed. "Calling Ralph? Yawning the technicolor yawn? Need me to hold your hair back?"

Ivy made no move to open the door. She sat on the toilet, holding her stomach, her head between her knees, afraid she was about to cry. Celine wouldn't understand tears on a night when they were having so much fun. Ivy hated secrets, she hated the secret pickled baby soon to be dead in a secret abortion. "I'm sorry," she whispered.

"For what?" Celine asked. "You don't want to go? Fine, I'll tell them. Just come out the bathroom, will you?" She shook the door so hard the entire row of stalls jiggled. "Hurry up."

"Is anyone else in here?" Ivy asked.

"No."

"I'm pregnant."

"What? Just unlock the door."

Ivy reached out and turned the catch. Celine stumbled in and slammed the door shut by leaning on it. "How long have you known?"

"A couple months."

"You better get yourself taken care of, girlfriend." Celine grabbed Ivy's chin. "Planned Parenthood."

"I'm saving money."

"They'll help with the money. Get your ass over there, first thing Monday morning. I'll go with you."

Girlfriend. Go with you. Ivy stared at Celine's navel ring and felt a rush of love like she'd never felt for Gil or anyone. "That's when I was supposed to start work at the diner."

"So what? They're desperate. They don't fire anyone. We'll go in late."

"Thank you," she said.

"Now, come on," Celine nagged. "The guys are waiting. We'll be lucky if they haven't left us."

The restroom door opened. Giggling. Loud conversation. "So then, you wouldn't believe it, she stood on the table, in her pink platform shoes and danced!"

A stall door clicked shut. Water ran.

"Hey, what are you two doing in there anyway?" Someone hooted.

"Fuck you," Celine snapped, poking her head out the door. "She's sick, you mind?

"Stupid bitches," she whispered in Ivy's ear.

"I'm not sure I want an abortion," Ivy whispered back. If Celine hadn't bent over her, hadn't come so close, she might not have said it. If she hadn't said it, she might not have known she thought it.

"Who's ever sure?" Celine mouthed. The other women flushed and left. "I had a baby. It's worse that way, I think. Every day that goes by I think about her. If I'd had an abortion, it would all be over, I wouldn't have to wonder all the time. I wouldn't have to look around at every kid her age and wonder. I tell myself some day she'll find me and then I'll know, but still …"

Ivy stared at her flat, tan belly. "How old are you?" she asked.

"Honestly? Fifteen. You can't tell anyone."

"How about when you had the baby?"

"Thirteen and a half."

"Younger than my little brother," Ivy said.

"I ran away after that. Once the school slut, always the school slut. I couldn't deal with it. Come on, I'm tired. I want a bed tonight. These are nice guys, I can tell. We won't have to do anything we don't want to and I bet they'll even buy us breakfast, room service if I tell them to."

Ivy followed Celine out of the stall. She splashed water on her face. She looked the same as before she met Gil. No older or wiser. No bruises. No evidence of a baby. She'd have the abortion, pretend the whole thing had never happened. Go back to school. Finish her paper on *Romeo and Juliet*. Go back to the pool hall. Perfect her shots—banks, caroms, and combinations.

CHAPTER 4

In the time it took Bryan to meander from his locker to Martine's to the technical arts wing where he was supposed to meet Neal, the place had emptied out. High school hallways a half hour after dismissal had to be the most unnaturally still places in the world. He peeked through the window of wood shop door. Neal hunched over a work bench alongside Roger Blake, the fattest kid in the school. Roger couldn't keep his jeans up. They sagged into empty folds beneath his flabby ass and wide knees, leaving a rashy strip of back exposed, displaying the top of his butt crack. Neal demonstrated a light sanding motion on the slats of a rectangular box Roger held in an awkward grip. Roger tried it. Neal shook his head and showed him again. Shoulders stiff with effort Roger copied him. Neal grinned, slapped him on the back, and said something Bryan couldn't hear. Losers liked Neal. They hung out in the woodshop before and after school, at lunch and during breaks. Maybe that was why his mother and Neal were together. The way her life had been going she sure qualified for loser status.

Just the evening before, she and Bryan had been cleaning the refrigerator and she cut her hand on a shard of glass from an exploded champagne bottle.

"I thought Neal took care of all this," she'd said, staring into her sliced palm as blood dripped down her arm and onto the floor. "This glass broke ages ago."

The freezer door hung open. Bryan grabbed a dish towel, wrapped it around his mother's hand, and lifted her arm. "Keep it up high. You probably need stitches."

She couldn't drive; he couldn't drive. "Call Neal," she said without the slightest hesitation. Faster than an ambulance Neal arrived and drove her to the emergency room. Bryan stayed home. When they returned Bryan pretended to be absorbed in the late movie, though now, standing outside Neal's shop, he couldn't remember a thing about it. He did remember in painful and exquisite detail Neal's tone, the catch in his voice when he asked Bryan to stop by after school today, that it was time for a talk. Ivy would have demanded to know the topic right there on the spot. Or she might have waited until Neal left and grilled Carol. But Bryan hadn't wanted to know. He'd given Neal no indication he'd heard. He'd cleaned the freezer properly, taking everything out and putting it back, and he was tired.

Neal straightened up and noticed Bryan framed in the window. He beamed and winked, waving Bryan in. Roger looked over his shoulder nervously.

"The rest can wait till tomorrow," Neal was saying as Bryan pushed through the door. "Didn't you say your grandmother's birthday was Saturday? That'll give you enough time to finish sanding and stain it and give it a coat of polyurethane."

The tip of Roger's tongue poked out as he pushed the sandpaper into a hard to reach corner of his project. "What are you making there?" Bryan asked to be polite.

Roger muttered something.

"Flowerbox," Neal said. He put a hand on Roger's back. "Time to stop for today. Come by tomorrow. What do you say I get you out of gym class?"

Roger grinned and shuffled over to the shelf of unfinished projects, placing his flowerbox between a birdhouse and a three-legged stool. "I can sweep up here," Neal said. "Don't worry about it." He held out his hand for the sandpaper as Roger passed on his way out of the room.

"Thanks, Mr. Richards." Roger said looking Neal right in the eye. Something passed between them that made Bryan want to smash Roger's stupid flowerbox.

"Close the door there, will you?" Neal said. "Have a good evening." The window glass rattled as the door banged shut.

"Kid like him needs gym class," Bryan said, brushing aside the sawdust with his hand and sitting on the workbench. "You shouldn't be getting him out of it."

"It's the last thing he needs." Neal took a push broom from the closet. "Humiliation. No one gets anything good out of being humiliated." The broom's yard long span of bristles seemed too big for the small amount of sawdust on the floor. Bryan brushed the pile beside him on the workbench down onto the linoleum. Neal maneuvered the broom behind it. "When I was in basic training there was always the guy everyone ragged on, the small guy, the guy that swings across ten rungs of monkey bars and falls in a heap, scrambles partway up the wall again and again, can't get his leg over the top. The drill sergeant calling him all the names he calls everyone else, but worse. Other guys joining in. One day you wake up and the guy's gone, bed smooth like no one slept in it. You think, finally, they sent him home where he belongs, only to find out, he tried to smash the drill sergeant's skull with an entrenching tool. People can only take so much."

"When were you in basic training?" Bryan felt a flutter of interest as he tried to calculate Neal's age. Maybe it had been the same time as his dad. "Were you in Nam?" He liked the casual way he managed to say it. Nam.

Neal cleared his throat, leaned on the broom, and studied the pile of sawdust. He looked about to say something.

"What?" Bryan asked.

"I'll tell you about it sometime," he said. "But that's not why I asked you to meet me."

"I'm not asking you to tell me all about it," Bryan said. "Just answer the question."

"It's not so simple." Neal passed the broom handle to Bryan and went for a dustpan.

When Bryan made no move to sweep the pile in, he took back the broom and did it himself, dumping the sawdust into the barrel.

Bryan folded his arms across his chest and crossed his ankles.

"Context is everything," Neal said.

"What's that supposed to mean?"

"I was drafted. I went to basic training. As it turned out I didn't go to Vietnam. I promise I'll tell you all about it. But not now." Bryan felt a twinge of satisfaction as Neal's usually mild voice sharpened and what little could be seen of his cheeks over his beard reddened. Roger's clumsy sanding efforts couldn't aggravate Neal, but Bryan's questions could.

"My dad joined up, the minute he was eighteen." Bryan regretted the little boy boasting quality of the words the moment he heard himself. "So what did you want to tell me?"

A shadow of reluctance passed over Neal's face. Bryan resented himself for resenting Neal and for wanting so badly to know what it was Neal had to say. He wished he could toss a "See ya' later," back over his shoulder and let the door fall shut behind him, the shaking window glass a rattly echo in Neal's ears.

"Let's go for a walk," Neal said. "I'm finished here."

"I don't feel like walking," Bryan mumbled.

"A drive then. My truck's out back. Come on."

I know what he's going to say, Bryan thought, and I don't want to hear it. But he accepted the armload of notebooks and folders Neal handed him and followed him to the teachers' parking lot.

After working at the diner for a month and a half, Ivy had her favorite customer, the tall man with a cowboy hat who called her Ma'am and always ordered three little boxes of Rice Krispies. She told Bryan about it on one of the postcards and couldn't help smiling when she set the little boxes on the counter beside a small metal pitcher of milk, hearing Bryan's incredulous voice, "Can't he make that himself, at home?"

"The man pays for my company," she'd say, imagining Bryan beside her.

"Like a prostitute?" he'd ask.

She really should call home. She longed to hear his voice, even her mother's voice, but she wouldn't know what to say about the baby.

"No." She'd give her brother a quick jab with her elbow. The coffee she was serving, sloshed into the saucer. "He likes me," she'd say. "I'm a good waitress, fast, accurate."

"Not hard to be fast or accurate serving cold cereal." She could see his lopsided grin.

She'd stopped feeling sick the day they woke up in Destin and George's hotel room and eaten a giant breakfast, all four of them cross-legged on the bed she and Celine had shared. The boys gave them their phone numbers in New York and seemed satisfied with the evening. Afterward Ivy remembered feeling vaguely disappointed that they hadn't kissed more or anything.

Ivy checked the clock near the swinging door to the kitchen, really a garish ad for Bacardi rum with a tiny clock face in the corner. It didn't even have numbers, just marks where the twelve, three, six, and nine should be. She'd gotten better at reading it. Ten after one. More than six hours down, less than two to go. "Pick up!" hollered Robert, the cook. He shoved three full plates of the pork chop special through the window, bending to wink at her.

Celine brushed past, dreadlocks tied up in a huge topknot, larger than her head. "That customer over there is mine," she whispered. "Don't even pour him a refill."

Ivy nodded. She didn't need reminding. Celine guarded that silver haired man with a strange ferocity. He walked with an easy loose limbed charm like a much younger man. When he removed his mirrored sunglasses, magnetic blue-green eyes flashed in his tanned angular face. He came in every day at the same time for lunch.

The owner's well fed and usually complacent son, Beauregard Bellamy Jr. sat at the counter with a pinched expression, watching Celine flirt. Ivy slid the plates onto the table in front of some pale tourists, a mother, a father, and a fidgety son. While taking orders, clearing plates, chatting with customers, she watched Beau watch Celine.

Everyone loved that mysterious girl, especially Ivy herself. Lately Celine had seemed even more full of secrets. She'd stayed out all night from the shelter the last two weekends and wouldn't tell Ivy where she'd been. She'd stop Ivy's questions with torrents of advice and reminders and warnings about waiting too long for an abortion. Ivy felt the nagging as love; in some ineffective but sincere way Celine was taking care of her. Instead of picturing Celine holding her hand as the doctor scraped her uterus, Ivy imagined her painting the baby's room, soft yellow or pale lavender. Ivy rushed around the diner hefting armloads of dirty plates, all the while furnishing the apartment full of light she and her baby would share with Celine.

The silver-haired man laughed. Celine slid into the booth across from him. The boss's son scowled. Ivy wouldn't dare to sit with a customer during a shift, though she'd been invited many times, especially the few times she worked nights and people had been drinking. Whenever she asked about that man, Celine changed the subject so skillfully it wasn't until later, Ivy even realized it. As a result, Ivy knew nothing about him.

The man fed Celine a forkful of key lime pie. Beau Bellamy leaped to his feet. Midstep Ivy changed her route to the kitchen to cut him off. He shoved past her missing the pot of coffee she carried in her right hand, knocking against the pot of decaf she held in her left. "God damn it!" he yelled, as coffee stained his white linen pants and cream colored loafers. Everyone in the restaurant looked at him and Ivy. "Watch where you're going!" He grabbed a hunk of napkins from a dispenser on the nearest table, blotting at his pants. His breathing was loud in the sudden silence. No silverware or dishes clanked, no water ran, conversation stopped. Ivy stood frozen, spilled coffee hot on her hand.

A familiar tinkling laugh. Then, "Seems like you're the one who needs to watch where he's going!" Celine's voice was calm and matter of fact, but in the quiet restaurant it might as well have been an announcement over a loudspeaker.

Beau Bellamy muttered furiously to himself, a vein throbbed in his fore-head. Ivy fought back a giggle. He looked just like a cartoon. Next he'd be slip-ping on a banana peel or stepping on a rake.

He threw the wad of napkins on the tourist family's table. It landed in the boy's plate and he began to complain, but his mother shushed him. Beau Bel-lamy scurried across the diner, focused only on Celine and yanked her from the booth. "You're fired!" he screamed. "Get out of here."

"Just a minute!" The elegant old man rose from the table.

"Don't involve yourself, Terry," Celine said. "He's not worth it. Let's go." She put her hand on the man's arm.

Wait, Ivy wanted to shout, you can't leave me here, but she stood speechless, arms beginning to ache from the weight of the cooling coffeepots.

"Ivy," Celine said over the heads of all the customers, making her a part of the play instead of just another member of the audience. "I'll meet you at the wall after your shift."

Ivy nodded.

Celine whispered something to Terry. He held the heavy glass door open for her and she paused, perfectly framed in the doorway, silhouetted by the bright sunshine. Heat blasted into the restaurant. "And all of you who eat here," Celine announced, "should know that this place is run by a pervert who thinks that being a boss gives you the right to fuck any waitress that strikes his fancy. And to fire any waitress who refuses."

Ivy, the only waitress on the floor, flushed. She felt everyone looking at her. Thinking what? Wondering why she still had a job? Bellamy had never both-ered her. Let him deal with the scene he'd started. She walked steadily toward the kitchen where Robert peered through the food window. He met her as she passed through the swinging door and took the coffee pots from her hands.

"That's a chick with *cojones*. Put that hand under cold water, see how red it is. You burned yourself." Robert turned the tap and cold water crashed into the deep metal sink.

"I should quit in solidarity," Ivy said.

"Listen, she may have found her sugar daddy, but you need the money don't you?" Robert slowed the stream of water. "Here, put your hand there. It's not the worst burn I've ever seen, but that's going to hurt for awhile."

"What do you mean, sugar daddy?" Ivy asked.

"That man, Terry Supp, owns one of the biggest yachts you've ever seen. Houses in Miami and Greece and Capri and the French Riviera. He is so stink-ing rich I wonder why he bothers eating in a place like this."

"You think Celine and he …" Ivy hand stung. "Celine's not … he's old."

"And rich," Robert said. "Keep it under there. You should have run back here right away, when the coffee spilled. I don't know how much it will help now. Except that show was too good to miss."

Beau Bellamy burst into the kitchen fuming. "Get out there, Ivy. People are waiting for their checks."

"Take it easy." Robert's unflappability was calming. "She's hurt."

"Let me see." Bellamy turned off the water. "It doesn't look so bad. Let's bandage it up." He rummaged in a drawer for the first aid kit, found some gauze and began wrapping it haphazardly around Ivy's hand. The combination of the pain, his clammy touch, and the shock of the whole scene brought back Ivy's nausea. Before she could turn back toward the sink she vomited on the floor splashing Beau Bellamy's coffee splattered shoes and slacks.

"Jesus Christ!" he yelled, leaping back against a counter.

Robert winked at her. "Maybe we should close early," he said.

Bryan sat beside Neal in the messy cab of his truck. Empty coffee cups littered the floor—rags, broken cassette cases and tapes, coins. To make a space for Bryan, Neal had tossed a pile of newspapers into the space behind their seats.

"Where to?" Neal asked.

"This was your idea," Bryan said.

Neal shifted into reverse, then pulled out of the lot. "Want ice cream?"

"I'm a not a little kid," Bryan said. "Just say what you're going to say."

Neal's lips tightened. He eased the truck into afternoon traffic on the River Road. They approached Rivertown Billiards, the gravel parking lot half-full, people stopping for beers on their way home from work. Ivy had gone there all the time. And before her, their dad. Bryan had never set foot in the place.

"Let's shoot some pool," Bryan said.

Neal followed his gaze as they passed the wide entrance to the lot. "Never was much good at it," he said.

Bryan rolled his eyes.

"But we can if you really want to." Neal signaled a turn into a driveway.

"No, that's okay." All those stories about Ivy hanging out there as a baby, yet Johnny MacKenzie had never brought him. Bryan didn't want to walk into Rivertown Billiards for the first time with Neal Richards. He'd wait for Ivy to come home and get her to go with him, introduce him to people as her brother, Johnny MacKenzie's son.

Neal flicked off the turn signal. "Well, then."

"Well," Bryan resisted the urge to pull out his harmonica.

They drove along the River Road to the dam and back without speaking. Neal made a few turns through a ramshackle west side neighborhood Bryan had never explored, and parked the truck in the driveway of a large grey house. "Thought we could stop a minute and use the facilities," Neal said. "Maybe grab something to eat and a football."

"I hate football."

"Frisbee?"

Bryan sighed loudly.

"Want to come in or wait here?" Neal opened the door.

"Where exactly are we?"

"My apartment," Neal said. "I live up there." He pointed. "In the attic. Mary Worthington, the guidance counselor, lives downstairs with her sister, Agnes, the retired principal of Lincoln School."

"Miss Worthington? She was Ivy's guidance counselor. And the other one—my dad told me she used to hit the kids with Hot Wheel tracks instead of yardsticks 'cause they didn't break."

Neal snorted. "I heard that too."

"She's legendary."

The summer before Bryan started kindergarten, the summer of Johnny's accident, he told Bryan several times how lucky he was that Agnes Worthington had retired. Johnny's laughter, as he related tales of being dragged to the principal's office by the ear, forced to sit with his nose against a dot she'd painted on the wall for that purpose, and whipped with the same bright orange pieces of track Bryan and Ivy raced cars on, confused Bryan. The stories seemed more terrifying than funny, but he obliged his father with a forced chuckle. On the first day of school he stood by the chainlink fence and cried. When his mother yanked his arm he held his breath until he grew dizzy and she ran for the school nurse. The principal, not Miss Worthington at all, but a tall red-haired man with a kind face, came instead and squatted beside Bryan, offered him a cherry cough drop, and gently coaxed him into the building. What Mr. Pelham did and said mattered less than the fact that he wasn't Miss Worthington. Bryan remembered worrying that his father up in heaven could see how foolish he'd been, not a brave and strong boy at all. And how could Bryan have forgotten he'd been told a hundred times that Miss Worthington had retired.

"This is their house," Neal said. "I finished the attic apartment for them and in return, they've let me live here for practically nothing for the past, what is it now, going on five years."

Bryan slid down from the seat and followed Neal up the walk, trying to peer in the dark windows to catch a glimpse of Miss Worthington. Neal caught his eye and grinned.

At the back of the house they climbed up three long steep flights of stairs. "I sure won't miss this climb," Neal said breathing hard.

"What do you mean?"

Neal didn't respond and the back of his head revealed nothing, yet Bryan now knew he was right. Neal was going to move in with them. That little slip confirmed it.

Bryan didn't want to like the apartment, but he couldn't help it. "Your house is a lot neater than your truck," he said.

Neal laughed. The place was perfectly scaled for one person. The built-in shelves and cabinets in the sky lit kitchen were well stocked with jars, cans, and boxes of food. A huge ceramic bowl of mail filled the center of the table. Bryan recognized his mother's handwriting on a folded note. Neal tossed a package of fig newtons onto the table. "Help yourself. If you want something to drink, take it. Refrigerator's under there." He sped off to the bathroom.

Bryan hated fig newtons. He bent to open the little refrigerator. A carton of milk, three cans of beer. He found a glass and filled it with water.

"So," Neal returned. "A little frisbee then?" He popped two fig newtons into his mouth and chewed.

"Neal." Bryan carefully set his half-empty water glass on the table. "Let's not make a big deal out of this. You're moving in with my mom and me, right?"

Neal pushed the plastic tray of cookies back into the bag. "Yes, we're getting married."

"Married!" Bryan slapped the table. "Why didn't she tell me? What about Ivy? Don't you think she would want to know? I hope you're going to wait until she comes home! Married!" He paced the little perimeter of the room, bumping his head once against the eaves. Neal stood dumb as a cow, folding the top of the cookie bag, creasing it over and over. "Haven't you heard of living together? To make sure it'll work out. Why do you want to marry my mother anyway?"

He stopped. This was a question he really wanted an answer to. "I mean, I love my mother, but she's a wreck. Our family's a mess. You've never seen her fight with my sister. And I was only little, but even I could tell my father and her didn't have the greatest marriage."

"Bryan, I'm forty-eight years old. In danger of turning into a lonely old man. I love your mother. She's caring. She's smart. She's funny. She's here. How many attractive, available women do you see walking around Rivertown?"

"There are other places."

"I love my job. I've lived in this town almost ten years and in the valley, my whole life. I don't want to go anywhere else."

Ivy sat on the wall hoping hard that Celine would show up alone. She listened to the fountain's feeble splash and splutter and closed her eyes. Maybe it was time to go ahead and get the apartment. With the abortion money she had enough for a down payment. She'd tell Celine as soon as she showed up. She'd tell her not to worry about losing her job. Ivy would pay two-thirds of all expenses, because of the baby. Even though a baby didn't take up a whole third of the space, Ivy would still offer, at least until Celine found a new job. She'd share her baby with Celine too so it would be almost like Celine had her own baby back. Or maybe they could find Celine's baby, by now she would be a toddler, and she could be an older sister to Ivy's baby. They'd be a family like the one passing Ivy right now with a heavy cooler and a beach blanket and cheerful colored sand toys.

"Hey, girlfriend!" Celine sang out from the other direction.

Ivy turned from the family.

"Do I deserve an academy award for that performance today or what? A nomination anyway!" Celine hopped up next to Ivy.

Ivy gave the laugh Celine expected, then asked abruptly, "Who's Terry?"

"You know who he is, my favorite customer."

"Robert called him your sugar daddy."

"He treats me right."

"Well …"

"He's a very private man, Ivy. I can't tell you every little thing about him. Listen, I'm not even supposed to tell you this, but …" Celine stopped. She gave Ivy a searching look. "Do you swear you won't tell anybody?"

"I swear." Who would she tell? Celine was her only friend.

"He's taking me to France."

"How do you know he means it?"

"Because we're leaving. Tonight."

"What? You can't do that. You need official papers, I think. Like a passport."

"People rich as Terry can get that kind of thing fast. Money buys everything, haven't I taught you anything in all these months? We'll sail around Florida for awhile, then when everything's set, off we go. Au revoir."

"I'm not going to have an abortion, you know."

"It's too late for an abortion."

"It is?"

"You're what, four months along?"

Ivy considered the calendar etched in her brain. "A little more I think."

"Nobody's going to give you an abortion this late."

"Well, good."

Ivy kicked the wall with her heels. Celine jumped up. She had trouble sitting still.

"Do you speak French?" Ivy asked with an edge to her voice.

"I just said au revoir, didn't I? Chevrolet, cafe, croissant, oui, oui, ooh-la-la." She spun around. "Pirouette, that's French too. See, I know a lot." She stopped. "Not many girls go from a cot at the Salvation Army to a bed in a yacht. Be happy for me, Ivy."

Celine pulled a thick wad of bills from her worn beach bag. "I want to give you this since I'm set for now. Five hundred dollars. You don't want to be bringing a baby home to the Salvation Army."

Home. The word made Ivy sick. She cracked her knuckles one by one.

"Here, take it." Celine stuffed it into Ivy's front pocket. "And don't you be afraid to apply for welfare. Aid for women with dependent children, food stamps, all that. You'll be okay. You're tough, like me."

Ivy wanted to slip the tip of her pinky through Celine's navel ring and keep her close. An apartment alone with the baby frightened her. What would she do if the baby wouldn't stop crying? What would she do if her baby didn't like her?

"I really do hate good-byes," said Celine. "We need to get this over with. I have a present for you or the baby or you and the baby, whatever you want." She rummaged deep in her bag and pulled out a cylindrical object wrapped in crumpled tissue paper.

Ivy squeezed it. Soft.

"Go on, open it, I'm getting old here. I didn't have any tape."

Ivy unrolled a piece of beautiful blue cloth.

"So do you like it? It's a shawl or a baby blanket, whatever you want. Cashmere. The real thing. And don't you love the color?"

The weave was so fine that Ivy could see the shadow of her hand through it. The deep blue color was exactly the shade of the top of the sky when you're waiting for the first star and you realize you don't need stars, that blue is enough, all you can stand. In spite of the sticky heat, Ivy wrapped it around her.

"Thanks," she said afraid that if said anymore she'd end up pleading with Celine to stay, revealing the intricacies of her plan for their life together, showing herself as the pathetic loser she was, always imagining futures for other people without them knowing.

"Hot as hell out here." Celine grinned. "It's a lot nicer on the water, I'll tell you."

"I should call the police on Terry," Ivy whispered. "For kidnapping an underaged girl."

"You wouldn't!" Celine slapped Ivy's leg. "You'd better be kidding. Come on. Try to understand. You know what it's like to want to go somewhere."

Florida. Paris. Everybody wanting to be somewhere else. Gil or an old guy. What was the difference? The old guy was rich. He hadn't hit Celine. Not yet. Surely he knew enough to use condoms. Maybe he'd even had one of those operations so he wouldn't get anyone pregnant.

"Why didn't you tell me before?"

"Because I knew you'd be upset. I wasn't going to tell you at all." Celine wrinkled her nose. "Sorry." She frowned. "Paris! Paris! I just have to get there. Everything will be okay. We all do what we got to do." Celine pulled the shawl back off Ivy's head and dropped a light kiss onto her hair.

"What about your stuff?" Ivy asked.

Celine held up her bulging beach bag then turned, wiggling her rear to show her toothbrush poking from her back pocket. "Listen. I've got to go. I'll miss you. We had some fun."

Ivy nodded. In Rivertown you knew the same people your father had known all his life. You watched neighbors grow old, have children and grandchildren. People knew your grandmother even if you never did. They told you that you had her chin or her walk. People left your life when they died. Otherwise you saw them at the grocery store, mowing their lawns, trick or treating, buying fried dough at the carnival in the mall parking lot. People didn't disappear.

"Maybe I'll send you a postcard. To the Three Aces." She patted Ivy's belly. "Good luck with junior."

"We're going to be okay." When Ivy said nothing, Celine went on. "We're tough, you and me. Survivors." She bit her lip. "You know, you're making this really hard."

"I'm sorry." Ivy couldn't afford to acknowledge the flicker of fear she thought she saw in Celine's eye, the shaky bravado of her laugh. She tried to smile. "Bon voyage."

Celine saluted and took off across the square. She threw a penny in the fountain and yelled, "That's for you. Make a wish, Ivy." She tossed in another, "That's for me," waved, and crossed the street.

Ivy sat. The shade had moved. Her loneliness burned as hot as the late afternoon sun on her face, as hot as her bandaged hand. The family that had passed earlier hadn't stayed long at the beach. The mother pulled a squalling toddler by the arm, beach blanket bunched and dragging. The older boy dropped a sand toy and whined for ice cream. The father, lugging the cooler, cursed loud enough for Ivy to hear. Lightheaded, she began the long walk to the bus stop, wondering if she'd make it.

She rested against a telephone pole. The dizziness passed. She opened her eyes to a sign on a plain square building. 'Holy Church of Christ, heartwarming messages in air-conditioned comfort.' She didn't go to church. She didn't think she believed in God. But she was hot and when she tried the door it opened easily.

The small, empty sanctuary, cool and dim, sucked her in. She slid into the nearest pew, leaned back, and prayed for a sign that she was making the right decision. She prayed and prayed, silence holding her like pond water. She buried her face in the soft folds of her shawl and listened to the determined beat of her heart.

Carol, home from work just long enough to slip off her shoes and flip through the mail, recognized the particular rasping squeal of the door of Neal's truck. She stepped onto the porch, but before she could wave or call out, Neal had pulled away from curb leaving Bryan still standing in the road. Not a good sign. She'd hoped that the two of them would have their man-to-man talk, Neal would slap Bryan on the back, Bryan would grin, and they'd all have supper together out in the yard.

Bryan's knapsack hung from one shoulder. He tapped his harmonica against his thigh and looked past her.

"Did you have a nice time with Neal?" she asked knowing how aggravating her words must be and still unable to stop herself. "Did you have a chance to talk?"

"Mom," Bryan sat on the bottom step, deliberately giving her his back. She might be annoying, she could admit it, but he was infuriating. "Why couldn't you tell me yourself? You know me a lot better than he does."

"Well, I …" Carol groped for words. He was right. Why hadn't she? Some sexist idea that it would be better for a boy to hear it from a man? Or still another sexist possibility … that Neal had to get Bryan's approval. She wouldn't have asked Neal to tell Ivy. Telling Ivy. Carol shuddered. "You like him, don't you?" She still had the mail in her hands, all junk.

"I like him. That doesn't mean I want him living with us."

"Well, I like him and I do want to live with him."

"I see that. You don't have to marry him."

"He wants to get married."

"Why? Why can't you live together? You can't get married without Ivy. Can you imagine—she comes home—oh by the way, you have a stepfather—a whole new member of the family. It's not fair. You can't." He stood and faced her.

Carol took a long breath. They were outside on a warm evening. The neighbors had their windows open. She would not make a scene by shouting.

"Don't talk to me about fairness when it comes to your sister." She enunciated each word. Bryan cringed a little and she didn't care. Damn Neal for driving off. This was supposed to be a celebration. "If she runs away, gives us no phone number or address, we're under no obligation to tell her a damn thing. And if she comes home and finds I've gotten married, she's just going to have to deal with it."

Bryan blew a few notes on his harp and sat back down on the step as if determined to ignore her. She threw the mail onto the mat and went down the steps to sit beside him.

He stopped playing and looked at her. "I wish she were here," Carol said. "But she's not."

Bryan played a few bars of a familiar blues song she didn't know the name of.

"And we don't know when she will be."

The harmonica shrieked and wailed. Bryan stamped his foot and rocked.

"It's not like it's going to be any big deal wedding," Carol said. "Just a city hall kind of thing."

She put her hand on Bryan's leg, the one that was still. "Listen," she said. "Can't you just be happy with me? Something good has finally happened."

She thought he hadn't heard, that he successfully blocked her out with his music just as his father used to do. As she moved to get up, take some aspirin for her blossoming headache, and call Neal, Bryan launched into a version of the wedding march. He gave a sidelong glance to check out her reaction. An edge of a smile showed against the harmonica, between his moving hands. She slapped his knee and actually blushed. When he finished the song she'd talk with him about wedding cake. She knew her boy well enough to know he wouldn't be able to feign indifference to that.

CHAPTER 5

Ever since Johnny died, summer had been Carol's saddest season. The sticky humidity reminded her of the long steamy nights she paced their stifling house while he lay unconscious in the air-conditioned hospital. The thick smell of rain on asphalt brought back memories of Ivy and Bryan begging her for money for the ice cream man when the workman's comp hadn't come through, and she worried about every single cent. The flicker of lightning bugs in the backyard made her think of her mother sitting on the back porch, lips pressed together to keep "I told you that man would come to no good end" from slipping out. Carol wouldn't have chosen summer as a time for a wedding and honeymoon, but Neal didn't want to wait.

"I'm more relaxed when I'm off from school," he said. "We can go away for a week or two. Wherever you want."

Carol imagined going to Miami. Ivy's occasional postcards came from there. Florida wasn't a place to go in the summer, and they'd spend much too long driving there and back. Instead they decided to spend a week on Cape Cod and reserved a romantic little motel cabin in Hyannis. At the last minute Bryan's trip to Everett's cottage fell through. Carol's hours on the phone trying to find a motel suite or a place with two available rooms proved futile, so they ended up, the three of them together, in the original cabin, Neal and Carol promising each other a real honeymoon someday.

Bryan wouldn't take his shirt off on the beach. Neal told her not to bother him about it. "Boys are as self-conscious about their bodies as girls," he said. "Leave him alone."

Still the sight of her skinny, bespectacled son dismayed her. He wouldn't swim, just sat alone on large rocks and played his harmonica, the picture of adolescent alienation.

Carol brushed sand from her feet before stepping into the crowded cabin—one room, with a double bed, a couch where Bryan slept, and a small kitchen area. There was barely space to walk. Neal lay on top of the covers in his boxer shorts reading a paperback detective novel. "Where's Bryan?" he asked.

"Out there somewhere." Carol shivered in the sudden cool of the air-conditioning and pulled the door shut behind her.

"Why don't you lock that?" Neal said. "Three days into our honeymoon and we haven't officially consummated our marriage yet."

"I thought we agreed this wasn't our real honeymoon," Carol said, but she pushed in the button on the doorknob. Nights of frustration, lying beside Neal feeling him hard against the small of her back, his hands on her breasts, Bryan's asthmatic breathing a few feet away as effective as any chastity belt. If Neal didn't resent her son, and he really didn't seem to, how could she? She was a mature woman, not some horny teenager.

Neal held out his arms. She told herself sand in the bed was no big deal, she'd shake the sheets out later, they might not have much time until Bryan came back. She shed her beach robe and bathing suit. Neal wriggled out of his shorts, and she bent over him. She'd grown to love sucking and licking every part of his body, his little sounds made her feel powerful and lucky. They usually took their time making love, but the possibility of Bryan's return itched at the back of her mind. As soon as she felt the stirring and dampness between her legs, she moved up Neal's slick body to press her lips to his.

"A condom?" His whisper muffled by her mouth, she lowered herself onto him. Excruciatingly aware of him inside her, of every place his skin touched hers, she rocked on top of him, moaning, willing Bryan to stay at the beach just a few moments longer while Neal filled and held her. She pressed her hands against his chest and sat up tall, pulling him up inside with deep muscles she'd forgotten she had. Worried Bryan might be outside she swallowed her screams. Neal pulled her down, cupping her bottom tight and stifled his cries by biting her neck.

The door knob rattled. "Later," Neal called in a strangled voice.

"Give us a couple minutes, will you Bryan?" Carol tried to make her voice normal, cheerful, as if Bryan were waiting for them to drive him to school.

Neal gave a final whimpering sound and Carol let her body go limp on top of him. He held her close.

"I hope he's not upset," Carol whispered. She rolled off Neal.

"We are married," Neal said. "He's fifteen. He knows about sex."

"Still, it's different when it's your mother."

"Don't worry so much." Neal pulled the sheet up over them. Carol felt sand scratching her skin already. "Bryan's fine."

"I think you should talk to him."

"About what? I do talk to him."

"Since the wedding he's seemed more quiet than ever. Brooding, that's it. He broods."

"Brooding is normal when you're fifteen."

Carol touched a sore spot on her neck. "Did you give me a hickey?"

Neal lifted his head, moving back so he could see without his glasses. "Guess I did."

Carol pressed the spot with her index finger. "A thirty-seven-year-old woman with a hickey? I feel ridiculous." But she didn't really, maybe a little, but mostly she felt desirable and loved.

"Make that two." Neal touched another place on her neck and she felt a thrilling twinge.

"We should put some clothes on," she said. "And unlock the door. You'll talk to Bryan when he comes."

"You're the one who needs to talk to him." Neal's voice had an edge. Carol climbed out of bed and grabbed her robe. She pulled off the sheet to shake it, but there wasn't enough space in the cramped aisle next to the bed.

She had spent the past ten years ignoring the questions in Bryan's withdrawn silences. They had been easier to overlook eclipsed by Ivy's fury, the clamor of her demands. Ivy let the world know she missed her father. Ivy raged against Carol, against the universe, but she didn't seem to ask the questions Bryan wanted answers to, and Carol had no idea what those questions were.

"I don't know what to say," she said.

"Here, let me do this." Neal stripped the bottom sheet from the bed. "I'll shake them outside. Go find Bryan."

Carol would have rather made the bed, but she rinsed off in the tiny shower, slowly, giving Bryan every chance to return, and dressed in a tee shirt and shorts long enough to hide the patch of veins near her left knee. The light had changed to the golden glow of later afternoon. Neal stood on the little porch.

"Isn't that him?" He pointed over to a large boulder, a hunched shadow seated on top.

"That's where I left him earlier."

Neal touched the small of her back, a nudge in Bryan's direction. "When you come back, we'll get supper. At that fish place you liked."

She walked across an emptying parking lot toward the sand fiddling with the neck of her shirt, trying to adjust it to cover the hickeys. It was still too hot for her hooded sweatshirt. She saw that Bryan was playing his harp, but the music was lost in the sounds of the wind and sea.

She felt her neck again and determined that if she sat on his left side he'd be less likely to notice anything. "Hey," she said and scrambled up beside him.

He stopped playing and slapped the spit out of his harmonica without looking at her.

"You hungry?" she asked.

He shrugged.

Thankful for the seagulls' squawks and the pounding of the waves Carol tried to think of something to say next.

"Must feel a little strange to be on your mother's honeymoon," she ventured finally.

"Hah! A little?" He whacked his harmonica against the flat of his palm again and again in a regular rhythm, staring at the horizon.

Carol tried ignoring the blush spreading across Bryan's face. His ears were bright red.

"I would have been fine at home," he said.

She wanted to say the right thing. What would Neal say? Something that wouldn't make him mad. Something to get him talking. Out of the corner of her eye she noticed the fine layer of dark hair on his upper lip. How had she missed that?

"I didn't want to leave you alone," she said.

"I'd rather be alone than in the way," he said. "You two should have run off to Las Vegas or something."

"I thought the wedding was nice." Even a city hall wedding was personal in a place like Rivertown. The party at the house afterward was small and satisfying, a few teachers from the high school, people from the bank, some neighbors. The three tiered cake Bryan made and decorated with orchids was more beautiful than any they could have ordered from a bakery. Bryan's friends, Everett, Casey and Martine, had come and helped clean up afterward. Carol remembered Bryan laughing, serving the cake, sharing the recipe with Everett's mother. After everyone left he had seemed sad, but what was she supposed to do about it on her wedding night? She and Neal had retreated into her/their bedroom, but Bryan's mood filled the house like a bad smell, and she hadn't been able to make love or even fall asleep. In the car, on the way to Cape, his silence had continued. He spoke when spoken to, complained a few times, and that was it.

"I thought the wedding was nice," Carol said again.

"I heard you."

"Bryan, let me teach you some social skills. This is when you are supposed to say 'yes, it was.' Do you think you can do that?"

His nostrils flared.

Carol tried to stop herself. Ivy would have a nasty retort. Justified in her anger, Carol would snap back. On and on until they were both screaming. Bryan's silences just made her feel like an idiot. Sarcasm is toxic, Neal had said to her once.

"I'm sorry," she said. "What was it about the wedding that bothered you?"

"Ivy should have been there," Bryan whispered. He brushed at his eyes. "You could've waited."

"I already told you how I feel about that!" Carol felt anger swelling inside her again.

"You asked, Mom! You asked what bothered me. I told you. Why don't you go away and leave me alone? Just pretend I'm not here. Or take me to the bus station. I really want to go home. Please?" He still hadn't looked at her.

What would Neal say now? She had no idea.

"When I married your father I was already pregnant with Ivy, so in a way she was there. She got to go to one of my weddings and you got to go to the other." That's it, she told herself, humor, not sarcasm, not anger.

Bryan almost smiled. "What was that wedding like?"

"I was so young," Carol said. "Nineteen. Your Dad was ten years older than me. Sometimes I think I married Johnny as much because I wanted his mother as I wanted him. She took care of people the way my own mother never had. Then she went and died before Ivy was even born. Your Dad had a hard time with that. So did I."

"What was the wedding like?" Bryan asked again. "I've never seen any pictures."

"There are a few somewhere that your grandmother took," she said. Trying to keep the bitterness from her voice, after all this was Bryan's father she was talking about, she went on. "I was young and scared and pregnant. He agreed to marry me, everything else was up to him. We got married and had the

reception, if you could call it that, at Rivertown Billiards. My mother was hor-
rified. So was I, but I couldn't admit it even to myself."

"Rivertown Billiards?" He turned to her, a smile twitching at the edges of his
lips.

"I never told you that?" She knew she never had. It was too embarrassing.
She was surprised he hadn't heard it from someone else. Curly must have mentioned it to Ivy.

"Did Dad talk about the war?" The way the question popped out Carol
knew Bryan had wanted to ask it for a long time.

"Not to me," she said. "By the time we met he'd been back almost ten years.
I'd try to bring it up sometimes, but he made it clear he wasn't going to tell me
anything beyond the talking he did in his sleep. But there's a box of letters he
wrote home to your grandma. I didn't find out about them until after he died.
He'd hidden them from me, like a lot of other things."

"I've seen those letters," Bryan confessed in a quavery voice.

Carol wasn't surprised. She'd kept the box on the shelf over the washing
machine, right in the open. "They don't say too much, do they?" Carol remembered the excitement she'd felt when she'd found the letters, hoping for some
deeper understanding of her husband, and the disappointment that followed
as she read them—sentence after sentence about how he hated the heat and
missed his mother's cooking. The only letter that really said anything that mattered she kept folded in her wallet. She'd never shown it to anyone.

Again, Carol tried to neutralize the bitterness that over the years had shriveled her heart. Johnny had been a lousy father. If he'd lived longer his kids
would have figured that out. Instead he was the glorified recipient of their
undying devotion, while she, the one who got up to go to work every morning,
the one who bought the groceries, the one who cleaned the house, the one who
arranged appointments, the one who took the car in, the one who did every
repetitive, thankless job of being a parent, received nothing but grief.

Bryan stood, balancing on the rock, put his harmonica in his pocket and held
out a hand to help her up. "Neal's probably wanting to get something to eat," he
said. "You shouldn't leave your husband alone so long on your honeymoon."

He gripped her hand and pulled her to her feet. He squinted at her neck,
rolled his eyes and blushed again, before leaping to the sand. Neal met them on
the beach and tossed her the hooded sweatshirt. It had cooled off enough to
wear it.

❀

Ivy stood, belly against the glass door of the empty diner, feet aching, watching the beginnings of a tropical storm, branches snapping, whipping across the empty parking lot, contents of the dumpster picked up and tossed through the air. The boss' son, Beauregard Bellamy Jr., closing early, sat in a booth adding up the day's receipts. Robert had left almost an hour earlier. "I'll give you a ride if you wait until I'm finished here." Beau wiped his broad, gleaming forehead with a paper napkin. He'd never bothered her the way he had Celine, and her back hurt from being on her feet all day. She nodded and sat, stretching her legs across the seat of the booth behind Beau. He pushed buttons on his calculator. She rubbed her belly and stared at the worn toes of her sneakers as she rotated her ankles.

"All set?" He turned suddenly, voice harsh, his face inches from hers. Something—a wart, a pimple, skin cancer—grew in the crease beside his nose. He noticed her noticing it and frowned, rubbing it with his finger. "Let's go then."

She slid her heavy body out of the booth. She'd have him drop her off a block away from the shelter. No reason for him to know where she stayed. Saving all the money she could, she planned to rent a room just before her baby's birth.

He clicked off the lights, she followed him outside. The smell of rain on hot asphalt filled her lungs. The baby kicked. She sank into the plush seat of the car. It had been a long time since she'd sat on something so comfortable. You could fall asleep in a seat like that.

Minutes away from the corner where she figured she'd ask to be let out, Beau turned into a deserted park. Banyan trees with their strange roots lined the road. Rain pounded the windshield and roof.

"Not really the right weather for a day in the park," Ivy tried to joke. "You think you could take me home now?"

"A little Yankee girl like you should experience a real Florida storm," he said. "Not quite hurricane season, so this is unusual." He drove on, windshield wipers slapping.

The vegetation changed to broad bands of marsh crowded with tossing reeds. Ivy rubbed fog from her window. Wind tore through the trees and swamp grass.

"Nasty out there," he remarked in the same tone he'd use to say 'beautiful day.' His fingers wiggled like stubby tentacles as he gestured proudly out his window. As if the weather was his show. A stone, Ivy thought it was probably fake, glittered on his pinkie.

"I should probably be getting back … home," Ivy said. "If you could just …"

"Only going to get worse," he grinned. He turned off the road into a small parking lot surrounded by a high wall of rustling, swaying green.

Beau turned off the engine. The wind screamed, a large, fringed leaf blew against the windshield, then away. He pushed a button locking all the doors.

Ivy guessed why he'd brought her there, hating herself for not realizing it sooner. Her mind raced to find an escape. Her body filled with a heavy mixture of rage and hopelessness.

"Now I know I can't shock a little slut like you," he said, unzipping his pants. "I'm not the kind of guy to rape anyone. You suck me off and I'll take you right home."

Her hands massaged the perfect swell of her belly. Outside wind and rain ripped bright, deep throated blossoms from plants she never wanted to see again.

"Now, come on." Voice sharp, Beau held his stiff penis in one hand.

Ivy closed her eyes and bent over him. The baby stopped kicking. She would never go back to the diner. She'd learned it wasn't hard to find a job if you weren't fussy, and she wasn't.

Bryan bought a used guitar with money he earned working at a job Neal had gotten him hauling bricks. Every afternoon and evening he sat on the porch steps, teaching himself to play. He could tell the time by watching the shadows move. He noticed the days getting shorter after the solstice. He learned chords, practiced picking, bought a harmonica rack so he could accompany himself. He sounded pretty good. When he banged away on the guitar and blew his lungs out he felt sadness in the purest way, like it was meant to be felt, no words attached. His father was his too, not just Ivy's and Mom's.

He'd gotten used to every day being the same, up early, sweating all morning at the construction site, shower at one, and the rest of the time, music. Everett came by once in awhile. They'd swim up at the res but Bryan couldn't stand seeing Martine and all her friends tanned and laughing in their tiny bathing suits. His own body looked better tanned and work had built up more muscle in his arms and chest, so he wasn't as embarrassed with his shirt off as he used to be, but he felt a new awkwardness with Martine. With so much of her beautiful body right out there, he could hardly breathe, never mind think of any intelligent conversation. Sometimes, at night, dressed in shorts and tee-shirts, she and Casey would walk down the street and stop to see him. That was all right. When they ran out of things to say, he could play them a song. They'd clap and tap their sandaled feet and with the music all around them, Martine had no way of knowing how much he ached to touch her.

Early afternoon, the sun burned hot, so Bryan sat on the porch, in the shade against the house, just thinking. The mail carrier didn't see him as she slid the stack of junk mail and bills into the box. A small, grayish envelope that looked like a real letter from a real person, fell beside him.

"I'll get that," he said, leaning over from the shadows.

She jumped, hand against her chest, mailbag swinging so it almost hit Bryan's head. "Didn't see you there. You scared me."

He stared at the postmark, Florida. It was addressed to Ivy. He opened it anyway. Gil, the letter was from Gil.

Ivy, Ivy, Ivy,

Buteful lady, buteful girl, you don't know how much I miss you how sorry I am about everything. I'll do anything for you baby. You know I will. You wanted to go to Florida. We went. Just like that. How many other guys would leave a good job to run off with a wild lady like you. Your so buteful maybe a lot of men but I'm the one that did it. When I came back to that room and found you gone I thought I would die. When my own mother left me I didn't feel so bad. I didn't know what to do without you. That guy, Freddie, remember him, the one who hardly ever talked. He talked. He talked me into robbing a conveneyence store and we got busted, filmed on fuckin video. We got put away for a year 'cause Freddie had a gun. What do they expect us to rob a place with? No one hurt and a year of my life to pay for it. Don't seem fair. Remember the first nite, walking home in the snow from Curly's and we stopped in that 7-11 to get condums. You bouhgt those fluffy pink marshmellow things and gave me one and it stuck to my mustach and you licked it off right there on Main Street. And then we went upstairs and I couldn't believe it when you told me it was your first time with a man, a bold, little tuff girl like you. But that just shows you. God wanted you to wait for the right guy and I am him. And I cant forget how wet and warm and tight you feel around my fingers, my tongue, and my cock like you were made just for me. Like two puzzle pieces. In my dreems I fuck you and lick you and we're together like we should be. And meentime I don't know where you are, my love, my angel. I'm thinking youll go back home so I'm writing you there. When I get out I'll find you. Your the best thing that ever happend to me girl. Please rite. It sucks in here. Send me some cigarette money. I love you. I love you. Wait for me. Don't let any other guy tuch those buteful tits, that gorjuss ass. YOU ARE MINE, LADY. When I get out of here, I'll make love to you again. Wile

I'm stuck in this place, I'm making love to you all nite, every nite, in my dreems. Feel me, in yours. I'm there.

Love,

Gil

P.S. I'd drag my balls across a mile of broken glass just to fingerfuck your shadow.

Bryan finished reading, embarrassed that he was turned on. He read the letter again, thinking of Martine at all the sexy parts, imagining he was saying those things to her. He had to go inside and jerk off before he could even think.

Up in his room, he took out the dagger, unwrapped it, and lay it beside the letter on the blue and white quilt his mother had made him when he moved from a crib to a real bed. He had never told Carol or Neal about the knife. He had to tell them about the letter. They'd want to see it, but he couldn't show that stuff to his mom. Maybe he could seal it, so she wouldn't know he'd read it, save himself some embarrassment, but when he'd torn it open he hadn't planned ahead, and the envelope was ragged. He'd play some tunes and what to do would come to him. At least Ivy wasn't with Gil. Good. Why hadn't she come home when she left him though?

No air circulated in his small bedroom but Bryan didn't want to go back outside or downstairs. He wanted to be in a small, dim place, with the door shut. He turned on the fan, angled it toward the edge of his bed, sat down and anchored the letter with the dagger. It fluttered under the sharp, bright blade at the edge of his vision, like the percussion section of his one-man band, while he played "You Can't Lose What You Never Had," "I Just Want to Make Love to You," "Can't Hold Out Much Longer," "Mean Old World." Then he made up his own songs, singing, saying everything he wanted to Martine, to Ivy, Gil, Mom. He felt better until he heard his mother's car. When she called his name he played louder. When he heard her step on the stairs, he stopped playing. He hid the dagger back under the mattress and stuffed the letter in his pocket. Carol knocked.

"Come in," he said, casually plucking a few notes on his guitar.

His mother stood in the doorway, hot and rumpled. "What are you doing in this stuffy room? Smells like old sneakers."

"Stay awhile, you get used to it." He smiled at her.

"Neal's bringing home some steak to grill."

"Okay."

"Do you want to make a salad or anything?"

He shook his head. Her face said she was worried about him. He hadn't cooked in awhile. It was too hot and he didn't like cooking outside. "I'll make one then," she said. "And maybe some potatoes?"

"Whatever."

"Are you okay?" She sat beside him. He watched his fingers move over the strings, listened to the sounds they made. "Is it okay for you? Neal living here?"

"He's okay."

She took a breath so deep, the mattress shifted. "He's a great guy, don't you think? I'm glad he's here, that's for sure."

'Cause he fucks you? Bryan thought. Do you fit together like puzzle pieces? He imagined thousand piece puzzles of Gil walking Ivy through the mall, Neal's hand on Mom's cheek like she was a precious thing, the sun making the drops of quarry water on Martine's tanned belly sparkle like diamonds.

His mother knew he liked Neal. Why was she trying to make him say it? He didn't want to. Ivy wouldn't have. Bryan felt mean.

He put down his guitar. His mother leaned forward, waiting. He pulled Gil's letter from his pocket and held it out.

"What's this?" she asked.

Read it, he said with his eyes.

She flattened it against her thigh. He plucked at his guitar. He couldn't watch her read those words. He couldn't guess what would happen next, so he made a little music, to accompany the whirring of the fan. He played three and half songs before she said anything.

"This came today?" Her voice shook.

He nodded.

"Where do you think she is?" Carol crushed the letter in her fist. "Where the hell is she?" She stood up. "At least she's not with him. At least she had the sense to leave him. Why hasn't she come home?"

She paced, as if his room were a cage. He wanted to run.

"We don't know anything. The only hint she's alive are those stupid postcards."

Bryan sat, paralyzed. To leave he'd have to make it past her. The room was so small, she paced so fast, an escape would require split second timing. He stayed where he was.

"I'll call the police. Now we have at least this information. She must be somewhere near this jail. Maybe now, they'll be more helpful. A girl on her own."

"Good, Mom." Bryan wanted her out of his way. He'd go to the mall, see what was playing at the movies.

She left. He leaned into his guitar, listening to her in the downstairs hall, picking up the phone. Neal was coming, with steaks, the cheerful sort of man born to stand over a gas grill brandishing a long fork. If you wanted your meat rare, that's how he made it. Ask for well-done, he didn't leave a spot of pink. Even chicken. The guy could barbecue chicken to perfection without precooking it. Bryan snapped his guitar into its case and tied his sneakers. He slammed the screen door while his mother was on hold.

CHAPTER 6

The bus rolled across the Connecticut line from New York, and Ivy vomited into the box of doughnut holes. They'd seemed like a good idea at the last rest stop. Milk, an afterthought—something for the baby. Not that a doctor had told her to drink milk. In the seven months of her pregnancy she hadn't been to a doctor. Maybe milk wasn't even good. You never knew anymore with all the pesticides and hormones what caused cancer, heart attacks, birth defects.

She wiped her mouth, folded shut the box and set it on the floor, hoping it wouldn't leak. No one sat next to her. She'd slept most of the way from Richmond. With no one to meet her in New Haven, she'd walk a few blocks to the green and catch the local bus to Rivertown.

She longed for her own bed. At the shelters they forced you up by seven, out by eight. In her mother's house she'd sleep all day. Bryan would bring meals to her room. They'd probably be mad she'd never called, but they'd get over it. She'd help out and wouldn't fight. The baby kicked hard. She didn't know how she would squeeze her swollen feet into her sneakers or how she'd even retrieve the shoes from deep under her seat.

The trees along the highway hinted at the colors to come. Her baby would miss it all this year. She calculated her due date to be sometime in mid-November. The leaves would be on the ground by then, trampled, crumbled, beginning their transformation into whatever it was they turned into during the long winter under snow. Snow. She'd forget everything that had happened since she last saw snow, especially the Three Aces Diner and Beau Bellamy Jr.

The bus finally lurched to a stop in New Haven. Somehow she reached her sneakers and loosening the laces fit them on, untied. Everything else she owned was in the belly of the bus, in the duffel bag she'd shared with Gil. The driver looked worried as she slung it over her shoulder. After what she'd been through, it was easy to lug an almost empty bag the few blocks to the green where a Rivertown bus waited. The clock outside the bank said four fifteen. Her mother would be home when she arrived. Bryan would be fixing dinner unless things had changed. Her huge belly led her down the sidewalk. A lot could happen in seven months.

Ivy stepped off the bus at the corner store, turned onto her street, her house appearing in sharp focus halfway down the block, smaller, as if seen the wrong way through binoculars. It was supper time. The street and yards were empty, but that didn't mean her arrival would go unnoticed. Her pregnant homecoming would make juicy table conversation behind the windows.

The porch, even the lizard shaped piece of concrete missing from the edge of the top step, looked exactly as she remembered it. The mailbox hung empty by the freshly painted, dark red door. If Gil were looking for her, he'd call or write here, the only address she'd ever had.

She'd never written once, or even called. The baby pressing on her bladder told her to get to a toilet. Ivy considered knocking, then seized the doorknob.

She had played this scene over and over in her head on the long bus ride, sleeping and awake. Nobody home. Bryan home alone. Mom home alone. Mom and Bryan home. Happy to see her. Angry. Indifferent. She'd imagined it so many times, so many ways, this felt like another dream. She pushed open the door a crack. If she didn't like this version, she'd make up another one. Voices drifted from the back of the house. Listening intently, she almost missed Neal Richards asleep in the naugahide recliner.

She blinked. He breathed big, slow breaths. The chair fit around his bulk as if he'd worn a place for himself, over a long, long time, like feet on stone stairs. Ivy struggled to remember when she'd last slept deeply in a spot where she knew she belonged. Tears she'd thought were all used up, gathered in her eyes.

"Oh my God!"

Ivy swiveled toward her mother's voice, revealing her belly. Carol gasped.

"What happened?" Bryan called from the kitchen.

Carol's arm shot out, the flat of her hand smacking Ivy's cheek. "You never called. Just those God damned postcards with no return address." She hugged herself as if to keep from hitting Ivy again or to keep from breaking apart. "Just letter after letter to you from that jerk in jail."

"Gil?" Ivy asked. Her face stung.

"You're back," Bryan said. "Just like that."

"What were you thinking?" Carol asked. "You have no idea what you've put us through, do you?"

"You read my letters?" Ivy wondered what they had said. She remembered why she'd left.

"Here you are," Bryan sounded almost angry. "A regular day. Any old day. A Thursday, after school. Open the door and here you are. Just like that." He shook his head.

"And not alone either!" Mom pointed at Ivy's belly. "Who is responsible for that?" Her eyes opened so wide she looked like a cartoon. "Gil? If he weren't locked up, would you have brought him home with you? If I ever see that …" She pressed her hands flat against her own abdomen, as though she had a sudden cramp.

She hates me, Ivy thought, hugging herself to keep from stumbling. "Why did you read my mail?"

"Ivy!" Bryan said. "What do you expect? We had no idea where you were. How you were doing. Shut up about the mail."

"Hey." The recliner squealed into an upright position. Neal's voice sounded sure, in charge. A gold ring glinted on his left hand. Ivy tried to remember where a wedding ring should go. Her mother's hands hid under her crossed arms.

"Got to use the bathroom," Ivy mumbled, escaping upstairs as Neal put an arm around her mother and led her to the couch.

An electric razor and shaving cream on the back of the toilet. A man lived here. Ivy remembered Neal's beard, remembered Bryan towering over their mother's shoulder. Maybe Bryan shaved, at fifteen. She flushed the toilet and counted toothbrushes. Three. She pulled her own red one from her jacket pocket, pasted it with the familiar tube of Crest, squeezed and rolled tightly from the bottom. In her mother's house it wouldn't occur to anyone to squash it from the middle. After brushing her teeth she slipped her worn brush into the last empty slot in the rack. She was home, fighting and all. She wanted those letters. Gil in jail. What had he done? How long would he be there?

Neal smiled at Ivy as she plodded down the stairs, his eyes crinkling at the corners. Bryan paced back and forth, shaking his head. Mom dabbed at her eyes, huddled beside Neal, her cheek against the worn flannel of his plaid shirt. His hand covered her knee.

"We've met before," Neal said.

"Only once," Ivy perched on the edge of the recliner.

"We'll be seeing a lot more of each other," Neal smiled. "Your mother and I are married."

Ivy stared into his bloodshot blue eyes. Only seven and a half months. Babies and jail terms and weddings. Carol's face was buried in a hand held nest of shredded tissue. Bryan, blankfaced, slapped a harmonica against his palm.

"Did you have a fancy wedding?" Ivy asked. "You should have invited me."

"They got married at city hall," Bryan said.

"We didn't know where you were." Carol cried, her face blotchy. "We had no idea where you were."

"How could you do this, Mom?" Ivy asked. "You just met him."

Customers at the bank had asked Carol out all the time, men liked her, friends of her dead husband, even a man in front of her in the grocery store express line. She'd scolded him for having more than twelve items. He moved to another cashier, then chased her across the parking lot to ask her to lunch. She'd mention the men to Ivy and Bryan only in passing. She went on dates, always home by ten o'clock. When Ivy and Bryan asked about her evening, she'd tell them where she'd gone, a detailed description of the restaurant and everything she'd eaten, entire movie plots, never mentioning the men themselves and when either Ivy or Bryan asked if she'd had a good time, she always, always answered 'fine' with the same dismissive wave of her hand, discouraging further questions. Ivy never imagined her marrying someone.

"Shut up," Carol said. "I don't owe you any explanations."

Ivy swallowed her protest.

Bryan breathed into his harmonica, filling the room with the sounds of an approaching train.

"I guess that means you're my stepfather."

"Not necessarily." He rubbed Carol's shoulder. "I'm her husband. That's all. We'll see about the rest."

"Hah!" Ivy said, relief mixing with disappointment.

Carol's head shot up. "What is so funny about this? Bryan, stop it!"

Bryan kept playing. Ivy smelled smoke from the kitchen. Bryan used to listen to their mother. He never let anything burn.

"Bryan!" Carol yelled. Ivy winced.

"Hey, Bry," Neal said, his low voice rumbled through the wailing. "Take it outside, will you?" His small, sharp nod and raised eyebrows made it an order.

Bryan's cheeks blew in and out, his slow progress toward the door the only evidence he'd heard. Music drifted back from the porch as though over a long distance, through closed windows and the door, solid wood painted red by Neal Richards, her mother wouldn't have chosen that color.

"Want something to drink?" Neal asked.

"Yes, please," Ivy whispered. "Water."

"Sweetheart?" He stopped, turning, halfway across the room.

Carol shook her head. Neal disappeared into the kitchen.

"Your father would be sick if he were here to see you," Carol said.

"Well, he's not." Ivy said. "You are. If he was, maybe none of this would have happened. You never think of that."

"Who?" Neal appeared with her water. Laughing, orange dinosaurs circled the glass. Ivy's favorite. Did it send out some signal he'd responded to without being aware of it? Was it just an accident? She let the weight of it, the feel of it, sink into her hand, then swallowed until the glass was empty.

"Her father." Carol answered while Ivy drank. "Her father's not here."

"He hasn't been," Neal said. "Must be strange for you, with me here and all but we didn't have a way to tell you." He took the glass from her. "We've been wondering when you'd be back. Waiting."

"Not when—*if*!" Carol screamed. "*If* she'd be back. We were so worried. Seven months. We had no idea. I had no idea. If you were dead in a gutter somewhere. Raped. Hungry. You could've called. You could've called collect. And look at you! Pregnant. That's just what we need."

"It's been hard," Neal said. "All the wondering."

"Are you apologizing for me?" Carol yelled. "I don't need you to apologize for me."

"I'm explaining," he said. "That's different."

"I wouldn't be here now," Ivy yelled back. "But I didn't know where else to go. It's my last resort. Very, very last. And I don't plan to stay long. Only until I can find a place of my own." She stormed out the door, home fifteen minutes and already she was furious and leaving.

"Visit over?" Bryan asked stopping her short. He sat where the porch railing met the house, a frozen, half smile on his face.

"I don't know what the hell I'm doing," Ivy said. She plopped down on the step. Bryan said nothing. She remembered his silences, how long they could last. "Coming back here could be the biggest mistake I've ever made."

"I doubt that." Bryan eyed her belly.

"Shut up," Ivy held her head. Bryan slapped his harmonica against his leg in a steady rhythm.

"So how long have they been married?" she asked.

"Let's see, it's September … they got married in June, right after school let out." Bryan came and sat beside her. "But he's been around a little longer than that. Since you left, actually. He's the kind of guy obsessed with helping people—like a savior complex or something. I think he goes for sad women. Mom was pretty sad."

"She's not too happy to have me back either."

"What did you expect?" Bryan's voice had deepened in Ivy's absence. And hardened. "Why didn't you call?"

Why hadn't she? Ivy couldn't remember. "I don't know. I couldn't."

"Finally we almost forgot we were doing it—the waiting. And Neal came, with his toolbox, every weekend. Rebuilding the porch where the boards had rotted, fixing leaky faucets, plastering cracks in the walls, barbecuing. After he'd been coming over for a little while he said something, I don't even remember what it was, and Mom smiled. I hadn't realized she'd stopped until I saw her face that day." He sat beside Ivy on the step.

"She stopped smiling long before that," Ivy said. "At least at me."

Bryan cleared his throat. "Mom's been weird lately, anyway. I don't think it's Neal or worrying about you. Something else is going on."

"She shouldn't have hit me." Ivy rubbed an ache in her lower back. "What do you think of Neal?"

"Like I said, he has a thing about taking care of people. He's so nice you want to piss him off just to see what he'll do but I don't think it's possible. If it is, you'll find a way." Bryan smirked. She slapped his arm.

He considered the row of holes in his harmonica. "It's easier with him here. Yeah, he's okay."

"Ever think what if Dad hadn't been killed? What if he'd been standing some place else when that concrete fell? He could've been standing somewhere else, two feet over in any direction." Her voice thinned. "Why was he standing right there?"

"I hardly remember him," Bryan said. "I'm glad Mom has somebody, now. Neal built me a shelf for my CD's. It's got handles cut into the ends so that if the house burns down or anything I can just pick it up and run. We were talking one night about what we'd take with us if the house was burning. The next day I found the shelf on my desk."

Ivy rolled her eyes. "What did Mom say she'd take?"

"First she said she'd let it all burn, but when we pushed her she said she'd probably take the quilts she'd made."

"And Neal?"

"His tools."

"You actually sit around talking about stuff like that?"

Bryan looked embarrassed. She hadn't meant to sound critical. That was the trouble, or at least part of it, with her family. They expected her to complain, to find fault with everything.

"Did you see the letters?" she asked. She wanted those letters. "You better give them to me."

Bryan blushed, nodded.

"Well?"

"There was a lot of stuff about how he ... uh ... wanted ... you." Ivy couldn't help grinning. "And how he's sorry. For what?"

"Never mind. Why did he go to jail?"

"He robbed a convenience store, near Tampa I think."

Ivy nodded. "How long's he in for?"

"About a year, maybe." Bryan blew a chord on his harmonica. "Do you love him?"

She looked at her rounded belly, where her belly button poked up under her shirt. "Don't know," she mumbled. "He said he loved me. When someone loves you and needs you, you feel like you're worth something. You matter."

"She ripped up most of the letters." Bryan sounded sorry. "There were lots of them but they mostly said the same thing. I saved a couple, and he'll probably send more."

"She's always messing with what's mine," Ivy said. She wouldn't have answered them, but still, her mother shouldn't have read and thrown away her mail.

Neal stepped onto the porch, hands in his pockets, Carol just behind him. "Looks like that baby's going to be born soon," he ventured. "Not that I know so much about babies or pregnant women."

"November," Ivy said. "I should see a doctor."

"We'll find one," Neal said. "Might be nice having a baby around. I never had kids. Always thought I'd like to."

"You haven't been to a doctor yet?" Her mother shivered, though the evening air was warm.

Ivy shook her head. "I'm ... I ... I hope everything's okay in there." She patted her belly.

Her mother bit her lip and flushed.

"Go ahead," Ivy sneered. "Tell me, I should've gone to a doctor. You think I don't know that already?"

"You don't know as much as you think you do," Carol's voice rose.

"It's okay." Neal slipped an arm around his wife.

"It is not okay," Carol said. "It really isn't." She looked at each of them. "I'm pregnant," she went on, voice threaded with disbelief. "Barely three months. And she comes back and makes me a pregnant grandmother. I'm sorry, Neal, I meant to tell you first. I don't even know why I'm saying it now." They all stared at her flat belly.

"Well," Neal beamed. "Well. Good thing we got married when we did!" He smiled his delighted pleasure at Carol, Ivy, and Bryan.

"I know why you're saying it now," Ivy said. "You can't stand that I came home and wrecked your happy little family, your little surprise. You want to make sure I know how much I've ruined everything."

Her mother glared at her with narrowed eyes and pursed lips.

"Carol." Neal glowed, a sappy grin showed through his beard. He hadn't even heard Ivy. Bryan fiddled with his harmonica. "Honey, I'm so happy."

"Aren't you a little old to be having a baby?" Ivy couldn't stop.

"Aren't you a little young?" Carol snapped back.

"Thirty-seven isn't old these days." Neal skipped down the steps and back up, tousling Bryan's hair. "I can't believe it. I'm going to be a father." He paused. "I'm the one who's old—pushing fifty."

"Forty-eight," Carol said.

"A father and a grandfather," Bryan said. "You'll be a step-grandfather first. I'll be an uncle and an older brother. Weird."

"It'll be great," Neal bounced on the balls of his feet. "Two babies in the house."

"I don't know." Bryan pulled his knees into his chest and wrapped his arms around them, rocking. The end of the harmonica poked from his tight fist, reflected a ray of the sun low in the sky.

"I told you, I'll be moving to a place of my own as soon as I can," Ivy repeated through clenched teeth.

"You're being ridiculous," Carol's voice was shrill. "None of you know a thing about babies. The crying in the night you can't stop, ear infections, teething. Just when you think you've made the house safe, they discover new dangers. You can't keep up. A person can't keep up with one baby, never mind two."

"But that's the beauty of it," said Neal, still beaming. "We'll outnumber them, two to one. Four adults ought to be able to manage two babies. What do we have to do? Feed them. Hold them. Change their diapers. Carol, I'm so happy."

"I'm not changing any diapers," Bryan said.

Carol brushed her fingers against Neal's beard, stroked his arm and held his hand in both of hers. Ivy's chest burned and it wasn't heartburn. Or maybe it was. Her mother was loved and in love. Her mother's new baby had a father. Her baby didn't. She didn't.

"Chicken's probably charcoal by now," Bryan jerked his head in the direction of the kitchen.

"We could go out," Neal suggested. "Celebrate."

"What would we be celebrating?" Bryan asked. "Babies?"

"Take your pick." Neal waved his arm to include the setting sun, the darkening top of the sky, the row of houses across the street, the black dog lifting his leg near the fire hydrant. Ivy willed her mother to smile at her, to believe they had something to be happy about.

"Ivy is back," said Carol, swallowing hard. "Tonight we can all get some sleep." She sat beside Ivy on the step, laying a hand on her thigh.

"Sleep." Neal laughed. "We'll celebrate sleep."

Ivy imagined stretching out in her own bed, getting up to pee, following the same path to the bathroom she'd followed all her life, carefully avoiding the nailhead protruding from the floorboard just outside her door. Neal might have hammered it down by now. She stared at her mother's hand, her wedding ring, her fingernails shiny with clear polish, against the dirty fabric of her jeans and wondered why she'd never thought to bang that nail—years of torn socks, scraped toes.

Carol stood. "Valenti's would be my choice."

Ivy nodded. She preferred the River Restaurant but kept quiet. Her leg held the warmth of her mother's hand, like a stone holds heat when the sun has stopped shining.

After a dinner during which they were all careful with each other and ate too much pasta with clam sauce, Ivy sat, propped against a stack of pillows, exhausted with a case of real heartburn, thoughts racing. She wondered if Gil's box was still in the basement. She hoped Carol hadn't thrown it away. Everyone slept. She could get it, bring it back to her room, see what she had left of him besides his Aerosmith tee shirt and the baby doing gymnastics inside her.

She sneaked downstairs. The basement had been transformed into a workshop, power tools and all. Must be where Neal made Bryan his CD rack. She had to look hard, but high on a shelf over the washing machine, she recognized the box. It wasn't heavy.

Back in her room she unpacked his paintings, photographs of his cats, his sketch pad. He'd shown her his drawings that first night in his room, the self portraits. She loved them. He had the face of a person who knew things, things she couldn't know but wanted to, like how a child left home alone tied to a chair could grow up to laugh and tell a good joke, how a man could love a woman and beat her, beat a woman and love her.

She turned the page to find herself, naked, the picture he'd drawn the day they left. She'd wanted to take it with them but had been too shy to ask. The girl in the picture looked a lot younger than Ivy felt.

She threw the sketchpad in the box with everything else. The flaps wouldn't close. Nothing fit, the way she'd tossed it all in. She pushed it to the back of her closet. The photos and broken glass she'd glued to the wall when she was seven, believing her magic circles could protect her father, keep him alive, were still there. Every day that summer, when Bryan napped, she hid in her closet with the pictures of her father and her glass collection. Her mother discovered it a couple years later, during a spring cleaning. Ivy expected her to have a fit and braced herself as she folded and stacked outgrown clothes to take to Goodwill. Instead, Carol crawled out of the closet, sat on the floor, silent. Ivy piled up eight sweaters waiting. They toppled and she restacked them in two shorter piles before her mother spoke. "I remember Grandma Harrington saying you were spending a lot of time in the closet. I thought you were in there sulking." Grieving. Praying. Bargaining with God. She'd wanted to tell her mother, but she'd cut up the photo albums and wrecked the closet wall with glue and felt lucky not to be yelled at. She said nothing. Her mother stood up, left the room, and punishment never came. She wondered now, what would have happened if she'd spoken up? The usual argument or a glimmer of understanding?

Ivy noticed the pool cue. Her old life, she'd thought, when she packed for Florida. I won't be needing it. Another mistake. Her big belly made it hard to clamber out of the closet and stand. Far across the room, her rumpled bed waited, the fuzzy, pink blanket she'd had all her life, her baby quilt folded at the bottom, the stack of pillows that held the shape of her, but she knew she couldn't sleep.

Carol lay rigid and silent as Neal clambered into bed beside her. "That was a nice, dinner, I thought," he said. He rested on an elbow and tucked a tendril of hair behind her ear.

She had the urge to snap at him but no justification for it, so she kept still.

"How do you feel?" he asked.

She widened her eyes to dry the tears collecting in the corners. The ceiling needed painting. Even in the dim light of the bedside lamp she could see flecks of peeling paint next to the smoke alarm which probably needed a new battery. Wasn't that what the blinking red meant?

"Carol, how do you feel?" Neal ran a finger along her jawbone.

She unclenched her teeth. "Tired."

"You're happy, right?" he asked. "About the baby?"

Under the sheet she placed her hands thumb tip to thumb tip, index finger touching index finger, against her flat stomach. Ivy and Bryan were born before she knew what it was like to be the parent of teenagers, before she knew that a sleepless night due to a baby crying was a picnic in the sun compared with a sleepless night waiting for a kid out past curfew or gone for months. Bad enough the fears of SIDS, choking, toddling into the street. There was a time in her life she'd thought changing a diaper would be a challenge. She'd wondered if she'd be able to deal with the stink of it. Anything could happen to this baby inside her, smaller than her little toe. She had no illusions that parents could keep their children safe.

Yet this time there was Neal—a father who understood older kids and liked them, an impossibly unselfish and mature man—responsible, a partner in parenting. This man wouldn't leave her home alone at night with no car, a sleeping preschooler, and an asthmatic baby to hurry to the emergency room. Neal didn't feel the world, or Carol, owed him because he'd fought in Vietnam and come back an alcoholic insomniac.

"I'm okay," she said.

"Ivy seems all right," ventured Neal.

"Depends on what you mean by that," Carol said. "Most parents wouldn't think a pregnant seventeen-year-old high school drop out was all right."

"She can finish high school. She's got a good family to support her."

"This house is too small."

"I can finish the basement," said Neal. "Let yourself be glad she's home."

"What's wrong with you?" Carol asked. "You always think things are going to work out."

"They always do, don't they?" Neal placed his hand on the sheet covering hers. "One way or the other."

"I love you," Carol said. She wished she could organize her thoughts the way she stacked money at the bank, in neat piles, the founding fathers all facing the same way. Her numbers always added up. People wouldn't cooperate. She had never even been able to get them to do something as simple as pose for a family photo at the mall. Three years in a row Ivy screamed that the dress Carol had sewn with smocking and ruffles and fabric that matched the dress she'd made for herself itched, Bryan stared into space, his diaper leaking on to his gray corduroy trousers, also sewn by her, and Johnny was late, off at Rivertown Billiards oblivious first to her hints, then her demands, that all she wanted for Christmas was a classic photograph of all of them. Candid shots were okay for the scrapbooks, but every mother deserved a formal portrait of her family to put on the wall or the TV.

Neal kissed her ear. When the baby was born she'd insist on a family photo at Rivertown Studios. Neal could get everyone there in good spirits. Her husband, her three children. She remembered her grandchild and moaned.

Misinterpreting the sound Neal pressed his lips to hers, his body against her side. Sex might help her sleep, she thought kissing him back.

"Strange to think there's another person here," he whispered. "We are not alone."

"I wouldn't call it a person yet," Carol said.

"It's okay to make love?" Neal leaned over her with his look of concern—wrinkled forehead, two deep lines between his eyebrows.

"Yes."

"Just checking."

Carol told herself she was a lucky woman; everything would be all right if she just relaxed.

Bryan heard the turn of his doorknob, the creak of the door opening. Ivy. Just like her not to knock. "Hey," she whispered. "Are you awake?"

He considered pretending to sleep and knew she'd just barge in, on tiptoes, but barging nevertheless, and proceed to wake him. "Bryan, I need to see Gil's letters."

She sat at the foot of his bed, gripped his toes and levered his foot back and forth.

"Hey, stop it!" He threw his pillow at her. She caught it.

He could just make out her face in the glow from the streetlight. Her belly strained against the white tee shirt she wore. He tried not to look at her breasts, also straining, or her bare legs.

"You've got to give me the letters," she said.

"I told you Mom ripped them up."

"You said you had a couple."

He was embarrassed, glad she couldn't see him blushing in the dark. The three letters he'd managed to save were full of sex. He'd folded and unfolded them so many times she'd have to be able to tell.

"Bryan, they're mine, they were addressed to me. Do you know it's a serious crime to open someone else's mail, not to mention very bad manners." She tickled his foot through the sheet. "Are you going to give them to me?" She tickled harder. He considered kicking her, but the thought of hurting the baby stopped him.

"All right. Let go!"

"You promise?" She held onto his foot; with her other hand she untucked the covers and reached for the skin of his bare sole.

"Yes! Will you let me turn on the light? Let me go. I don't have them in bed with me." Thank goodness. There had been nights he'd fallen asleep with them under his pillow. What he did have was an embarrassing erection he didn't want her to see. He couldn't get up until it went down.

He reached for the lamp on his bedside table.

"Weird Mom's pregnant, huh?" he said to distract her and himself from the letters for a minute.

"I can't believe it," Ivy said. "I mean what do they see in each other. They're so old. Mom's such a cold bitch and Neal is like ... like Dopey from the seven dwarves."

Her words, her smug expression, made Bryan want to punch her. His stomach filled with a familiar and inflating ball of rage. She thought she knew everything, had the right to judge.

"If you think Mom and Neal are so bad," he said. "Why did you come home?"

Her stunned expression satisfied him for the briefest of moments before he felt sorry. It was as if he had punched her, right in the solar plexus.

He climbed out of bed to get the letters from the back corner of his bottom dresser drawer where he kept them with two of his father's letters, the one with a sentence at the end about seeing wounded or dead guys and realizing that skin was just a bag to keep our guts from spilling all over, and one describing C-rations in detail, tasteless scrambled eggs in a can, coiled and gray like brains.

She was up from the bed and looming over him as he squatted by the drawer.

"Give me all of them," she said.

"Here they are."

"All!"

"Those aren't yours. They're personal." He slammed the drawer shut and deliberately seated himself on the floor, back against the dresser.

With a shake of her head that told him she thought he was pathetic, she swept out of the room with her letters. Bryan sat where he was, gulping for air.

A quiet tap and Neal peeked around the partly open door. "You okay?"

Bryan nodded. He wanted Neal to go away and he wanted Neal to come in. He couldn't decide.

Neal's belly stuck out like Ivy's over worn white boxer shorts, stretching his tee shirt. Tufts of gray and brown hair sprung from the V neck. The hair around his head stood out in all directions. He did look kind of dopey. He put on his glasses, focused on Bryan, and plopped down onto the floor beside him. Bryan fought the urge to rest his head on Neal's shoulder.

"Quite a day." Neal folded his hands in his lap and studied them. Bryan breathed easier. Neal knew when not to look at him. His mother was always staring at him as if she wanted something.

"Ivy …" Bryan began not sure what he was trying to say.

Neal waited.

This always happened. Bryan desperate to talk, without words. Neal's waiting didn't feel as pressured as most people's, but still …

"Remember when you asked me about basic training?" Neal said finally.

Bryan nodded, glad Neal was talking. The subject didn't matter.

"The third day, I know because I counted every single one, we were running and a guy fell down. The drill sergeant ordered us to run right over him, no swerving around. I was directly behind the guy, my instinct was to stop and help him up, but I would have been trampled myself. I'll never forget the feeling of his body under my boot. That moment changed my life. I wasn't going to be a guy who, thinking only of myself, trampled on people. From what I can see, your sister hasn't had that moment yet. Lots of people haven't, unfortunately."

"Lots of people never will," Bryan said. "Lots of people think that's what life is about. Besides how did you survive the army with that attitude? My dad told my grandmother that he hated killing people but when it's them or you, you don't stop to think about it." That sentence came just after the one about skin being nothing but a bag. Bryan had that letter memorized. "Why didn't you go to Vietnam?"

"This is a long conversation for another day when we're not so tired," Neal said. "But, no, I wasn't. My third day of basic training I knew I had to file for CO status."

"Conscientious objector?" Bryan couldn't believe it.

"It was a long ordeal, but I finally got it. No disrespect to your dad. It was a strange time. People did what they had to do."

"Didn't you feel like a wimp? Like other people were dying for you? My dad hated conscientious objectors." He'd mentioned that in the letter about the eggs.

"Choosing not to be an aggressor doesn't make you a wimp." Neal's tone was mild and sure.

Bryan mouthed the words to make sure he'd heard right. He felt the same stomach clenching shame, relief, and possibility he felt at the quarry when Martine made a space for him to sit on her towel even though he was the one guy who never tried to wrestle the girls off the ledge into the water.

Neal tapped Bryan's knee. "What do you say we get some sleep?"

Bryan nodded, too exhausted to speak. They hoisted themselves to their feet.

Neal switched off the light before smoothing the sheet over Bryan's shoulders and giving his back a quick rub and a pat. "Good night," Neal said. The door closed with a soft click before Bryan realized Neal had tucked him in.

CHAPTER 7

"Hey, Chef Boyardee, did your slutty sister drop that kid yet?" Tommy Sparks, an overgrown senior, knocked Bryan against his locker with a pseudofriendly body check.

No one else had put it that bluntly. In the few weeks since Ivy'd been home Bryan had heard something from everyone. Only Martine and Everett seemed to care at all. Everett because he was Bryan's best friend and Martine, because possibly, he hoped, she wanted to be his girlfriend but probably, he feared, only because her brother, Leo, used to hang out with Ivy at the pool hall.

He turned his back on Tommy and fiddled with his lock, hoping he'd go away. No wonder Ivy never left the house. No wonder she hadn't even considered coming back to school.

"Asshole," Everett muttered as Tommy Sparks swaggered down the hall.

Bryan grabbed the books he needed and slammed the locker, imagining Tommy's head in the way.

"You want to go over to the field?" Ev asked. "I heard Martine and Casey say they'd be at the park. They said it loud, so I could hear. They want us to come. I know it."

"I don't know." Bryan would go anywhere to be near Martine and her tan belly and tinkly laugh, but he didn't want even Ev to know. It seemed pathetic.

They moved toward the door in the flow of people. "Osmosis," his science teacher always said, "is a process much like a crowd of people forcing its way through a small set of doors." He thought of it every day when he left school.

The afternoon sparkled, one of those blue and gold, early fall days. He could imagine Martine's hair lit up and glowing like on a commercial, her teeth white. "What the hell," he said nonchalantly. "Let's go." At home, Ivy would be sitting in the living room, staring at the TV. Bryan could make something quick for dinner, a stir-fry, and practice guitar later, when it was dark.

"We could go by your house. Get your sister," Ev raised his shoulders. His tiny, careless shrug didn't make his words less of a surprise.

"Ivy?" Bryan stopped, a rock in the stream of people. "Why?"

"Why not?"

"She never goes out." He couldn't imagine Ivy in the sunlight, reaching up to pick a Frisbee from the air, bending to retrieve it from the grass, laughing. Any relief she felt about being home had worn off fast. She shuffled from room to room, muttering to herself, like a lonely old woman. He stayed out of her way.

"That's what I figured," Ev said. "Maybe she should. Martine and Casey are dying to see her. I heard them talking."

"Oh, I get it," Bryan said. His stomach felt like the bowl of an electric mixer set on high. "My sister, the freak. Should we charge them?"

"What's the big deal?" Ev bumped him with his hip. "Mostly I just thought Ivy would like it."

"You want to gawk at her too, don't you?"

"It's hard to imagine her all fat and everything," he admitted.

Why not? Let everybody see her. Maybe then they'd stop wondering and whispering. Besides, she deserved it. But Bryan didn't. He didn't deserve any of it. He did what he was supposed to. Ivy did whatever she wanted. The last thing Bryan wanted to do was play Frisbee with Ev, Martine, and Casey. No one believed him when he said he didn't like the game. No, that was the second to last thing. The last thing was to play with Ev, Martine, Casey, and Ivy. But he'd do it. Ivy wouldn't come anyway. Not if a stupid talk show was on TV.

He said, "If you want her to come, you ask."

When Everett and Bryan stepped into the house, Ev said, "Hey, Ivy. Haven't seen you in awhile."

Ivy grinned. "Little Everett, you've grown since I last saw you." She seemed happy to see him. Bryan wanted to punch them both. "I guess I shouldn't talk," she added, standing, turning from side to side to show off her huge stomach. It pushed against the shapeless black overalls their mother had bought her. Bryan could swear she stuck it out even farther than it naturally went.

"Wow!" Ev's mouth hung open.

She took his hand and laid it flat against her. "It's kicking," Ivy said.

Before Bryan could say anything, Ev began to babble. His face shone. "Oh my God. It is. I can feel it. I really can." You'd think he was the father. Or the uncle.

Ivy smiled, a gigantic, genuine smile. Ev put both hands on her belly, as if it was a basketball and he was aiming a foul shot.

"We're going to play Frisbee," Bryan heard himself say. "You want to come?"

"Me?" Ivy seemed shocked.

Ev stepped back and rubbed his hands together. "Come on," he said. "It's beautiful out."

"What the hell? Just let me pee first. That's the worst thing," she turned to Everett, confiding, "I have to pee constantly."

He nodded as if he understood perfectly and watched Ivy's ass as she climbed the stairs.

"Where's the Frisbee?" Bryan asked.

"In here." Ev jiggled his pack on his shoulder. "Something the matter?"

Bryan kicked the bottom stair. Something was the matter, but he couldn't even say to himself what it was. He was ashamed of his sister and possessive too. It didn't make sense. "Let's wait outside."

"I thought she'd look all …" Everett stopped. "It's kind of amazing, really."

"Oh, yeah," Bryan said. "What? What's so amazing?"

"How it moves around and everything."

"Yeah. So, what?" Bryan wouldn't know. He'd never felt it. Ivy appeared in her jean jacket that didn't even come close to buttoning.

The three of them headed toward the park. They used to play together a lot around the time Johnny died and after. Everett didn't have any brothers or sisters. Bryan always thought that was lucky, but Everett never minded being bossed by Ivy.

"You never made it to Indochina," Ev said.

"What?" Ivy looked confused.

"That summer," he said. "You had Bryan and me digging all day long. To Indochina. You promised us all the fortune cookies we could eat once we got there. And tigers. You said we'd see tigers and water buffalo and rice paddies. We'd wear big straw hats and walk barefoot."

"Oh, yeah." It sounded more like a sad kind of sigh than words.

They could see Martine and Casey on the swings, legs pointing to the sky, then folding, pointing, folding.

"How was Florida?" Ev asked.

"Hot," Ivy answered.

Martine and Casey pretended not to see them at first. They started tossing the Frisbee around on the baseball field. The girls stopped swinging and made their way over. "Want to play?" Ev asked.

They threw it around without talking much until Martine said she was tired and plopped down behind second base. Ivy joined her and one by one they all sat in a ragged circle.

"How is it? Being back?" Martine asked.

Ivy looked toward Bryan for a moment before answering, as if she wanted him to say something. Then he realized she was just staring in his direction, through him, considering. He hunched forward, eager for her answer.

"Rivertown sucks," she said. "But being alone and pregnant with nowhere to live was worse."

Everyone looked at the grass. Ev picked at it. Martine ran her fingers though it like it was hair. Casey plucked a wide piece and pressed it between her thumbs to make a whistle. Ivy had seen so much they hadn't. She picked a three leafed clover and threw it away.

"Are you going back to school?" Ev asked.

"Never," Ivy shook her head.

"What will you do?" Martine asked.

Ivy looked thoughtful. Bryan held his breath.

"Take care of the kid, I guess. Take care of Mom's kid. Our little brother or sister."

"Could be fun," Martine said. "But maybe you should see about going back to school …"

"I'm never going back to that school," Ivy practically spat out the words. She stared at each of them through slitted eyes. No one contradicted her.

"Leo's wondering why you haven't shown up at Curly's," Martine risked saying. "Tells me he hasn't had a good game since you left."

Ivy yanked at clump of grass, shaking her head. Bryan wanted to push, ask again, why she hadn't gone to the pool hall. Another one of those questions that got caught on something inside and never made it past his lips.

"So what should I tell him?" Martine pressed on. She ignored the don't-ask-me-about-this-one, barriers people put up. It was one of the things Bryan liked about her.

Ivy cleaned dirt from under her nails. Casey and Everett rolled their eyes at each other. Martine and Bryan watched Ivy.

"Tell him …" Bryan tried to read Ivy's lips as they moved without sound. She didn't seem to know what to say and was silently trying a number of possibilities. "I don't know," she said, finally. "Maybe I quit."

"But …" Bryan scrambled onto his knees. "You can't. You love playing pool." He knew what he was talking about. She did love playing, the way he loved cooking and music and you didn't just give something like that up. She had no right to look at him like he was pathetic or wrong. He was sick of her looking at him that way. She'd given him that look their whole lives.

"You'll be back," Martine said. "I'll tell him." Ivy didn't argue. She lay staring at the sky, her belly rising up like a hill.

"Is it moving now?" Ev asked.

"No," Ivy patted the baby. "But it will. Whenever I lay down, it starts moving."

"You guys should feel it," Ev said.

"Can we?" asked Casey, inching closer. The four of them surrounded Ivy, on their knees.

"Go ahead," she said. "It's kicking now. Or punching or something."

Bryan could see her belly ripple. Ev and Casey placed their hands on it. Martine too. He put his hand beside hers, his little finger almost touching her thumb.

The late afternoon sun shone on Ivy's face. She closed her eyes. It was like they were casting a spell, all of them, on their knees, waiting, covering his sister's belly with their flat palms. Then, it moved. Bryan felt it. Martine felt it. Her eyes got huge. Her face glowed in the golden light.

"That's it!" Ev yelled. Casey laughed. They all were laughing. The baby moved some more. Ivy looked proud even with her eyes squeezed shut. She was smiling again. She wasn't the one amazing everybody. It was the baby. Not her. Bryan moved his little finger so it touched Martine, pretending the baby had pushed it.

The red, orange, and yellow leaves glowed against the drizzly, early morning sky. Carol glanced at Ivy who, three blocks from home, was still trying to buckle her seat belt around her big belly. Carol had scheduled their appointments with the obstetrician first thing in the morning so she wouldn't have to be too late for work.

"I give up." Ivy let her seat belt ratchet back into its slot.

"Wait, I'll pull over."

"Mom, just go. We'll be there in five minutes."

Carol hesitated at the stop sign. A truck blasted its horn behind them.

"Just go!"

"We don't want anything to happen to the baby, when you've made it this far, everything you've been through." Ivy had seen Dr. Cardullo twice already and the baby appeared to be fine. Ivy had been pronounced healthy too—the luck of the ignorant or the young.

"Go! We're more likely to have an accident sitting here. That truck's going to run right over you!"

"Us, you mean." Carol remembered Neal's advice about humor and teenagers. "There's four of us in this car."

"Oh, Mom." Ivy rolled her eyes, but the tension melted out of her voice.

A school bus turned a corner ahead of them. Carol congratulated herself for not asking Ivy when she planned to go back to school.

The office lot was almost empty. Carol parked the Honda next to the handicapped space, two spots from the door. "Voila!" Inexplicably proud of her success she congratulated herself again. They'd hurry in and out, she'd drop Ivy off at home and get to work less than an hour late.

Neal had wanted to come, to find out the results of the amnio, but he had a meeting with the principal. The school department was threatening to cut the Technical Arts budget by more than a third.

Carol held the vestibule door open while Ivy took her own sweet time walking the few feet from the car. She didn't yell or nag. What happened to all these words she wasn't saying? She hoped the baby didn't absorb them; it couldn't be healthy. Stand straight! Couldn't you be bothered to brush your hair this morning? Didn't you even notice that shirt is missing a button? If you insist on wearing those ratty sandals you could at least take care of your feet; I'm not talking toenail polish, just washing the dirt off would help.

"Did you take a shower yesterday?" Carol asked as Ivy passed through the door. What would Dr. Cardullo think of her mothering skills? Not only had her daughter gone out and gotten herself pregnant, she'd never been taught to bathe before a doctor's appointment.

"Did you?" Ivy asked.

Carol didn't bother to respond. Ivy knew she showered every morning.

They opened the door to the suite. Just as Carol planned they were the first appointments of the day. No waiting.

Ivy fell into a chair and put her feet up on a table, messing the fan of magazines, and closed her eyes. Carol sat down beside her resisting the urge to rearrange the reading material. It wasn't worth Ivy's scorn. Better the doctor think she'd raised a careless, ill-mannered daughter than fight with Ivy. She didn't have to live with the doctor.

"Who's first?" Dr. Cardullo, a young woman with a long dark braid and large horn-rimmed glasses, appeared at the door leading to the examining rooms. Carol wanted to suggest contacts. The doctor had a beautiful face, but you had to look around the glasses to see it and other people might not bother.

"Go ahead," Ivy said, head resting back against the wall, eyes still closed.

Carol gave the doctor a wide eyed, what-can-you-do look and followed her in.

She stopped at the restroom to urinate in a paper cup, stepped on the scale to be weighed. Dr. Cardullo marked the charts. After the doctor pronounced her blood pressure normal, and listened to the baby's heart, Carol asked about the amnio results.

"Everything looks good. No problems detected." Dr. Cardullo patted Carol's knee as if proud of her, as if she'd brought home a good report card. "Congratulations." A pleased smile floated up from deep in Carol's chest and spread across her face.

The doctor consulted her notes. "You wanted to know the gender?"

"Yes," Carol said. At first Neal wanted to wait, but Carol convinced him she'd had enough surprises.

"A girl."

"Oh no!" Carol's face hurt. The smile dissolved. She could feel it evaporate, condense into the lump of tears in her throat.

The horror that flashed across Doctor Cardullo's face before she smoothed it into a look of mild, professional concern, remained visible in her eyes, even behind the glasses. Carol realized she'd said the words aloud, words she didn't even know she was thinking. "I mean, girls are so much harder than boys." She wanted the doctor to stop looking at her if she were a terrible person. "Maybe not for fathers, but mothers and daughters … especially when they're teenagers … I mean …"

The only thing to do was leave. "Well, speaking of daughters, Ivy's waiting." The windowless white room tightened. Carol tore at the edges of the paper on the examining table.

"How are you feeling?" the doctor asked peering into Carol's eyes. "Still tired?"

Carol nodded. Her eyes filled.

Doctor Cardullo ripped a sheet off her clipboard and handed it to her. "Stop at the lab for a blood test. I want to make sure you're not anemic. Are you taking your iron pills?"

Carol nodded. She did skip them occasionally. They made her constipated. But already feeling so ashamed, she couldn't admit it to the doctor.

"See you again in a few weeks. I'll call with the test results." Dr. Cardullo followed her down the hall to the waiting room door.

"Ivy, your turn." The doctor sounded warm—maternal. No, Carol thought, pregnancy was making her stupid, paranoid. She attributed motives and feelings to people that really weren't there. She tried to dismiss the thought that the doctor disapproved of her and sympathized with Ivy, but as Ivy passed through the door, Dr. Cardullo touched her daughter's shoulder with what looked to Carol like love.

Walter, the lab technician, stabbed her efficiently, filled and labeled a tube of blood in moments. Carol appreciated people who were good at their jobs. Back in the waiting room she tried not to think about being late for work and wondered how the plant in the corner stayed so green without any natural light. She was about to get up and inspect it more closely, to determine if it was real, when the door to the examining rooms opened and Dr. Cardullo called her in.

"Is something wrong?" Carol asked with, she thought, appropriate motherly concern.

"Everything's fine," the doctor said. Carol couldn't detect any judgment positive or negative in her tone. "But we need to talk about something and Ivy thought we could do it now, the three of us."

Carol suddenly knew exactly what it meant to drag one's feet. Ivy had told the doctor what a bad mother Carol was, how mean and unsupportive. Something would happen now. Carol clenched her teeth, told herself to relax, and unclenched them.

Ivy sat fully dressed and huge on the examining table. Her sandaled feet dangled. Her deliberately bored expression gave nothing away. Doctor Cardullo gestured to a chair and seated herself on a rolling stool. She looked at Ivy, as if signaling her to start. She waited and when Ivy continued to sit, sullen and silent, the doctor turned to Carol who was beginning to relax. If she had even the slightest insight and sensitivity, the doctor had to see how difficult Ivy was.

"Ivy's baby could be born at any time now and survive just fine," the doctor said. "Ivy and I have been talking about the birth. She needs to be prepared. She needs to think about who she wants with her, a labor coach can be very helpful."

"Usually it's the baby's father," Ivy said. "She's trying not to say that, but it's true."

"Often it's the father." Dr. Cardullo nodded. "But many women want some-one there who has been through it, had a baby herself. They want their moth-ers. Ivy seemed hesitant to ask you, but did agree it might be a good idea."

Carol looked toward Ivy for confirmation, but her daughter was staring at her belly. In the seven weeks since Ivy had come home, the house pulsed with feeling and trembled with Herculean effort to get along, make it through the days. Neal and Bryan had the stress of beginning a new school year, Carol had been sick and pregnant and furious and relieved and learning to live with a man again. Ivy had her own problems. That had to explain why Carol hadn't once thought of her daughter actually giving birth and who would be there.

When Ivy was born, Johnny had slept in a chair at Carol's laboring side. The nurses had coached her. He woke up to share the joy, to marvel at Ivy's loud cry, her thick dark hair, her eyes the color of the sky before it storms. With Bryan he'd been home with Ivy. Again the nurses helped, competent, kind pro-fessionals. Carol never would have considered having her mother at her births. A stranger off the street would have been more welcome.

"So," the doctor continued. "Ivy was wondering, right Ivy? If you wanted to be there when she has her baby."

Ivy nodded, still focused on her belly.

"I hardly remember my own births," Carol said. "I don't know how much help I'd be."

"Forget it," Ivy muttered.

Before the reflexive spark of Carol's anger could catch, Dr. Cardullo nudged her with a meaningful look. "But I'd love to be there to do whatever I could," she said.

Ivy's swinging foot hit the metal table with a vibrating thunk. Dr. Cardullo stood up. "She needs you," the doctor said. "All you have to do is be there. There's a birth class for women and their labor coaches. Most people take it earlier in the pregnancy, but nurse practitioners do offer an alternative, inten-sive two Saturday class at the hospital that would work for you. Next week and the week after. As long as this baby waits until its due date, that should be fine. Okay?"

Carol pulled out her datebook. "What time?"

"I'll check on it. I think it's nine to one."

Carol wrote it in while Ivy slid down from the table. She stood straighter than when they'd walked in. The doctor must have talked to her about the importance of good posture. Carol could say anything, but until Ivy heard it from someone else, she wouldn't listen.

"Want to see the wedding pictures?" Neal tossed the envelope of photos into Ivy's lap and set a bulging plastic CVS bag on the floor. "Some good ones in there. One I want to enlarge and frame."

Ivy still wasn't used to Neal coming in the door after work, arms full of groceries and mail, kicking off his shoes, hanging his coat in the hall closet. If she'd never left, he would be the outsider. She might have stopped them from marrying. Who would want a loud, almost grown stepdaughter fighting with his new wife? Since she'd come back she usually felt too tired to fight. Or too scared, her position so precarious, she couldn't risk alienating anyone. Neal hung over the back of the recliner. The envelope lay, untouched on her thighs.

"Go on," he urged. "Check 'em out. Your mother's been bugging me to pick these up—with good reason, I guess, it's what, four months ago, now. Had to finish the roll first."

Ivy picked at the sticky flap, unable to bring herself to open it. Neal waited, his breath hot on her head. Finally, she tore it open and dragged out the stack of pictures. Her mother, dressed in a stylish, off-white suit Ivy had never seen, with a corsage of tiny, red rosebuds pinned to the jacket, looked back at her. She wore her black, low heeled shoes, the ones she wore to work. She looked happy. A woman not thinking about a run away daughter. A woman who had no idea she was about to be a thirty-seven-year-old grandmother. She looked like a happy woman marrying a man she loved, a man who loved her. Neal, his face beaming, looked stuffed into a too-small suit.

"Did Bryan take this?" Ivy asked.

"He took all of them, except the one he's in. The justice of the peace took that." Neal leaned over farther. "Your mother told me to get a new suit, one that fits. Told her I hadn't worn one since my high school graduation." He squinted at himself. "Considering that it's been over twenty years, it doesn't look that bad. Your mother, she always looks good."

Ivy flipped to the next picture.

"That's it," Neal said. "That's the one I thought I'd frame."

Carol between Bryan and Neal. A happy little family. Bryan, sport coat over a white button down shirt and his baggy pants, looked surprisingly handsome, grown up. His smile seemed genuine. Mom had her arm linked through his.

"It was your wedding," Ivy said, moving it to the bottom of the pile. "Yours and Mom's. You should frame a picture of the two of you together."

"Yeah, but I knew when I married her, I was marrying a family," Neal said.

"I wasn't there."

"I wish you had been," he said, sounding like he meant it.

"Well, I wasn't." She shuffled through the rest of the photos, the ones he'd taken to use up the film—Bryan clowning in the kitchen, holding out a panful of something; Carol posing vamplike in her kitchen chair, legs crossed, arms behind her head, chest out, chin tilted up, Bryan again, a closeup of the frying pan. Ivy recognized the stir-fry they'd had three nights before. Another close-up—this one of Carol's face partially hidden by her hand gesturing the camera away. Ivy had eaten that same dinner, sat at that table, that night, but she wasn't in those pictures either. They must have taken them before they'd called her down.

Ivy shoved the photos back in the envelope and staring at the TV, held them over her shoulder toward Neal. He cleared his throat once, but didn't say anything.

They watched an entire McDonald's commercial before he retrieved the CVS bag and shook it. "I got a bunch of Halloween candy here." Ivy had forgotten it was Halloween. "Do you usually get a lot of kids trick or treating?"

Ivy tried to remember last year, before she'd met Gil. She'd spent Halloween at the pool hall. Curly, a pair of devil horns stuck to his bald head, poured anyone who came in costume a free beer. Too young to drink, she hadn't bothered to wear one. "I have no idea."

"What about when you were a kid?"

"No, I mean yes. Neal, I'm trying to watch TV, you mind?"

Halloween when she was a kid. As was true about everything else, before Dad died it was one way, after he died, it was another. Even the things that were the same were different.

"Look what else I got." Like a magician, he pulled a fake jack o' lantern from the bag. She glanced at it, then back to the television. Careful not to block her view, he felt around behind it for an outlet. She thought of carving pumpkins with Bryan and Dad, taking turns deciding on shapes for the eyes, nose, and mouth. After Dad died, they still carved pumpkins, just the way they had with him, taking turns, Mom holding the knife until they insisted they could do it themselves. They always had more than one pumpkin. Strange that they hadn't each made their own. No, always back and forth, taking turns. The eyes never matched.

Neal set the glowing pumpkin on top of the TV and admired his purchase.

"Nice, huh? No mess and it'll keep until next year." It wasn't natural for someone to be so perpetually pleased with himself.

"It's fake," she said, wanting to scream. Too perfect, like their little family wedding photo. No slimy tangle of pumpkin seeds or smell of candle and smoking pumpkin flesh. The plastic jack o'lantern grinned its symmetrical grin. She wanted to smash it but it would probably just bounce.

Neal turned toward the kitchen with his photos and Halloween candy. "I'll put this in a bowl." His voice drifted back. "Your Mom said you liked M&M's. Figured we might as well have candy we like."

Feeling mean she clicked the remote and stared at the blank TV under the jack o'lantern's cheerful leer. Mom would be home soon. Bryan, too. They'd eat. The doorbell would start ringing. Neal would leap up with the candy, talk to every kid, pretend to be scared of the little ghosts and witches and monsters.

They never merely gave out treats in the years before Dad died. He'd decorate the house, put cardboard graves in the front yard, set up speakers blaring spooky music, enact creepy scenarios on the porch. Mom said he'd done it since he was a teenager. The neighborhood had come to expect it. Ivy remembered older kids lined up on the sidewalk jostling each other, shouting—a hazy, thrilling memory, like a scary movie seen from the safety of her Dad's lap.

Carol and Bryan came in together. "Hey, where'd we get that?" Bryan made a beeline for the jack o'lantern.

"We should move it to the window," Carol said. "Some kids are already out."

"It's not even dark yet," Ivy said.

Carol laughed. "Don't you remember how hard it was to wait? You were always too excited to eat dinner." Neal came from the kitchen with a bowl full of candy. "Trick or treat," Carol teased. He kissed her. Bryan rolled his eyes. Ivy tried to roll hers but she felt tears welling up and blinked instead.

"You like the jack o'lantern?" Neal stood beside them, Carol in the middle, just like the wedding picture. "I just thought it would be easier, with all of us getting home so late."

"I was home all day," Ivy said.

"I forgot about buying candy until I saw the kids up the street. Glad you remembered, honey." Carol patted Neal's arm.

"So who's going trick or treating?" Neal asked.

Carol laughed. "We had some costumes over the years. I'd always be up half the night sewing ruffles on a gypsy skirt or yarn on a lion's mane. You kids always had great costumes."

The costumes. Always Carol's choice, Carol's idea. Other kids in the Halloween parade at school had store bought costumes of shiny fabric and plastic masks that really looked like their characters, usually from TV. Ivy always had to explain who she was.

"Those costumes really lasted." Carol congratulated herself. "You used them afterward for dress ups. They're still around. The babies will be able to use them." Neal laughed.

Ivy vowed she'd let her kid be whoever or whatever she or he wanted to be for Halloween, even if the costume fell apart before stepping out the door. She'd fix it with tape and staples. Halloween costumes weren't meant to last for years.

"So who's going trick or treating?" Neal repeated.

"Yeah, right," Ivy said, lifting her shirt. "I'll draw some black triangles on my belly and go as a jack o'lantern."

"Good idea!" Neal grinned, ignoring her sarcasm.

"We're all a little old for trick or treating," Bryan said. "Why don't we have dinner here in the living room and give out candy when the doorbell rings?"

"Food!" Carol said. "Good idea. And I need to change my clothes before I do anything else."

"I picked up the wedding pictures." Neal hurried to get the envelope. He looked like he expected Carol to pat him on the head and say good boy.

Bryan reached for the packet. "Let me see." Their three heads leaned over the photos, Neal's bald and shiny, Bryan's nondescript, light brown and messy, Carol's smooth and blonde, as if she'd just combed it.

"Neal, I told you to buy a new suit," Carol said.

"I look pretty good," Bryan took the picture and held it toward the light from the pumpkin.

"You were right, honey," Neal said, "as usual."

Carol smiled and moved to switch on the light.

Neal stopped her. "Let's look at these later. Get changed. I'll make us some sandwiches and then show you my costume idea."

Carol kissed him. "You're just a big kid," she said heading up the stairs.

"You know," Bryan said, flipping through the photos, one side of his face glowing in the pumpkin's steady shine, no flickering shadows like a candle would have thrown. "I don't think this wedding would have happened so fast if you'd been around."

"What do you mean?" Ivy sat up straight. "You think I would've scared him away?"

"Maybe," Bryan said, flipping through the pictures again. "You have to admit you were giving Mom a hard time about going out with him."

"Not really," Ivy said, holding her belly.

Bryan shrugged. "Anyway, that's not what I meant."

"Well, what?" She hadn't given her mother a hard time about Neal. It was Mom's forgetting Dad, ignoring his birthday.

"You know how careful Mom is. If she hadn't been so sad and worried and hysterical she wouldn't have let him move in on her so fast."

Bryan peered at the photo in his hand. "You running off made her upset enough to let her guard down."

"Is there anything that happens in this family that isn't my fault?" Ivy said. "Don't blame me for this."

Bryan gave a short laugh and set the pictures on the TV. "Blame? I'm not blaming." Carol's footsteps sounded in the upstairs hall. Ivy's face burned. "I can't even talk to you," Bryan whispered. "I didn't say anything about blame."

Ivy pushed back in the recliner and squeezed her eyes shut.

Neal came in with a plate of sandwiches.

"What's your idea?" Carol asked him, coming downstairs. Ivy wondered if they'd notice she had her eyes closed.

"I'll show you," he said. "Grab a sandwich and come on. I think I've got everything we need in the basement. Bryan? Ivy?"

"I don't think so," Ivy mumbled.

"Come on, I thought of this as I was driving to work this morning. It's great."

"No, thanks," Ivy wouldn't budge.

Bryan wavered. "What is it?"

Ivy opened her eyes.

"I'll show you. Come on." Neal moved toward the basement door. Carol and Bryan followed. "Coming, Ivy?"

Ivy shook her head.

"Leave her alone," Carol said. "She can stay home and give out candy. Someone should."

From the basement she heard her mother's giggles, Bryan's laughter, banging and clattering. Her mother passed through the living room and went upstairs, coming back with an armload of Neal's work clothes. She walked right by without a glance. The doorbell rang a few times and Ivy struggled to her feet, wordlessly held out the candy bowl. She considered joining the fun in the basement, but it seemed too late. She sat at the end of the couch nearest the door so she didn't have as far to walk.

Finally, Neal and Bryan emerged with paper bags over their heads and a rope strung from one to the other. Bryan wore a bird house on top of his bag. Carol stood between them, peeking through Neal's shirt, its empty sleeves clothespinned to the rope. All of them laughing.

"There's room for another set of clothes." Bryan's words came muffled from under his bag. "It's more fun than you'd think, Ivy."

"No," Ivy said. "You go."

"She doesn't want to," Carol said through the shirt.

But I do, Ivy thought. I really do. I just can't. Help me, Mom. She shifted on the couch. Maybe she was going crazy. She couldn't really want to walk around the neighborhood looking like an idiot. She'd already done enough of that.

"All right," Neal sounded resigned. "If you're sure."

"She's sure," Carol said. "Come on. If we're going, let's go."

The doorbell rang. Ivy opened it. "Trick or treat." Familiar voices. Two beautiful witches. Martine and Casey. Now Bryan would feel like a jerk, tied to his stepfather with a bird house on his head.

"Is Bryan home?" Martine looked past Ivy.

"Bryan, is that you?" Casey laughed. "What a great costume! A clothesline!"

Bryan bowed. The birdhouse leaned with him. The girls laughed.

"We were just heading out around the block," Neal said. "Would you like to come with us?"

"Sure," Martine's teeth shone white and silver in her green face.

"We won't go far," Carol said. "Maybe Bryan can detach himself and go on with you—as a telephone pole."

Ivy stepped out of the way as they filed out of the house. Bryan hesitated but when the rope pulled tight, he followed. They laughed and chatted their way off the porch leaving behind a lonely silence and the grinning fake jack o'lantern. She plopped back onto the couch, sinking into the cushions. Mom and Neal and Bryan had everything. Things to do all day, wedding pictures, a clever Halloween costume. She had a flow of letters from jail she wouldn't let herself answer, a huge baby inside a body only meant to hold one person, and a bowl of candy in her lap. She opened one of the little bags of M&M's and poured them into her mouth.

The doorbell rang, a reason to get up. She had a responsibility. A woman she didn't recognize hung behind a little girl with whiskers painted on her cheeks, a pink tutu, purple feather boa, glittery net angel wings, and black pointed ears stuck to a headband. "I'm a fancy, ballet dancer, angel cat," she said.

"Say trick or treat," the woman prompted from the shadows.

"Trick or treat," the girl smiled. Her two top teeth were missing.

Ivy stood frozen. "A fancy, ballet dancer, cat," she repeated slowly.

"A fancy, ballet dancer *angel* cat," the little girl corrected, reaching for the candy.

Ivy offered the bowl. The girl grabbed as many bags as she could hold. "These are my favorite."

The woman stepped forward, "I told you, only one. Only take one. Put those back."

The girl's hand tightened around the candy. Her narrowed eyes met Ivy's.

Ivy nudged the bowl over the girl's bag and tipped it. The candy slid in, a rustling, crackling avalanche, settling heavy in the bottom, the mother's protests small and far away. The little girl's eyes widened. She had to use both arms to lift the bag. Ivy hugged the empty bowl and slammed the door.

She turned off all the lights, unplugged the jack o' lantern, and sat in the dark, listening to the doorbell ring, wishing she saved a few packs of M&M's for herself, hoping the little girl and her mother weren't fighting about the candy.

CHAPTER 8

For the third day in a row Bryan walked Martine home from school. They walked past the foundry in a cold drizzle and up the hill past the park. The trees had lost most of their leaves and dark came early, especially in the rain. Moisture beaded on Martine's red fleece jacket and red-brown hair. In the gray afternoon, through Bryan's rain spattered glasses, colors shone. He wanted the walk to last longer than the mile and a half. He needed more time to prepare to drop his arm over her shoulders or reach for her hand.

"Hey, Bryan!" Martine sounded angry.

He stopped, midstep, and turned toward her.

"You're not listening."

He didn't know how to tell her he was listening; he loved hearing her voice and let it wash over him, so like music he didn't even listen to the words, just the changing tone and pitch.

"I'm boring to you." She pouted and began walking a step ahead of him, the set of her back scolding him. If he didn't do something she'd march home and into her house. He followed her for a block. At the corner she had to stop to let a car pass before she crossed the street. Bryan touched her elbow. She turned toward him.

Later, going over and over the moment in his head, he couldn't remember how it all happened. He would have thought a kiss took more planning than holding hands or an arm around a girl, but this was Martine and there'd been a layer of energy between them since their pinkies had touched. He kissed her against the telephone pole, her leg between his, pressing against his aching crotch. Even through layers of clothing he felt her nipples rub his chest. Her mouth. He'd expected softness, not the hard urgency of teeth and gums. Kissing her, touching her tongue with his, licking her teeth, pulling air in through his nose was more like playing his harp than he'd ever have thought. Unlike the inanimate harmonica, she kissed back. The music in his head swelled and crashed. It was like a movie—the drizzly, darkening corner, the cone of street light, the beautiful girl. And the man bent over her.

"I have to go," Martine said and slipped out of his grasp. Through his steamed up glasses all he saw was a red blur as she stepped away.

"Wait." He reached for her arm and missed.

"I'm late," she said. By the time he wiped his glasses on the edge of his shirt and put them back on, she had turned the corner.

Bryan almost skipped home. Next time he would take his glasses off before he kissed her. Next time maybe they would be without coats. His hands remembered the feel of her shoulder blades. He adjusted his jeans around his hard on and pulled out his harp. He blew a long string of notes into the November air.

He planned to head right to the shower, to slip by Ivy, who, as usual, would be lolling in the recliner watching TV with her feet up. If the bathroom hadn't been on the second floor, she wouldn't have had any exercise. Pregnant women got away with anything. He wouldn't have been allowed to sit around like that.

"Bryan?" Ivy said, before he was all the way in the door. She sat upright in the chair, arms wrapped around her belly, ignoring the TV. "I can't do this. I don't want to have a baby." He'd never heard his sister's voice so small.

"But you have to. Don't you?"

She looked up at the ceiling, rocking her upper body back and forth. "It's all stupid. The whole world is stupid."

He took a step toward her, not knowing what he'd do when he reached her side. "You've been watching too much TV." She stopped rocking to look at him. "TV makes the world look more stupid than it is," he said.

"You're stupid, Bryan. How am I going to raise this kid, with no job, no one to help me?"

He picked up the remote, pressed numbers until he found Julia Child. Some things on TV made sense. Julia whisked a cream sauce, smooth and white in a shiny pan. "Why did you run off with the biggest asshole in Rivertown? Why did you sleep with him? Why didn't you use any birth control? I'm not the stupid one around here."

He'd just had his first kiss. He wanted to relive it in the privacy of the bathroom. Ivy took everything away from him, and she didn't even realize how selfish she was.

Ivy covered her ears and screamed a scream that raced through his brain like electricity along a wire. A scream that sounded as if it had been gathering force and volume during all the past weeks in the chair. He froze as she flung her head back over and over against the recliner and wailed.

Then, with a huge sigh, more like a gasp, she stopped and struggled to her feet; a wet stain spread down the legs of her jeans. Her waters had broken. He knew it from the past few months of baby conversation. He didn't know if she realized what was happening or if he should point it out. All the screaming couldn't be good for the baby. Bryan felt sorry for him; he knew it was a boy. He had trouble feeling sorry for Ivy but feeling sorry for the little guy was easy. Ivy was right about it being a stupid world. The baby didn't even know what he was getting into.

"Shit!" Ivy cried. "I'm soaked." She looked as though she expected Bryan to do something. "This is it."

"I'll call Mom," he said.

"In the birth class they said over and over that first babies take a long time. Get me some dry clothes first, then call her. She'll be home any minute anyway." Ivy closed her eyes, rocked, standing.

Bryan raced upstairs, glad for something to do. Ivy's floor lay buried under a layer of clothes, knee deep in places. Sticky cups and glasses sprouted from the dresser. Candy wrappers and empty tortilla chip bags and an envelope covered with pen and ink drawing littered the bed. He recognized it as one she'd received from Gil the week before. No one knew how often Gil wrote since only Ivy was home to get the mail. If she received one letter on Saturday in front of family she made a show of throwing it away unopened. For the first time he wondered if she retrieved them from the trash later. He'd thought of doing that himself.

Her black pair of overalls topped a pile of laundry. He wondered what people wore to have a baby in. In the closet hung a long row of dresses their mother had made for Ivy, some loose and smocky, never worn. Shuffling through them, Bryan couldn't choose. Nothing would be right. The pool cue, leather case dusty, still rested on the closet shelf. He imagined handing it to her, imagined Ivy leaning over a pool table, big belly in the way. Maybe her pool playing days really were over. He'd never heard of a mother shooting pool.

"Where are you?" Ivy yelled. "Bring a towel. Come on. Hurry up!"

He ripped the nearest dress from a hanger, yellow with yellower flowers, and snatched a towel from the hall closet as he rushed by.

Ivy paced the living room, rocking her pelvis, rubbing her belly.

"Here." He tossed the dress toward her.

She pulled off her jeans, right there in the living room. He tried not to look at the weird elastic panel where a snap and zipper should have been or her sticking out belly button. He wiped up the chair with the towel.

"Fuck the chair, Bryan," Ivy held out her hand.

He gave her the wet towel, hunching his shoulders, sure she'd complain about the dress but she slipped it over her head without seeing it. He looked at the tangle of wet jeans and underwear. "I'm calling Mom."

Ivy nodded.

An answering machine informed him that banking hours were from nine to five and he should call back then. He looked at the clock. Carol had to be home any minute. Neal too.

"She'll be here soon," he told Ivy. She stopped pacing long enough to nod.

Bryan kept checking out the window, listening hard for the sound of Neal's truck or Mom's old Honda.

"I don't feel good," Ivy croaked. In the moment it took Bryan to turn around, she was on her hands and knees, vomiting.

Like a dog, he thought without disgust, putting a towel under her, praying for their mother to walk in.

"They never said anything about puking," Ivy sobbed. "Where's Mom?"

"She's on her way," Bryan said. "Lie down, I'll get a wet rag. Want some water or anything?"

"I want Mom," Ivy choked. "I want Mom." She lay on her side, in the silly, yellow dress, tears streaming down her face.

"Shh." He knelt to brush her hair off her forehead. She grabbed his hand and hung on tight.

Fingers aching, he prayed harder for their mother to come, tried to remember if she'd said anything about errands after work.

Ivy's eyes stared, wide open and strange, looking at things he couldn't see, the baby, the inside part of herself. She moaned. "Are you having a contraction?" he asked and realized though he knew the word, he didn't know what a contraction was. She moaned again and again.

Ivy vomited, still on hands and knees, her face sweaty. Her hand crushed his, pressing it to the floor, so he couldn't clean anything up. The room smelled sour. Her vomit soaked into the rug. Finally, the sound of Neal's truck rumbling into the driveway, door slamming, Neal's solid footsteps on the porch, the most beautiful beat Bryan ever heard.

"Whoa!" Neal took in the scene.

"I want Mom," Ivy whimpered.

"She's coming." Neal knelt beside her, across from Bryan. "She'll be here."

Bryan put a hand on the small of Ivy's back and when she leaned into it, he rubbed hard.

"I'll call Doctor Cardullo." Neal said.

"Mom." Ivy hollered. "Where is she?"

"I already tried Mom," Bryan called after Neal. "Tell the doctor the water broke." He checked the clock. "About an hour ago."

Bryan turned to see their mother opening the door, her own rounded belly tucked under her tan raincoat, She crouched next to him. "So it's happening," she whispered, her voice shaky. "How you doing, Ivy?"

"Doc says, bring her in," Neal announced.

"Hear that, honey? Time to go to the hospital," Carol said. She still had her purse hanging from her shoulder.

"Mom," Ivy said. "Mom. Mommy. Mom."

"It's okay." She tried to help Ivy to her feet. "Come on, Neal. I need your help."

"I'll help," Bryan said, grabbing Ivy's arm harder than he meant to.

"Oww," she cried.

"Bryan," Carol snapped. "Be careful. Neal?"

He loosened his grip, fixing his body next to Ivy's. She leaned on him. "You can start the car," he said to Neal.

"Thanks, Bryan," Carol said. "Help me get her to the car. We'll take her to the hospital and call you as soon as anything happens."

"What?" Bryan stopped. Carol didn't. Ivy stumbled.

"We'll call you," his mother repeated.

"I'm coming," he said, suddenly wondering if he was, if there was some rule against brothers. Ivy rocked and moaned. He wrapped his arm more tightly around her waist.

"This will probably take hours," his mother said, slowly as if explaining something to a little kid. "Neal will come pick you up as soon as the baby's born."

"No," Ivy said, before Bryan could. "He's coming. I need him."

He half-guided, half-lifted her to the seat of the Honda. He slid into the back seat still holding her hand.

Bryan always thought having a baby was pushing it out. He didn't know that most of it was just waiting through pain while a body did its inside thing. Afterward, trying to describe to Everett, Martine, and Casey the noises Ivy made, he ran through his memory bank of animal sounds and nothing matched. He experimented with heavy minor chords on his harmonica, but those weren't right either. Her noises had been somewhere between animal and music. The sleepless time in the dim hospital room blurred into a collection of images—the tightening and loosening of Ivy's hand around his, the prickly exhaustion in his legs from standing at her side first while she lay in bed, then while she squatted and finally Mac was born.

Exhausted and beaming Ivy handed Bryan his nephew, John Bryan MacKenzie, wrapped like a burrito in a flannel blanket. He couldn't believe how solid the baby felt. Their mother fussed over Ivy. Neal burst in with flowers he dropped onto the nightstand and fussed over Carol. Ivy's hands rested against the damp sheet. A mother's hands now. His sister was a mother.

"Mac," Ivy said. "We'll call him Mac. Between those last pushes, I heard Dad whispering in my ear, 'Name him after me.' I thought, 'No offense, Dad, but I don't like the name John.' He told me to call him Mac." She craned her neck to look at him. Bryan held the baby close to his heart. He'd seen Mac enter into the world, understood he'd come from Ivy's body, he was hers, but the deep gray, blue eyes searching Bryan's face held the width of the sky, the depth of the ocean, the black hole at the center of the galaxy, a piece of everything that had ever happened. He peered into Mac's face, wobbling on an edge of understanding something important.

"Give him here." Ivy held out her arms.

Bryan could have kept the baby forever, but he laid him against his sister's breast. Needing something to hold he reached for his harp, then stopped, remembering where he was.

"Look at his little mouth," Ivy marveled. "His fingers."

"All that hair," Neal said.

Carol leaned close to her grandson. "His ears are perfect."

Bryan wished they'd be quiet. He had to think. Neal, with his bushy beard and big belly, was a baby once. Someone had pushed him into the world. And Ivy herself. And Mom. Grandma Harrrington, that disapproving voice on the telephone every Sunday morning, had done what Ivy just did. And long before that, before Grandma Harrington ever said a mean word or even thought one, she was small and slippery, bundled in blankets and diapers. Everyone, every single person in the world, had been a baby once. He came from a long line of babies. A line stretching back to the first baby. He was a part of things. He belonged here. Everyone did. His head filled with the songs he'd play for Mac as soon as he came home.

"Turn the light out, honey," Carol said. She had to work in the morning, but would leave at lunchtime to pick Ivy up at the hospital. Even with the nap she'd managed earlier, she felt exhausted. Her baby gave a sloshy little flutter. Neal slept with his hand flat on her belly and still hadn't felt it.

"She's swimming." Carol lay on her side, Neal faced her. Rain pounded the windows—hard, cold November rain. Her bedroom, for years a battleground, then a lonely place, had become a haven—the gentle glow of the lamp on the squares of the quilt she'd made for Johnny's mother, IJ; Neal's ever reassuring bulk beside her as she fell asleep, all through the night and when she woke in the morning. When he woke to pee or left the bed because he couldn't sleep and didn't want to bother her, she always knew and woke with a startled adrenaline rush. She hadn't told him and never would. She feigned sleep well.

Neal lay his bearded cheek against the curve of her belly. "Stay there," Carol rested her hand on his bald head. "You'll feel her, just wait."

"Seeing Mac makes this more real to me than it would've been," Neal said. He pressed his mouth against her. "Hey, girl, it's your Daddy. You going to move a little, let me know you're in there? I'm saying hello to you. Come on, wave, knock on the walls."

"It was watching Ivy that made it more real to me," Carol said. "I can't believe I did that twice. You really do forget. Now I remember and I'm trying not to be anxious."

"I'll be there."

"I know." Being there had not been Johnny's strong suit. He talked about being there. He promised to be there. In stories, after the fact, he inserted himself. But most often, when she needed him and when she didn't he'd been at Curly's pool hall, and after one humiliating scene when she'd borrowed a neighbor's car, packed Ivy and wheezing Bryan in without car seats—Bryan just a baby, flopping over the seat belt that couldn't be adjusted tight enough, three-year-old Ivy propping him up with uncharacteristic silent obedience born of fear, she vowed she'd never go looking for him again.

Carol had pulled right up to the door of Rivertown Billiards, left the car running and went in to get Johnny. She had hidden her hysteria, approached him at the bar with a pleasant smile. "We need to take Bryan to the hospital."

"How'd you get here?" he asked eyes too bright, not just drunk she knew but speeding on something. "Don't I have the car? Who's with the kids?"

"Be a gentleman. Buy your wife a drink!" someone hollered.

"Please, Johnny." The edge of panic she'd tried to keep hidden sharpened. "Bryan's having an asthma attack."

"MacKenzie, you're up," someone called from the pool table.

"Carol." Johnny purred her name the way she used to like, before she knew he was being more manipulative than loving.

"Fuck you," she said and slammed out the door. Even with the jeering at her back, more aimed at Johnny than at her he tried to convince her later, she expected him to follow. He didn't.

He came home after the bar closed, when Bryan breathed almost normally thanks to the nebulizer treatment, and hours of humming and back rubs had finally relaxed Ivy's rigid body enough to let her sleep. He passed out right away without speaking, woke up in time for work—he prided himself on never missing a day no matter how drunk or high he'd been the night before—and when he came home that afternoon full of apologies and played tickle monster with Ivy and skipped a night at Curly's to rock Bryan to sleep and make gentle love to her, it was easier to accept his apologies, take what he had to give, than fight. She'd manage.

"So what will we name this girl?" Neal asked.

"Do you mind that Ivy named the baby after John?" Carol asked.

"Of course not," Neal said. "I think it's nice. I was thinking that maybe we could name this baby Josephine after my mother." His eyes without his glasses shone unfocused and hopeful.

"That's a nice name," said Carol.

"Maybe it's too old fashioned," he said. "Too big a name for a little baby."

"We could call her Jo," Carol said. "Or Josie. I like it."

"You do?" He kissed her. He rubbed her shoulders.

"Time to sleep, Grandma," he said.

The nurse wheeled Mac in for a feeding. She lifted him from the plastic tray and handed him to Ivy who had been trying to sleep but couldn't. Her belly felt crampy and her bottom sore.

"After you feed him I'll take him back to the nursery," the nurse said. "You need your rest. There's a reason they call it labor."

Mac's tiny reddish face wrinkled between the white of his blanket and the blue of his cap.

"I hear he's nursing like a pro, already," the nurse said. Ivy wished, for hundredth time that day, that the nurses wouldn't be so relentlessly cheerful. It made her nervous.

Her breast was bigger than the baby's head, but somehow he clamped his mouth around the nipple and sucked. "Terrific!" the nurse chirped. "Give him both sides. I'll be back."

As if he knew the nurse was gone, Mac let go. "Come on," Ivy whispered brushing her nipple against his cheek the way she'd been taught. "Latch on, fella, come on." He stared up at her with his otherworldly expression and she worried for a minute he was being stubborn or didn't like her.

"What are you thinking?" she whispered. "Come on, eat, you can do it."

He kept staring at her face.

"I'm your Mom," she told him. "You could have picked a better one. But I'll do the best I can." She wondered when he'd ask about his father. It seemed impossible that a man's child could be born and the father wouldn't sense it somehow. She tried to picture Gil in jail. He said they wore one piece coveralls—space suits, he called them. He said he finally had the dental work he couldn't afford on the outside. He played handball. He wrote about guys laughing at his jokes, trading cigarettes for his stories. She'd never written back, knew she couldn't, but the letters kept coming. Sometimes they slowed to a trickle or stopped for a couple weeks, then in one day she'd get three, all professing his undying love and imploring her to write.

If she didn't support Mac's head, it flopped. He nuzzled against her, his lips parted. She vowed silently to put off mentioning Gil as long as she could and began in a whisper to tell him about the rest of his family.

He began a rhythmical sucking. "You have an uncle, Bryan. When you start eating regular food he'll cook for you, anything you want. He made baked Alaska when he was seven years old and it came out perfect. And your grandmother, well, she can get pretty angry, but it's usually at me. I don't think she'd yell at you that way. Besides, now that she has Neal treating her right, she laughs more. She used to sew to relax. She made some beautiful quilts. Maybe she'll make you one someday when she's not so busy and tired. You know, she's pregnant with—your aunt." Ivy stopped to imagine Mac and her little sister playing together the way she and Bryan had. Digging in the yard. Mac wouldn't be older by much, just—she calculated—four months. "You'll be like twins." With all these people to love him it might take a while for him to notice Gil's absence.

She missed her father every day of her life, but she'd had him until she was seven. Mac wouldn't know what he was missing. No one could tell a joke or story like Johnny could, except maybe Gil. April Fools Day had been her father's favorite holiday. He loved to trick Ivy and Bryan. "There's a dollar on the ceiling," he would say. At seven years old Ivy knew he was April fooling them and persuaded Bryan not to look up, no matter how many times their father repeated, "There's a dollar on the ceiling." Bryan couldn't resist a peek and, in the dim hospital room, Ivy smiled remembering the glee in her brother's voice as he pointed to the bill their father had taped to the kitchen ceiling earlier, though at the time, she'd felt foolish. Johnny loved springy snakes in cans, flies in fake ice cubes, plastic vomit. Her mother didn't laugh at any of it.

She turned Mac so he faced her other breast. He didn't seem interested, just sleepy. She didn't know if she should wake him up. Tomorrow she would take him home. She was reluctant to leave the safety of the hospital room with its army of too cheerful, yet capable, nurses just outside the door.

CHAPTER 9

Carol unearthed her sewing machine from the basement and set it up on a card table in the corner of the living room. It was time to start quilting again—a constructive nervous habit, something to keep her from nagging Ivy about her parenting skills or lack of them, something to calm her until Neal came home and they could together figure out how to handle the fact that Bryan had a girl in his bedroom with the door closed. Her foot weighed too heavy on the pedal and the needle raced up and down along the short seam. She was working on a seven stars pattern, a difficult one to piece together, even for her expert hands, so she had to pay attention, go slowly, not let her anxiety manifest itself in trembling hands or a lead foot.

Her driving teacher had told her that, "Carol, honey, you have a lead foot," and it took her awhile to realize it wasn't a compliment. Ivy wanted to learn to drive. Neal suggested they use drivers' ed as incentive to return to school. He did know what he was doing when it came to teenagers. She smiled down at the red print diamond in her hand and thought about the quilt she'd make for Neal someday after she finished this one for Mac and another for their baby. She wouldn't start their baby quilt until Josephine or whoever was born. No sense tempting bad luck by expecting the best.

She added a yellow diamond and smoothed the partially completed block on the table to admire it. The colors she'd chosen worked well together. The sound of Bryan's guitar wafted down from his room. If he and Martine were making music they weren't making out. That's all they needed—another pregnancy in the house, though she couldn't imagine Bryan having sex. She couldn't imagine Ivy doing it either, but obviously she had. Neal said parents had trouble seeing their kids as sexual beings and vice versa. Should she go up and knock on her son's door or leave him alone? After this past year she no longer trusted her instincts if she ever had any. If only Neal hadn't accepted that remodeling job on top of teaching; he came home late every day now, but they did need the money.

As if she didn't have enough to worry about, her mother would be coming for her annual Thanksgiving visit next week. Carol's leaving home and settling in a "dying mill town," then marrying a man with "less than no prospects" had confirmed Babe Harrington's not so humble opinion that her daughter had wasted her life and rendered the damage that pregnancy and child rearing had done to Babe's figure and fragile marriage all for "a great big nothing."

Carol sewed too far and had to tear out over an inch of tiny stitches. Surely her mother would approve of Neal. Everyone liked Neal. She'd think he was too fat and bald. But even Babe, with her constant "I question your judgment," would see how good he was for her and Ivy and Bryan. She tore a hole in the fabric with the seam ripper.

"Shit!"

"And you tell us not to swear," said Ivy switching on the TV. "Did you eat yet?"

"I thought I'd wait for Neal. Mac asleep?"

"Mmm." Ivy held up the baby monitor without turning from the TV then set it on the table beside the recliner and lay back.

"Do you like these colors together?" Carol brought her a finished block.

Ivy barely looked at it. *The Simpsons* was starting. She'd seen every episode more than once, but she couldn't shift her eyes for one moment to admire the quilt her mother was making for her baby. "Nice." Ivy aimed the remote and turned up the volume.

Carol slapped the quilt square onto the card table and bit her lip to keep from fighting.

"What's the matter?" Ivy peeked around the back of the big chair.

"Nothing." Carol tried not to hiss through her clenched teeth. Breathe, she told herself.

"No, what? You're mad." Ivy muted the TV during the commercial. Upstairs the music had stopped.

"No, I'm not mad." Carol turned off the light on her machine and stacked the finished blocks matching the edges.

"Then why'd you make that big sigh? You're always mad at me."

"Ivy, I am not mad." Carol pronounced each word. The show would start back up in a minute and Ivy would turn around. Carol would escape to the kitchen, set the table for herself and Neal, even light candles.

"The quilt's nice, all right? I like it. I'm just tired and I want to watch this show, you mind?" Ivy pointed the remote at Carol as if about to turn her off.

The front door opened and Neal was there, an outside smell of leaf mold and wood smoke clinging to his jacket. Carol crossed the living room, slipped past Ivy and into his arms.

"How's everybody?" he asked.

"Shh," said Ivy.

"Let's go in the kitchen," Carol said.

He poured himself a glass of water. Carol put a plate of left over lasagna in the microwave. "Bryan's in his room with Martine," she said. "I think you should go talk to him."

"Uh oh," he laughed. "You mean the man-to-man sex talk?"

She handed him two plates and he put them on the table. "That, but for right now, maybe you could tell them they have to leave the door open."

He grabbed a plastic bowl of salad from the refrigerator.

"Later, Carol. After dinner."

"Can't you do it now? I was waiting and waiting for you." Her stomach tightened. She wouldn't be able to eat.

"No! I'll talk with him later. After she leaves."

"But then it's too late." The microwave beeped.

"Too late?" He looked genuinely befuddled. He had no idea what she was talking about.

She was alone in a houseful of people who thought she was crazy. They thought she worried too much. In a world so full of danger and trouble it was the people who didn't worry who were crazy.

"Carol," Neal said. "Let's eat. I'll talk to Bryan, later. Are you going to get that lasagna out?" He put two candles on the table. "It's nice to have dinner just the two of us."

She pulled the lasagna from the microwave burning her fingers. By the time she reached the table, Neal had lit the candles, dimmed the lights and was forking salad on to his plate. She wiped her eyes with her napkin before unfolding it on her lap.

"I'll talk to him," Neal said around a mouthful of lettuce. "Eat. Come on. Feed that baby."

Carol took a small bite of lasagna and chewed it for a long time. Somehow it slid past the lump in her throat and she took another.

Bryan and Martine sat on his bed, his guitar dropped into its case, his harmonica rack with the harp still clipped in on the floor beside it. The spoons Martine was learning to play clinked together on his quilt as she moved close to him. The music they'd been making hung in the air like cooking smells. It had been two weeks since their kiss. He'd expected the second one would happen even more easily, but for some reason, it hadn't.

Their bodies heated the three inches of empty space between them. He could almost feel her. She made the hair on his arms stand up. All he had to do was shift his weight, the mattress would sag, she'd lean toward him. Once they touched all the rest would follow, like it had under the streetlight. He hoped that just because they were in his bedroom with the door shut she wouldn't expect more than kissing.

"I can't believe Mr. Richards lives here," she said. "Isn't it weird—your mother married a teacher?"

"It's not like I ever took his class," said Bryan.

"Still …" Martine twisted a piece of her hair and sucked the end. He hoped his hard on wasn't obvious and considered picking up his guitar except that if they began to play music again it would be like taking steps backward. "You know, when Leo heard I was coming over he said I had to tell Ivy to come back to the pool hall. I told him to tell her himself and he said he would but no one ever sees her. Doesn't she go out?"

"Not much," Bryan said. "Mac's only two weeks old. She'll go out eventually." He wondered if she would.

Martine rummaged in her bag. It was made of worn black canvas and so covered with buttons it rattled when she walked. "Do you have a tissue?" she asked finally. Her eyes flashed green and full of light under heavy dark eyebrows.

He couldn't find one so he went to grab some toilet paper. When he came back she was holding a bottle of red nail polish. He handed her the paper and she blew her nose. "Thanks." She tucked the tissue in her bag. If she'd thrown it in the trash he would have taken it out and saved it, that's how much he loved her.

"I have an idea," she said. The mischievous glint in her eyes made his heart beat fast.

"Take off your socks."

He sat back down on the bed, realizing too late that he missed his chance to settle closer to her. He hesitated, more out of fear that his feet would smell than any reluctance to grant her strange request. "Come on." She bent over and scooped up his feet with her forearm, knocking him flat on the bed. She shifted to a cross legged position facing him, his feet in her lap and peeled off his socks. "I'm going to make you beautiful." She unscrewed the cap to the nail polish. The acetone smell filled the room and he stopped worrying about foot stink.

She held the bottle up and pointed to the label. "Decadence. I don't know why they can't just say red or pink. Someone gets paid for coming up with these names. I swear they've used every flower or fruit or mixed drink name in the book. I have another one in my bag …" She leaned forward to reach it and her breasts almost rubbed his shins. His heels were practically in her crotch. He kept his feet still. "Here it is—pinkalicious. You have a choice, decadence or pinkalicious."

"You decide," he said.

A bottle in each hand she looked back and forth considering. "The red I think. Decadence."

Martine attended to each toe, concentrating so hard the tip of her tongue showed every couple minutes. He wanted to make a clever joke about nail polish colors based on what she'd said, some funny, unlikely name, something about blood and accidents or pink being a girly color, but the glimpses of her tongue and the feeling of her fingers on his toes turned his thoughts to pure and pleasurable lust. Her hair fell around her face as she bent over first one foot, then the other. He wished he had a thousand toes.

"Now don't move," she said. "It has to dry. When I do my own I always put cotton balls or tissues between my toes to keep them apart. Spread your toes and don't move." She screwed the cap on the nail polish, tossed it into her bag. Cupping a heel in each palm she slipped to standing and arranged his feet on his bedspread. "I got to go or I'll be grounded. See you tomorrow." She was gone—the shiny red of his toenails proof he hadn't dreamed the whole strange thing.

He heard her say good-bye to Neal, probably passing on the stairs. A knock on his door. He folded the bottom of his bedspread over his feet. He hadn't thought about people seeing them, people's reactions. His mother or Ivy had to have nail polish remover, but he didn't want to remove it.

"Bryan?" Neal said.

"What?"

"Can I come in?"

"Sure." Bryan adjusted the spread and sprawled back against his pillows attempting to look relaxed. He reached down for his guitar and picked at the strings.

Neal stood over him. "What's that smell?"

"Drugs," Bryan said. Neal didn't laugh. "Martine's nail polish."

Neal nodded. "You eat yet?"

"I'll come down in a few minutes."

"Your Mom asked me to talk to you." He shifted from foot to foot, then sat next to Bryan's feet almost dislodging the covers.

"So what else is new?"

"The sex talk," Neal said.

"Oh, please." Bryan played a loud chord. He'd been smart to grab the guitar.

"Do you have any questions?"

All he had were questions, but he didn't want to ask Neal. If a girl paints your toenails and leaves, does she love you? How do you initiate a second kiss when you're pathetically shy? What would she think if she knew he got hard just looking at the glistening tip of her tongue? What was to keep her from liking Everett better when Ev made her laugh and talked to her so easily while Bryan just stood mute?

"I think the main thing," Neal said, "about sex and all, is not to do anything you aren't ready for. Pay attention to your feelings and hers. And remember," here he began to sound like a public service announcement, "When the time comes use a condom. Sexually transmitted infections are serious. Pregnancy happens."

"You think I don't know that?" Bryan asked. "I'm surrounded by the evidence."

Neal laughed. "I guess so. Come eat, will you?"

"In a minute."

When Neal left Bryan kicked off the spread and admired his feet. Tommy Sparks would give him a rough time if he saw them and their gym teacher was a fascist about showers. If Neal allowed Roger to skip gym by hiding out in the shop, he should let his own son. Bryan wiggled his toes and wondered how long he could make the polish last.

At the sound of the doorbell, Neal put down the stack of plates he was counting, Carol set the coffee pot on its burner, Bryan laid the greasy turkey baster in the sink. Ivy, at the table, lifted three week old Mac to her shoulder. They all moved toward the front door clumped together.

Through the lace curtained glass, they saw Grandma Harrington's frowning face. "So, I'm about to meet your mother," Neal whispered.

Carol sighed.

"It'll be fine." Neal wrapped an arm around her shoulders, kissing her hair.

"We'll see." Carol shrugged him off.

Bryan squeezed past them to open the door. Ivy hung back. They hadn't seen Grandma Harrington since last year. Ivy had left the table before pie—and she loved pie, especially Bryan's mince, which he only made on Thanksgiving—to escape to the pool hall, returning late, after she was sure Grandma had left. Carol hounded Ivy for weeks about disappearing. "Your Grandmother drove all that way. She's only here for a few hours … The least you could do …" Grandma Harrington drove four and a half hours each way, all in one day, to come for dinner once a year. She never stayed the night, insisting on sleeping in her own bed. No one else's sheets were clean enough or mattresses as firm as her own.

"Thought you would never open the door." Grandma thrust a huge cooler at Bryan who staggered under the weight. She shook out her arms, purse waggling on its short strap. "Well, here I am. And lucky I didn't injure my back standing there. Would've sent Bryan out to the car for the cooler if I'd known I'd have to wait so long. He's certainly grown tall enough to manage the job."

Carol, Neal, and Ivy parted, letting Bryan through to the kitchen. "Now, let me show you what I've got in there," Grandma hollered. "Don't you go opening it without me." She craned her neck to watch Bryan's back disappearing with her cooler into the kitchen.

"Mother." Carol put a hand on Grandma's arm. "I'd like you to meet Neal."

"Oh, yes, the new husband." Grandma inspected Neal. "Maybe you learned something from the last time." She snorted. Carol paled, then reddened, muscles in her face tight. Ivy cupped Mac's head in her hand, fighting an urge to run upstairs and hide him safely in her room. Grandma reached out as if to tug Neal's beard, but stopped a few inches from his face and shook a finger at him instead. "Her first husband's idea of a Thanksgiving dinner was a bottle of wild turkey. Before the meal was over, he'd be off with his friends."

"That only happened once." Carol's voice shook. "Why do you have to bring it up every year? Why do you have to bring it up now?"

Grandma's pursed lips didn't disguise the smirk quivering at the edges of her mouth. "You know I've been careful not to mention it in front of Ivy and Bryan, but this young lady is obviously old enough to hear it now, being a mother herself."

Ivy swayed, rocking Mac. Compassion for her mother mixed with a how-do-you-like-it-when-someone-criticizes-your-man feeling. She didn't blame her father for leaving early either, having done it herself.

"Let me take your coat," Neal said.

Grandma turned her back toward him and shrugged off her navy blue wool coat. "I've had this coat for thirty years," she said. "Buy quality, take proper care of it, it'll last forever."

Neal took longer than he needed to hang the coat in the closet.

Carol nudged Ivy forward.

Grandma smiled. "So here you are, Miss Ivy. All grown up. With a baby. You know, I was twenty when I had your mother, not so young in those days. But aren't you seventeen?"

"I turned eighteen in August," Ivy said. "Old enough to vote."

Grandma shook her head. "I couldn't believe it when your mother told me. And no father." Her bright blue eyes pierced Ivy, reminding her of Gil's, pinning her to the wall. "You've got a long row to hoe, young lady, a long, hard row, by yourself. Good luck. And look at you," she turned to Carol, laid a hand on her rounded belly. "I hope you know what you're doing. A baby, at what, thirty-seven years old. I hope you're up to it."

"Don't you want to see your great-grandson?" Ivy croaked past the lump of rage choking her. "Want to see Mac?"

"I see him," Grandma leaned over. She smelled of Hall's eucalyptus drops. Sucked them even when she didn't have a cold. The medicinal odor brought Ivy right back to the summer of Dad's accident, Grandma ordering Ivy and Bryan in for a nap, in for dinner, while they missed their parents so much they couldn't admit it or they'd never stop crying. Her stomach turned.

"Lots of hair," Grandma observed. "Make sure you put baby oil on his head. I think I see some cradle cap there. Not a pretty sight—a crusty head like that. Let me go see about my Jell-O mold. I hope it made the trip. Should be okay—I packed plenty of ice. Not ice but those plastic things you freeze. Much better than ice, no melting, avoid all that water ..." She headed for the kitchen. Neal squeezed Ivy's hand. She squeezed back.

"She didn't even look at Mac," Ivy whispered. "What is her problem?"

"I don't think she likes babies," Neal said, trying to make it sound like a joke.

"She hates them," Carol hissed.

"Some people just don't know what to do with a baby," Neal said, hugging Carol. Ivy wished he'd hug her too. "Don't take it personally, Ivy. It says more about her than anything else. Carol, why don't you just sit and relax? Bryan's got the meal under control. I'll help."

"It's better if I keep busy." Carol led them into the kitchen.

Grandma and Bryan leaned over the open cooler. "Now, I made two molds," she was saying. "The one I always bring and this new one I saw in my paper."

Which paper? Ivy wondered. That long ago summer she'd read Grandma's tabloids late at night, by flashlight, copying words she didn't understand into her little pink, spiral notebook, notorious, sodomy, cult. She'd looked up the words in a dictionary. After a few weeks, frustrated by definitions as confusing as the words, she ripped the dictionary to pieces and buried it in the trash.

"Wow!" Bryan said, wincing as Grandma unwrapped a fishbowl filled with blue Jell-O, bright gummi fish suspended throughout.

"Don't worry," Grandma said. "I bought the fish bowl special for this. It never had a live fish in it. When you think about it, it's just another bowl really. Could be used for anything."

"Is this dessert?" Bryan muttered. He was probably worried about how it would look on the table. At least Grandma's traditional mold, full of cranberries, oranges, celery, and nuts, fit with Thanksgiving. Ivy preferred gummi fish over walnuts and celery.

"We should keep it cold, until dinner," Grandma said.

"I'll put it in the refrigerator," Ivy offered. She cradled Mac on one arm and lifted the bowl with the other. Grandma hurried to open the refrigerator door.

"Be careful, dear," she said.

"Why don't we turn on the Thanksgiving parade," Neal suggested. "You'll be more comfortable in the living room, Mrs. Harrington."

"Oh, call me Mother," Grandma smiled.

Ivy saw Carol roll her eyes. Bryan poked a potato and pronounced it done. He drained the pot, boiling water and steam splashing in the sink.

Neal settled Grandma in front of the TV.

Ivy sat at the kitchen table holding Mac. "He's Dr. Jekyll as long as someone holds him," she said. "Mr. Hyde the minute he's put down." Being a mother had been a lot easier with the baby inside. She'd been tired, but not like now. Her arms ached. She discovered a new pain she thought was from nursing, near her left shoulder blade. Her nipples hurt.

Bryan took the turkey from the oven. Carol set the dining room table, dusted crystal relish trays, filling them with pearl onions and watermelon pickle—Grandma's other contribution. Without them on the table, it wouldn't be Thanksgiving, even though no one liked them.

Ivy would have been happy to mash the potatoes, pour water, anything but feed and hold, and change a baby. She thought of Celine every day, thin and in Paris, drinking cafe au lait, beret over her dreadlocks. By now she'd probably left the creep she went with and found a romantic attic room with slanted ceilings and a window overlooking the Eifel Tower. Ivy breathed in the clean powdery smell of Mac's head. He'd grow up. She'd lose weight. For now, he was here with her, his first Thanksgiving. She tried feeling thankful. She was thankful. Really.

In the living room, Grandma talked back to the announcers in a loud voice. "So what, it's cold out there. We don't need to hear your complaining. Who cares how much air is in the purple dinosaur? You think anybody wants to know about that?"

"You'd think Grandma could hold him. She's just sitting there on the couch." Ivy jiggled Mac and stretched to drink coffee without bringing the hot liquid near him. "Him being her only great-grandchild."

"Ask her," Neal said.

Grandma Harrington had never held Ivy or Bryan or hugged them beyond a quick squeeze at the beginning and ends of her visits, never, even when their father died, when everyone, including their mother, could have used a hug.

Ivy drained her coffee cup and brought Mac into the living room. Grandma perched on the edge of the couch, shaking a finger at the TV. "Look at those girls with their backsides hanging out. They must be freezing, never mind, they should be ashamed."

"Could you hold Mac until dinner?" Ivy asked.

Grandma looked down at her cream colored, crepe blouse. "I don't know, dear. I'm not very good with babies. They spit up … that sour milk smell. The stains … Oh all right. Give me that diaper."

Ivy helped arrange the diaper on Grandma's shoulder. Mac stared at the lacy shadows on the wall. Grandma held his head in her hand. She had jeweled rings on three fingers.

"Maybe because I was a bit older than you when I had your mother, I knew enough not to do it again," Grandma said. She sat straight and stiff. "I hope, for your sake, you arrive at the same conclusion."

The rings pressed against Mac's soft, dark hair, his little round head. Ivy wanted him back.

"Learn from your mistakes, Ivy," Grandma said. "It's the best anyone can do."

"Mac is not a mistake," Ivy snatched him from her grandmother's arms, turning her back on the woman. The old lady didn't know what she was talking about. Even if Mac hadn't been planned, Ivy was glad to have him. A baby, a person, wasn't a mistake. If Carol hadn't been born, Ivy wouldn't have been born, or Bryan or Mac. Mac would do good things. He'd happened. He was a happening. Grandma Harrington stared at the TV shaking her head. Ivy strode back to the kitchen.

If Dad's mother was still alive, she'd love a great-grandson. She would have helped take care of him. The last check in her checkbook had been for Ivy's highchair. Carol had told Ivy the same story with the same intonations her whole life. "We had finally agreed to name you Jane, even though it reminded us both of the girl in the first-grade reading books. The night of Grandma's funeral, your father insisted that if you were a girl, we call you Ivy. In this day and age! A name like that. But under the circumstances, what could I say? I agreed and prayed you'd be a boy." She'd laugh, never noticing Ivy didn't laugh with her.

"Grandma Harrington is horrible," Ivy said. "She's an old witch."

"Be quiet, Ivy," Carol said, filling a tray with glasses and cloth napkins. Neal sliced the turkey. "Don't push it. I told you before. She can't stand babies."

Bryan turned from the stove, gravy spoon in hand. "You're dripping," Carol said. Neal hurried to wipe the floor.

Ivy held Mac tight. Imagine saying your own mother hated babies. That would mean she'd hated you. The mistake. Carol seemed happy with Neal and being pregnant. Today with Grandma Harrington here, she shrunk and tightened, like those spongy toys squished into capsules. Wait until someone poured on the water. Carol should have told her mother not to come if she couldn't be nice.

"You're burning that." Carol peered into the gravy pan.

"Ma," Ivy said. "Leave him alone. He makes gravy better than you."

Carol slapped a handful of spoons onto the counter, startling Mac. He whimpered.

"Come on, Mom." Ivy pleaded, patting Mac's back. "Look what you did." Carol bristled.

Neal laughed the too hearty laugh he used when Carol and Ivy edged toward a fight. Sometimes it worked. They'd glare at each other and stop. Bryan poured the gravy into a small pitcher, biting his lip. He'd told Ivy the only thing he didn't like about Neal was that laugh, like the braying of a donkey.

"I'd like to see you do some work around here, Miss," Carol said. "A little cleaning. A little cooking once in awhile."

"How could I? When Bryan's not in here, you are." Ivy stood.

Carol shook the dessert forks at her. "Do some dishes then. Clean the bathroom. Since you've come home, all you've done is sit on your rear and expect to be waited on."

"Jesus Christ! I just had a baby." On cue, Mac started screaming.

"Well, let me hold the baby once in awhile," Carol yelled, her pale skin blotching red. "I'm his grandmother. I know how to hold a baby. You act like you don't trust me."

"Calm down, Carol." Neal put an arm around her. "Of course she trusts you."

"You don't know if I trust her or not," Ivy yelled over Mac's wailing. "Stay out of this. It has nothing to do with you." She thrust the baby at her mother. "Hold him then. Here." Carol held Mac against her shoulder, hand on his back still clutching the bouquet of forks.

Bryan set the gravy on the counter, as if afraid he'd spill it. "Everything's ready," he said.

Mac kept screaming. Carol jiggled him.

"Please," Bryan said. "Let's eat."

"You act like dinner is the most important thing happening here." Ivy glared at Bryan.

"Well, it is Thanksgiving." He glared back. "It's not just any dinner. I've been up since five, cooking."

Neal's hands looked ridiculous hanging at his sides. His lips twitched as he fought his instinct to laugh and soothe. Mac wailed. Ivy, Bryan, and Carol waited, daring Neal to try to make it better. He shook his head, lifted the turkey platter, carried it to the dining room, Carol behind him. "Is something wrong?" Grandma called. "Will we be eating soon?" Bryan moved to follow with the gravy, then stopped, looking back at Ivy, forcing a staring contest.

They'd had them as kids, usually on long car trips at Ivy's command. Of course, she always won, gloating as his eyes flickered down or toward the window. He'd try to refuse to play, 'I don't have to if I don't want to,' but he always did.

Through Mac's screaming they heard the announcers of the Thanksgiving Day Parade. "The holidays are here now. It's official. People have outdone themselves. Look at those happy faces." Ivy narrowed her eyes at Bryan. She knew how to make him crack. He looked back unflinching. Staring through his glasses, into his brown eyes Ivy saw he knew her. He knew her better than anyone. Startled by the realization she almost blinked. Tears clumped in her throat, gathered in her eyes. Bryan had cried after losing a contest but neither one of them had ever cried during one. If she could keep from blinking, she could still win. Rules said nothing about tears.

Mac stopped wailing. Ivy wriggled her nose, stuck out her tongue, in a last ditch effort to beat Bryan. He stood firm.

Voices filtered in from the other room. Grandma's and their mother's sharp, Neal's reassuring.

Bryan was stubborn; he wasn't going to give up. He'd sit for the rest of the day peering into her soul, reading her private thoughts, watching tears spill down her face. "All right," Ivy said, rubbing her eyes. "You win … this time."

Bryan exhaled. He'd been holding his breath. "You're really mad, aren't you?" he said. If he laughed, she'd punch him. He didn't.

Ivy flopped into the chair. She wouldn't look at him.

"I'll just bring in the rest of the food," he said. "We'll eat in a minute."

"What does everyone want from me?" Ivy whispered. "I have a three week old baby. I never sleep. I'll move out as soon as I can."

"No one wants you to move out," said Bryan. He didn't sound like he meant it. "No one said anything about moving out.

"When Mom's baby is born and you're helping out watching both babies, it might feel better, like you're working … earning …"

"Why doesn't anyone care about me?" Ivy asked, eyes filling again. "Don't you see how hard this is? Why does everyone always have to be doing something for money to have anyone think they're doing something important?"

"Should I put out the Jell-O molds?" Grandma hollered.

"I'll take care of it," Bryan shouted back. "Relax."

"And why is she even here?" Ivy asked.

"She's leaving tonight." Bryan rested a hand on Ivy's shoulder, surprising both of them. He took it back. "Then we can be thankful."

"Why does she come?" Ivy asked.

"Mom invites her."

"Yeah, why? Why does Mom invite her?"

"Because she's her mother, I guess," Bryan said.

Ivy's sore back muscle twinged. In the dining room, Mac chortled. By deciding not to have an abortion, had she earned herself a lifetime invitation to

Thanksgiving dinner? Was it her or Bryan who'd be inviting Carol for the rest of her life? And what about Neal? Were stepparents included in this cosmic deal?

They assembled at the table. Ivy collected Mac from Carol before they sat down.

"Turkey's a little dry," Grandma frowned at Bryan, then Carol and Neal and Ivy, as if determining who to blame.

"Have some gravy," said Neal.

"You're spoiling that baby," she said.

With Mac on her shoulder, Ivy maneuvered a forkful of potatoes to her mouth, already an expert. "If I put him down, he'll scream," she said.

"Exactly, and if you ignore him, he'll stop. He'll know who's in charge."

They concentrated on chewing turkey. Neighbors took more interest in Mac than his great-grandmother did. People on the street stopped to admire his dark hair, his ruddy complexion, the way he slept in the stroller with his fists curled near his face. Ivy glanced at her mother, who chewed slowly, face flushed. Since Carol was Grandma's baby, Grandma must have left her to cry until she gave up. Ivy wondered if her mother had done that to her. Maybe. She wondered if she was a mistake. Was Bryan? Maybe when Bryan was born, Mom switched to taking care of him. How could someone take care of two little kids anyway? When Bryan was born, Carol must have had to hold him all the time and left Ivy to Johnny. That could explain why Bryan never seemed to miss their father as much as Ivy did.

"Why did you come here?" Bryan turned to his grandmother. Everybody stared, forks in midair. "You don't like us. Why did you drive so far to have dry turkey with people you don't even like?"

His mother coughed. Ivy gulped. Bryan never said things like that. She did.

"Nothing wrong with this turkey, Bryan," Neal laughed. "Anybody want more?"

Grandma studied the wall above Bryan's head. Ivy braced herself for a sharp reply. When none came she felt a flicker of compassion, squelched by the sight of the mounded watermelon pickle. Leave it to Grandma to bring something no one liked. Frugal to the point of stinginess, her specialty a pickle made from the part of the fruit most people threw away. She probably collected it out of the trash. She hadn't brought a present for Mac. The Jell-O filled fish bowl glistened in the center of the table. She had bought a fish bowl and she'd want it back, empty and clean. She probably had her name in permanent marker on a piece of tape stuck to the bottom.

Ivy and Neal resumed eating. Carol pushed food around her plate looking like she was about to speak if she could only think of exactly what to say. Grandma Harrington, a tall woman, seemed smaller.

"I thought I was welcome in my daughter's house," Grandma said, still staring at the wall.

"You are," Neal said. "Of course you are."

"Of course," Carol echoed. At the insincerity in their mother's voice, the barest edge of buried rage, Bryan and Ivy's eyes met. More confirmation of what they'd known for years—she tells us to be nice to Grandma, their looks said to each other, and she can't stand her either.

"I'm sorry," said Bryan, as if reminded that it was only a game, he'd play. They weren't expected to like their grandmother, only to be polite. Grandma nodded.

"Pass those pickles around," she said.

Ivy handed them to Carol on her right. Grandma watched as they made their way around the table. As each person took one, she gave the barest nod. When Ivy took the dish from Neal, she only hesitated a moment before spearing a piece.

"Pass the Jell-O," Ivy said and scooped herself a generous helping full of bright fish. It quivered on her plate next to the mashed potatoes. She looked up in time to see Carol cover a weak smile with her napkin, a smile of approval, for her.

CHAPTER 10

Bryan emptied the overstuffed mailbox. Nine envelopes of varying size all addressed to Ivy. Valentines. He dumped them in her lap.

"I hate this holiday," she said, pulling her nipple from Mac's mouth, lifting him to her shoulder. Bryan tried not to look at her breast but he couldn't help it. His own sister. He swore she left it out on purpose.

"How many you think he's sent you?" Bryan asked, remembering Martine's breast against his arm as they sat squashed together in a booth at the Pizza Pavilion.

"Oh, I don't know." Ivy flicked an imaginary speck off her nipple and tucked it back into her bra. Mac burped. "Last time I counted it was up to forty-nine but that was a few days ago."

"I didn't even get one," Bryan mumbled.

"And how many did you send?" Ivy asked.

His face got hot. For weeks he'd agonized whether or not to send Martine a card. They spent time together with Ev and Casey, but they'd only kissed seven times in the past three months. A lot of the time it seemed she just wanted to be friends. He finally decided that Valentine's Day was a chance to let her know he wanted more and spent three hours making a card of cut paper and fancy stickers from the mall card shop. Instead of listening in Spanish class he'd spent the week looking at the back of her neck, trying to compose a verse for the card, finally resorting to 'Happy Valentine's Day.' He flunked the Friday quiz. The card still sat in his desk drawer.

"Martine or Casey?" Ivy teased. "Who's the lucky girl?"

"I'd never tell you," he said, resolving to tear up the card as soon as he went upstairs. "You know that."

"Come on? Who do I see? I never leave the damn house. I wouldn't tell anyone."

"You'd never shut up about it. I know. I've been your younger brother for about sixteen years, remember?"

"Oh well," Ivy checked Mac's diaper. "Martine, Casey, who cares?"

"You do." He picked up a large square envelope. "Are you going to open any of these?"

Ivy shrugged. "Go ahead."

Bryan tore open the card and pulled out an elaborate, pen and ink, anatomically correct drawing of a heart stabbed by an arrow, blood dripping from it. "'You've done this to me,'" he read. "Did he make this himself? The guy can really draw." Bryan held it toward Ivy who waved it away. He opened another, also an anatomically correct picture of a heart, this one torn in two, resting in a pool of blood. "'You rip up my heart.' I detect a theme here."

"Open them if you want," said Ivy. "But you don't have to read them out loud. I got the idea after the first one."

Bryan opened card after card, each one, carefully drawn and shaded and full of movement. "Something about these …" They thrilled and repulsed at the same time. He thought of the card he'd made for Martine, construction paper and shiny stickers—the work of a child.

"Throw them away," Ivy said, suddenly furious. "I'm sick of them. They give me nightmares."

"Seems like he really loves you," Bryan said.

Ivy looked like she might cry, then her expression hardened. "He's obsessed. And in jail with nothing to do."

"Have you told him about Mac?" Bryan had wanted to ask since he'd handed Ivy the first of Gil's letters months ago.

"Are you kidding?" Ivy's hand cradled the baby's head. She curved her body around him. "And as far as he knows I'm still in Florida somewhere. That's how I want it to stay."

Bryan imagined Gil in a jail cell, a father and not knowing it, drawing pictures of his heart, wrecked by Ivy, still pulsing with warm, bloody life. "I never liked him," Bryan said. "But Mac's his son."

"Gil's a sperm donor," said Ivy. "Not a father."

"Still …"

"You think I haven't thought about this? What am I going to tell Mac as he gets older? You think I don't want a father for my baby?" Ivy touched the top of

Mac's ear. "See this little point. Gil has one just like it." Bryan had to look away from the complicated sadness in her eyes.

He dropped the cards onto the pile. "I'd be happy if I'd gotten even one valentine," he mumbled.

"Depends on who it's from," Ivy said. "Valentines from the wrong person are worse than nothing."

He turned his harmonica over and over in his hand. "At least you know someone loves you."

"Bryan." Ivy shook her head. "Love and obsession are not the same thing."

"Well, what exactly is the difference?" He heard Martine's liquid laugh, felt the pressure of her fingers on his wrist.

Ivy gave Mac her other breast. "I don't know," she said finally.

They heard a car pull into the driveway. Bryan checked the clock. "Did Mom say anything about coming home early?" he asked from the window.

"No." Ivy chewed on a fingernail.

"Why is she here then?" Their mother sat in the battered gray Civic, slumped over in the driver's seat. "Something's wrong. Come here, quick."

Ivy jerked the recliner to an upright position and struggled out of it to stand at the window beside him. He waited for her assessment of the situation, trying not to panic.

"Maybe she's tired," Ivy said. "You get tired when you're pregnant."

"She's crying. Her shoulders are shaking. See? She's crying hard, if we can see it from here."

"When you're pregnant, you get all emotional," Ivy explained. "It's too much. Even with a husband. Maybe she sees how hard it is with Mac and she's afraid." Bryan heard the edge of worry in Ivy's voice even if she didn't seem to notice it herself. Carol didn't sit in her car and cry.

"I'm going out there," Bryan said.

Ivy put a hand on his arm. "She wants to be alone. Or she would've come into the house."

Bryan pressed his forehead against the cold window pane and closed his eyes. "We should call Neal," he said.

"If she wanted Neal, she'd have called him." Ivy turned on the TV. "Or she will, when she comes in."

"What do you think is wrong?" He couldn't stop staring out the window, across the lawn, through the windshield at their mother with her head resting on the steering wheel.

"I told you what I think," Ivy snapped. Mac whimpered.

Neal's truck pulled up in front of the house. Bryan's initial sense of relief dissolved into panic when Neal leaped out and opened Carol's car door.

Bryan pulled hard on the curtain. "Something is wrong. Neal knows what it is." He went outside. Ivy could follow or not.

He could hear Neal talking to Carol in a tight, coaxing voice. "Just come inside, honey, we'll call the doctor. If she says to come in, then we'll go."

"No," their mother answered from the driver's seat. "Just get in the car. Get this over with."

She lifted her head, eyes narrowed and angry. "You don't get it do you? You still think everything could be okay, don't you? Everything peachy until proven otherwise." She glared over Neal's shoulder toward Bryan, but showed no sign of noticing him. "You're almost fifty years old and you still don't know that sometimes there is no bright side. Get in the car. Please." Bryan flinched to hear her talk like that to Neal. He felt Ivy breathing heavily on the porch right behind him.

"We need to tell the kids," Neal said.

"Should we say something?" Bryan whispered.

"Just get in the car," Carol begged.

"I'll drive," Neal said, stepping back to let her out. They spotted Bryan and Ivy and Mac. No one spoke. Bryan walked down the porch steps.

"The baby's dead," Carol said, voice clear, carrying across the driveway, the road, the neighborhood, the whole town.

"You don't know that," Neal insisted. "You don't know for sure."

"It hasn't moved in hours." She ran her hands over the sides of her belly. "It's dead. They wouldn't tell me over the phone. But when I go in there and they check for a heartbeat they don't find, they'll say it then. It's dead. She's dead."

Bryan shivered. Babies used to die all the time, mothers too, in the days of covered wagons. But not now. If Ivy could have a healthy baby and never even go to a doctor the whole time she was pregnant, their mother's had to be okay.

"You don't know that!" Neal shouted, banging the roof of the car with a fist.

Carol gave him a pitying look. Bryan wanted to put an arm around Neal. He stood close to him instead.

"Look at you." Carol shook her head. "You stand there hoping, hoping, hoping. Well, I'm the one with a dead baby inside me. And I want it out. Now." She gestured toward Bryan. "We've told the kids, all right? Satisfied?"

Neal squeezed his shoulder. "We're going. Bryan, we'll call when we've talked to a doctor."

"We already know what's going on. At least I know." All the times Carol had gotten hysterical over Ivy or even way back, when she fought with their Dad, Bryan had never seen her so distraught. Bryan wondered what would happen if she died too, if Neal would have to be their father, all by himself. Imagine marrying someone and ending up without her—with two kids and a grand-child to take care of.

Bryan glanced at Ivy who stood frozen on the porch, clutching Mac in front of her. The baby waved his arms and kicked his feet. Bryan wanted to yell, "Hide Mac. Get him out of sight." A perfect baby, suddenly obscene.

"Please, Neal." Carol nudged Neal with her shoulder.

"Okay, honey." He tossed a look of despair over his shoulder toward Bryan.

The sound of the engine faded to silence. "It's freezing out here," Ivy said. "Come on." She held the door open for him. "Hurry, I'm letting the heat out."

"Did you hear all that?" Bryan flung himself onto the couch, trying not to cry. "Do you think Mom will be all right?"

"She'll be okay." Ivy sat beside him. "She always expects the worst. Let's wait and see what the doctor has to say."

"Don't you think she'd know?" He held out a finger to Mac who gripped it hard. "It's her body. Couldn't she tell?"

"She doesn't know." Ivy winced. "She doesn't know anything."

Bryan wiggled his finger and Mac held on. Strange to consider losing a little sister when you never even had one. "It's too hard," Bryan said out loud. "I was looking forward to that baby."

"The baby's okay!" Ivy stood suddenly. Mac's grip loosened and Bryan's finger felt exposed.

She grabbed the remote and flipped to the food channel. Instead of a relaxing or inspiring cooking show, three enormous men were competing to eat the most hotdogs. "Gastronomic gladiators," the announcer called them. After the hotdogs—hopefully it was taped on another day—they ate pies. They'd moved through burritos and onto beer when the phone rang.

Bryan raced to answer it, Ivy right behind him. The TV announcer's excited voice blared after them.

"Cord accident," Neal said. He sounded small and strange.

"What does that mean?" Bryan imagined electrical wires and outlets, shocks.

Silence. Bryan waited.

"A knot in the umbilical cord, baby moves a certain way, it tightens. At least that's what they think. They know she's dead."

Ivy hovered beside him, all raised eyebrows and mouthed questions. He turned away from her, trying to concentrate on Neal's words.

"They're going to induce labor now," Neal said. "It could take a long time. I'll call you if anything happens."

Bryan hung up. His limbs felt heavy, like bags of sand. "Mom was right."

"Oh, God." Ivy jiggled Mac who grabbed his finger again, a squirming, breathing link, holding everything together.

Somehow the rest of day passed in half hour increments—food show after food show. Mac nursed, but Ivy and Bryan watched people cook and never felt hungry. Bryan called the hospital twice and their mother was still in labor.

"I wonder if hurts as bad as mine did," Ivy said before climbing the stairs to bed. "I can't imagine going through all that knowing the baby is dead."

"They probably knock her out," Bryan said.

"I hope so." Ivy tucked Mac's blue blanket around the sleeping baby. Bryan never understood why she called it a shawl. "I'm going to try to sleep too," she said.

Something smashing in the basement woke Bryan before it was light. He thought he'd never fall asleep but he had, on the couch, after more TV he'd watched without seeing. He pulled aside the curtain and saw his mother's car in the driveway. He hadn't heard anyone come home.

He stood at the basement door and listened to sounds of splintering wood. A low moaning. Smash. Quiet, the furnace clicking on. Moaning again. Smash. He sneaked part way down the stairs.

Neal swung a hammer against what was left of the cradle he'd been building, three different hardwoods, pegged together, carved, sanded, months of work, shattered into a pile of splintered boards. Neal looked up, hammer dangling from his hand, the grief in his eyes hitting Bryan as hard as a punch to the gut. Bits of wood stuck in his beard.

"Hi," Bryan said.

"Hi." Again Neal's voice sounded too small. He looked at the mess around him as if someone else had made it.

"How's Mom? Is she upstairs?"

"She'll be okay. She's at the hospital. Sleeping. She'll come home tomorrow. I mean today. Later." He raised the hammer as if to pound something and stopped midswing. "What a fucking waste. What a God damned, motherfucking waste."

"Is it … is she …" Bryan couldn't find the right question. Neal didn't swear.

"The baby's out, born, whatever. Little girl, tiniest thing. Sweet little wrinkled face. But cold. She was warm and then cold. Just like that."

Bryan wanted to move from his spot on the fifth to bottom step, uncurl Neal's fingers from the hammer, and set it down, but he stayed where he was. All his practice comforting his mother had taught him nothing about how to help a grieving man. "That was a beautiful cradle," he heard himself say.

"She was a beautiful baby." Neal swung the hammer, the wood leaped into the air. When the dust settled, he said, "You build. Things break. You fix them. You can even build beautiful things, then something like this happens to show you how powerless you are and you wonder why you even bother. Doesn't feel worth it." He stooped to pick up a piece of what had been the headboard, carved with hearts and flowers. "Sometimes you just have to smash things," he said.

"Are we going to have a funeral or something?" Bryan asked.

"Yeah." He sighed. "Got to figure all that out in the next day or so." He dropped the piece of wood, switched off the basement light, and rubbing his head sunk to a seat on the stair just below Bryan. "Reminds me of the time my baby sister died. Never think much about her. Eva. She choked while I was watching her—on a sponge. I was cleaning up a spill and she wanted to do it too. She put everything in her mouth but I never thought she'd bite a sponge. Her body felt cold, like the baby's. You know what it felt like? A raw mushroom."

Bryan put his hand on Neal's bald spot, a gesture like tousling someone's hair only there wasn't any. Neal reached up and placed his hand on top of Bryan's.

"A body should never feel so cold. I remember my mother and father, shaking the body, pushing on her heart. Me screaming not to hurt her. On some level they never forgave me."

Bryan wondered if that was why Neal never talked about his parents. "How old were you?" he asked.

"Six."

"Why did they let a six-year-old watch a baby?" Bryan asked. "It was their mistake, not yours."

"That's what your mother says." He sighed. "I think that was when I first knew I loved her, when she said that. She said it was easier for them to blame me than themselves. I still feel I could have done something."

"You couldn't," Bryan said, not sure he spoke the truth. "You were a little kid."

"My parents never got over it. I spent the rest of my childhood trying to make it up to them."

Pale gray morning brightened the basement windows. Bryan wondered who else knew about Neal's sister or his parents. He'd never be able to cook with mushrooms again.

"I always wanted kids of my own," Neal said into the shadows. "Probably not going to happen now."

You've got us, Bryan thought, wondering how it would feel to hug Neal and be hugged back. With an ear pressed against Neal's chest or even his back, Bryan would hear his huge, sad heart beat, doing its job. He thought of Gil's illustrations and imagined Neal's heart looking like them. He remembered the way his own heart pounded as he'd cut and glued red paper for Martine's valentine, how it shrank when he tucked the card away in the desk drawer, afraid to give it to her. Neal tightened his lips. He set his shoulders, and with only the light from the stairs and his push broom, swept together the splinters, the broken boards.

Bryan had almost destroyed Martine's valentine to keep it from Ivy's prying eyes, or maybe to keep from giving it to Martine. Bright scraps of envelope and card, the letters spelling her name, shredded confetti in the waste basket. No. He had made something beautiful for the girl he loved. He'd give it to her, whole.

Dr. Cardullo and the nurses all assured her that the undertaker would take care of the baby's body, but Carol couldn't help thinking she should do it herself. It was so small. It would fit in the plastic shopping bag of supplies that stood on the window ledge of her hospital room—all the things they thought she'd need like giant sanitary napkins and vitamins that would choke a horse. She should be taking her baby home, Neal's baby. When Ivy and Bryan were born the hospital had given her a goody bag of baby lotion, formula, diapers.

She sat on the edge of her bed in her flimsy hospital gown, all the discharge papers signed. Neal was late with her clothes. The dress she'd put on yesterday morning when she was still a pregnant woman, merely beginning to wonder and worry, just starting to think she hadn't felt the baby move during the night, was a rumpled mass in the bottom of the wastebasket. She eyed the phone and was about to dial their number when the half open door swung wide.

"Oh, you are still here?" A thin elderly man in a white uniform hesitated. "They say you are gone."

"Not yet," Carol said. Her baby was gone but she was here. "I'm waiting."

He continued to look at her skeptically from behind his cart of cleaning supplies.

"For my husband," she said. "My clothes."

When the man still didn't move, she wondered if she should offer to wait in the hall, but she knew there were live babies out there being wheeled back and forth and she couldn't stand to see them.

"Carol?" Neal shoved past the man and his cart as if they weren't blocking the doorway. "Here." He pushed the plastic bag of clothes at Carol, then paced back and forth by the window without looking out.

Carol opened the bag. The cleaning man, seeming unimpressed and unmoved by misfortune as terrible as theirs, still waited in the doorway. "Can't you come back later?" she asked. "I need to get dressed."

"They say you are gone."

"I will be gone in a few minutes," Carol slid off the bed, holding the front of her gown together. "Please?" She turned toward Neal, but he was staring at his empty hands. "Get out of here!" she shouted. "Give me a minute to get dressed."

"Okay, I come later," the man said. He backed out through the door dragging the rattling cart. Neal's helpless, defeated silence filled the room, surrounding her.

She couldn't move. Neal had tossed any old thing in the plastic bag without thinking to ask her what she wanted. Before the flutter of panic in her chest could begin flapping hard, she forced herself to open the bag and take out the khaki slacks that would never button or zip around her bloated waist and a scratchy wool sweater. She turned the bag over and dumped a pair of underpants onto the bed. No bra, no shirt, no socks. "What were you thinking?" She tried for a light tone, even a trace of a laugh, and it didn't work at all. Even without looking at him she knew she'd made a mistake.

She took the clothes into the bathroom and shut the door. Sitting naked on the toilet, bleeding, stomach stretched flabby and empty, she wished she'd never married Neal. She hadn't wanted a baby. Maybe that was why it died. It was her fault for doubting the rightness of it. Neal probably blamed her, and if he didn't he should. No, he didn't blame her, but he couldn't take care of her. He was supposed to take care of her. She was the one who felt scared and anxious and he was the one who reassured—an unspoken agreement she hadn't even known they had until it was broken.

After Johnny's mother died, only his sadness mattered. He didn't care or even care to know that Carol felt devastated too, that IJ was supposed to be the loving mother she never had—an accepting mother. Everyone felt sorry for Johnny. It was sad. It was tragic. And it had given Johnny license to drink heavily again, to hide behind his jokes and stories and pool game leaving her alone.

Carol put on the sweater. At least it was long and covered her unfastened pants. Neal stood blank faced in the same place between the bed and the window. "I'm ready," she said. When he didn't reply she reached past him for the plastic shopping bag. She took his hand. "Neal," she said. "Let's get out of here."

She led him past the cleaning man and the nurses station, through several sets of swinging doors, to the elevator, through the lobby, to the parking lot. The cold air slammed against them.

"Where's the car?" She eyed the rows of vehicles, seething with pity and rage, willing herself to be patient and kind, like Neal, to give him time to respond.

"The truck." His voice sounded husky and strange. "It's here somewhere."

"Over there." Once she knew to look for the truck she spotted it right away. It wasn't locked. Neal paused at the open door.

"Do you want me to drive?" Carol asked.

When he nodded mutely she realized her offer had been more sarcastic than sincere. She had just been through labor. She deserved a man to drive her home. She circled the back of the truck. Every time her foot hit the asphalt she whispered to herself, "be kind." When she reached Neal, his hand frozen to the door handle, his eyes watery behind his glasses, his head bare in the cold she stopped. If she'd been standing immobilized by grief, Neal would know exactly how to help. He would say nothing or the right thing. This was all wrong.

"Give me the keys," she said. "Get in."

He fumbled in his jacket pocket, then the other one. When he moved on to his pants pockets, Carol dropped her shopping bag and wrapped her arms around him. The heat of her cheek freed the icy tears caught in his beard.

The silence in the truck cab weighed less heavily than the silence in the hospital room. They shared it. When Carol pulled into the driveway, Ivy and Bryan were waiting at the window.

Neal climbed down from the truck and walked up the steps beside her. Bryan and Ivy opened the door, faces anxious. Neal passed by them and went straight upstairs.

"Is he okay?" asked Bryan. "Are you?"

Ivy took the shopping bag and helped Carol take off her coat, small kindnesses uncharacteristic of her daughter. And where was Mac?

"Are you hungry?" Bryan asked.

She was hungry. She was starving. The smell of Bryan's minestrone hit her—and something else.

"We made bread," Bryan said. "I taught Ivy how. It came out okay. And soup."

The three of them sat at the kitchen table and ate without talking. The baby monitor crackled. They could hear Neal's footsteps pass Mac and Ivy's room and the bathroom door close. They heard him pass by again and the bedroom door close. Carol finished her soup. "This was delicious. I'll bring some up to Neal," she said. "Thanks." She wanted to be safely in her bedroom before Mac cried.

Ivy pressed her ear to her mother's bedroom door. Nothing. If it weren't for the brief morning, before work, clatter and late-night, back and forth murmurings, she would hardly know her mother and Neal still lived in the house. She turned the knob, easing the door open a crack. Still no sound. After the baby's funeral, just a simple graveside ceremony, they went back to work, but spent their time at home in their room. Ivy, exhausted from the effort of keeping Mac silent and invisible, had begun to feel invisible herself. Neal hadn't come home yet trying to make up for lost time on his construction job. Bryan had gobbled his dinner and gone out to meet Martine, Everett, and Casey at the mall. She had to get her mother out of bed. The long, narrow lump under the intricately stitched quilt didn't move.

From the darkness at the top of the stairs, Ivy had watched Carol work on that quilt. She was ten and waking regularly with nightmares. She had sat, her dead father's tee shirt stretched over her chubby knees, trying to be satisfied with watching her mother's head drawn toward the light of the sewing machine like a flower toward the sun.

Her mother's work basket sat, forgotten, under a chair in the corner of the dark bedroom, an unfinished baby quilt spilling from the top, a seven-stars design, bright diamonds on white. Ivy turned to leave. What could she possibly say? How would she have felt if Mac had never breathed? Her breasts ached and throat tightened just thinking about it.

Her mother had Neal. They talked at night. After enough nights had passed, things might be normal again. Then Ivy thought of Mac and all the days ahead between now and normal. She stepped closer to the bed.

"Mom, are you asleep?"

"No." Flat on her back, Carol folded the quilt edge to below her shoulders and looked at Ivy.

"Do you need anything?"

"No."

"Supper?"

"I'm not hungry."

"Bryan's worried you're not eating."

"Neal makes my lunches. I'm not too hungry these days."

Neal had taken care of everyone until the baby died. Now he slunk around the house barely speaking. Bryan said kids at school hovered outside the door of the shop at lunch arguing about how to help Neal, wondering if they should leave him alone or ask to work on something, then, unable to figure it out, wandered off.

Carol lay still in the bed and stared at the ceiling, eyes large, chin sharp and pointed, shadowy hollows around her long, white neck.

Get up, Ivy wanted to scream. Instead she asked, "How about some tea? Or water?"

All her life when Ivy felt there was nothing she could do, she'd done something anyway, the loudest, biggest thing she could think of. But her baby slept in the next room and she wanted him to keep sleeping. Yelling wouldn't make her mother talk. Ripping off the covers would only reveal her mother's empty belly and skinny arms and legs. Ivy shut her eyes and swallowed.

"What do you do in here?" she asked.

"Nothing."

Ivy waited.

"I think. I cry. I tell myself to move. My body refuses. I pull the covers over my head and wonder why I should bother getting up, ever. It's all I can do to drag myself to work and back."

I hate you, Ivy thought.

Then her mother asked, "How's Mac?"

Ivy pictured Mac naked, kicking and pink and laughing after his bath, his dark curls, plastered to his head. Or his tiny feet tucked into a fuzzy stretchsuit. "Sleeping." Ivy sat near the foot of the bed, on Neal's side.

"I've been thinking about when your father died," Carol said.

"So have I." Ivy straightened.

"I had to keep going. My world had collapsed. I had to remember to buy milk, take you to the dentist, keep track of library books. I had to make those things count, so I did. All that hurt and loneliness. It won't go away, even when you ignore it." She sat up against her pillow.

Ivy remembered Bryan saying, "Mom can't just be." Now for two weeks she'd barely moved except to go to work and use the bathroom. No books lay open. No radio or TV played.

"Remember how you'd come downstairs?" Carol said. She reached for Ivy's hand. "I needed that time, that bit of time I thought should be mine."

Ivy could still hear the irritation in her mother's voice, see the reproach in her eyes as she turned from the sewing machine. Why was this miserable girl bothering her? How did she end up with this frowning, fat daughter? This girl who broke her sewing machine and couldn't stitch a beanbag without throwing it across the room, beans scattering everywhere. This girl who never had a favorite blanket or stuffed animal, who collected broken glass, and slept in her dead father's tee shirts.

"I'd be so angry, so tired, needing to lose myself in the sewing ..."

"I couldn't help it," Ivy said, a sudden lump in her throat. "I had nightmares. Bad ones."

Carol pushed back the ragged cuticle on Ivy's index finger. "I was so tired ... overwhelmed."

"I needed you," Ivy squeezed out the words. "I missed Daddy."

"I missed him too."

"You liked Bryan."

"Ivy!"

"It's true! Daddy liked me best." 'And I liked him best' was what she didn't say, but they both knew.

"No." Carol shook her head. "No. You'll see. Someday you'll understand."

Ivy wouldn't. She'd gone over and over and over it her whole life. She'd had her father, for only seven short years. Whenever she felt her mother's disappointment, she'd take out her father's grin and play it over and over.

"It's not a liking best. In some ways your Dad was an easy going guy, fun loving anyway. He liked a little spark. That was you. Full of fire, right from the start. Bryan was easier for me. That's all."

"You held Bryan. You didn't yell at him."

"He was easier."

"So you loved him more."

Carol stared at Ivy's hands, red and cracked, casualties of a cold, dry winter and constant diaper changing.

"I'll never forget, Ivy. I was sitting there wishing I was sewing, furious at being interrupted and you held my sleeve, your nails and cuticles chewed down, fingers covered with dirty Band-Aids. You said, 'I like it when Bryan's asleep. I like being here with you. It feels like we're the only people in the world.'"

Ivy remembered. The nightmares. Night after night. Mewing kittens buried to their necks in sand. Impossible to walk without stepping on their heads. The dark in her room. Knowing she was a bad girl, the worst, but unable to stop herself from bothering her mother. Needing. Needing. Needing. Bad, bad girl.

"You still bite your nails," Carol said.

Ivy listened hard for criticism, preparing her answer.

"Those cracks must hurt." Carol reached for a small, cosmetics jar. "This helps. Put some on."

Ivy unscrewed the lid, staring at the cream.

Some nights, if she was lucky, her mother had let her lie on the couch. Ivy pretended to be asleep. Pretending well enough to fool her mother required all of her ten-year-old will. She couldn't miss the moment just before her mother went upstairs, when she kissed her forehead and said she loved her.

"If I don't use this every night," Carol snatched the jar from Ivy. "My hands crack as bad as yours. Let me."

She rubbed dense green salve into Ivy's sore hands. It smelled of damp earth and growing things. Ivy closed her eyes and remembered walking in the woods on the hill with her father, following the stream to its beginnings. The woods were still at the end of their street. When she was a little girl, they seemed a wilderness. She and her father had scrambled up boulders, bushwhacked through brambles, identified edible plants, Ivy filled with the thrilling sense anything could happen in such a wild place, yet sure of happy endings because Dad was there. Her favorite place. She wouldn't play there after her father died.

Carol's fingers massaged Ivy's knuckles, slid over her palms, eased salve into the cracks around her ragged fingernails.

"Okay?" Carol screwed the cap on the jar. Ivy held her hands to her face and breathed. "Smells nice, huh? Here. Keep this jar. I have more. You have to take care of yourself especially now that you're a mother." As she settled back against her pillows, her face relaxed into a weak smile.

You're a mother, too, Ivy thought. Get up. I want you to rub cream into my hands every day. Seven years had passed since the nights she'd beg to sleep on the couch while her mother sewed. Seven years, and a child of her own. She stretched out on the bed, burying her face into Neal's pillow. Seven years ago her breasts, now pressing uncomfortably into the mattress, leaking milk, had barely begun to grow.

Gil had hurt her but he fed her cupcakes and brushed tangles from her hair without pulling. He'd told her she was beautiful and, in bed with him, she believed it. She didn't want to raise her son alone, resenting him and his nightmares for interrupting her carefully planned and desperately needed quiet time. Mac didn't even have the option of preferring one parent to another. She knew how much it hurt to have a hole in your life where a father should be.

"Is that the baby?" Carol asked, hearing Mac a moment before Ivy did.

Ivy couldn't answer.

They listened as the cries escalated, perfectly pitched to get results.

The mattress shifted. Carol sat on the side of the bed. She put a hand on Ivy's back. "I'll get him," she said. "You're tired. Rest."

Ivy rubbed her hands over her face and breathed in the smell of her mother.

CHAPTER 11

'Fight!' The large red letters pulsated on the screen. Eight months old, Mac didn't need quarters to have a good time at the arcade. Bryan held him around the waist, his bare toes on an upside down trash can. He poked at the buttons, squealing at the parade of cartoon bad guys and their kicking, punching, falling down, the splashes of blood appearing and disappearing like fireworks. He grasped the joystick, laughing.

Bryan scanned the doorway for Martine. She sometimes came by after her dance class. She liked seeing him with Mac, said he looked cute holding a baby. Since Bryan had given her the valentine, he'd kissed her eleven times, three of them at the CYO dance on Friday, the end of a long school year. It was time to stop counting kisses. She'd probably call herself his girlfriend, but they hadn't said anything like that to each other yet. They would though. Summer stretched, long and lazy, in front of them.

Mac fidgeted, bored by the screen full of letters advertising CD's and comic books. "Don't worry, little guy." Bryan brushed his lips across his nephew's soft hair. "The action always starts again, you know that, don't you? Hey, don't do that!" He lifted Mac to keep him from sucking on the joystick. "Let's take a break."

Bryan squinted into the dim center of the mall. A few people strolled past. No Martine. No Everett. "Oh well, Mackie, it's me and you. How about some pizza crust? I could use a slice." Bryan glimpsed the tensely muscled back of a tall man in a tank top, low slung jeans, an 'I know you're going to try to mess with me and I'm ready' walk. "Gil's in jail," he reminded himself, squeezing Mac too tight.

Baby screams cut through the ringing clatter of the arcade games. Bryan loosened his grip. "Sorry, guy. Didn't mean to squash you. Ssh. Pizza, okay?"

Mac stopped crying. He always agreed with his uncle.

The only time Bryan had seen Gil, the guy had a coat on and was wrapped around Ivy. There was no reason to think he'd be recognizable to him now by the shape of his body and way of walking.

Bryan shook open the umbrella stroller and strapped Mac in, tried not to look at his pointed ear, Gil's ear, Ivy said. He thought of Ivy's ears, how she'd come home with a scar where an earring used to be. When he'd asked her about it, she told him to mind his own business. When he'd mentioned it to Martine, she guessed someone had pulled Ivy's earring until her ear tore.

Hands tight on the hooked handles of the stroller, Mac happy to be rolling along, Bryan told himself to relax, to breathe. The flow of letters from Florida had stopped recently. Gil might have given up. Or he might be out of jail, looking for Ivy. What would he do when he found out he was a father? How much blood came from a torn ear? How long had it taken to heal? What did Ivy think when she looked at the knot of earrings in the wooden box Neal had made for her?

Bryan stopped in front of a wall of one way glass so Mac could admire himself. He wriggled and laughed, arms and legs straining to grab his reflection.

Bryan studied himself: floppy brown hair, wire rimmed glasses, cute nose according to Martine, dimples he'd never liked until she touched them with her thumb and grinned. He smiled, turning his head, to check them out. The face passed inspection. Even with the glasses and a pimple or two. Martine had pimples now and then herself. Pushing the stroller close so Mac could slap at the mirror, Bryan considered his body. Definitely not okay. In the past year he'd grown, taller than Ivy, taller than his mother, and hadn't gained a pound. He ate enough, anything he wanted and more, but his elbows sat like baseballs halfway up his arms. Underneath his baggy pants his knees bulged wider than his thighs. Without sucking in his breath, he could feel every rib under his tee shirt.

"Who's that baby, Mac?" Bryan asked, to make it clear to anyone watching he wasn't standing there to look at himself.

The muscle man approached eating a slice of pizza, ignoring the signs posted everywhere forbidding food outside the food court. Bryan had been told once by the security guard to sit at a table or take his pizza outside. He sat to eat ever since.

He watched in the mirror as Muscleman scarfed his pizza. His heart slammed against his ribs. Gil's blue eyes, sharp and unforgettable, met his. If only the mirror were a video screen, Bryan could push buttons to kick and punch, throw fireballs. He'd be big and colorful and as tough as his opponent. He glanced at his hands, knuckles white on the stroller.

"Hey." Gil slapped him on the shoulder. He'd finished his pizza, all but the crust.

At the sound of a new voice, Mac turned and said, "Ga." Bryan stood silent, the stroller supporting him.

"So how you been?" Gil asked. His teeth gleamed. Bryan stared, remembering a missing tooth, brown spots.

Gil smiled wide, tapping his teeth with the pizza crust. "Like these choppers? Courtesy of the state of Florida, Department of Corrections." He pushed them forward with his tongue, then clicked them into place. Bryan felt sick and tried to keep his face from showing it.

"So how's your gorgeous sister?" Gil waved the pizza crust as he spoke. Mac reached for it.

Gorgeous sister. Ivy, so fat she could hardly get out of the recliner when Oprah was over. Eyes deep in her head, dark smudges underneath. So lazy she never left the house.

"Have you heard from her? Has she gotten my letters?"

Gil didn't know Ivy was home. Bryan wouldn't tell him. He'd want to come and pick up his box. The dagger lay under Bryan's mattress. He took it out sometimes, late at night, when he knew no one would walk in on him, and standing on his bed, pretended to stab at his reflection in the small mirror over his dresser. He could look pretty tough. He'd die if anyone found out. "No," Bryan said, beginning to walk away, Mac twisting and whining, eye on the crust in Gil's hand.

"So where is she?" Gil fell into step beside him. "I've been counting the days till I'd see her again. We belong to each other. I'm your future brother-in-law, you know." Bryan wondered if Gil carried a knife or a gun.

He swallowed the bile rising in his throat and pushed the stroller as fast as he dared. Mac wailed, clutching the air for the pizza crust. Shut up, Bryan thought. Usually Mac and he understood each other. Please shut up.

With easy strides, Gil stayed with him, his biceps proclaiming 'white and proud' barely an inch from Bryan's ear. With Mac yelling his head off, Gil had to start noticing him. "Listen," Bryan said. "Last I heard, you took her to Florida. I gotta go."

"Baby-sitting?" Gil asked.

Telling himself he only imagined the knowing edge to Gil's voice, Bryan answered coolly, "Yeah."

"Thought girls did that," he said.

"No," Bryan stared straight ahead, at the door.

"You know where your sister is." Gil gripped his shoulder. "Tell me. She's my woman. I'll find her. God means for me to. You could make it easier." Mac's screams pressed against Bryan's ears as hard as Gil's fingers dug into the hollow beneath his collarbone. "I'd appreciate things being easier."

"Shut up," Bryan hollered, his voice echoing through the mall. Mac stopped. In the sudden silence, Gil held on.

"I'll find her," he whispered. "I can always go to the bank and get your mother to tell me. Maybe I should just stick with you. You'll go home eventually. When you're finished baby-sitting." He seemed to see Mac for the first time. "Whose baby?" He squatted in front of the stroller. Mac snatched the crust. Gil laughed. "Greedy little fucker, aren't you?"

Bryan jerked back the stroller. "I gotta go."

Gil wrapped an arm around him. Bryan smelled sweat and cigarette smoke and felt the heat of the man's body. He wanted to dissolve into tears, tell everything, so he'd go away. But then Gil would be the one pushing the stroller. Bad enough the pizza crust he'd gnawed with his evil looking dentures was dissolving against Mac's tiny teeth and pink gums.

"Listen." Bryan's voice picked up strength. "We haven't seen my sister since you took her away. And if you come by the house, my mother'll call the police. She hates you."

"Hah!" Gil threw his head back. "Ivy took me away, is the truth of it. She hated this place. Only way she'd have me was if we left. Me take her. That's a laugh."

"My mother doesn't see it that way. Neither does my stepfather," Bryan added.

"No law says I can't come by your house," Gil's eyes narrowed.

Restraining orders, Bryan thought. Ivy can get a restraining order. He shrugged, catching Gil by surprise. He lost his grip on Bryan's shoulder.

"See you," Bryan said, swiveling the stroller to push open the door with his hip.

Gil stopped in the doorway. Bryan blinked in the bright sun, moving as quickly as he dared between the few cars. Iridescent puddles steamed on the asphalt. Dead rainbows he used to call them. Heavy rain had done nothing to cool the air. Out of sight of the mall, he tore the gooey crust from Mac's hand and threw it into the bushes.

"You don't need that," he said, when Mac cried.

He stopped in the shade of a stone wall near the library. A stone wall his father had helped build. "Come on, little guy." He unbuckled the safety belt, lifted his squalling nephew. Bryan blew raspberries against Mac's neck and belly and plump thighs until crying turned to teary giggles. He eased the baby up to his head and tickled him against his hair. Knees weak, Bryan leaned against the wall and hugged Mac tight to his chest. Mac reached over Bryan's shoulder and patted the stones, fingers playing over the cool, rough surfaces and mossy mortar between them. Bryan patted the baby's back and stared at the sidewalk.

Worms lay on the pavement as if scattered by a cruel or careless hand. When he was young he'd made a mission of rescuing them, always late to school after a rain, picking countless worms off the concrete, gently placing them on lawns. Now he had the urge to squash the stupid things. Couldn't they figure out how to get back where they belonged? He nudged a large one with the toe of his sneaker. It wiggled, going nowhere. He picked up his foot, ready to grind the fleshy worm to pulp. Mac wriggled around. Bryan put his foot down, beside the worm. Mac pointed, "Da. Da. Da."

"Yucky," Bryan told him.

Mac insisted, babbling louder, faster.

Bryan leaned forward, picked the worm off the pavement. It twitched wildly. He wanted to whip it against the wall, fling it through the air. Mac struggled against his arm, reaching for the worm. He wondered where Gil was staying, when he'd come to their house, when he'd realize he was the father of the best baby in the world.

"Daaaaaaa!" Mac lunged for the worm and almost grabbed it, almost slipped over Bryan's arm onto the sidewalk.

"You really want that, don't you?" he said, adjusting his hold on both the baby and the worm. "You don't even know what it is but you want it."

"Worm." He dangled it closer to Mac who pinched it and tried to bring to his mouth.

"No," Bryan laughed. "Easy there." He held Mac between his knees, held the baby's hand in his, loosened Mac's grip on the limp worm. He flattened Mac's palm and draped the worm across it, where it moved again. Mac laughed.

"Worm," Bryan said again. "Worm."

"Wuh," echoed Mac. "Wuh."

"That's right." Bryan laughed. The best baby and the smartest baby. "Worm."

Mac prodded it with his finger, shrieking when it wriggled.

"I'll tell you what to do with worms," Bryan said. "If you're not going fishing. If you find one on the sidewalk like this, you pick it up and try to find the nearest dirt." He looked around, concrete everywhere. Except at the base of the wall, a thin ribbon of damp earth. He set the worm down on it and they watched as it burrowed to safety.

Carol shouldered open the door, arms full of groceries. Ivy lay in the recliner, living room curtains closed, watching TV with the volume on high, and nursing Mac. She deigned to look up only when, with an exaggerated crash, Carol dropped one of the bags on to the hall telephone table.

"I'd help, Mom, but as you can see, I'm nursing the baby."

Always that tone. Well, not always, Ivy had been subdued again for awhile after the baby died, but her sarcasm seemed to be edging back and Carol's resentment grew right along with it. Bryan at least did the cooking and worked with Neal at the construction site twenty hours a week. He even watched Mac, more than Ivy did if you didn't count the hours nursing or sleeping.

Ivy laughed along with the laugh track. In the five months since the baby died there hadn't been much joy in the house. Any there was came from Mac—he radiated contentment. Carol had never known such a happy person. His face broke into a huge grin whenever she approached him. He gurgled and laughed and held out his arms. She didn't remember Bryan or Ivy being so full of delight. Neal talked about her trying to get pregnant again, she wasn't getting any younger, but she wasn't ready, might never be ready, and meanwhile he poured his love all over Mac, to the point where Carol thought he might be trying to prove something to her about what a good father he'd be.

"Any more bags?" Bryan asked as she dumped the groceries on the counter. Water splashed in the sink over something in a colander. His haunted expression didn't make sense.

"What's wrong?" she asked. "Is Neal all right?"

"What's wrong with Neal?" Bryan asked.

Carol carried around a chronic worry that Neal would be injured at work. She reminded herself how unlikely it was he'd be injured renovating a barn. Besides, if there had been an accident Ivy would be upset too.

"I don't know. Something's wrong."

"No, did something happen at the site? Mom?" He approached her, water still running, TV blasting in the room.

"Bryan, wait." She tried to explain. "I was asking you about Neal. I haven't heard anything. You looked … panicked, and that was the first thing I thought of."

"No. It's not Neal. I didn't know if I should say anything." He lowered his voice. "I haven't said anything to Ivy. But at the mall today … I saw Gil."

"Gil?" Carol leaned against the counter for support. "At our mall? Are you sure it was him?"

"He talked to me."

"What did he say?"

"Mom, Mac was with me."

"Oh." She had to sit down. She felt her way along the counter.

"I didn't tell him anything, but he wants to see Ivy. He'll come here."

Carol sunk into the nearest chair. "He will not come here. Do you understand me? He will not come here." Even as she said the words she wondered what could prevent it. Neal. "What time is it?" she asked even as she looked at the wall clock.

Bryan glanced up with her. Neal wouldn't be home for a few more hours. In the long summer daylight he worked late.

"Don't tell your sister," Carol said. "We'll think of something."

After waking in the sticky heat to nurse Mac, Ivy couldn't fall back to sleep. She'd dreamed of Gil making love to her and it was worth trying to remember the details; Celine's blue shawl, soft neon light, his tongue behind her knees and between her legs, his promises that, in the dream, she knew were good. When his letters stopped three weeks ago, she missed them, regretted throwing all the others away. He'd said he would come to River-town, looking for her. Deep down she'd been waiting. All those shredded drawings, sketches of her. He remembered what she'd looked like. He made her beautiful. If he saw her now, he might not think so. Heavy, tired, stuck. Hungry, always hungry. She had to get up, eat something.

She crept downstairs to the kitchen. Moonlight pouring through the window reflected off the white stove and refrigerator, leaving everything else in blue shadows. She slapped together a sandwich. A year and a half ago she thought she couldn't survive in this house another moment. Slumped in the chair she wondered how she'd ever survive outside it. Someone's feet hit the floor over her head.

"Can't sleep?" Neal stood in the doorway, his boxer shorts as white as the appliances. He rooted through cupboards, drawers, and the refrigerator assembling crackers, peanut butter, milk, a knife, a glass, a paper towel. He sat and arranged everything in front of him before unscrewing the lid on the peanut butter jar. Without his glasses, he looked wide eyed, defenseless. Ivy looked away, glad he knew enough not to switch on the light.

"Haven't slept straight through a night since ..." Neal spread peanut butter to the edges of his cracker and wedged it into his mouth.

Ivy nodded, scooped a fingerful of peanut butter from the jar.

"Your mother though," Neal said after a gulp of milk. "She sleeps. For her sleeping is easy. You wouldn't think so, someone as tense as she is but like everything else ... she does it right."

Ivy licked her teeth. So Neal realized Carol wasn't perfect. Ivy smiled inside.

"Worried about this Gil character?"

She picked peanut butter from under her fingernail. How did Neal know she'd been dreaming of Gil? She smiled to herself. Worried, yes, but at the moment, more hungry for him, sex starved, desperate, aching for someone to get her out of the house, out of Rivertown, out of her life. She smiled harder imagining Neal's face if she ever told him what she was thinking.

"Got me worrying some, I have to say. Could make trouble for you, about Mac and all." Neal poured another glass of milk. "Now I never met the guy," he continued. "Do you think there's anything to worry about?"

She sucked another fingerful of peanut butter. Neal waited, spreading cracker after cracker, lining them up on the paper towel. Of course there was something to worry about. There was always something to worry about.

Gil wouldn't come. Follow through was not his strength. "Don't worry," Ivy said.

"Hard not to."

"You're not my father." As soon as she'd said the words, Ivy wondered where they'd come from.

Neal studied his crackers. "No," he said. "But I care about you. And I care an awful lot about that baby of yours. And I love your mother. We don't need any more trouble around here."

He chewed, cracker crumbs spilling onto his beard. Ivy waited, expecting him to go on. Neal fixed things whether you wanted him to or not. After he swallowed, he would outline his plan, a good one, as foolproof as a plan could be. A way to make sure Gil couldn't get to her. She watched and waited to hear it.

"Guess I'll try to get some sleep," he said when his crackers were gone. He brushed crumbs from his beard, picked up the peanut butter jar. "Should I leave this out for you?" Hadn't he heard her mother telling her how fat she was? How she had to stop eating? Was that all he had to say?

"Put it away," she said, voice hard. His nearsighted eyes met hers. The shadows made it easy to ignore the question she thought she saw there. He moved around the kitchen, cleaning up.

"Good night," he said, pausing near Ivy's chair.

"Night," she answered, unmoving.

She heard Neal climb the stairs. No sound from Mac. She wanted her own house, where her own man could walk around in his underwear. Gil never wore underwear. Naked then. Neal could get him a job. He'd done some construction work. If he didn't drink, and he'd said a million times he wanted to quit, they could make a life together. People could change. She had.

At the sink, Ivy splashed her face and neck with cold water. Hoping for a breeze, she slipped onto the porch, settled on the top step, wrapped her cotton nightgown around and between her sweaty thighs, and leaned against the railing. Full of moonlight and the sound of insects, the heavy air shimmered and hummed. She closed her eyes and wished as hard as she could for someone to love her and make her feel beautiful.

A shadow fell across her eyelids. "Hey." Gil bent over and gripping her shoulders, kissed her hard. During the past sixteen months that voice had sounded in her head, threatening, promising. She'd even felt his kisses, but without the solid smell of cigarettes, beer, and salty skin. He'd found her, like he'd said he would. The inevitability of it all eclipsed any surprise.

Her mouth searched his. Her cotton nightgown stuck to her, soaked with sweat and milk. She touched the bones of his face, the line of his jaw, remembering.

"Oh God. Ivy. I've dreamed about you for so long." Words more moaned than spoken. She began to cry, everything turning liquid in the heat. Tired of holding, stroking, feeding, she wanted to be held, touched, desired. By a man, not a baby. But Gil was a baby. Gil needed her too much, had tantrums—scary, in a one hundred and eighty pound, six foot body. No one else had ever kissed the soles of her feet. No one else had ever run his tongue around the inside whorl of her ears, buried himself between her legs. No one else would be courageous or foolhardy enough to come to her mother's house in the middle of the night and begin making love to her on the front steps. In the stagnant air he was a hurricane wind. She was a wave swelling to a crest, easier to let herself crash against the sand than try to resist.

Then they were moving, standing, walking, down the middle of the street. The smooth tar held the heat of the day. She led him toward the woods. Among the trees, near the creek, the spongy ground sucked at her feet. She stepped on skunk cabbage, releasing its musky scent. Full of silvery shadows, the woods spread around them. She wouldn't talk and ruin everything, not until they loved each other with their bodies; they used to be good at that.

She pulled away from Gil. His hair was shorter than she remembered, his teeth whiter and strange looking. His eyes, colorless in the moonlight, scared her. She slapped away mosquitoes from her face.

"I was afraid you wouldn't love me anymore," he said. "You didn't answer my letters."

Ivy stepped back. He knelt in the mud as if it were soft carpet and wrapped his arms around her waist, his head against her breasts. "I missed you," he said. "Don't ever leave me again, baby. Promise."

She combed her fingers through his hair wanting to say okay, I promise. She wanted to marry him, to show him his baby, to live happily ever after. Why hadn't he said anything about the milk leaking from her breasts? Or the thirty pounds she'd gained? Had he even noticed?

And if she said, no, I can't promise, would he twist her arm around her back until her elbow popped? Would he throw her down in the mud and kick her with his boots?

"I love you," he murmured.

If she promised, keeping her fingers crossed behind her back, and didn't say anything else, he'd love her the way she needed to be loved, at least for tonight.

The creek tumbled over rocks as it had all of Ivy's life, gurgling like a happy baby, like Mac.

She touched Gil's hair, his neck, he stroked between her legs. They rolled and tussled on the muddy ground. She ignored the buzzing in her ears and let herself enjoy him.

CHAPTER 12

Hours later, the sun beat on the backyard. The summer had been so hot and dry Neal had almost given up trying to grow a lawn. Ivy dragged the battered, plastic wading pool from the basement and filled it for Mac. If it hadn't been for the purple imprints of Gil's mouth on her neck and chest, itchy bug bites, her filthy nightgown stuffed under her bed, and the sense of fullness, contentment, glow, she felt in every pore of her body, she'd have been convinced that the time in the woods had been an extension of her dream. She plopped down on the scorched grass, setting Mac in the pool. He splashed and crowed.

Every night she promised herself she'd apply for food stamps. Every day she broke her promise. Between her first night back, eating out at Valenti's, and last night in the woods, she hadn't left the yard except for doctor's appointments, the hospital, and the afternoon at the park with Bryan and Ev. At home, she had TV. The people living on screen couldn't see her, ask questions, judge. A touch of her thumb to the remote control and they were gone.

She dipped her head into the pool. Mac patted it and laughed. She brushed her wet hair back with her hands and let the water run down her neck, onto her tee shirt. Gil and she had played in the stream the night before, naked. She hadn't said a word to him, about anything. She knew she'd have to. She knew it would be soon, today. She knew Gil.

"Maamaa," Mac said. "Maa maa maa."

"Here comes the fishy." Ivy pushed a rubber fish toward him, tickling his belly. He grabbed it and put it in his mouth.

A slow day full of baby time stretched before them. She'd keep him in the pool as long as possible, then lunch, then nap. They floated and sunk bright plastic boats, ducks, fish. The heat made them sleepy.

A familiar humming sound jerked her up straight. The light seemed to change; colors flashed brighter, then too bright. She closed her eyes. He'd come for her, for Mac.

He strode into the backyard as if he lived there, as if she and the house belonged to him. Seeing Ivy next to the pool, he stopped.

"That baby," he said. "Your brother had him yesterday."

Dizzy, Ivy plucked Mac from the water and stood holding him close.

"Ivy," Gil said, staring hard at her blank face.

She wanted to run. She remembered how she'd run to the yard when her mother told her dad had died, to the hole in the dirt. She hadn't made it to Indochina then. Now, the hole was filled in.

"Ivy," he whispered. "Whose baby?"

She tried to read his face, ran through possible answers and his probable responses. 'Hers but not his.' He might kill her. 'Hers and his.' They'd be locked together until … Baby-sitting. She was baby-sitting. She'd lie and lie and lie even if he didn't believe her, she'd lie, the only thing to do.

"He's …"

Mac patted her breast with both hands. "Maa maa. Naa. Naa." He butted his head against her, sucking at her shirt.

Ivy faked a laugh. "He always does this. Thinks I'm his mother. He practically lives here. Even Bryan watches him sometimes."

"Don't lie to me," Gil's jaw tensed. "You think I'm stupid? Anyone can see he's yours. What I need to know, what you better tell me is who's the father. Who's the god damn father? Who's the lucky son of a bitch?" He bounced on the balls of his feet, eyes blazing.

Mac's whimpers escalated.

"He's …"

"Is he mine? Or are you a whore?"

"I'm not a whore," Ivy whispered. "Not a whore."

"Is that my son?" Gil's voice softened. He stepped closer, stroked her shoulder.

Sobs drummed in Ivy's chest, Mac bounced. Tears streamed onto his wispy hair, his bare back.

"Come on, Ivy. Tell me, sweetie, is that my son?"

"Maaa maaa," Mac wailed.

Ivy nodded, one slight movement of her head.

"He is?" Gil beamed, seemed to grow larger. "That's my boy?"

Gil's hand on her hair, her cheek, was gentle.

"My God, Ivy, he's perfect. Please, please. Come on, let's sit down."

Mac cried. Ivy let Gil guide her to the slice of shade under the pear tree. She sat and began to nurse Mac.

Gil watched. She felt herself become beautiful, important. A real mother. Part of a family. When Mac finished nursing, she would hand him to Gil. While he napped they could make love. Or Gil could stay with him and she could go out. Out. They would have money. Take turns working. An apartment of their own. She wouldn't need food stamps.

Mac's eyes rolled under his half-shut lids. Gil's desire pulled at her. He wrapped his arm around her shoulders and laid a hand on her thigh. She told herself everything would be okay and leaned her head on his shoulder, felt his breath on her ear.

"I'll take care of everything," he said. "We'll get married, right away."

Ivy shivered.

"Why didn't you tell me, Ivy? Why didn't you answer my letters?"

"I don't know," Ivy said. "I was confused. I was afraid of you."

"Me?" Gil's surprise seemed genuine. "Why?"

"You hurt me, Gil." She cradled the sleeping baby, pulling her tee shirt down. "A lot of times." If he tried to deny it, she'd point to the scars.

"I stopped drinking … everything but beer. I'll never hurt you again. I swear. I'm sorry, Ivy. How could I hurt the mother of my son? My wife."

Ivy touched the point on Mac's ear and realized Gil hadn't asked the baby's name.

"Hey!" he noticed. "That's my ear. The guy has my ear." He laughed. "Can I hold him now? Will he wake up?"

Ivy laid Mac against Gil's chest. "I've never held a baby before." His voice caught. "Ivy, honey, this is all I've ever wanted." The baby sighed, then settled. Gil grinned.

Ivy stood, stretched her arms, rolled her shoulders, and spun around. An urge to laugh rose in her throat. Maybe Mac was exactly what they both needed. Maybe tonight they'd put him in the stroller and head to Rivertown Billiards to show him off. Gil shook out a cigarette and lit it with one hand, careful to blow the smoke away from Mac's face.

"I should put him down for his nap," Ivy said, splashing pool water over her head.

"Tell me everything," Gil said. "How old is he? Where was he born? Why did you leave Florida, Ivy? You know no one could ever love you like I do."

She hadn't even begun to answer when Bryan and Martine, deep in conversation, appeared on the back porch. Bryan leaned over the rail, towels in hand, reached for the clothesline and spotted Ivy and Gil. He froze.

Ivy stood in front of Gil and Mac shielding them from her brother's eyes.

"I'm calling the police," Bryan yelled. "Get out of here."

"Wait," Ivy hollered.

"Why? What?" Martine peered over Bryan's shoulder.

"Relax, will you?" Gil boomed. "There's no problem here."

Mac, startled awake, whimpered.

"Get out," Bryan said, less sure of himself.

"Ivy, tell him to relax?" Gil nudged her.

"You better go," she whispered. His eyes flashed. She saw his grip on the waking baby tighten. "I mean, just for now, okay? I'll talk to Bryan."

Gil hesitated. "All right. Until tonight."

Mac began to cry. Gil handed him to Ivy and the cries slowed to a stop. The knots inside her loosened with Mac's sticky body back in her arms.

"I brought you something," Gil said, fishing in his pocket. "Here." He tossed her a small white box. "See you later," he whispered. He kissed her hard on the lips, Mac sandwiched between them.

"Later, Buddy," Gil said to Bryan. "Nice looking lady you've got there. You take care of her. I'll take care of your sister, okay."

Bryan scowled from the porch.

"I take care of myself," Martine said.

That's what I used to think, Ivy thought.

Gil laughed. "Everybody needs someone to take care of them. Not just girls. Ivy and I, we'll take care of each other." He glanced at Mac. "And our son."

Bryan turned to Ivy, eyes wide. Gil flexed a muscle and grinned. "Later, all." He rounded the corner of the house.

"You told him," Bryan said, coming down the steps. "Are you crazy?"

"Shut up, Bryan," Ivy said.

He hesitated, clenching and unclenching his fists. Martine stood beside him. Ivy stared at the dry grass.

"I have to give Mac some lunch." Ivy tried to walk past them but Bryan blocked her.

"You can't …" he said.

Mac reached out toward Bryan.

"You've got to stay away from him," Bryan said, ignoring Mac.

"It's my life," Ivy said.

"Yeah, and it's going to suck if you go with that asshole. Can't you see that?"

"Maybe." The lump in her throat formed again. "It's going to suck no matter what."

Mac whined. Bryan took the baby without noticing.

"You're only eighteen," Bryan said. "The guy beat the shit out of you. You're going to let him near Mac?"

"You don't know what you're talking about," Ivy said, anger dulled by exhaustion.

Mac slapped at Bryan's cheeks. "Hey," Bryan said.

"Can we give him his lunch?" Martine asked.

"Sure." Ivy swallowed tears. "He really likes those green grapes. Cut them in half so he doesn't choke."

They took Mac inside.

Alone in the hot yard, Ivy remembered Gil's gift, jammed into the pocket of her shorts. She opened it, a pair of dangly, rhinestone earrings hung from her shaking fingers. Gil knew how much she loved rhinestones. He must have forgotten she'd stopped wearing earrings.

During the lunch hour rush at the bank Carol closed her window to take an emergency phone call leaving a long line of disgruntled customers waiting for Bernice, the only other teller. Bryan told her Gil had just been at the house holding Mac. She paged Neal at the construction site and paced circles in the staff room waiting for him to call her back. Everything in the tiny room—the Coke machine, the molded plastic chairs, the folding table with its peeling, contact papered surface she set her lunch on every day, looked alien. When the phone rang she snatched it.

"Hey, honey, what's up?" Even sounding slightly concerned Neal's voice reassured her.

"Meet me at home right away, Gil Thompson came to the house. Bryan came home and saw him with Ivy and Mac in the yard."

"Did he try anything? Was he violent?"

"He didn't have to be, Neal. That girl's judgment is so bad all he has to do is ask and she'll go back with him. I'm telling you. If only we'd got her back to school, a job, anything, but what does she have? We can't let her do it."

"Okay, I'll meet you at the house, but honey, she's eighteen. I don't know how we can stop her if that's what she wants to do."

"I won't let her take Mac. She can ruin her own life, but I'm not letting her ruin his."

The sign over the parking lot read 101 degrees. Carol rolled down the car window. She'd be home before the lousy air-conditioning had a chance to work. She practiced aloud what she would say to Ivy, phrasing and rephrasing, knowing anything she said would lead to a fight. Her daughter didn't deserve that beautiful baby. Maybe she herself didn't deserve one either, but Neal did. Why had Ivy's baby lived and Neal's baby died? The question formed in front of her as clearly as if it were written across the billboard on top of Pulaski's Appliances. Fate made Gil Thompson, and Johnny MacKenzie for that matter, fathers but not Neal, who was man enough for the job. Ivy had the baby, and Carol, who might have learned enough to do it right this time with Neal's help, wasn't given the chance.

She pulled into the driveway, relieved to see Neal's truck there already. He, Bryan, and Martine clustered around Mac's high chair distractedly feeding him grapes and crackers and something in a sippy cup. They kept glancing out the window over the sink into the backyard.

Martine answered Carol's unasked question. "Ivy's out there crying."

Neal, covered in sweat and sawdust, added, "We were waiting for you to figure out who should go talk to her."

"If someone even should," Bryan said. He stirred hot water into a bowl of baby cereal for Mac.

"Someone should," said Martine.

Carol leaned against the sink beside Neal. Ivy was sitting in the baby's wading pool, with her clothes on, knees tucked up against her chest. Her sobbing escalated, and she threw something glittery across the yard.

Neal didn't offer. It didn't seem fair to ask him. He'd just begun to come out from under the sadness weighing on him since the baby died. Ivy was her responsibility, her daughter, her former baby. "I'll go," Carol said. "I don't need an audience."

She approached Ivy from behind. "That's one way to beat the heat," she said, Neal-like, to let her daughter know she was coming. She squatted next to the pool and dipped her hand in the space under Ivy's raised knees.

Ivy gave her a guarded look.

"So Gil is back?"

Ivy nodded.

"What are you going to do?" Neal, again. A question instead of an order.

"Don't know," Ivy whispered. She splashed water on her face.

Words pushed against Carol's closed lips—words she knew she shouldn't say. She sorted through them to try to find the least provocative, the ones her daughter might listen to. "You know, your father was the kind of guy who liked, above all else, to have a good time."

"Yeah, so?"

"It's not that there's anything wrong with a good time, but when you're a parent the kids come first, at least for a while. Someone has to put the kids first anyway. And it's a lot easier to do that if there's two people to take turns putting the kids first. Or even more than two. Here, with us Mac's got you and me and Neal and Bryan. With Gil he'll have you. I'm not saying this to make you mad, Ivy. Anyone can see Gil's not ready to be a father." Carol stopped there.

"And I'm not ready to be a mother," Ivy said. "Why don't you just say it? It's what you think."

Carol almost threw up her hands. What advice would Neal have for her about Ivy reading her mind? Her legs hurt from squatting so she sat, even though she'd have a hard time getting the grass stains out of her skirt.

"Besides you never appreciated Dad. He was a good father to me. He showed me stuff in the woods. He took me to the pool hall. He loved me." Her eyes dared Carol to deny it.

"He did," she said. It had cost Carol a lot to be sitting there sweating under her daughter's hostile gaze. Her boss would be understanding, but only after an explanation Carol dreaded having to give. And she probably shouldn't have bothered Neal who couldn't afford to lose an afternoon on a project already behind schedule, but his presence in the house helped her not to fight. "And I love you too," she said.

Bryan sat, sweating in the dark living room, feeding Mac a bottle. He'd been lying in bed, too hot to sleep when he heard the baby wail. Ivy wasn't in her room. Out with Gil he guessed. Should've let Mac cry until he woke Mom or Neal but he couldn't do that to his nephew. Moonlight spilled through the screen door.

Footsteps hit the porch. The door squeaked.

"Where the hell have you been?" Bryan asked. Ivy had twigs and leaves in her hair. Mud streaked her nightgown and legs. She glowed in the silvery light.

Mac, in his lap, threw the half-empty bottle to the floor and reached toward her. "Maa maa." He sounded like a little goat.

"Yeah," Bryan said. "Some Mama you have. Leaving in the middle of the night." Ivy made a face. "You could at least let someone know when you're going out. Ask someone to listen for the baby."

"What are you? My father?" She lifted Mac. Torn lace dangled from the neck of her nightgown. "I don't have to answer to you. You're not my boss."

"You do this every night? Sneak out with the psycho killer?" Bryan sounded stupid even to himself, but he couldn't stop. "You're crazier than he is."

"Shut up," She stuck her breast in Mac's face. He stopped fussing and nursed. "I don't have to listen to you. Go to bed."

"Who will you listen to?" Bryan leaped from the couch, stood over her.

"Worry about yourself."

"I'm worried about Mac." He made a fist, jamming it into his other hand over and over. "I don't give a shit about you." His voice wobbled. "It's Mac we're all worried about."

"Thanks for getting up with him," Ivy said, as if she hadn't heard him. "I wish everyone would trust me a little more," she said. "I made it this far."

"Gil's a jerk. You're making the same mistake over again." He had to make her listen. "He's nuts. Martine said her brother heard he tried to shoot somebody."

"Martine's brother is full of shit," Ivy frowned. "Besides, now that he knows he's a father, Gil's completely different."

She couldn't really believe that.

Bryan didn't know what to say. "Right, a father ..." He stared at Mac's small fingers spread over Ivy's breast.

"What's going on here?" Neal paused halfway down the stairs, Carol behind him.

"Ask her what's going on," Bryan said. "With Gil Thompson."

"Still the little tattletale," Ivy narrowed her eyes. "Anything else you think they want to know?" She looked as mean as ever. "Jealous, Bryan? 'Cause you don't have the nerve to sneak off with Martine. You wouldn't even know what to do if you were alone in the dark with her. You're just a baby."

Bryan wouldn't let her get to him. "Screw up your own life if you have to. But don't wreck Mac's."

"We should all go back to bed," said Neal. "Talk about this in the morning."

"Wait a minute, Neal," Carol said. "Ivy, is this true? You've been sneaking out with Gil Thompson?"

"No one approves of him being here at the house," Ivy said. "So, yeah, I guess it's sneaking. Yes, I have to sneak. Since it's not okay with any of you for me to see the father of my own baby." She laughed a crazy sounding cackle.

"We just want what's best for you. And for Mac," Carol said. "You're afraid of him. You left Florida to get away."

"Who told you that?"

"Come on, Ivy," Neal said. "He's got quite a reputation. He's a scary guy. Even if you say you love him, of course you're afraid. It doesn't take a genius to figure that out."

"No." Ivy glared at Bryan. "Someone told you. Someone who never learned to keep his mouth shut."

"Does it really matter?" pleaded Neal, moving down the stairs. He snapped on the light.

"I thought I taught you a long time ago that everyone hates a tattletale. Some people never learn," Ivy jeered.

Stop acting like you're six years old, Bryan wanted to say. I'm not afraid of you anymore. But he couldn't say it. So maybe he was. "If it were just you," Bryan said. "I wouldn't even care. But I'm not going to let you ruin Mac's life."

"Ha!" Ivy said. "You don't have anything to say about it, so shut up." She talked big but she looked ashamed. Maybe she was worried about ruining Mac's life.

"Ivy," Carol said. "Stay away from that boy. Go back with him and you're signing up for a lifetime of hell."

"Why can't any of you see my life is hell now?" Ivy whispered.

"Hell!" Carol threw up her hands. "You call this hell? A full refrigerator. A roof over your head you don't even pay for? A family who loves you."

"I'll pay you back!" Ivy screamed. "I'm sorry I can't pay now."

"No one's asking you for money." Neal put his arm around Carol.

"Growing up without a father sucks. Maybe none of you noticed. I don't want that for Mac. I don't want to live stuck in the same house I lived in my whole life, like I never grew up."

Bryan's head pounded. Tired of Ivy acting like losing their father had made no difference to anyone else, like missing him was her exclusive right, as though their father dying gave her permission to be a nasty, selfish bitch all the time. He felt in his pocket for his harmonica. It was upstairs by his bed.

Ivy looked from Bryan to Neal to Carol. "At least with Gil I have a chance."

"A chance of what?" Carol knelt in front of Ivy. Bryan thought his mother should be madder. She put one hand on Ivy's knee, brushed Mac's hair off his forehead with the other. "Chance of what?" Carol insisted, frowning up at Ivy.

"I don't know." Ivy shook her head. "A life. A husband. A father for Mac. A house. Maybe a garden." Ivy didn't know anything about gardening.

"Ivy," Neal was saying. "Your mother wants what's best for you and the baby."

"Your mother … your mother," Bryan mimicked. "She can say for herself what she wants. She spoke fine for herself all the years before you came along." He sounded like his sister. Maybe he was going crazy too, but no one paid any attention.

"Neal's right," Carol said. "We've lived longer. We know a few things you don't. I only want what's best for you and Mac."

"But how do you know what that is?" Ivy demanded. "Why does everyone, everyone, think they know what's best for me, for my son?"

Carol sighed and shook her head, taking her hand from Ivy's knee. Ivy moved as if to grab it and hold on, then seemed to stop herself. "We might as well go back to bed," Carol said. She headed toward the stairs and Neal. "Four o'clock in the morning is no time to talk about anything. Get some sleep, Ivy. You know Mac won't sleep late."

Bryan watched Ivy brush away the tears trickling down her cheeks. The stairs creaked as Neal and Carol went to their room, whispering to each other. Mac stirred and whimpered, breathing deeply. Ivy and Carol used to fight to tears and shouting, even smashing a plate now and then. Ivy rubbed the spot on her knee where their mother's hand had rested. Maybe Carol was finally just too tired. Tired of it all. Tired of Ivy. Maybe she didn't care if Ivy ran off again with a man who had hit her. Maybe she was tired of Ivy freeloading, taking up space in the house. Bryan was.

Put the baby to bed, you idiot, he wanted to say. Instead, he began pacing the living room. How could Ivy even consider going back with that guy? What did he do all day? He lived in the rooming house over the Capital Theater, spent his nights in the woods with Ivy. She'd given him back the stuff he'd left in the basement.

"Even if you're stupid enough to see him and let him put his hands on you, you better keep Mac away," Bryan managed to blurt out.

"You've got no right to say that." Ivy gave a short laugh. "Mac's his, not yours."

Bryan pounded the arm of the couch so hard he hurt his fist. "Just leave him home when you hang out with Gil, okay. I'll babysit. Whenever you want."

"Gil is Mac's father and if he wants to see him, he will." She lifted Mac to her shoulder and stood easily. Full of purpose she lifted the diaper bag from its hook by the door.

"What?" Bryan asked. "What are you doing?"

He followed her up the stairs. Still holding Mac, she stuffed tee shirts, underwear, and shorts into the bag. It expanded to hold all she needed and more—Mac's clothes, diaper wipes. "Ivy?" Bryan asked, afraid of the answer. "What are you doing?"

Even her pool cue fit.

"Don't worry," Ivy said. "You can babysit sometimes."

Bryan opened and closed his mouth.

Ivy hesitated. When she spoke her voice was strong. "Things are different now. We have Mac. Gil knows I won't put up with any of his violent shit. He wants me. He wants his son."

"No," Bryan said. He blocked the doorway. "I'm waking up Mom and Neal. They'll stop you."

"No, they won't," Ivy said. "They can't." She sounded sure but she hurried anyway, pushing past him, waking Mac, who began to cry. Moving faster, down the stairs, out the front door, faster, diaper bag swinging wildly. She strapped Mac into the stroller, carried it down the front steps, and through the growing light, flew up the street in her dirty nightgown. He knew if he yelled she'd only run faster and he'd wake the neighborhood. Neal said it, she was eighteen, and Ivy did whatever she wanted. Always had. She turned the corner. He stared at the empty sidewalk.

CHAPTER 13

"Shh." Ivy hushed Mac so he wouldn't wake Gil, who was curled against her back. The first night she and the baby showed up, just a week ago, Gil liked the idea of the three of them together in bed. The second night he told her to make a bed for Mac on the floor. Every time she tried to put Mac on the sleeping bag he began whimpering. When Ivy began to cry from exhaustion, Gil relented.

"Quiet," she whispered. "Come on, I'll change you, and we'll go outside." She gave him a handful of Cheerios.

Two diapers left. Gil wouldn't be happy when she told him they needed more. Ivy carried the wriggling baby through the stifling hallway lined with closed doors, to the bathroom they shared with two floors of withered men and one cranky woman.

Fumes from decades of piss rose from the cracks in the linoleum. Ivy held her breath. At home her mother yelled at Bryan and Neal to wipe the toilet and floor if their aim was off. Mac strained to reach the string dangling from the ceiling's light bulb, as she stood him in the sink to change him. She held him while she used the toilet, careful not to sit on the seat. In the whole past week, she'd gone to the bathroom alone only three times.

Thankful for the toilet paper, often the roll hung empty, she tore off a hunk for later and stuffed it in her pocket. She dropped Mac's wet diaper into the metal wastebasket where it added to the room's stench. She hurried to the open window at the end of the hall, climbed onto the fire escape and gulped fresh air.

Mac waved to a man unloading cases of beer at the rear entrance of the package store, pointed at a passing train, chortled as a bread truck pulled up to the back door of the River Restaurant where Gil had landed a job as a dishwasher. Sometimes they spotted Gil on a cigarette break sitting on an over-turned milk crate. Ivy looked past it all. If she could, she'd wish away the row of stores beneath them, East Main, the train track, and put nothing but grass and trees between herself and the river. One of these days she'd wake early enough to see the sun rise. Already it shone over the hill, a daytime sun burning in a cloudless sky. Another hot day. But not as hot as Florida. And she wasn't throwing up.

"Let's wake Daddy now," she said. "We'll take you to the park. Daddy will buy you a pop."

"Pah. Pah. Pah."

Mac twisted in her arms. She wished she could put him down.

"At the park you can swing, play in the sand, practice your crawling. Let's get Daddy."

"Daa Daa," said Mac slapping at her cheek.

"Let's show him how you say that," Ivy smiled. "Daddy."

"Daa."

"We won't be living here long, little guy," Ivy climbed back through the window. "Daddy has a job. We'll save money. We'll have our own bathroom. I'll buy you a yellow rubber duck. And for me, bubble bath that smells like lemons or vanilla."

They climbed onto the bed where Gil slept on his back, arm hooked over his eyes. She'd grown used to the way his night time mouth without dentures shrunk into itself. She kind of liked his wispy goatee. For almost a month now he'd been working hard and barely drinking. One night from the fire escape she'd seen him out back of the restaurant sharing a joint with a red-haired waitress, but before she could figure out a way to talk about it he'd come home and made love to her, kissing her behind her knees, scratching her back, whispering how sexy she was, how he burned for her. He was careful not to wake Mac. She decided not to mention the waitress. Everyone needed friends.

"Da. Da." Mac poked at his face. Ivy curled herself around him. She kissed his neck.

"What time is it?" he groaned.

"No idea." She moved her arm. Already sweat glued them together. "Hot though."

"You're hot." He grinned, turning toward her. "Hand me my teeth, will you?"

"Watch out for the baby." Ivy caught Mac before he tumbled off the bed, and picked Gil's dentures from the window sill. "Did you hear him say Daddy?"

"No." Gil popped the teeth in, then wrapped his big hands around Mac's waist and waved him around in the air. "Did you say Daddy? Did you say Daddy, fella?"

"Da da." Mac drooled.

"You know your Daddy, don't you?" Mac squealed as Gil tossed him. Ivy giggled. Gil made engine noises. Someone in the next room pounded the wall.

"Fuck you," Gil hollered.

"How many paychecks do you think it'll take until we move out of here?" Ivy asked.

"Don't know." Gil swung Mac in figure eights. "Look in the paper. See what's out there. What is it now? End of July? September first we'll be in our own place."

Another month. Ivy could wait. She'd lived long enough to know it took time to turn a dream into reality. If only she could work too, they'd make twice the money, but who would watch Mac? Once they had a place of their own she could work at home. Meanwhile they needed diapers.

Mac laughed, displaying his four little teeth, as Gil swooped him through the air. Gil's arm muscles bulged. Ivy's breath caught to see her son and his father in a scene so right. She wanted to make love with Gil right there, right then. In Florida, between the bad times, there were long moments during sex when, bodies tangled together, she forgot they had troubles. Now by the time Mac was sleeping she was usually sleeping too, exhausted after days of roaming the streets, the park, the mall, having to think about when and where to do laundry and bathe, what to eat, how to pay for everything.

Diapers. "Gil?"

"Da da," Gil prompted the baby, smiling. "Say, da da."

Mac drooled, flapping his arms.

"Gil. We need another pack of diapers."

"There's a twenty in my pants. Bring back some coffee and a box of donuts too, okay."

Ivy blinked.

He sat Mac on his stomach and bounced him. The baby laughed.

"Cigarettes." Gil added. "Cigarettes before donuts if there's not enough. We'll save so much money in a place of our own. A whole pound of coffee costs as much as five cups out."

"We could get a hot plate," Ivy said.

"We could." Gil grinned. "First paycheck, we'll get one. You know we're going to be able to live off the food I bring home. That'll save some bucks too."

"Too bad we don't have a refrigerator," Ivy found the crumpled bill and dropped Gil's jeans.

"Only a matter of time, angel." Gil reached toward her.

She liked how simple it sounded. Only a matter of time. Mac crawled onto her back, wrapping his hands in her hair and Gil folded his arms around them both.

Gil worked eleven to seven. At four o'clock, when Mac had been awake for two hours after his nap with three more hours to go, she missed him. She missed TV. She even missed Bryan and how he used to come home in the late afternoon and pester her. She passed the time pushing the stroller through the streets, imagining the pizza or spaghetti Gil would bring for dinner.

She crossed the street when she passed the bank where Carol worked. She avoided the construction site on the hill where Neal's truck was parked. She needed air-conditioning too badly to stay out of the mall. So far she hadn't seen Bryan. Only Martine, once, from a distance before she swerved the stroller into Bradlees where she could lose herself in the housewares department.

Ivy plopped Mac in the middle of the unmade bed with a handful of plastic spoons Gil had brought from the restaurant and a tennis ball they'd found at the park. She folded clothes clean enough for another wearing and stuffed the laundry into a trash bag, uncovering her pool cue. J. MK., the tarnished name plate read. Mac's initials. She'd never considered changing the letters to her own. When Mac grew up, she'd pass it on, and the name would be right.

Ivy unsnapped the clasps. The hinges squeaked. She stared at the cue stick for a moment before screwing it together.

"Ma ma?" said Mac.

With the stick in her hands, a yearning for the pool hall and her old life filled her. She leaned over the bed, aiming at Mac's tennis ball. He laughed. It bounced off the wall. Ivy caught him before he fell off the bed trying to reach it and put him on the floor. She shot the ball against the baseboards. Mac crawled after it.

"I know," she said, leaning limp against a wall, pulling Mac into her lap. "We'll leave Daddy a note to meet us at the pool hall. It's time for you to meet Curly and the guys."

"Gai. Gai." Mac gripped handfuls of her tee shirt, pulling himself to a standing position.

"Look at you!" Ivy beamed.

Mac bent his knees, in a wobbly bounce. "Gai. Gai."

Ivy counted back. The last time she'd played pool was the night she met Gil, about a year and half ago. She had been home almost a year. Time to get her game back.

She scribbled a note for Gil, wondering how rusty she'd be after so many months. Her cue tucked back in its case, tight under her arm, Mac on her hip, stroller in her hand, she almost forgot the diaper bag.

For two curvy miles, they walked in the shade of the trees lining the River Road until Rivertown Billiards appeared, a ramshackle gray building with a rusting Coke machine in front, plunked in the middle of an almost empty parking lot. If only she'd come here, back in September, instead of to her house … all those mornings and afternoons and evenings stuck in the living room chair, afraid to be seen in public, with the pool hall barely three miles away. Gravel sprayed from the stroller's wheels as she sped toward the door. Mac shrieked and clapped his hands.

Dusty streaks of late afternoon sun fell across the green felt. The juke box stood silent. Curly lay under a pool table, his feet in their high top sneakers with the rubber toes cut away, sticking out. Rattlings and mumbled curses. The coin mechanism shook. Ivy breathed the smell of chalk, beer, and stale coffee. She tried to swallow the lump in her throat before Curly emerged.

"Gai. Gai." Mac said.

"Huh?" Startled, Curly bumped his bald head, sliding from under the table. "Oww."

"I'll get some ice," said Ivy moving toward the bar.

Curly's frown turned to a smile so warm, Ivy felt the heat. "I heard you were back, lady. Where have you been?" He stopped rubbing his head and hugged her, stumbling over the stroller. "And you've brought the little one. John MacKenzie. You look a little like your grandpa. You sure do."

"Same name as his grandpa too, but I call him Mac." Ivy put a handful of ice in a dish towel. Curly waved it away.

"I'm fine." A red lump blossomed on his forehead. He tickled Mac's bare toes. "Should be able to get yourself a game soon." Curly eyed the Budweiser clock over the bar. "Been playing much?"

"Hah."

"Guess you've had other things keeping you busy. Want a Coke?"

"Thanks." Ivy unstrapped Mac and followed Curly to the bar. She settled on a stool.

"He want anything?"

"He's fine."

"When you were about as old as him your Dad would bring you down here once or twice a week. Never too young to start hanging out. Now that you've finally showed up again, don't be a stranger."

"I won't."

"Ivy." He leaned close to her. "Are you okay? I've heard …"

She didn't want to know. "I'm fine. Everything's great." She swallowed, sure she was about to cry.

The door slammed behind Leo Leveaux, Martine's brother, and a shorter, dark skinned man Ivy had seen around. "Look who's back," Curly's voice echoed in the empty room. Ivy wished someone would play a song or something.

"Ivy MacKenzie!" Leo slapped her on the back. "You didn't like Florida?"

Ivy flushed remembering why she'd stayed in the recliner so long.

"Hate Florida myself," said Leo's friend. "I'm Miguel." He stuck out his hand.

Ivy shook it, her ragged fingernails and torn cuticles red against his smooth brown skin. He smiled with his eyes. "You're a legend around here. Can we play?"

Ivy would have liked to play Leo first, someone she knew. Curly squeezed her shoulder. "Go on. I'll keep the little guy happy, at least until it gets busy. You've got time for a game."

She fumbled with the clasps as she opened her case. Her heart beat fast. When she broke, splitting the balls apart with a satisfying crack, sinking two, she almost shouted. Instead she bounced up and down on her toes hugging herself. She missed the next shot.

Miguel leaned over the table. He reminded her of Destin, that nice boy in Miami, no taller than she was, compact, turtle-like. He moved like a turtle too, deliberate, no hurry. He sank one and grinned, shot again.

They circled the table. Ivy scratched. Miguel won with only one of Ivy's balls left. "Good game," he smiled, holding out a hand.

She shook it, nodding.

"Another?" He grabbed the rack.

"I should check on Mac." Ivy tilted her head toward the bar. "Just for a minute."

"Great. I'll buy you a beer."

"He won't let me drink."

"Who?"

"Curly. I'm underage."

"How old are you?"

"Almost nineteen, end of August."

"Guess how old I am."

Ivy looked him up and down. High tops, Converse, black, jeans, white button down shirt with the sleeves rolled up. Short hair. He seemed older, boys didn't wear tucked in, button down shirts to play pool. And they were always looking for something. Miguel's brown eyes observed and appreciated, laughed. Contented eyes.

"Twenty?"

"Twenty-three."

They neared the bar. Mac held out his arms for her. Curly handed him over. "So how's it feel?"

"Definitely out of practice." Ivy stood Mac on a bar stool, hands around his belly. "But it's coming back. Next game, I'll beat this guy."

"Gai," said Mac.

Miguel ordered a beer. She wanted to ask what he was doing here, how long he planned to be around but it wasn't her business, she was Gil's woman and had to be careful not to give anyone the wrong idea. Gil! Six thirty. Maybe they could squeeze in another game before he showed up.

"Ready?" she asked.

Curly fed Mac goldfish crackers and pretzels.

Miguel and she chalked their cues. She racked the balls. He won the break. Ivy's blood buzzed through her veins. She made every shot, one after another and won, with all his balls still on the table.

"Wow," he said.

Flushed she looked up. He applauded her. She hadn't noticed the place filling with people. Over Miguel's shoulder, like a disembodied head, hung Gil's angry face.

Miguel turned. Curly, Mac in his arms, rushed over from the bar. "Hi," Ivy said. "I thought it was time to show off our little guy." Taking Mac, she snuggled against Gil's side. "Do you want a beer?"

"Hey." Curly slapped Gil on the back. "Had to beg old Ivy to give us a game. Nice son you've got here. Have a beer, on the house." He maneuvered Gil toward the bar. Miguel winked at Ivy before slipping away toward a table where Leo sat with two women.

"While I'm slaving away," Gil whispered near Ivy's ear. "You're out shooting pool with other guys?"

"Gai," said Mac. "Gai."

Curly opened the beer, set the sweaty bottle on the bar, busied himself close by. Gil made everyone nervous, except Mac who rested his head on Ivy's shoulder, sucking his thumb. She wanted everybody to relax, play pool, laugh, have a good time. Unless it was Gil's party, that couldn't happen. He had to be in charge.

His pale throat gleamed as he lifted his bottle. Ivy imagined decorating it with a necklace of bruises, like he'd given her, not lovebites, the fingerprint kind. For a minute she wished she could go back in time and deny, deny, deny, he was her baby's father. Mac grew heavier as he slipped into sleep. She turned on the stool, to rest her back against the bar. Over in the corner, Miguel chatted easily with Leo and the women. She averted her eyes before Gil could follow her gaze and accuse her of flirting. She wished he could understand, she didn't want another man. She wanted to play pool. She wanted a life outside of their room.

"Why don't you play a game now?" she asked. "We both need to have fun."

"Mac's asleep," Curly said. "Let me fold up a blanket for him back here and you both can play."

Gil's eyes flashed. Ivy waited. He slammed the bottle down on the bar and nodded.

Ivy brought the baby around the bar. Curly made a bed for him in a small alcove where he stored cases of liquor and did his bookkeeping. "Let me know if he wakes up." As soon as she set him down, Mac stretched out, arms and legs flung wide. Curly covered him with a couple of towels.

Ivy wanted to close the door, barricade it with cases of tequila and rum, lie down with her son and sleep. Or leave him with Curly, or anyone who might keep him safe in a way she sometimes thought she couldn't.

"Ivy?" Gil's voice cut through the hum of the bar, the music. "Table's free."

"Your father would've expected me to help you," Curly said, as they watched Mac sleep. "If you need anything …"

"Thanks," Ivy broke in. "I don't need anything right now."

"But if you do …" She wouldn't look at him but Curly bent over, tipping his head so he could peer right into her face.

"Okay," Ivy mumbled, meeting his eyes for an uncomfortable moment. "Thanks."

"Come on, Ivy!" Gil called.

As she ducked under the counter, Gil slipped an arm around her shoulder. "You're right," he said. "We need some fun. Come on, I'll kick your ass!"

Even though she'd pushed it to the corner of the kitchen, Carol focused on the empty high chair every time she entered the kitchen. It blamed, saddened, and angered her, yet bringing it to the basement seemed too final. Ivy still lived in town. She'd glimpsed her on Main Street. Neal, with the patience of a stone, assured her Ivy would come back—if not to live, then for regular visits. "It's too hard right now," he'd said. "She's trying to separate, to make it on her own, be an adult. We have to let her make her own mistakes. She knows we're here."

"Easy for him to say," Carol told the high chair. She'd acted as her best self the days just before Ivy left; she'd tried so hard, thought she'd succeeded, and ended up losing again—two people this time.

Maybe it wasn't easy for Neal either. He seemed more resigned than happy. After asking her once about trying again for a baby, he'd stopped. She hadn't even said no, only not now.

"My life is like a soap opera," she said. "Suddenly I'm not even in it anymore, just watching."

The high chair tray gleamed.

Bryan and Martine argued their way down Main Street through heat waves shimmering over the sidewalk. "We never have any fun," Martine whined. "All you do is worry about your sister. If you want to know what she's doing, ask her. Doesn't she live right there?" Martine pointed to the Capital Theater, across the road. "Or you can find her at the pool hall. Leo sees her there."

"Who says I want to see her?" He wanted to see Mac.

"She'll come back," Neal had said just the night before at supper. "The less we pressure her the better. We know where she lives. Want to visit?"

"No," Carol said poking at her food. "She hasn't given me the address. She hasn't even called."

"Don't you miss Mac?" Neal asked. "I'm worried about him."

Carol threw her napkin onto her plate, on top of a mound of spaghetti, pushed her chair from the table with a loud scraping sound and left the room. The white, cloth napkin soaked up sauce. Neal had looked at Bryan eyebrows raised, shrugged, and cut into a meatball.

Bryan and Martine squinted at Ivy's building, into the bright sun. The windows stood open at different heights. Bryan wanted to adjust them all to the same level. Nothing moved inside. Every time he walked through downtown, he stopped and stared; he couldn't help it, not knowing which room was theirs. He concentrated, trying to send Mac a message, listening hard for an answering cry. "Why don't we stop and see if she's home?" Martine said. "I'm sick of it, Bryan. Maybe if you see that she's okay, you'll relax and we can have some fun."

"It's Mac I want to see."

"Let's just go in and look for them." Martine tugged his arm.

"I … I can't," he said. "She hasn't invited me." He sounded like his mother.

"God, Bryan, it's your sister. Since when do you need an invitation?"

Bryan remembered Gil's breath in his ear. The guy had taken his box of stuff. He'd probably figured out by now his dagger was missing and who'd taken it. "What if Gil's there? He doesn't like me."

"So? You don't like him either. You have the right to visit your own sister. And nephew."

"If Ivy wanted to see us, she'd have come home by now." Bryan wiped his forehead with his hand.

"Then let's go to the pool hall, Bryan," Martine said. "All you do is worry about Ivy. I'm sick of it. We might as well go find her."

"I told you. I am not worried about my sister!"

A baby cried. Bryan's arms broke out in goosebumps and he began shivering, even though the sun beat down.

"Sssh." Martine cupped her ear, that ear he licked when they made out by the quarry. "Did you hear that?"

A car passed. A few blocks away a trash truck rumbled.

"What?"

"Sssh."

Wailing.

"That's him," Bryan said.

"Let's go," Martine dragged him across the street. She pushed the heavy glass door. "Unlocked. Good thing. I don't see any doorbell."

He breathed the suffocating air and couldn't speak. Their eyes adjusted to the dimness. She went on. "There's no list of names and apartment numbers. How do you know where to find anyone?"

A muttering old man stumbled down the stairs on his way out, pushing past them.

"Yuck." Martine wrinkled her nose. She led the way up the grimy stairs.

"I can't believe how hot it is in here," Bryan said. He'd never seen a slum but thought this must be what one was like.

"Shh. Do you hear the crying?" Martine asked.

Sounds from a TV came from behind one of the closed doors. Traffic noises. Toilet flushing.

"Let's go," he whispered. "There's no air."

"Come on, Bryan," Martine said. She was about to laugh at him. "We've come this far." Before he could stop her she yelled, "Ivy MacKenzie. You have visitors."

From behind a door, halfway down the dim hallway, Ivy appeared. Seeing her, Bryan knew he hadn't believed she actually lived there.

"What are you doing here?" She didn't smile. Her hair needed washing. She'd lost weight. "What do you want?"

Martine nudged him forward. Ivy's eyes, the tilt of her head, her arms folded across her chest, all said leave me alone.

"Just came to say hi," he said, grabbing Martine's hand.

Mac peeked from the door Ivy had left open. He crawled to her and holding onto her legs, pulled himself into a standing position.

"Mac," Bryan said.

His little buddy whipped his head around. "Daaaaa," he squealed. On hands and knees, he raced toward Bryan.

Bryan squatted and flung his arms out to receive the baby. He hugged him close, breathing in the yeasty smell of his head. He told himself not to cry as Mac's arms locked around his neck.

"He's missed him," Martine said. Ivy nodded, frowning. Bryan didn't know if Martine meant he'd missed Mac or Mac missed him.

"Might as well come in," Ivy said. Newspapers covered the bed. She folded them together to make space for everyone to sit. Bryan stared around the room. A bed, a dresser with a missing drawer. No chairs.

"All three of you live here?" he asked.

"Yeah, but not for much longer." Ivy pointed to apartment ads she'd circled in the paper. "September first, we're out of here. Gil's been working. I've even been earning a little shooting pool."

"Is Gil at work now?" Bryan hoped he didn't sound like it mattered one way or the other.

Ivy nodded.

"What's he doing?" Mac bounced on Bryan's lap. Martine tossed him the tennis ball. Bryan felt Ivy watching him every time he tried to look around. He wondered where they cooked, ate, kept their food.

"Working at the River Restaurant," Ivy said. "Decent pay. All the pizza and spaghetti we can eat. Steak. You name it."

Bryan remembered sitting on a booster seat in the River Restaurant's dark red booths. "Dad's favorite restaurant," he said. "He liked the pitchers of Coke."

"We all had to drink the same kind of soda," Ivy said. "And that weird ice cream they always gave for dessert." Ivy would pick the nuts and maraschino cherry halves from her silver dish of spumoni and arrange them on his napkin. She ate all the ice cream, picked smooth. Bryan ate the fruit and nuts, one at a time.

"What a team," Johnny would say.

"Jack Sprat and his wife," Carol always added.

"No," Ivy pounded the table. She didn't want to look like the fat lady in their nursery rhyme book. Even at four Bryan knew that and couldn't understand why Mom didn't.

"So ..." Ivy said.

"Well ..." He squeezed Mac's pudgy knees. "I just wanted to see how you were doing."

"Did Mom and Neal send you?" Ivy sounded almost hopeful.

"No," Martine said. "I told him he should visit. We were just passing by."

"Oh." Ivy jumped to her feet, disappointed. Bryan could tell.

He swallowed. "You know, that night you left ..." he started.

Ivy looked out the open window.

"I don't know," he went on. Mac was drooling on the tennis ball. "I never thought you'd just leave. When you first took off for Florida, Mom made me crazy. It was hard. I hated you for leaving. Neal comes, things get a little better, you come home and everybody's all upset again. We all get used to that and having Mac in the house and everything's okay and ..."

"Well, it wasn't okay for me!" Ivy said.

Mac looked worried.

"Is it okay now?" Bryan asked. "Here? With Gil?"

"We're getting an apartment September first."

"Where?"

"I haven't found the right one yet."

"If you want, I'll come over and cook dinner for you," he offered. "Once you're moved in. Or I could help you move."

"We don't have much to move," Ivy said. "But okay." She brushed at the tears on her face. "I don't know why I'm crying. Everything's okay, really. Tell Mom I'm getting an apartment."

"I think," he hesitated. "I think, if you wanted to, if you ever did want to come home ... Mom and Neal would like having you back."

"No!" The word burst in the air. Mac whimpered. "I mean," she said, widening her eyes and smiling at Mac. "I'm with Gil. We're getting an apartment.

God, Bryan, I'm almost nineteen. Too old to live with my mother. Tell her I'm fine."

"I will."

A heavy silence surrounded them. He didn't want to leave Mac. He pictured Ivy watching them from the window and wanted to take her too.

"How come I don't ever see you anywhere," he asked.

"I take Mac to the park. I walk around a lot. And sometimes I go to the pool hall. It's nice to have a place where I can bring the baby. Curly plays with him, says it reminds him of when Dad brought me."

Bryan had always hated thinking about Ivy as the center of attention at the pool hall, and he hated the idea of a stranger taking care of Mac when he was the rightful babysitter. He picked up the tennis ball and flung it at the wall, swallowing his jealousy. "Want to come out for a while?" he asked.

"Gil's getting out early today. I told him I'd be here."

"Leave him a note."

"I can't." She looked at the floor.

After a moment she added, "You can take Mac for a while if you want. I can tell he's really glad to see you." On cue Mac grabbed Bryan's shoulders and stood in his lap, gurgling.

Bryan smiled, imagining himself and Martine and Mac strolling through the mall. He pictured the look on his mother's face if he brought Mac home for dinner. Next time.

"What are you going to do for your birthday?" he asked.

"It's still a couple weeks off." She walked over to the window. "You remembered."

"Bryan remembers everybody's birthdays," Martine said.

"Come home for dinner. I'll make you a cake."

"I'll probably be doing something with Gil." Ivy waited.

Bryan couldn't do it. He couldn't say bring him along.

"How long can we have Mac?" Martine asked.

"How long do you want him?" Ivy's shoulders sagged. Bryan studied the warped floor boards to avoid looking at her.

Martine checked her watch. "How about we bring him back at four? That's two hours."

"Fine." Ivy handed her the diaper bag.

Bryan wondered what she'd do, by herself in the room. "Guess this'll give you some time to look for an apartment."

"Yeah." She cleared her throat.

"Well, then …" He lifted Mac onto his shoulders. "Bye."

"Bye. Bye." Bryan didn't have to see him to know that Mac waved and smiled as if he were in a parade. Martine took the stroller.

Bryan couldn't look back, but he felt Ivy watch them walk down the hall. Out on the hot sidewalk he was sure she was peering from the window even though he couldn't see her.

"Glad to be out of there," Martine flapped a hand in front of her nose.

When they tried to strap Mac into the stroller he fussed and clung to Bryan's neck. They headed toward the air-conditioned mall, Martine pushing the empty stroller, Mac a welcome weight in Bryan's arms. He wished he dared to take him home.

"She's getting an apartment," he said in a loud voice, almost a shout, as if Martine had said she wasn't.

CHAPTER 14

When she woke on August thirtieth, Carol's clenched toes and achy womb knew it was Ivy's birthday before her mind registered it. Neal slept beside her. Nineteen years ago at this time she'd been in the same bed when her water broke, Johnny snoring heavily, passed out after a long night at the pool hall. He woke up eventually, enough to drive her to the hospital through the beginnings of a hurricane, but he slept through the labor. And then there was Ivy.

Neal shifted onto his side. Carol watched shadows of maple leaves flutter on the pulled shades. In third grade, before Mrs. Flaherty began a filmstrip about tadpoles growing into frogs, Ricky Maganello, who made the best shadow puppets with his hands, tricked her into sticking up both her middle fingers in the white light for all to see. He'd told her that was how to make a giraffe, her favorite animal. It was the only time she had ever been scolded by a teacher. It wasn't the scolding that shamed her as much as her own gullibility. Neal said to be patient, Ivy would be back. She was beginning to feel foolish for believing him.

Feeding Ivy mashed carrots with a small spoon, rubbing smelly ointment on her diaper rashes, sewing her dresses for the first days of school, painting her bedroom three different shades of pink until it was exactly right, every day and night doing whatever was required to keep that girl healthy and safe, Carol couldn't have imagined that Ivy would run off. She never thought her daughter would be living in the same small town, just blocks away from the bank, and never even wave hello. Bryan wanted to make a birthday cake, invite Ivy and Mac over for dinner. Carol knew she wouldn't come without her creepy boyfriend, but she was not going to let that man in her house. Neal, Mr. Forgiving, Mr. Flexible, Mr. Look at the Best Side of Everyone, would have allowed it, but she wouldn't give him the chance. He did know something about teenagers after all his years of teaching, but his "leave her alone and she'll come home wagging her tail behind her" approach wasn't working.

She switched off the alarm clock a minute before it was set to ring and nudged Neal.

"Oww," he said.

"Time to wake up."

"You don't have to hit me."

"It's Ivy's birthday," she said, and wondered why she said it.

Neal swung his feet to the floor and rubbed his face. "Have to get to school. Got a day of meetings ahead and I need to set up …"

Carol followed him down the hall to the bathroom.

"You want to go first?" he asked her at the door.

Stopped short, she shook her head and continued on down the stairs. She wanted a fight, she wanted comforting, she wanted her dead baby to be six months old like she was supposed to be, and she wanted her birthday girl home to blow out nineteen, no, twenty candles, one for luck. Carol measured coffee into the filter basket and filled the pot with water. The empty high chair mocked her. Carefully, she set the glass pot of water on the counter. She didn't walk across the kitchen or stomp or run; it was as if she were carried across on a giant's palm, as she stood ladylike, contained, posture perfect. The high chair wasn't heavy. She sailed with it, back across the shiny linoleum, opened the cellar door and flung it down the stairs. It landed with a satisfying clatter. Confident it had suffered damage, she poured the water into the coffee maker.

Every birthday of her life, Ivy woke feeling that something good would happen, even the worst one right after her father died and the last one in Florida, pregnant and slaving away at the diner. Birthday girls deserved something good. So she wasn't surprised when she found the perfect apartment on the afternoon she turned nineteen. In two days, on September first, they'd move in, just as Gil had promised.

"Wait'll we tell Daddy," she said, pushing Mac's stroller along. "A washer and dryer in the basement, space for a sandbox. Did you feel the breeze through that screened porch? And that little yellow room. It's perfect for you. Doesn't even need paint." She laughed out loud in the middle of Main Street, forcing herself to walk by the River Restaurant. Gil's boss didn't like her coming in, even if it was her birthday and she had big news. She'd hug it tight like a corked bottle of champagne, until Gil came home, then pop it open and share.

Finally, she had something to celebrate. She'd told the landlady she'd bring the first and last month's rent that evening. They'd both go so Gil could see the kitchen with its stenciled cupboards.

"What's happening to me?" she asked Mac as she lifted him from the stroller. "Why am I excited about designs on a cupboard or a dryer in the basement? I'm turning into my mother. Why am I so happy?"

"Ma ma," he said. "Ha pee Ma." Gil had tried to teach him to sing happy birthday before leaving for work. "Ma ma."

Gil greeted them at the door of their room, shirtless, beaming, his grease and sauce spattered pants low on his hips.

"Da da," said Mac.

"What are you doing here?" Ivy asked. Had he quit his job? Been fired? Her stomach knotted.

"It's your birthday. I got off early."

"Well, I'm glad." She kissed him, handing off Mac. "We have a lot to do. I have great news."

"So do I!" Gil put Mac in the middle of the bed and moved toward her.

Right away, Mac started to fuss; Gil frowned.

"He's probably hungry." Ivy rummaged through the pile of laundry until she found a towel. "What's for dinner?"

"For him?" Gil pulled foil containers from the bag on the bed, peeking under their lids. "Spaghetti. For us, veal parmesan. Nothing but the best. Here, Mackie." Ivy slipped the towel under Mac. Gil put the spaghetti in front of him.

"Uh oh," Ivy laughed, as Mac stuffed handfuls into his mouth, sauce covered strands dangling from his fists. "Maybe we better get a rag. This is going to be messy."

"Never mind about that," Gil took her hand. "Close your eyes. Time for your present."

"But, I have to tell you … you won't believe it. I already got the best …"

"Shh." He pulled her against him, covering her eyes with one large hand, his body hot and urgent against her back.

"Keep your eyes shut," he said, reaching into his pocket, holding her hand, unfolding her fingers. A warm band of metal slid down the length of her ring finger and stopped. "Happy birthday, sweetie," he said, kissing her.

Her throat tightened, tears collected behind her closed lids.

"Open your eyes now," he said, voice full of pride.

She wiped her eyes and looked at her finger. No one had ever given her a ring before. Gil beamed. She should squeal, hug him, smile. "Gil, is that a diamond?"

"The real thing!" He grinned like a kid handing his mother a bouquet of wilted dandelions.

"It's beautiful." Ivy tried to keep the anxiety from her voice. "It doesn't mean … it's a birthday present, right?" She'd gotten as far as imagining daily life with Gil, not marrying him, forever and ever, till death do you part, like her parents had married, like Mom and Neal. When she imagined family she saw Mom and Bryan and Mac and Dad.

"You think I'd spend a thousand dollars on a diamond that was just a birthday present? This is an engagement ring, baby."

A humming began in her head. "Gil! You used the apartment money."

"It's not so bad living here."

The limp flowered curtains stirred in a slight breeze. Gil's garish paintings decorated the walls.

"Maamaaa?" Mac cried.

"I found a place today. A perfect apartment," she said dully.

"So? There'll be others. Ivy, it's your birthday. You're my woman, my truest love, I wanted to give you something special, make you happy."

"But I am happy!" Ivy shouted.

"Happier, then. I want to marry you."

"I'd rather have a decent place to live than wear a diamond ring."

"We'll get a decent place to live. Ivy, I love you. It doesn't matter where we live as long as we're together. I want to marry you,"

"Take the ring back."

"Don't you want to marry me?"

"Just take the ring back. Get the money."

"I can't take it back."

"Why not?"

"I got it from a guy who …"

"This is a stolen ring? You spent our savings on a stolen ring?" The airless room grew smaller, hotter.

"Got a bigger one that way. Better deal."

"How could you? Our apartment money. Our whole savings."

"Our savings? That money was mine, Ivy. Mine. For some asinine, idiotic reason, I wanted to buy you, my woman, something special for your nineteenth birthday."

Mac dumped the spaghetti and cried, waving the aluminum container so hard it rattled.

"You wanted, you wanted. Are you some kind of loser? Even on my birthday you don't think about what I want? What Mac needs." She bent over the baby, prying the container from his fingers.

His arm arced back. She watched his fist travel toward her face in slow motion. She stepped out of range, falling onto the bed and Mac's spaghetti. Gil's fist swooped past Mac whimpering on her chest, and brushed her cheek. No sound of bones crunching. No loose teeth. She'd bitten her tongue, that was all. She swallowed the blood, thick and salty.

Ivy rolled over, shielding Mac, burrowing her face against his little shoulder and sticky neck. He'd crawled toward danger instead of away, thinking she could save him, fix things. Gil gripped her arm, hard.

"Ivy, I'm sorry." Gil relaxed his fingers, voice tight. "I'm sorry. You should know better than to call me a loser. Anyway, I didn't hurt you." His short laugh didn't cover the sob underneath. "You've got sauce and spaghetti all over the back of your shirt. Change and we'll go out. Shoot some pool. Mac. Mackie, baby." Gil's breath burned hot on her neck as he peered at Mac. "Daddy was only fooling. I didn't mean it. Come on, little guy." He pushed at Ivy's shoulder trying to see Mac's face. "Daddy's sorry."

You're a sorry loser, Ivy thought. Still hugging Mac, she worked the ring off her finger. "Maybe you can sell this. Take it."

"I will," he said. "That's what I'll do. I'll sell it and we can still get an apartment. I didn't know you wanted one so bad."

"How could you not know? Since I moved in here, that's all I've talked about. Don't you ever listen?"

"I listened, Ivy, I'm listening now. I'll sell it. I'll get the money." He stroked her hair and peeled strands of spaghetti from her back.

Mac whimpered against her chest. He sucked his fingers and tweedled his hair. Ivy wished she could shrink inward, hide way inside. Bryan could. Lots of people could, but not her, never her. Gil wrapped his arms around them both.

"What do you say, honey? Give me the baby. Change your clothes. We'll go out. To Curly's. I'll even let you win."

He could hurt me, Ivy reminded herself. He could hurt Mac.

"Put the ring back on," Gil said. "At least for tonight. For your birthday. Show all the guys down there what I got for you. Let it shine against that pool cue."

"Keep it," Ivy said. She wriggled out from under him. He flipped over on his back, arms behind his head. She dropped the ring on the bed.

"You don't understand," he said to the ceiling. "You're my woman. Plain and simple. God's truth. Accept it, baby." He lowered his voice. "Remember how it feels when we're making love. We fit together, you and me. We should never be apart. You have to see that." He sat up, reaching for her.

Ivy leaped from the bed. Mac sobbed. She grabbed the diaper bag and her pool cue. "I don't see it that way."

Clutching Mac, she slipped out the door, leaving the stroller, her clothes, Mac's clothes. She had to stop running. Every time she ran she lost something.

"Ivy, get back here," Gil hollered.

She ran down the hall, Mac wailing.

"Get your ass back here, where you belong!" Gil's footsteps clomped behind her.

"I love you, you stupid bitch!"

Outside, on the street, with witnesses, she'd be safe. He wouldn't hurt her in public, not with jail still fresh in his mind. She only had to make it down the stairs. Why had she moved in with him? Why had she ever thought it could work? Now that he knew Mac was his son, she would never be free of him. She made it downstairs without stumbling.

"Ivy," he bellowed.

She hesitated in front of the building. Which way to go? Gil burst onto the sidewalk.

"Ivy, just listen, please." He fell to his knees in front of her, his face pleading. Mac touched his hair. Ivy held the baby tighter as if she could pull him in through her skin. "I'll sell the ring. I'll get the money. I'll get you an apartment. Come on, Ivy. Give me a chance. One more chance."

Cars passed. People stared.

"No," she whispered. "No. No. No. No." Each time she said it the sound came from deeper down until she was shouting. Mac cried harder.

"No more chances. I gave you more than I ever should have." She stepped back, bruising her elbow on a parking meter. "Stay away from me."

"You can't keep me from my son."

"You stay away from both of us. We don't need anything from you." Ivy stared unflinching. "I mean it." She'd dropped the pool cue and the diaper bag. Gil jumped up, kicking them into the gutter.

"You can't do this." He grabbed her arms and shook her. "You can't just throw me away like a piece of trash."

Ivy tried to protect Mac's head by curving her body around him while Gil tugged at her folded arms.

A truck screeched to a stop at the curb across the street. Neal's truck. Over Gil's shoulder Ivy watched Neal leap from the cab and race toward her. A car swerved around him and honked. Colors sharpened and a hectic pounding filled her ears. Neal looked like a cartoon character, but he'd almost been hit by a real car, and he waved a real wrench in his hand.

Ivy screamed and Gil released her. He turned, saw Neal with arm raised, and lunged. Ivy would've tried to stop him, but her arms were full with Mac. Neal slammed the wrench into Gil's shoulder. Gil knocked Neal into the street. The wrench flew out of Neal's grip and clanked against the hubcap of a parked car.

A small crowd gathered. Neal, glasses askew, lay in the street, breath knocked out of him. Gil clutched his shoulder but bounced on the balls of his feet like a boxer. "Mind your business, you old fuck," he said.

Two men from the furniture store made a barricade of their bodies in front of Gil. They didn't touch him though. Another man helped Neal to his feet. A police car sped up, blue lights flashing and parked against traffic, near Ivy. Mac's sobs subsided as he sucked on a fold of her shirt sleeve.

Two cops jumped from the car. "What's the trouble, here?" asked the younger one. Ivy knew him from the pool hall, Mike Kelly.

"This old guy tried to bash my skull in with a wrench," Gil hollered. "I had to defend myself."

"Mr. Richards?" said Mike, and Ivy knew he'd had Neal for shop in high school. "Is that true?"

Neal pushed at one side of his glasses with a finger, trying to get them to sit right on his face. "This man was abusing my … stepdaughter. I had to do something."

Ivy felt a swelling in her throat. She loved Neal. He looked ridiculous in his cockeyed glasses, but he hadn't even stopped to look when he crossed the street to help her.

The older policeman hovered near Gil. He seemed ready to twist Gil's arms behind his back and handcuff him. Ivy looked away.

"Baby, tell them, we're getting married. Tell this guy to leave you alone."

Mac stared at the lights on the police car and gripped her shirt.

Neal spoke softly to Mike Kelly. Together they retrieved the wrench. Mike nodded. Gil's voice kept on, "I love her. Ivy, I love you. Everyone just go. Don't you have your own wives and kids waiting for you?"

"He's threatening me," Ivy said to the older cop. "I'm trying to go home with my son."

"This is her home," Gil waved toward the dirty glass door.

Ivy looked into the officer's concerned brown eyes. She'd stopped thinking of policemen as her friends in fifth grade when one caught her exploding cans of soda against the wall of her school and lectured her all the way home, yet here she was confiding in one.

"My stepfather came to get me," she said. The cop escorted her over to Neal and Mike Kelly.

Gil was fuming. She could hear his breath.

Ivy concentrated on Mike Kelly's badge. All her life Carol had given her names like Miss High-and-Mighty, Miss Know-It-All, Miss I-Don't-Need-Any-Help-From-Anybody. Now she'd be showing up with no money, no hope. It had been bad enough last time. If she had an apartment, everything would be different.

"I could arrest you," the older cop warned Gil. "If you threaten or hurt her again, I will. Stay away from her, from her house. If I were you, I'd think about leaving town. Make a fresh start somewhere else. We all know you around here."

"You don't know me," Gil took a step back.

Ivy pointed to her pool cue and diaper bag in the gutter and the older cop retrieved them. "Take her and the baby home, Mr. Richards," Mike Kelly said. "We'll take care of this guy. Show's over, people." The spectators obliged and began to drift away.

"No car seat. Sorry," Neal said when they were in the truck. "You okay?"

Outside, Gil was arguing with the cops. It was hot in the cab, but Neal and Ivy rolled up their windows at the same time. Neal started the truck. Gil shouted at them.

They drove a few blocks; even Mac was silent.

"Some birthday," Neal said. "Your mother'll be glad to see you."

"Will she?" Ivy asked. Mac chewed on the seat belt crossing her chest. It was strangling her.

"Yeah." Neal swallowed. "I didn't just happen to be driving by, you know. Drove back and forth a couple of times, hoping to find you. To see if you wanted a birthday party. Or at least cake. Nothing fancy."

When she didn't answer, he went on. "Didn't expect a scene like that though. Listen to me. You've got to take this seriously. Guys like him—they're dangerous. Don't let him near you. Mike was telling me a lot of women, they take restraining orders and then talk to the guys when they call or come over. Get a restraining order, then don't have anything to do with him. Everyone knows he's bad news."

Ivy, heart racing, shifted Mac on her shoulder. "I'm not an idiot," she said, voice steady.

"I'm not saying you are," Neal said, gripping the wheel. "It's just …"

"We're almost home," Ivy said. Tears threatened to fall. "Can we not talk now?"

Neal let out a loud breath, and turned into the driveway. He strode up the walk ahead of her, probably to warn her mother.

Mac squirmed. Ivy held him tight and followed Neal. "Well, Mac, here we are again," she whispered.

Late summer afternoon light. Long shadows. Cooling asphalt. She stepped over the hump the elm tree roots had made in the walk. Miss I-Admit-I-Need-Help-Or-I'll-Have-To-Leave-Your-Grandson-On-Your-Doorstep. Neal was already inside. Bryan appeared in the open door.

"What the hell!" His voice made Mac grin. "Ivy, happy birthday. I was just thinking about you. Wondering what you were doing …" She handed him the baby. "What happened?"

Tears slid down her face. She didn't want to cry. Not in front of her mother or Neal. "Mom home yet?" she whispered.

Bryan nodded his head. "Yeah, Neal's talking to her in the kitchen."

The living room smelled like home. "Play with the baby," she managed to say. "I need a shower."

Mac patted Bryan's face, bouncing in his arms. They sat on the floor. "Ivy," Bryan asked. "What happened?"

"Don't ask me, please. I'm okay." His eyes bored into her. "I'm okay. Stop looking at me like that."

"He hurt you, didn't he?"

"He didn't."

"He better not," Bryan said. "I'll kill him."

"I left him," Ivy said. "If Mom will let us stay here, I'm back. Until I can figure out what to do next. Now, I really need a shower." She headed toward the stairs. She could stand in her mother's gleaming white bathtub without smelling piss and mold.

Mac started to cry.

"He's not used to me anymore," Bryan said.

She had to be alone to think. She'd take a bath. Stretch out and soak in cool, clean water. No one could care for a baby without help. No one. It was too hard.

She ran water until the tub almost overflowed and sank into it. Her nineteen year old body, old and tired, used up. She closed her eyes, slid low in the tub, laid her head back, her hair floating, spreading like sea weed. She pretended she'd died. Drowned. Relief.

If she died, they'd be glad to take Mac. They'd be sorry. Gil would be sorry. She slipped lower, submerging her face and thought more about being dead while listening to the amplified sounds of her breath and her pulse. Living might be bearable surrounded by water. After a long time, muscles relaxed, dirt and sweat and spaghetti sauce rinsed from her skin, she lifted her head and smelled chocolate. She heard her mother, Neal, and Bryan. Mac seemed quiet. She got out and opened the bathroom door a crack.

"What makes her think she can come and go like this?" Carol's voice shot up the stairs. "It's not good for Mac."

"It's not good for anyone," Bryan said.

"And it's hot to be baking," Carol complained. "You could have run to the store …"

"Shh, Carol, I told you—"

"You've told me a lot of things," Carol's voice was sharp. "Usually I listen. Usually you're right."

"If you were there …" Neal hesitated.

"Did you really go at him with a wrench?" Bryan asked.

They must be talking in the living room. Ivy could hear every word.

"It's not something I'm proud of, Bryan." Neal's voice was a strange combination of weariness and a trace of something else. Pride.

"You should have killed him," Carol said.

"Don't say that," said Neal.

"Besides if you did, there would be all kinds of trouble," said Bryan.

Ivy remembered Neal crumpled on the ground. He'd barely hurt Gil. If the cops hadn't come, Neal was the one who might have been seriously injured. Or Ivy herself.

"We've got plenty of trouble with him alive," Carol said. "I don't want him anywhere near here. Now that Ivy's back he'll show up sniffing around, whining, like a stray animal."

Ivy slammed the door to let them know she'd been listening and leaned against the sink, towel wrapped tight around her. She shouldn't have let Neal bring her here.

A knock on the door. "Ivy, happy birthday." Neal. Neal always saying the things her mother should have said. "You going to be done in there soon? Bryan wants to know what you want for your birthday dinner."

Answer. Just answer. She couldn't find words.

Steps on the stairs, a whispered conference. Bryan's voice. "Hey, Ivy, come on. The cake's in the oven. Neal's thinking of barbecuing."

"Okay," Ivy croaked.

"Earlier today," Neal said, "we were talking about you. Your mother was telling me about the day you were born. The hurricane warnings. The big rain. How your Dad worried about getting to the hospital."

Ivy shivered in the warm bathroom. She hadn't brought clean clothes in with her. She'd have to find some old thing in her room. When they went downstairs, she'd make a dash down the hall. And then?

A sharp rapping. Her mother said, "Ivy, other people have to use this bathroom." The doorknob rattled. "Come out."

"Hey, little guy." Ivy heard Bryan say. "Let's go make some barbecue sauce. You can help me." His footsteps clomped down the stairs.

"I'll get the fire going." Neal followed.

"Ivy, I mean it," Carol said. "Open up."

"Mom," Ivy said through the door. "Don't you care about me?"

"You're my daughter. You don't listen to anybody. When I let myself care, I go crazy, can't sleep, can't concentrate. Do you know all the mistakes you've caused at the bank? Everything was working out all right," tears filled Carol's voice, "until that monster showed up again."

"It wasn't all right," Ivy said, teeth clenched. "It wasn't all right for me."

"Well, it would have been after awhile. You're too impatient. Always have to have everything right away, right when you want it."

"You're always criticizing me," Ivy shouted.

Silence.

"Ivy, listen. You did the right thing. Coming home. Please open the door."

Ivy cracked open the door, and Carol pushed it wider. She stepped into the bathroom, still in her work clothes. She flipped down the lid of the toilet and sat, crossing her legs, studying the toe of her shoe. "All day, I've been thinking about you. My first child. The day everything changed, forever. I remember your little toes, everything new and perfect and how hard I worked to keep you safe. And how many times I realized I wasn't the parent I'd imagined I'd be, the parent I hoped I'd be."

Ivy adjusted her towel. She wasn't the mother she hoped to be either. She didn't even have a house for her son or a father or a job so she could buy him what he needed. She rubbed the row of bruises on her upper arm, tears in her throat, chest—her whole body full of tears. If she began to cry, she wouldn't stop until the room flooded and nothing remained inside her. Nothing.

"Please come downstairs," Carol said. "Please. I'm glad you came home. You did the right thing."

"I didn't know what else to do," Ivy whispered.

"You did the right thing," Carol repeated.

"My life is a mess," Ivy said.

"It'll work out," Carol stood beside Ivy. They looked at themselves in the mirror. "If you can keep yourself away from Gil."

Ivy bristled. Before she could snap back at her mother, Carol put an arm around her bare shoulders. "All a person can do is try," she said. "And too much of the time our best isn't good enough. I'm trying, Ivy. Please."

"I need to get dressed," Ivy said. "You didn't get rid of my clothes, did you?"

"Your room is the way you left it," Carol said.

The next morning Bryan wiped globs of oatmeal from between Mac's fingers. Ivy hadn't come downstairs yet, but you could tell she was back. The house felt full, satisfied full, like a stomach after a meal you were really hungry for.

What was left of her birthday cake sat on the counter. Knowing Ivy, she'd eat it for breakfast. The party turned out all right. Martine came by, her pockets full of Chinese finger traps she won playing skiball. She'd given up saving for the goose lamp. She hadn't expected Ivy or a party but thinking fast, as she always did, she called the little tubes of woven plastic party favors and gave one to each person. They lay heaped on the counter next to the cake. Bryan handed a couple to Mac to distract him from finger-painting with the oatmeal so he could wipe the dented highchair tray. Mac threw them onto the floor and laughed.

Ivy and Carol had laughed twice together at the party. Once, when they both tried to yank their fingers from the traps, Ivy shrieking she couldn't believe she'd forgotten how to get out of them, and once when they figured out how easy it was, just relax and do the opposite of what instinct told them. Yes, the party was a success. Ivy told Martine and Bryan that she planned to take

Curly up on his offer of a job at the pool hall even though there was some question about her being underage. Carol, Neal, Ivy, and Mac all went to bed. Martine stayed to help with the dishes, but they'd used paper plates. After throwing them in the trash, she and Bryan had plenty of time to make out in the living room.

Bryan lifted Mac out of the highchair. Just thinking about Martine and his hands inside her shirt made him crazy to see her. He'd change Mac's diaper, put him in the stroller and head down to the mall. On a day as hot as this one Martine was sure to show up there soon to take advantage of the air-conditioning.

"God damn it!" Gil's voice ripped through the house followed by a pounding on the screen door's metal frame. "Ivy, I know you're in there. You can't keep me from my son." Bryan pulled Mac's sweaty body tighter.

Carol flew into the kitchen. "Didn't take long for him to show up," she whispered. "Take the baby out the back. Get out of here."

"Where's Neal?" Bryan asked.

"I want my son!" Gil bellowed.

"Go!" Carol whispered. Without looking back she headed for the front door, hollering, "Get off our porch, now. Or I'm calling the police."

Bryan didn't want to leave his mother with just a latched screen between her and Gil.

"Fuck the police!" yelled Gil.

"Neal," Carol called. "Dial 911."

So Neal was still home, unless she was bluffing.

"Ivy's left you," Carol said, voice firm. "For good. Accept it. Get on with your life."

"What life?" Gil sounded like he was crying now. Bryan felt a pang of something he couldn't identify poke through his panic, not exactly pity, but almost.

"Ivy," Gil blubbered. "I know you're in there. Talk to me. Please. Just come here and talk to me."

"Are you leaving?" Carol asked. "I promise that if you're not off this porch in three seconds, the police will be escorting you off."

Bryan hung back, ready to disappear into the kitchen. He kept a hand over Mac's mouth, but the baby didn't make any noise—as if he knew he had to be quiet. Gil stomped away. Everything had happened so quickly, but Bryan knew he didn't imagine it. If he had, his mother would've been the one holding Mac, and he, dagger in hand, would have ordered Gil off the porch.

Carol closed the wooden door over the flimsy screen, even though the day was hot. She slumped onto the stairs. "Is he gone?" Ivy called from the upstairs hall.

"For now." His mother sounded defeated as if she'd used up all her tough determination on Gil. Bryan wanted to congratulate her for getting rid of him with just words. She'd won.

"Where's Mac?" Ivy traipsed downstairs in the oversized tee shirt she slept in. Bryan wished she'd think to thank their mother. He didn't expect her to say anything to him about the birthday cake or watching Mac so she could sleep in, but their mother had just defended them all from a dangerous felon that Ivy had brought into their lives.

"Mamamama," Mac said. Bryan handed him to her.

"I woke up and he wasn't there," Ivy said. "I didn't hear anyone take him out of the crib. How could I have slept so hard?"

"You were tired," Bryan said.

Ivy held Mac and peered out the window. "I've got to go down to the pool hall and tell Curly I need that job. I have no money now. I need a job."

"You can't go now!" Carol said, exactly what Bryan was thinking. "Gil's out there. And mad. And high on who knows what. It's not like Curly's going to give the job to someone else if you wait a day or two to tell him."

"I can't let Gil keep me trembling in the house."

Sometimes it seemed as though his sister had an addiction to trouble.

"Listen to me for once," Carol's voice rose. "I'm not saying you should stay in the house forever. Just today, this morning. Just until we can get a restraining order or talk to the police."

"I need to go. I can't let him think I'm afraid."

"Why not? That makes no sense," said Bryan. "Why do you care what he thinks?"

"Because then he's beat me. I planned to go to Curly's today and I'm going."

"This isn't about winning and losing," Bryan said, knowing he was right, but he didn't know what it was about and wished he did. If he knew, he might be able to help her, and himself. He'd know something about life.

"Ivy, he could kill you." Carol pulled at Ivy's arm as if trying to drag her deeper into the house.

Bryan thought of the pearl handled dagger under his mattress, wondered if Gil had gotten a replacement, if he'd even need one with those fingers, long enough to wrap around Ivy's neck.

Ivy shook off Carol's hand, dumped Mac back into Bryan's arms and disappeared upstairs.

"Where is Neal?" Bryan asked.

"At school." Carol absently rubbed the baby's head. "She can't be serious."

"Should we call him?" Bryan asked.

Carol didn't answer.

Ivy came down the stairs rubber flip-flops slapping. Bryan expected her to push past them, but she stopped, and the three of them stood sweating in a little clump by the front door.

"Mom," Ivy said. "I really need to figure out what's next for me. I really want to know I have this job. I can't sit trembling in this house. Will you take me to the pool hall if we stop at the police station on the way?"

"It's the courthouse," Carol said. "I looked into it. You get the papers at the courthouse."

"Curly told me the police station."

"Ivy, I'm sure—"

"What difference does it make?" Bryan almost shouted. "They're both in the same municipal building. Sorry, Mac," he added when the baby, brow wrinkled, leaned back in Bryan's arms to study his face.

"The paperwork is simple," Carol went on. "You can do it right there."

"People say it doesn't really help." Ivy looked in the hall mirror, pulled her hair up into a pony tail, and frowned at herself.

Bryan wished she'd be more hopeful. "It's better than doing nothing," he said as Mac squirmed to get down.

Carol had already found her purse and was hunting for the keys. "Let's go," she said.

They piled into the hot car. The buckle on Mac's car seat burned Bryan's hand. He climbed in the back beside him and pressed his face to the window to watch for Gil, but the street was empty in the bright heat. His mother stared at the road ahead and held her neck so straight that even from the back seat, Bryan could tell she was a woman on a mission. Ivy fiddled with the radio, finally switching it off before Carol could tell her to stop, then started messing with the air-conditioning.

Even with all Martine's urging, Bryan had never set foot in Rivertown Billiards. His mother wouldn't have liked it if she found out he'd gone there, it could be the last straw, the thing that finally broke her for good. And he didn't want to see Ivy in the place she'd met Gil, where all the trouble started. He hated the way she bragged repeatedly about Johnny bringing her there night after night, never Bryan, who stayed home with Carol. After Ivy rediscovered the pool hall at age thirteen, until she left with Gil, Bryan continued to keep his mother company in the evening. He may have been coming home early from the park and the mall to finish homework or cook dinner, but his real purpose was to show his mom she had one good kid, one kid who loved her, chose her over a dead man. He never thought he'd be seeing the inside of Rivertown Billiards for the first time with his mother along, her jaw clenched. Maybe she was planning to drop Ivy off.

When they passed the Capital Theater, Bryan shuddered wondering if Gil was in there. Ivy craned her neck to look at her old window. "I made those blue curtains," she whispered. Carol chewed her lip. Bryan wanted to ask Ivy what else she'd left in that room.

Carol swerved into the Rivertown Billiards lot and tried not to think about the last time she'd pulled in, could it be fifteen years ago, driving the neighbor's car, Bryan fighting to breathe. She recognized the only other car—Curly's rusting red Fiesta parked near the door of the shabby bar. Gil didn't drive though. He could be inside, waiting. The thought of the papers on file at the courthouse gave small comfort.

"Okay, thanks." Ivy opened her door before Carol had even come to a complete stop. "I'll be right back."

"Wait just a minute." Carol stopped short of adding 'young lady.' She tucked her keys in the side pocket of her purse and climbed out of the car, straightening her wrinkled, sweat-soaked skirt.

Ivy squinted at her across the roof of the car, "You're not coming, are you?"

"Thought we would," Carol said. "That way I can give you a ride home. It's hot. You can't expect us to wait here."

Bryan already had Mac unbuckled and out of the car.

"Go home," Ivy said. "You don't have to wait."

"We've come all this way." As soon as Carol said the words, she wondered what she meant. It wasn't more than three miles between her house and the pool hall. Ivy nodded and shrugged as if Carol's words had made sense and headed toward the door, scuffing up little dust storms with every step. Bryan, Mac and Carol followed behind her.

Before her eyes got used to the dimness, Carol heard a "Look who's here!" Not Gil, Curly. Curly, who avoided her window at the bank and crossed the street if he saw her coming. She'd seen him many times over the years but they never spoke. She'd forgotten the sound of his voice. He took Ivy's hand.

"I came to ask about that job," Ivy said. "I want it."

The air conditioner, an old window unit behind the bar, clunked and whirred but cooled the air effectively enough. The smell of spilled beer and stale smoke brought back bad memories. Three empty pool tables waited on the far side of the room, pool cues hanging along the wall behind them. Little tables with chairs turned over on top were scattered across the floor. No sign of Gil or anyone else.

Curly stared at Carol. Carol stared back. Ivy introduced everyone.

"I know your mother," Curly said, dropping Ivy's hand. "As beautiful as ever. It's been quite awhile since we've talked."

"John's funeral." The words slipped through Carol's tight lips.

"I know," Curly said. "How long ago was that?" He didn't wait for an answer, turned toward Bryan. "The last time I spoke to your mother." He rubbed his head again. "I remember the first time I saw her, too. Do you remember, Carol, when you came in all big eyes, and mussed up blonde hair, a Marilyn Monroe look alike, all upset about a flat tire? Any guy in here would have paid to help you, but John was quickest and the rest is history."

"Ancient history," said Carol. So ancient she wondered why it still hurt so much, why she couldn't muster up even a polite smile.

"And this is the boy. You look just like your Dad. Don't you think so, Carol? Spittin' image of Wild John MacKenzie."

Before Carol could respond, Ivy snorted. "Wild Bryan," she mouthed. Bryan flashed Ivy a look of hatred. At home she would have reprimanded Ivy for teasing, but the familiar strangeness of Curly and the pool hall paralyzed her.

Curly cooed and tickled Mac, making him giggle and thrash around in Bryan's arms.

"I know you didn't stop by just to say hello," Curly said. "Though I wish you had."

She might as well get right to business. "Ivy says you've offered her a job."

"Mom," Ivy said. "I can handle this. I told you not to come. I can take care of myself."

Carol chose not to contradict her.

Curly planted his hands on his hips. His Hawaiian shirt stretched across his big belly. "She's a natural, Carol. You should see this girl shoot pool. Good for business."

"So she'd be playing pool?" Carol had envisioned her daughter becoming a teacher or a dental hygienist or a nurse, at least until Ivy had changed her expectations by running away and coming home pregnant. "Doesn't she have to be twenty-one?"

"Waitressing mostly, but when it's slow …" Curly smiled at Ivy. "Yeah, she'd be playing some pool. And don't worry about the age thing. This is a small town, people help each other out. I do someone a favor, they do a favor for me."

"How's it good for business? So lowlifes like Gil Thompson can stand there and gawk at her, take her home afterward. Nothing good has come of anyone in my family hanging around your place." Carol folded her arms over her chest and challenged Curly with her raised chin.

"Don't blame Gil on him!" Ivy said. "He tried to stop me that first night. He offered me a ride." She looked at the floor, face red. Curly put a hand on Ivy's shoulder, his eyes sad and full of real caring. Carol remembered Dr. Cardullo and wondered why it was so easy for other people to love Ivy and so hard for her.

"Carol," Curly said. "You've been mad at me for years. Don't take it out on Ivy—an old grudge you can't shake off. Don't let it ruin her life."

"I'd hardly call keeping a girl from hustling in a pool hall ruining her life." Carol fussed with her skirt again.

Mac squirmed and whimpered. Bryan patted his back.

"Here, little buddy," Curly held out his arms. Mac lunged toward him. Curly carried him over to the bar and fed him a handful of goldfish crackers. "Anybody want a drink?" he asked.

Carol glared. He knew how she felt about drinking. "Water," she said.

Bryan wandered toward the jukebox and back. Ivy began taking chairs down, arranging them at the tables.

Curly sat Mac in Carol's lap on a barstool, hurried behind the bar, turned on the tap, scooped crushed ice into a glass. "No ice," Carol said, her words, clear, crisp, easily heard over the running water.

He dumped the ice. "Why don't you kids shoot a game while your mother and I work this out?"

"It's none of her business," Ivy complained, but she set down the chair she was holding and turned toward the wall rack. Bryan followed her. Carol lined up goldfish crackers along the bar for Mac. Curly sat beside her.

Ivy racked up the balls with a huge clatter.

Curly leaned toward Carol and said nothing.

"Break if you want." Ivy's voice rang out. Bryan muttered something in response.

Curly waited. Carol wanted to slap the look of concern off his face. He'd never been concerned as long as Johnny spent their grocery money, money for vacations they never took, money for house repairs, on drinks at the pool hall. She'd worked hard to make a new life, yet here she sat on a barstool, holding her grandson.

Words spewed from her mouth. "The last night he had here on this earth he spent drinking with you. Sober for two years, remember? Until then. He comes home just before daylight, draped over your shoulder. Do you remember the things you said to me? Because I do. I wasn't drunk. Exhausted, from waiting up all night. Furious. But sober. I remember every word you said." She took a sip of water and tried to calm herself down. She kissed Mac's head and rearranged his diminished row of goldfish crackers. Behind her she heard Bryan whoop. He must have sunk a ball.

Curly tried to hand her a napkin while staring at his shoes. For a moment she wondered why, then realized she was crying. Mac snatched the napkin, stuffed it in his mouth. Glad for the distraction, she tried to remove it, but the paper dissolved into wet shreds, and she wasn't sure she got it all. Curly sat too close, his words, his very being, reminding her of Johnny, of times before children when they had their moments of fun and times after, when Johnny disappointed her, enraged her, over and over again.

"You shouldn't have said those things," Carol said finally.

Curly's fingers drummed against the bar. "I tried to apologize at the funeral. Remember that?"

Carol moved her water out of Mac's reach.

"It wasn't so bad," Curly said. "If he hadn't died the next day, it wouldn't have been so bad. His dying made it matter, made it a bigger deal than it was."

"That's your opinion," Carol breathed. "He hadn't drunk in two years. Why then? You and your raising hell. Crawling home at four in the morning. Off to work three hours later. Still drunk, or at least hungover. No one can tell me for sure that wasn't why he died. So even if you hadn't said those things, I hold you responsible, partially responsible, for his death. I should have told Ivy as soon as she started pestering to hang around here. If it weren't for this guy you think is so great, your father might still be alive."

"Are you talking to me?" Ivy inserted herself between Carol and Curly, or tried to. Bryan stood behind her.

"If, if, if …" Curly's eyes bulged. "You can blame me for the things I said, but I won't accept any blame for his death. That had no more to do with me than it did with you or anybody else. If I didn't care about your daughter, his daughter, so much, I'd throw you out of here for saying that."

"You won't have to throw me out," Carol said. "Because I'm leaving. And I forbid Ivy to ever set foot in this hellhole again."

"Mom!" Ivy grabbed her arm. "Stop. Stop it. Please."

Mac started to wail, wet clumps of napkin stuck to lips and tongue.

"They hung out here every night when you were small," Carol turned to Ivy, ignoring Mac's cries. "Every god damn night. I was home."

Carol hardly noticed when Bryan lifted Mac out of her arms. He stopped screaming and sucked his fingers.

"John said he asked you to come," Curly said. "I told him to ask you. Everybody wanted to know you better, the beautiful blonde from Pennsylvania. We'd let people ahead of us in line at the bank to end up at your window. We couldn't believe John married someone from out of town, someone so beautiful and smart. And we were glad for him after all he'd been through, he deserved some luck."

"That's not what you said to me," Carol said. "And why would I want to sit pregnant in a smoky bar, watching a bunch of guys get drunk, when I had to work the next day. And then I had kids."

"He brought Ivy. I remember …"

"That's right, he brought Ivy. And left me home sitting in the steamy bathroom, with a coughing, wheezing baby who couldn't breathe no matter what I did."

"Listen to yourself," Curly's voice cracked. "You can't seriously blame me for—"

"I had no car to bring Bryan to the emergency room because it was parked here in your lot."

Curly cleared his throat. "That's why he finally quit, don't you think? Ivy was like a nagging little wife or mother herself at what? Four years old? She used to tell him to go home, that Bryan was sick. That you needed him. I'll never forget the night John packed up his pool cue in the middle of a game, they left and that was the last time he came in here. Until …"

"Come on, Curly," Ivy interrupted. "The things you said the night before Dad died. What were they?"

Carol realized the kids had heard everything, even while at the pool table, even over the sound of the air conditioner.

"You shouldn't have made him quit, Carol," said Curly. "He was a damn good player. A person's got to have some fun. Chance to do what they love most."

"He had fun at home," Carol said, doubting herself, but saying it anyway. "Or don't you believe that? You think I had the power to make him quit? He knew he was drinking too much. And for him the pool, the drinking, couldn't have one without the other."

"I've given up the stuff myself," said Curly. "All that was years ago. I never made John come in here. I didn't make him drink. You can't make a person quit drinking, then you can't make him drink either." He sounded as unsure as she felt. He searched her face, as if waiting for her to agree. "And I am sorry for what I said. Maybe I was jealous. John had everything I thought I wanted."

"You said I'd ruined his life," Carol said. "Remember? You said if he'd stayed with Lisa he'd still have his motorcycle, his buddies, his game. You called me the blonde bitch, the ice queen with her nose in the air." The tightness in her stomach loosened. She'd spent years trying to be a good mother, trying not to bad mouth Johnny, and look where it had gotten her. "And Johnny laughed. Remember that? You got him to the couch, took off his shoes, the whole time calling me names, and he laughed. 'Lisa,' he said. 'Lisa knew how to have a good time.' Then he passes out. Sneaks off to work the next morning without speaking to me. I don't even know how he got himself up."

"I set the alarm on his watch," Curly said.

"What a good friend." Sarcasm was surprisingly satisfying. Ivy's mouth hung open. Bryan looked pained. Carol kept talking. She'd waited years to say all this, without realizing it. Maybe the whole reason for Ivy playing pool was so Carol could follow her here and have it out with Curly. "His last words to me—'Lisa knew how to have a good time.' I prayed he'd get better, sat beside him all those weeks. If he had to die, why couldn't he have gained consciousness long enough to say something else, to …" Carol laid her head on the bar. No one spoke.

Carol didn't know what happened to people when they died. She didn't think Johnny was watching. Yet, she felt his presence on the bar stool beside her, sensed his hand on her back encouraging her to let go of her resentment. *Don't take it out on my old friend,* she heard him say. *I'm the one who was a jerk that time and I'm sorry. Forgive him. Forgive me. Life is good.* His touch disappeared.

"Water please," she said finally, lifting her head. It had never felt so heavy.

Curly and Ivy bumped into each other in their hurry to refill her glass.

"I don't want Ivy drinking in here," she said, straightening her hair.

"You tell her, Ivy," Curly said. He'd gotten to the faucet first. Ivy wet a paper towel for Carol's face. "Have you ever drunk alcohol in here?"

"He won't let me."

"Keep it that way." Carol took a long drink and sighed. "What are you going to do when Gil Thompson comes looking for her?" She poked at Curly's chest, the tip of her fingernail clicking against the button of his shirt. "And he will."

Curly lifted Carol's chin. She let her chin rest as if balanced on the very tip of his finger.

"I'll take care of it," he said looking straight into her unblinking eyes as if Ivy and Mac and Bryan weren't even there. "I already told Ivy. If she needs help, I'm here. There's no place in Rivertown she's safer."

Carol wondered if Curly kept a gun under the bar and surprised herself by hoping he did.

The door to the pool hall swung open, letting in a flash of sun and blast of heat, and Ivy jumped, expecting to see Gil lunging toward her. Leo Leveaux, in silhouette looked a lot like him, tall, slouching and muscular. His friend Miguel Rodriguez slipped in behind him.

Heart racing, but relieved, Ivy waved, and the two men waved back before sauntering toward the pool table and choosing sticks.

"It's only a matter of time before Gil comes here," Carol said.

"Okay, Mom." Ivy wished her mother would leave and take all her dire predictions with her. "Curly said he can handle it. And I won't even talk to Gil. Not one word."

"I have reason to be worried about you."

Ivy couldn't argue with that. "If he even steps inside this door I'll call the cops," she said. "I promise."

"Hey, Ivy," called Leo. "You want to play winner?"

"Maybe." Mac's diaper needed changing, and Ivy had left the diaper bag in the car.

Carol wrinkled her nose. Bryan held Mac out in front of him; the baby's legs dangled. Ivy grabbed Mac and held him close, stinky diaper and all. "After I change this guy. That is, if someone can hold him." She scanned Carol, Curly, and Bryan's faces for a volunteer.

"We saw your boyfriend," Leo said tapping the top of his pool cue against the floor.

"Careful with the stick," said Curly.

Miguel stood beside Leo and made faces at Mac.

"He was passed out on the steps of Saint Anthony's in a puddle of his own piss. The cops picked him up."

"He's not my boyfriend," said Ivy lightly. "And speaking of piss I really have to change this baby." A wet spot marked her shirt. "I'll be right back." No one offered to hold Mac so she brought him with her into the burning sun to the car. She could have asked someone to get the bag, but hadn't thought of it. They were probably all talking about her right now or about Gil—her baby's father a passed out drunk, in and out of jail. Mac would be teased about it in school. Kids were so mean. Better to hear stories about Gil assaulting his boss after being humiliated one too many times or making a threatening scene in front of Carol at the bank, wanting to see Ivy, his agony and need for her echoing off the high ceiling for everyone to hear.

She decided against changing Mac on the seat of the car, too hot. Gil had never changed Mac's diaper. Ivy tucked her nose against his sweaty neck and wondered what he'd remember of Gil, the man who walked in the world with the exact same bump in the exact same place on his ear.

People would have said Ivy grew up without a father, but her memories sometimes seemed more real than a living father would have been. If Johnny had been there every day he would have faded into the background the way her mother did. She wouldn't have thought about him all the time. She wouldn't have listened to his actual words the way she attended to his imagined criticism and advice. In the dusty glare of the Rivertown Billiards parking lot she could almost see him approaching, pool cue in its case under his arm, mischief in his eyes, ready to challenge her to a game. She'd hand him his grandson and the diaper bag, too.

Johnny MacKenzie would have understood Ivy's love of the game. To her mother it was only a waste of time and worse. But shooting pool conquered time, made it irrelevant. The only other thing Ivy knew that could do that was sex. Pool didn't lead you to love the wrong men—challenge them, beat them, lose to them, but not love them. Pool didn't get you pregnant.

Back inside, Leo and Miguel had just a few balls left on the table. Curly and Carol talked in low tones at the bar. Bryan hovered over the now plugged in jukebox. Ivy lay Mac on a table. He refused to stay on his back, twisting around, making her job not impossible, but a lot harder than it needed to be. She removed the heavy wet diaper, folded and taped it into a soggy ball, and maneuvered the dry one through his legs, all while trying to keep him from wriggling off the table. No one seemed to notice she could use some help. Mothers should know how to diaper their kids. Ivy tugged at his foot and flipped him onto his back. Outraged he began to wail and kicked the diaper bag to the floor.

Bryan must have heard it fall. Maybe he thought it was Mac; he was there to pick it up the moment it touched the floor. He made faces at Mac and tickled his belly while Ivy taped the diaper closed. He scooped Mac up and brought him over to the jukebox to admire the flashing lights. Ivy threw the wet diaper in the trash can behind the bar. It made a final sounding thud when it hit the bottom.

"You ready to play me?" Miguel called. "I beat his sorry ass."

"We can take Mac home," Bryan said. "Right, Mom? But don't stay too long. And make sure you get a ride home with someone."

Ivy, thankful for the babysitting, stopped herself from teasing him for acting the worried parent.

"We'll go. But since we're here …" Carol twirled around on her stool and leaned back, elbows on the bar. "We might as well watch one game."

Curly beamed, grabbed her glass and refilled it with water. Ivy's knees quivered. Now that the moment she'd barely dared to hope for had arrived, when her mother watched her do what she did best, she didn't want her need for approval to start screaming and mess things up. She sneaked a glance at Carol as she positioned the cue ball. She wanted to show what she could do and make her mother understand. She saw Carol bounce a little on the stool and give a soft clap when she sunk three balls in one shot, then she tried to forget people were watching. Ivy concentrated on the slide of the stick, the click of the balls and their changing position on the expanse of green felt, but every one she sunk was to show her mother. See, Mom, see how good I am at this.

"Your game," Miguel said. He didn't sound disappointed. "Another? Give me a chance to redeem myself?"

"We'd better be getting home," Carol said. She sounded like she always did. Ivy's victory hadn't impressed her, hadn't meant anything. "Neal will be wondering what happened to us. Go ahead and stay awhile, Ivy. We can take Mac. But I don't want you walking home alone."

"Someone will give me a ride," said Ivy. 'Don't you think I'm good?' she wanted to ask.

"Okay then, Bryan?" Carol said, Mac on her hip.

"Before you go," Curly said digging in his pocket. "I want to give you this." He handed something small and silver to Bryan. "It was your Dad's. Actually it was mine, but I gave it to him for luck when I found out he was going to Nam. And it must have worked 'cause he made it back." He laid the object, smaller than a quarter, on her brother's open palm and folded Bryan's fingers over it as if wrapping a gift.

Ivy kissed Mac on the nose to hide her dismay—Curly giving things to Bryan, her mother walking off without a word of praise. While Mac grabbed at her cheeks, she felt her mother drop a kiss onto the crown of her head. Ivy glanced up. Her mother's face looked softer, kinder, as if all these years she'd been hiding behind layers of bright makeup, meticulously applied.

"Be careful," Carol said to Ivy. Then she added, "Have fun."

"Don't be a stranger here, Carol," Curly said. "For you, water's always on the house."

"Thanks," Ivy managed to say staring down at her shirt. The wet spot had dried, leaving a faint stain. Loud feelings clashed in her chest as she watched her mother and brother and son move toward the sunlit door where they paused for a moment like small black cutouts and waved.

Miguel racked up the balls.

Bryan studied the silver charm, the head of a bull dog. Questions about his father filled his throat. If he weren't so careful, so worried about upsetting people, and was more like Ivy, he'd ask them. "Why a bulldog?" It did explain the nickname he'd puzzled over in the letters.

Curly's jukebox sucked. No blues. No rock. Just country, country, and more country. Bryan was surprised his father would have hung out in a place with music like that. Watching his mother watch Ivy play, he'd wanted Miguel to win and felt like a creep for thinking that way. He crunched across the gravel after his mother, Mac staring back at him over her shoulder.

"Why didn't you tell me Dad fixed your flat tire?" Bryan said suddenly. "Why didn't you ever tell me he was an alcoholic?"

Carol stopped short, eyes flashing. "Does it matter?"

"Yes!" He was shouting. He didn't want to scare Mac, but he couldn't stop himself. "It matters! It all matters!" The parking lot spread around them, hot and deserted.

His mother touched his arm. "I didn't know," she said. "You never asked. Ivy—"

"I didn't want to upset you," Bryan said, crying now. "You were always mad at Ivy. Or sad. I'd plan to ask something and it would never be the right time. You'd be tired. Ivy left and I couldn't ask then. And then Neal … I like Neal. I didn't want to … didn't think it would be right to talk about Dad when Neal was trying to get used to us and us to him and then I guess I just made myself forget I had questions. I found his letters and I tried to tell myself they were enough."

"Oh, Bryan," Carol said, resting a cool hand against his cheek. "Get in the car. Your Dad and I were so young when we got together. Neither of us knew what we were doing. Vietnam had messed him up. His mother spoiled him rotten. I think half the reason I married him was so she could spoil me too, and then she died. Your Dad was devastated." She reached for the door handle then seemed to change her mind. "So, you found letters? Neal mentioned something about that. I found them too, after he died. I was disappointed at how little they told me. Except one. I kept my favorite in my wallet. Here, take the baby. I'll show you." She opened her purse and from a zippered compartment of her wallet extracted a square of paper, two sheets worn at the folded places. She opened it and began to read aloud. Bryan leaned close to follow along, jiggling Mac to keep him quiet. The writing was careful and neat.

Dear Ma,

Only seventy-two days left and they've reassigned me to a job at the rear. Guess I earned it—all those days, weeks, months of walking point—not a man in our platoon would begrudge me this luck. I don't even want to tell you what my job is, but I have to so you'll understand where I'm coming from when I tell you I've been thinking about my life in some strange ways. Out in the boonies we had time to think but there it was all about survival, watching out for ourselves and each other. It was the job—keeping myself and my buddies safe. And you know me I also had to be the one man entertainment committee. Lay on the bull shit, Bull Dog, they'd say, and I'd tell them some story about something or other, like the time Joey lit a shot of wild turkey on fire and spilled it down his shirt and Curly sprayed him with the soda water nozzle. Course I embellish it a lot. I think of Joey every day out here now I know first hand what he went through. Anyway, part of my job, you don't have to tell anyone, in fact I wish you wouldn't—I take the wedding rings off the dead guys, the corpses and send them with any other personal items to their wives. It's a job that makes you think. If I get married, and I hope I do, I'll be looking at my ring thinking about dead guys.

Carol paused. "He was full of secrets. I have no idea if, at our wedding, he really thought about this or not. There was a lot about him I never knew. A lot I can't tell you 'cause I just don't know."

Sometimes you have to cut the rings off. Sometimes they slide. Sometimes the fingers are separate from the hands. I've seen a lot of sights I wish I never saw. When I get home I'm going to find me a bulldog puppy 'cause I give a lot of the credit I'm still alive——knock on wood——to Curly's good luck charm he laid on me the night before I left.

Bryan kept his fist closed around the charm while Mac tugged at his thumb.

That little silver dog has spent the war against my sweaty, filthy, bug bitten hide. I wanted to make a difference, that's why I came here, and I guess I did, but whether it's a good difference or a bad difference I don't know. If I'm ever lucky enough to have a son I'd tell him don't worry about being a hero, just be a regular good guy, love your mother——

"That's really what it says, Bryan, I didn't put that in." She grinned.

love your friends. If I'm ever lucky enough to have a wife I hope she never has to open a box with my wedding ring in it. Just bury me with the sucker on my finger. When I'm back home I want one of your pot roasts with those browned potatoes and onions, and my chances are better, knock on wood, of really coming home now that I'm smack in the center of this huge base. It's like a city. We got everything here. You know, it pisses me off all the guys playing with paper——filing, stamping, typing, signing, while us real soldiers are out there humping the boonies, but at least I know I wasn't a coward. I did what I came to do. I can call myself a man and sleep at night, unless the nightmares wake me up. Breathe easy, Mom, I'll be home to mow the lawn this summer. Love, Johnny

All it took was the slightest movement of her fingers and the letter folded itself back into its tiny wallet sized square. "I like how he was thinking of us and he didn't even know us yet," she said.

Bryan noticed Johnny hadn't written anything about a daughter, but he stopped his smug expression before it could begin to take shape. Once Johnny had known Ivy he'd loved her. Gil wouldn't dare come around if Johnny were alive. He hated remembering his father's delight at tossing Ivy into the air over and over while she laughed and screamed, because next came the more vivid memory, the one he felt in his stomach, the disgusted narrowing of his father's eyes as Bryan begged to be put down. He wondered if Johnny had loved him at all.

His mother pushed a sweat soaked lock of hair off his forehead and spoke as if she knew what he was thinking. "He loved you, Bryan. He'd be proud of you too. When you play the harmonica, you remind me of him. He loved you." Her soothing tone turned fierce. "He loved us all the best he knew how. Let's get out of this heat." She took Mac and ducked into the hot car to put him in his seat. Bryan fingered the bull dog charm in his pocket memorizing its edges.

CHAPTER 15

Between customers Carol checked her watch. The bank manager had given her permission to leave a little early this Friday afternoon. She'd have to close her window by four fifteen in order to pick Neal up at work and get him to the garage before it closed. It was the second time in two weeks that his windshield had been smashed in the teachers' parking lot. If it happened to old Mr. Hennessy who purposely humiliated students by calling them up to the board when they didn't understand the math problems or Ms. Korvac, the gym teacher who called the heavy girls names when they couldn't vault over the horse, people would have assumed students were responsible for the vandalism. But everyone agreed no student would wreck Neal's truck.

Carol scanned the line of people snaking between the velvet ropes. Mike Kelly, that cute young cop, was two away from the front. She'd wait until he was served. It was the least she could do. Whenever Mike came in he made a point of telling her Gil's whereabouts. He still had his room over the Capital Theater and worked, when he wasn't too drunk or high, washing dishes at the River Restaurant. He'd been picked up a few times for disorderly conduct. No one in the family had seen him. At least no one was admitting to it.

The tellers on either side called the next people in line and Mike was hers. She smiled at him.

"Cash this please." He handed over his paycheck. "How's it going, Mrs. Richards?"

She'd given up trying to tell him her name was still MacKenzie like her children's.

"You're my last customer. Neal needs a ride to get his truck."

"Hey." He slapped the counter. "Sorry about that. Can't believe it happened twice. You know I have a suspect."

"Gil Thompson, right?"

"Seems pretty obvious."

"I guess so." Carol counted out his money twice, once in her hand and again on the counter.

"He's the kind of guy we'd like to encourage to leave town, but nothing we've said or done has worked. Better a broken windshield than a broken head, though, right? Thanks, Mrs. Richards. Take care of yourself."

She put the 'use next window' sign up and went to the vault with her money tray. Now she was late. She checked out as quickly as she could, raced to her car feeling around in her purse for her keys as she ran, slid into the driver's seat, jabbed the key into the ignition and noticed a long crack running the length of the windshield at eye level.

"Shit!" she yelled, and pounded the steering wheel. "You bastard." She peered under and over the crack, out the side and rear windows, but saw no one, only newly shattered sideview mirrors. Breathe, she told herself. She'd drive Neal to the garage, then ride home in the truck with him, leaving her car there to be fixed. She was late.

Carefully, slouched in her seat so the crack wouldn't distract her, she pulled out of the parking lot and drove down Main Street. There, just before the turn over the bridge to the high school, on the corner by the travel agency, right near the curb, stood Gil. He was laughing with a red-headed woman—a waitress from the River Restaurant. Carol recognized the scanty uniform. She could turn the steering wheel, press the accelerator to the floor and run him down. Very tempting. She jammed her foot on the brake just to keep it off the accelerator. The car jerked to a stop in the middle of the road. Horns blared. Gil looked up, right at her, and smiled his shiny grin. If she hit him, she might injure or even kill the waitress too. But how dare he smile at her? How dare he make her afraid in her own town? How dare he smash their cars? In a fury she swung the car over to the curb beside him and parked. She leaped out and with the car as a shield, began yelling. "Don't smile at me! Admit you wrecked my car. Admit it. You owe me for this. You owe Neal. I'll make you pay."

The waitress looked bewildered. Gil sneered. "I don't owe you a thing. You don't understand. Ivy begged me to take her to Florida. Begged me. 'My mother's a bitch,' she said. Take me away. Your daughter begged me to fuck her. Yell at her, not me. We can go yell at her together. I've got some things I've been meaning to yell at her about." He made to open the door.

"Don't touch this car! Get your hands off my car!" Carol screamed, leaning into the open driver's side door to press the horn.

A police car parked behind her, no sirens or lights. A cop she didn't know with a big mustache climbed out, hand on his gun.

"All right," he barked. "What's the trouble?"

"I was standing here," said Gil quickly, "minding my own business and this woman starts accusing me. Right?" He turned to the red-haired woman who nodded.

"This man is responsible for the damage to my car."

"Whoa," said Gil spreading his hands in a calming motion. "I don't know where she got that idea."

"Listen, ma'am," said the cop. "Maybe you should file a report at the police station. Someone can help you out down there." He inspected the car. "You shouldn't be driving with limited visibility."

Carol wanted to holler that he was the one with limited visibility if he couldn't see what was happening here right under his nose, but Johnny had taught her to be deferential to cops, always. "I'm on my way to the garage, anyway. I'll drive right there." She glared at Gil who widened his eyes at her and draped an arm around the waitress.

"And, officer?" Carol worked to keep her voice pleasant. "The reason I'm going to the garage in the first place is to pick up my husband's truck which has had the windshield smashed twice recently. I don't think it's a coincidence. It's him."

The waitress laid her head on Gil's shoulder, and Carol noticed how tall she was. No feelings showed in the girl's face. Carol wondered if the she knew anything about the vandalism, Ivy and her bruises, or Mac. She wanted to order the girl into the car and warn her. At the same time she knew that this heedless girlfriend would do more to keep Gil away from their family than the restraining order.

The policeman was listening now. He looked questioningly at Gil who gave an elaborate shrug. "File a report," he repeated. "We'll be watching you," he said to Gil.

"Talk to Mike Kelly." Carol's voice quavered. "Talk to any other cop. They already are watching him."

Like a valet, the officer held her car door open. "Okay ma'am. Drive carefully, now."

Carol collapsed into her car. The blast of the foundry whistle told her she was late to meet Neal. She panicked when she couldn't find her keys in her purse or pockets, then realized they were still in the ignition. The dinging warning signal hadn't even registered. Or maybe that was broken too.

As she pulled out into the row of cars leaving the foundry she glanced in the rearview mirror to see Gil laugh, pull the red-haired girl close, and enfold her in a hug. Carol winced. Thank God Ivy wasn't with him anymore. She slammed on her brakes to avoid crashing into the car in front of her waiting to make a left turn. The driver, without turning around, gave her the finger. If that stranger knew how crazy she felt, how capable of using her car as a deadly weapon, he wouldn't be gesturing that way. People should be more careful. Johnny used to say that, used to tell her she didn't know all he carried around inside him or she wouldn't provoke him by expecting so much.

The line of traffic progressed across the bridge and thinned out. She made her way up the hill to the high school, mouth dry, face tight, needing to see Neal and knowing he'd have found a ride to the garage with someone by now if he had any sense. She parked haphazardly in the empty teachers' lot. The doors were locked.

She peered in the nearest window, the guidance office. Carol remembered sitting there at the end of Ivy's freshman year when she'd been called in to discuss her daughter's "academic performance." According to the high scores on the standardized tests, Ivy should be doing far better than the C's and D's she was earning in class.

"Ivy hates school," Carol had explained. "Her father was killed while building it. Maybe it has to do with that."

"Well, she's certainly limiting her options with this grade point average. Her teachers report she rarely does her homework. Perhaps you're not providing the structure she needs at home."

The poster on the wall behind Miss, never Ms., Worthington's perfectly coifed head was still there—a photo of a basset hound's droopy face and in a flowery script the quote, "When life gives you lemons, make lemonade." Carol remembered thinking that for lemonade you also need sugar, not to mention water, a pitcher, ice, glasses, the energy to stir it, someone to drink it with, a place to sit and put your feet up.

Carol was about to bang on the door one last time when Neal rushed out, breathless and red-faced. "I tried calling you," he said. "They told me you left. I kept checking the parking lot, and going back to the phone. Then I thought you might be waiting in front. Where have you been?"

"I could have killed him, Neal," Carol whispered. She glanced over her shoulder to be sure no one was near. The expanse of concrete steps, parking lot, and playing field were deserted.

Neal didn't ask who she meant.

"I could've killed him, too," he said. They stood face to face about a foot apart. "That day with the wrench. I was lucky he was taller, stronger, and younger than I am. Are you okay? Did he come into the bank?"

"No." Suddenly she couldn't bear the space between them. She wrapped her arms around his waist and squeezed. The stack of manila folders he'd been holding fell to the ground. They held each other tight. "He smashed my windshield too," she said.

"I called the garage." Neal said, his breath warm against her neck. "Tony was leaving, but he said to just take the truck and pay him tomorrow. We'll leave your car there."

"What are we going to do?" Carol asked. A paper blew free of a top folder and skittered across the steps.

"We're going to get through this," he said. She allowed herself to relax into him, to rest her head against his sweat soaked shirt and breathe his salty, woody smell. His beard rubbed her temple and cheek. She imagined it polishing her skin, smoothing her sharp edges.

Ivy punched in a song on the jukebox. "Crazy ..." Patsy Cline's mournful wail ripped through the empty pool hall. The Friday rush would start soon. She loved coming into work after a day at home with Mac, handing him over to Bryan. It was mid-October, over a month since Gil had smashed Carol's windshield, and he hadn't done anything else. She still looked over her shoulder and avoided the River Restaurant. Everyone said he had a new girlfriend. She'd heard he was planning to leave town. Ivy had seen them together once late at night holding hands as they walked along the edge of River Road, when Curly drove her home. Bryan mentioned seeing them on the bench by the monument passing an aluminum pan of restaurant leftovers back and forth.

Ivy began her trips to the back room to restock the refrigerator with beer, singing along with Patsy ... crazy for loving you. Craziness explained the twinges of disappointment that Gil had let her go more easily than she expected or why she'd been with him in the first place. Craziness explained a lot of things.

"Ivy," Curly slammed the cash drawer. "We could use some more change. I'll be back in twenty minutes. Unless you want to go."

"No." She checked the clock. "I'll manage here. You should make it back before the crowd." The door banged behind him. Bottles clanked in her arms and rattled as she arranged them in neat rows.

The song ended, the jukebox clicked and stopped. Too quiet. She fumbled in her apron pocket for more quarters. Coins warm in her hand she heard the door creak open. She stared openmouthed as the change fell from her fingers back into her pocket. Gil. Freshly shaved, with a haircut, low slung jeans, gray tee shirt clinging to his chest and muscled arms. Her heart pounded. He glared in her direction, then smiled. She folded her arms under her breasts. *Call the police*, she told herself. *He's not supposed to be near you.*

"Give me a beer," he said, sliding onto a bar stool.

She stayed where she was.

He glanced around the room. Nodding, as if satisfied no one lurked in the corners, ready to challenge his presence, he leaned against the bar, stretching out his legs.

"How you been?" he asked.

Ivy shrugged, not trusting her voice. All these weeks, imagining the moment they'd see each other again, his pleading with her to come back, herself standing firm, imagining his threats, the terror in her throat, and here he was. All she felt was wobbly and slow.

"What about my beer?" He smiled.

She moved carefully, not trusting her unsteady knees to carry her. She was finished with this guy. Finished.

She opened a Bud. She didn't have to ask what kind he wanted. He took a swig, poked at the label. "So …"

Ivy waited clutching the damp rag she used to wipe the bar.

"Came by to ask you to come back to me," Gil said. "Last chance. If you're not coming back to me, I'm leaving."

Leaving. "Where to?" she asked.

"California, this time. Fuck Florida." He finished his beer in a long swallow.

Gil looked good, sitting there on the other side of the bar, wanting her. She pinched earlobe, felt scar tissue. "No, Gil. It's over." She flinched, waiting for his reaction.

"Okay." He lit a cigarette, inhaled. "Thought because of the kid and all I'd give you one last chance." His words came out in a cloud of smoke.

The kid, Mac. Growing up in Rivertown where everyone knew his unhappy beginnings.

Ivy shook her head.

"How about one last game then?" Gil glanced at the clock.

"No." She wanted him to go. He kept staring at the clock behind her as if waiting for something. Muscles in her neck and shoulders, stiff with fear, reminded her why she'd left him, why she wouldn't go back. "Curly should be here soon," she said.

"You won't play with me?" he wheedled. "For old time's sake. Ivy, that night we met, I never felt that kind of love. You'll always be part of me." He looked from the clock to the door and back again. Was he worried about Curly? Why didn't he leave? She cut limes, glad of the knife in her hand, as small as it was.

The door opened. The tall, slim woman she'd seen him with stepped in, wearing jeans and a sweatshirt, her red hair pulled back in a loose ponytail.

Gil leaped up. "Hey!" The woman smiled, a generous, tooth-filled smile.

"This here beauty is Jennifer." Gil grinned at Ivy. "Take a load off, baby, have a beer." She perched on the stool next to Gil. He wrapped his arms around her waist, pulling her to him. Ivy's heart thumped. He'd been waiting for this woman the whole time. What if Ivy had said she'd come back to him? Would he have laughed in her face? Or would he have told Jennifer, forget it? "Single-handedly, this woman pulled me up from the depths of despair. The trash heap." He kissed her long neck through the ponytail. "Angel, this is Ivy."

Angel. Ivy had been his angel, the one who saved him. Nothing in Jennifer's smooth, scrubbed face, acknowledged the presence of an ex-girlfriend, the mother of her new boyfriend's child. Rivertown was not a big place. She had to know that Gil was violent, that he had a kid. Ivy wanted to ask why she was with him. Did she think he could change? Did she think she could change him? Was she afraid to be alone? So many questions. "What kind of beer you want?" she asked her.

"None for me," Jennifer said.

"Budweiser," Gil winked at Ivy.

She set a bottle down in front of him. Beer foamed up through the neck of the bottle, spilling onto the bar. Ivy wiped it up.

"Where's hers?" Gil asked.

Ivy said carefully, "She doesn't want one." She squeezed the beer soaked rag, staring him right in the eyes. Gil scowled. All their months together rolled into a single dense moment.

"Bitch," Ivy thought she heard him breathe.

A nervous giggle from Jennifer. "Oh, I might as well have one."

Gil beamed approval. Ivy opened another bottle, glad she was on her side of the bar. Gil stood, stretching his arms high over his head, his back muscles rippling under his tee shirt. Curly was taking a long time. If he were here Gil wouldn't be winking and lounging and showing off his body. Curly would throw him out. Gil strode over to the juke box.

"This song's for you," he said, crossing back to the bar.

Which one of us? Ivy had time to think before the first notes of "Help Me Make it Through the Night" hit the air.

"I love this song," Jennifer said.

Gil slammed his hand on the bar. Ivy winced, remembering the force of it against her cheek. Jennifer sipped at her beer and licked foam from her lip with the tip of the tongue that kissed Gil, that licked the secret places on his body where Ivy's tongue had been.

"You know," he said, staring at a spot on the wall over Ivy's head. "I'd ask about my son, if I had one. But when you sleep with sluts and they tell you their brats are yours, so's they can nail you with child support for the rest of your life, you know better than to believe it. So I have no son to ask about. Understand me?" His eyes glinted.

And Mac has no father, Ivy wanted to spit back.

Jennifer's eyebrows knitted together, her eyes full of questions now.

"Jennifer's brother rents roller blades in Venice Beach. He's expanding his business, wants to make Jennifer and me partners, right Jen?"

"Well, he's been asking me …"

"So we're heading out there," Gil interrupted. "Jennifer's got the tickets in her bag. California, here we come. Tomorrow we're out of here." He squeezed Jennifer's knee and planted another kiss on her neck. "Show her the tickets, Jen." Jennifer laid them on the bar. Gil flapped them so close to Ivy's face she felt the breeze. "No coming back to Rivertown this time. No reason to come back here. It's cold. No decent jobs. Unfriendly people. Bitchy women." Jennifer tensed. "Not you, sweetie." Gil pulled her close, slipped the tickets back into her purse.

"Good luck," Ivy said, handing Jennifer a bag of potato chips. Jennifer forced a smile, setting the bag on the bar as if she was allergic to it. She shifted on her stool, glancing toward the door.

Gil ripped the bag open and began to eat. "Thanks," he said.

Ivy wondered what he'd do when Jennifer dumped him, when the roller blade renting brother ran him out of town. She hoped he knew better than to come back. If he ever did, she had her family, Curly, and the law.

"That sounds good," she said. "I hope you … I hope you're really happy."

"I'm happy," he said. "I'm very fuckin' happy." He played with Jennifer's ponytail. "I've never felt this good. Never."

Ivy crushed the empty potato chip bag and turning her back to Gil, threw it away.

"So, sure you won't shoot one last game?" Gil slid off the stool. "Ivy and I used to play now and then," he said to Jennifer. "In fact, we met, right here. Remember that night, Ivy?"

"I kicked your ass," Ivy said.

"Yeah. You did," he admitted.

"And I'm a stronger player now. I've been practicing. You wouldn't have a chance."

He frowned. "I always have a chance."

"Do you play?" Ivy asked Jennifer.

"A little."

"You two go ahead." Ivy said. "I'm working. Got to finish setting up here before the crowds. Want another beer?"

"Does a bear shit in the woods?" Gil laughed. Ivy handed him a cold bottle.

"We could all play—cutthroat." He grinned.

"No thanks." Ivy wiped the bar.

"You sure you don't want to give me one last chance to beat you?" Gil asked, then hearing what he'd said, slugged his beer, avoiding Ivy's steady gaze. "Come on, Jen." He wiped his mouth with the back of his hand and chose two cue sticks from the rack.

"Eight ball's my game," he told her. "You know how it works?"

Jennifer smiled. "I've played before." They claimed a table.

People trickled in. Ivy waited on them and avoided watching Gil and Jennifer, their shots, their kisses, or hearing her giggles, his deep laugh. She wondered how many pictures he'd drawn of Jennifer. Had he come up to her after a long night at the restaurant with her likeness on a napkin? She didn't take the game seriously. She wasn't very good. Gil could win easily.

Curly burst through the door clutching the money bag. "Sorry, took forever. Friday afternoon is not the time to go to the …" He stopped, noticing Gil, threw Ivy a concerned look.

"Gil came to say good-bye," Ivy said. "He's leaving after this game." Her words rang out over the conversation, the music, the scraping of chairs.

Gil paused, midstroke. For one charged moment he and Curly glared at each other. Curly broke away to dump the money into the cash register.

"You okay?" Curly whispered. Ivy nodded. "He's not supposed to be here. We can get him arrested."

"He's leaving," Ivy said. She was okay. Gil stood a half a room away, his hand on a gorgeous woman's thigh and Ivy was glad it wasn't on hers. She ducked behind the bar to grab some glasses. Curly ducked down beside her. "Should I throw him out? Call the cops?"

"He'll leave. He has a plane ticket for California," Ivy said. "Let him go. He's finished with me."

"Glad to hear it," Curly muttered.

"And I'm finished with him," Ivy straightened up.

"God damn it!" Gil hollered. Curly laid a hand on Ivy's arm. "One ball left and I sink the god damn eight ball. Fuck." He kicked the table. Ivy's heart jumped.

"Come on, Jennifer, let's go." Gil threw his cue stick onto the table. Jennifer laid hers beside it. She'd won but she wasn't smiling. She followed as Gil approached the bar, hands spread in front of him as if motioning Ivy and Curly to take it easy. He leaned over, grabbing Ivy's hand, his mouth near her ear.

"I owe you nothing. Understand me?"

Ivy nodded. She wondered if she should bring up Mac's name, to have Gil deny him in front of Curly, another witness. Instead she said, "I understand." Maybe she should have stopped with that. "You owe for the beers though."

"I know that," Gil said groping in his pocket. "You think I'd stiff you?" He slapped a twenty down on the bar. Ivy got change from the register, counted it into his waiting hand. His fingers handcuffed her wrist. He pulled her against the bar and stuffed the change into her shirt pocket. His chest heaved up and down. Curly stood behind her. Jennifer watched, pulling at her lip.

Ivy jerked her arm away from Gil, rubbing her reddened skin, staring into his frantic blue eyes. Gil, afraid and not knowing it, a dangerous combination. Better to know your own terror. She knew hers. She wanted to find the words to keep him away forever. She stared without flinching until he turned away.

"Come on, Jen."

Ivy watched him go. He slammed the door so hard it shivered on its rusty hinges. A man at the end of the bar called for another beer. Curly served him and the other three guys, then came to stand beside her.

"I'm lucky," she whispered to Curly at the cash register. "So, so, so lucky."

"It's not just luck," Curly said, back to the bar. "You're tough." Tough. She'd heard that before. Celine had said it. Tough. Survivor.

The pool hall filled with people, music, smoke. Ivy served, no time for games. Finally, Curly shut down the jukebox, turned up the lights, ushered the last few customers to the door, and locked up. He sat at the bar, swung his short legs onto the stool beside him, and looked around the room.

"I can clean up in the morning," he said. "Sometimes it's better to put off until tomorrow things you could do today. I'll take you home. You don't look so hot."

Home. She'd screwed up, but she still had a place to live. She still had her family. So did Mac.

"Get your things," Curly said.

She followed him to his car. "It'll take you forever to clean up," she said, voice weak.

"Come in a little early tomorrow and help if you're so worried about it."

He opened her door and dumped the pile of junk on the seat into the back. He wedged a box onto the floor of the front seat. "Try not to step hard on that." Red in the face he extricated himself, rebuttoned the button that had popped open on his shirt.

"What's in there?" she asked, more for something to say than because she really cared.

"In the box?"

"Yeah." She leaned against the open car door. He looked embarrassed.

"That's okay," Ivy said. "You don't have to tell me, but now I'm dying to know."

"I'll tell you." Curly cleared his throat, circled the car, and slid into the driver's seat. Ivy buckled up beside him. "Bad habit of mine."

Ivy imagined drugs, sex toys, Oreos bought in bulk.

"You know how in the middle of winter they send those flower catalogs? Every year I order more than I can plant."

"You have a garden?" He didn't seem like the gardening type.

"Back of my house. I'll show you sometime if you want."

"So, what's in the box?"

"Bulbs. A few of everything." He pulled out of the parking lot. Ivy rested her feet lightly on the box. It filled the entire floor.

"You want them?" Curly asked.

"Me? Gardening?" Ivy frowned. "I don't know. The only plant I ever had, I killed." Bryan's venus fly trap, after one meal of hamburger it had shriveled and died.

"You should try it. Relaxing as hell." He took the curves in the River Road as if they were imprinted on a map in his brain. "What about your mother? There's a woman who needs to relax. Give them to her. A peace offering."

"She's too busy," Ivy said. "Who's Lisa?" She'd been wanting to ask. "Mom just said she was some girl and no matter how I pushed, that's all she'd say."

"She's right. Exactly right. Lisa. Just some girl your dad went out with for a while. Before your mother came to town."

"What was so great about her?"

Curly hit the steering wheel. "Nothing! Nothing! I just wanted to get to your Mom. John and Lisa had broken up ages before. She was just the first woman he hooked up with after coming back from Nam."

"Why did you want to get to my Mom? Why didn't you like her?"

He checked the rearview mirror. "It wasn't that I didn't like her. She didn't like me. For a lot of reasons, I guess."

At a stop sign Curly leaned his head back against the seat and closed his eyes.

"I offered to buy his motorcycle when it looked like she wanted him to give it up. He gave it to me. I tried and tried and tried, for years, to pay him, but he wouldn't take my money. Your parents could have used the cash and your mom blamed me. I tried giving it to her. Made more trouble. John mad at her. Her mad at me. John mad at me. I got fed up with both of them. Then the night before he died he came in, back to the pool hall. Can you imagine? After two long years, the best player in the valley." Ivy could imagine. Exactly. "We were all glad to see him. Everybody buying him drinks. Lining up for a game. He was my best friend. I'd missed him. So I get him home and there's Carol all pinched faced and mad, blocking the door. I didn't bother trying to see things from her point of view. I made a mess with my big mouth. For a little lady your mother can carry a big, heavy grudge." He shrugged. "Everybody has reasons for how they feel and what they do. I shouldn't have said what I said but if he hadn't died …"

"She's happy with Neal." Ivy didn't know if she was defending her mother or telling Curly not to feel bad.

"Well I'm happy for her." A car honked behind them. Curly pressed the accelerator.

"Ha."

"No, really. She's had a tough time of it. Losing John when you kids were so small. I see that now. It was tough for all of you. All of us."

His silence wrapped around Ivy and held her. He stopped in front of her house.

"Did my father ever talk to you about the war?"

Curly shook his head. "Carol asked me that too. He never talked to anybody as far I knew. Shot pool instead."

She shifted her feet on the box. "Is it hard, planting bulbs?"

"Hell of a lot easier than raising a kid." He laughed. "You dig a hole, you put the bulb in, you cover it. In the spring, you have flowers."

"Thanks for the ride." Ivy opened the car door, and with her feet on the ground, twisted to lift the box. She tucked it under her arm and waved good night.

The food section of the morning paper featured pumpkin recipes. Bryan read one for pie aloud to Neal and Carol, who sat at the table skimming the arts and leisure pages and sipping coffee. People should know better than to make a pumpkin pie with maple syrup. The maple flavor would dominate everything else. "I would never make pie like that," he said aloud. Mac, in his Jolly Jumper, bounced in the doorway.

"Doesn't anyone have anything to do around here?" Ivy appeared carrying a cardboard box.

"You're welcome for letting you sleep late," Bryan said. The recipe after the pie looked interesting—orange pumpkin bread, but it called for nuts. Martine hated them, said they made her sick. He could leave them out.

Ivy dropped the box onto the table. "Okay," she said. "Thanks for letting me sleep in."

"MaaMaa," Mac yelled.

Bryan tore out the recipe. He'd probably never make it; he rarely tried new things. People liked the old ones so why take chances?

"So, doesn't anyone have anything to do?" Ivy said again.

"It's Saturday," said Neal. "Give me a break. In an hour I'll be nailing up sheet rock." He had toast crumbs in his beard. "What's in the box?"

Ivy lifted Mac out of the Jolly Jumper. "Bulbs."

"Light bulbs?" Bryan peeked under a cardboard flap. "Oh. Like for flowers?"

Ivy settled Mac on her hip and poured some coffee. "What's wrong with flowers?"

"Nothing." Bryan picked up a bulb, flakes of papery, brown skin falling from it. "There's nothing wrong with flowers as far as I know. You bought these?"

"A present," Ivy said.

"From who?" Carol dropped her newspaper.

"Gil's gone, Mom," Ivy said. "Don't worry." Mac squirmed. "He's gone, really. He has a new girlfriend. Off to California."

Bryan reimagined Gil and the girlfriend on the bench, Gil shrinking under Bryan's threatening gaze, quaking when Bryan said, "If I see you anywhere near my sister or my nephew, you're history."

"You sure he's not just dreaming?" Carol asked. "Feeding you a line? How's he going to get to California?"

"I saw the tickets. He and the girl, Jennifer, came into the pool hall yesterday, to say good-bye. Why she's with him I don't know."

"Well," Neal said. "This is very good news."

Bryan rubbed at the newsprint on his fingers, relieved Gil was gone, disappointed he'd done nothing to make it happen.

"Men like him ..." Carol began.

"Mom, he's got someone else now," Ivy said, shoulders slumping, looking almost sad for moment. "California is far away."

Mac grabbed for a piece of toast and started tearing it into pieces he dropped onto the floor.

"He doesn't want the responsibility of a kid," Ivy continued. "He made that clear. That'll keep him away. He's afraid he'll have to give me money."

"Did you know the circus is in New Haven this weekend?" Typical Neal, jumping from big worries to circuses in a heartbeat. "Do you think Mac would like it?"

"He's too young yet," Carol said, picking up Mac's crumbs. "Wait a couple of years."

"I think he'd like it," Bryan said handing Mac another slice of toast. "I remember liking it." But thinking back, he'd liked it because he was supposed to. He fingered the bull dog charm he'd hung on a chain around his neck and realized he no longer fiddled with his harmonica.

"You were a lot older than Mac is now." Carol stood to clear her plate.

"He couldn't have been too old," Ivy said. "Dad took us, a bunch of times. Doesn't it only come once a year?"

Their father had sat between them, eyes on the trapeze artists, the lion tamers, the clowns. Ivy asked for balloons, popcorn, cotton candy never letting Johnny forget for a moment she was there. He'd sigh, reaching for his wallet. "Me too," Bryan remembered saying. "I want that too." Johnny would reach for his wallet again. Ivy kept her arm near their father's on the armrest, his watch with its stretchy gold band, his wedding ring. Bryan had watched them watch the circus.

"Ivy ate my cotton candy every time," Bryan said. "And he let her."

"You never finished it," Ivy said.

"I wanted to save it. Behind Dad's back you kept sticking your tongue out at me. It was all blue from my cotton candy."

"I'll buy you all the cotton candy you want the next time we go," Ivy said.

"So are we going?" Neal asked. "I'll call for tickets."

"Tonight." Bryan tilted back in his chair. "Let's do it." He'd like it now, pointing things out to Mac, making Ivy feel guilty so she'd buy Bryan the things she owed him.

"Can't," Ivy said. "I've got to work and you're watching Mac, aren't you?"

"We could take him," Bryan said. "Maybe Martine would want to go too."

Carol's fingers shredded the corner of the newspaper. She looked at Ivy. "For weeks after you kids went with your Dad, Ivy would dress up in her bathing suit and crack her jump rope in the air while Bryan leaped through her hula hoop. You both would look at the program until it fell apart."

Bryan remembered the bright pages, stiff and glossy, softening to the feel of worn cloth. Ivy kept it in her room. He had to ask to look at it. "How come you never came with us?" Ivy asked their mother.

"It wasn't easy, with little kids. Your father working all the time. Going out at night. I needed the time alone a lot more than I needed family fun." Carol raised her eyebrows in a can't-you-understand-that look.

"Well, it's time you went to a circus," Neal said, kissing the top of her head. "And I'm delighted to be the man to take you. I'll order tickets now."

Carol squeezed his hand. "Ivy has to work tonight. We can go tomorrow, all of us, together. Martine, too, if she wants."

"I'll ask her." Bryan landed his chair legs on the floor. He didn't know if Martine would think a circus was fun or a waste of time, but he might as well ask and find out.

Neal nodded.

Ivy swallowed a mouthful of coffee and flashed their mother a look of pure gratitude.

"Guess I'll plant some of these now." Ivy tucked the box of bulbs under her arm and held Mac on her hip with the other.

"You never did say who gave them to you," Carol said.

"Curly."

Carol pursed her lips.

"He suggested you take up gardening to relax." Ivy smirked.

Neal laughed. "You have to admit—"

"I don't have to admit anything," Carol interrupted. "He should mind his own business."

"Mom," Ivy said. "He's helped me so much. If it weren't for my job … Never mind. Do we have anything to dig with?" She rummaged through a drawer, clattering silverware, Mac squirming on her hip.

"There's a spade in the garage," Neal said.

Bryan expected Carol to yell at her, to forbid the using of any kitchen utensil in the dirt, but Ivy pulled out a big metal spoon, stood in the doorway brandishing it, and Carol didn't say anything. "That job has been good for you," Carol said finally, as if she just realized it.

"Sure has," Neal smiled. "Nice of him to give us those bulbs too."

"I might as well help plant a few," Bryan said.

"Plant some in the back," said Carol. "In that spot you dug when you were kids."

"Did you hear that?" Neal said. "Don't dig up the lawn."

"Maybe that's the way to make Neal lose his temper," Ivy whispered on the way out the door. "I really would like to see that, just once."

Bryan thought of the smashed cradle and changed the subject. "Remember when we were digging to Indochina and I found that bone? You said it belonged to Elvis Presley."

"I read a lot of Grandma's newspapers that summer." Ivy pressed the rounded tip of the spoon into the ground. "I could see myself on the cover, the headline blaring, 'Seven-year-old girl digs to Indochina with spoon.' Part of me really thought I could make it."

"I saw what you did with that glass collection."

"What?" She flashed a scorching look. "You've been going through my closet? What else did you find?" she asked, eyes hard as old baking chocolate.

"How long did it take you to do all that?"

She seemed to melt a little. "I did most of it while he was in the hospital, before he died. I believed it could save him if I made it right. I just couldn't figure out what right was, what colors, what shapes. I'd surround him first, that felt right, magic circles around his pictures but that didn't seem like enough. It wasn't enough. I ended up gluing and gluing, covering the whole back wall with glass, my hands cut, and he died anyway. I couldn't stand to look at it. Couldn't get rid of it. So I just blocked the whole thing, like it wasn't there, like I'd never done it."

"I had no idea you were making it," Bryan said.

"You were only five."

"You were only seven. Didn't anyone notice your hands were bleeding? Didn't anyone notice you disappeared for hours?"

"Guess not." After a moment she added, "Mom found it later. I thought she'd freak out, but she didn't yell or anything. She left it alone."

Mac sat on the lawn, ripping up clumps of grass. Bryan couldn't remember if their father had cared about the lawn, probably not. Ivy looked so sad. He suddenly understood why Neal tried to cheer everybody up all the time, but Bryan didn't want to be like him, laughing, telling people to look on the bright side, things could be worse, etceteras.

"It's good Gil's gone." As the words left his mouth Bryan wondered if he should have said them.

Ivy dug deeper. "Yeah."

"You don't sound happy about it."

"I am happy. I know it's the best thing. But sad too. For Mac. With no father."

"Better no father than a father like Gil."

Ivy's voice rose. "But I don't even have a picture of him, nothing to show Mac when he's older. It'll be like his father never existed." She jabbed at the dirt. "Maybe you should get the spade. I can hardly break the ground with this spoon."

"I don't know how we dug such a deep hole that summer," Bryan said. "You were really determined. And bossy." Let her try to deny it.

Ivy took a bulb from the box. "I don't even know which way these go. Which end is up?"

"I learned this in science." Bryan held the bulb, turning it in his hand, his mind on the dagger still hidden under his mattress. "Be right back," he told her.

His eyes, used to the bright sun, took awhile to adjust inside. He unwrapped the blade. All those months, he never really thought of it as his. He'd been waiting for Gil to claim it. Now it would be Mac's. Like Johnny's harmonicas belonged to Bryan. His memories of Johnny were vague, just a few of them startlingly clear and odd, like the arm hairs poking through the stretchy gold watchband on the armrest at the circus or his father's squinty-eyed look when Bryan disappointed him. But when he played, he felt Johnny playing along. When he touched the bulldog charm, it was like touching a piece of his dad.

Mac wouldn't remember Gil. All he'd have of his father would be a knife, a weapon. No looks—disappointed or pleased.

Bryan stared down from his window at Mac crawling around, plucking at the grass. Ivy scooped more holes, tucked the bulbs in, patting the dirt on top.

Bryan thought about rewrapping the blade; a weapon was a terrible present to give a child. He could bury it in the yard or in the trash, but it really should be Ivy's and Mac's. She was his mother. She could decide what to do with it.

Bryan brought it out to the yard, feeling heavy inside. Ivy sat back on her heels.

"A letter opener?" she said. "That won't work any better than a spoon. I thought you went to get the spade."

The heaviness burst in Bryan's chest. His face heated up. Letter opener? "It's Gil's," he said. "I took it from his box of things." He didn't tell her he thought it was a dagger. Gil could have hurt her with it anyway. "You could give it to Mac."

"You keep it." Ivy scooped Mac up and jiggled him. "I have no idea where he got it, what it meant to him, if anything."

"You can make something up," Bryan said. "What are you going to tell Mac about Gil? The truth?"

"There are a lot of truths," Ivy said. "I'll tell him as many as I can. You'll tell him some, Curly, Mom, Neal, they'll all have something to say."

Mac struggled to get down. Ivy let him crawl across the lawn.

"I still think Gil could come back," Bryan said. He gripped the pearl handled blade trying to decide if it looked as sharp as it had before.

"I'm telling you," Ivy said. "He doesn't want the responsibility of a son. He made it clear. Mac is mine."

"Ours," Bryan said. "All of ours."

Mac stuffed a fistful of grass in his mouth. Ivy pried his lips apart as he squirmed and turned his head away. "There," she said, dropping the half-chewed, soggy mess, wiping her fingers on her jeans. "You are a lucky baby, you know that?" He grabbed the spoon. In his pudgy, dimpled fist, it looked enormous. "You want to help plant the flowers?"

Ivy knelt beside Bryan, Mac between them. Bryan ducked to avoid his flailing, spoon-wielding arm. Anything could be a weapon, even a spoon in the hands of a baby.

Or not. He loosened the packed earth with the letter opener. Mac stopped waving his arms and scrunched his face in concentration as he prodded the ground. Dirt sprayed into the air. He laughed and tried again, delighted with the growing hole, the flying dirt.

"Look, Ivy," Bryan touched his sister's arm, squinting through the shower of earth. "He already knows how to dig."

Reading Guide

Introduction

Running away isn't hard for Ivy MacKenzie. She's been longing to break free of her small town, her nagging mother, and her tenderhearted brother for as long as she can remember. The hard part for seventeen-year-old Ivy is coming home.

Ever since the death of her father, a Vietnam veteran, Ivy's been looking for a way out of a life she hates and a family she resents. She spends her time at the local pool hall, and it's there she meets Gil Thompson, a stranger only too happy to take her away to Florida, promising flamingos, sunshine, and love. All too quickly, she discovers that Gil's rotten teeth match his rotten temper, and life out on her own isn't what she expected.

Ivy returns to Rivertown but finds her family rearranged. Her mother, Carol, has married the high school shop teacher, Neal Richards, and her brother, Bryan, is more interested in his new girlfriend than he is in her. She needs them all desperately now, even if she won't admit it. She needs them to save her from herself, and to save her from the man who says he loves her but will surely destroy her.

Digging to Indochina beautifully illuminates the complexities that bind family members to each other and deftly explores these most intimate relationships, delving into the consequences of secrets, silences, and the shadows cast by the past.

Discussion questions:

1. What do you think of the title of this novel—*Digging to Indochina*? What does "digging to Indochina" mean to Ivy? Does it mean the same thing to Bryan? Why do you think the author chose this title?

2. The author explores a tangle of relationships between mothers and daughters, mothers and sons, sons and daughters, and also lovers. What distinguishes parental love from romantic love in this novel? Compare the romantic lives of Ivy, Bryan, and Carol.

3. On page 14, Rich says to Ivy, "Don't tell me you're a good girl." In response, Ivy "raised her eyebrows, smiled, feeling shy and pleased. She'd left her mother and brother and taken off for Florida with her father's army duffel bag and a tattooed man she'd met shooting pool. Good girls didn't do that. Good girls didn't sneak out to the pool hall when their mother had strictly forbidden it, make their mother and brother miserable by talking about dead fathers every chance they got, storm around the house when their mother had a date. Good girls had friends and parties and their own date for the prom. She wasn't good, not at all." How does Ivy view "good" girls and "bad" girls? Do you think society has a common view of "good" girls and "bad" girls?

4. How does gender affect the interpersonal relationships of the characters? How is the father-daughter, father-son relationship different than mother-daughter, mother-son? How is the relationship between Ivy and Bryan different with Neal?

5. What role models does Bryan look to in his striving to become a man? He often assumes the role of caretaker or mediator in the family; why do you think he does so? Page 224 reads, "Bryan tore out the recipe. He'd probably never make it; he rarely tried new things. People liked the old ones so why take chances." Is this position reflected in his character? Does it hurt or help him and others in the family?

6. Do you think the author's portrait of a small town is accurate? How would the story have been different if it had taken place in a big city, or in your own community? Can you picture Rivertown and what it would be like to live there?

7.   How do you think Grandma Harrington's reaction to Mac affects the way Ivy and Bryan view Carol? "Lots of hair," Grandma observed. "Make sure you put baby oil on his head. I think I see some cradle cap there. Not a pretty sight—a crusty head like that. Let me go see about my Jell-O mold. I hope it made the trip. Should be okay—I packed plenty of ice. Not ice but those plastic things you freeze. Much better than ice, no melting, avoid all that water ..." She headed for the kitchen. (pp.126–127)

8.   On page 34, Carol reflects, "How stupid she was as a child, thinking parents have all the power. If a daughter could just take it into her head to run away, then the parent had no power at all. None." Ivy and Carol often argue. How does this power struggle damage the two of them and the rest of the family? Neal tries to intervene. Does he help or hurt matters?

9.   Mentioned immediately in the opening line, John is a powerful presence in the book. "Bryan's sister, Ivy, ran off the day after their father's birthday." What is his legacy? Ivy remembers him one way, Bryan another, and Carol still another. How do their feelings and relationships to him change over the course of the book?

10.   All the characters experience loss and go through their own versions of the grieving process. How do the ways they experience grief push them apart and/or bring them together?

11.   Why do you think Ivy is drawn to Gil? What does it take for her to leave an abusive relationship? Why didn't she simply go home after leaving Gil?

12.   Letters and postcards play a significant role in the novel: Ivy's postcards home, Gil's letters from prison, Johnny's letter from Vietnam. Discuss how the author uses these communications and how they affect the characters.

13.   What does the book say about violence?

14.   The novel is told from the perspectives of Ivy, Bryan, and Carol. How does this help you, the reader, understand the dilemmas each character faces? What would be added if the author told part of the story through Neal's eyes?

15.   Carol loses her baby while Ivy's little boy is the picture of health. Why do you think the author introduces a miscarriage? How does it

change the balance of power in the household? Does it change for better or worse?

16. Why is the pool hall so important to Ivy? What does she find there that she can't find at home? And why is Bryan's cooking and baking so important to him?

17. Neal builds things, Bryan cooks, Carol sews, but Ivy only watches TV. What do these activities say about each character?

Interview with Connie Biewald

Author of *Digging to Indochina*

1. Rivertown bears a striking resemblance to your hometown of Ansonia, CT. What was it like growing up there?

    I think the place where you grow up is in your bones, and Ansonia is certainly in mine. In a town like that everyone knows your family, for better and worse. It can feel stifling, no matter how good people's intentions are. I think I needed some degree of anonymity to figure out who I was and who I wanted to be—some freedom from people's limiting expectations. Somehow, maybe because I was a voracious reader from a young age, I was aware of the wider world. I ached to get out and see big cities, oceans, deserts, mountains, meet all kinds of people, have experiences I wasn't going to have in Ansonia, Connecticut.

2. What inspired you to create this story, one that's fueled by so much anger?

    Anger covers hurt and, for many reasons, I was a hurting little girl. My parents had an idea about what a family should be like and what I should be like and when I didn't fit that picture, my mother, in particular, had a hard time dealing with it. I was a feisty little kid from the start, and my mother was very controlling and still hurting from her own childhood wounds. It made for a tough time for both of us.

3. You have a line on page 88 in which Carol reflects, "She had no illusions she could keep her children safe." As the mother of two teenage boys, is that how you feel?

    That is exactly how I feel. The truth is we can't keep anybody safe. The only safety we can create is temporary—emotionally safe spaces in which people feel listened to and seen for who they are. Otherwise safety *is* an illusion. You realize that most vividly when tragedy hits or when you're lying in bed waiting for your teenager to come home. Cell phones help.

4. The intricate family dynamics in *Digging to Indochina* drive the story ever forward. Are there similarities between the MacKenzies and your own family?

There's a definite similarity in the emotional dynamic between Ivy and Carol. I also have a brother who shares some qualities with Bryan. He and I and our spouses share a two family house and have raised all our kids in an extended family situation. The saying, "it takes a village to raise a child," is one of the truest things I know. Neal is a composite of my dad, my husband, and other wonderful men in my life.

5. Speaking of family dynamics, what did *your* mother think of the novel?

My mother read an early draft of the book and hated it. She said no one would ever want to read about such an angry girl. I vowed never to show her anything else I ever wrote. Years passed. My own kids grew older. I began to appreciate some of what my mother went through in raising me. I added Carol's perspective to the book. I grudgingly let my mother read it. She said she wanted to talk to me about it but, still hurt by her earlier response, I put her off several times. Finally I said, "Okay, let's talk." She said simply, "I'm sorry." It meant a lot to me that she appreciated the emotional truth of the book, that she saw how hard our relationship had been for me. I thought it was interesting that when I wrote an angry, Ivy-centered book, my mom couldn't see that, but when I tried to appreciate my mom's point of view and wrote it with some compassion, she was able to have compassion for me.

6. Who is your favorite character in the book? Why?

There are things I like about each of them—even Gil. I like his optimism. I identify most with Ivy. I appreciate angry girls and know how little it takes in many cases to cut through that rage to what's beneath it. I love Bryan's tenderness and how he's relatively unafraid to show it. As a teacher and parent I think a lot about how our society limits what emotions are acceptable for girls or boys to express. In all my reading, I haven't run across too many male characters like Bryan.

7. You're known to have a fondness for pool halls. What is it about them that attracts you? As far as your character Ivy is concerned, is hanging out at the pool hall ultimately a good thing or a bad thing for her?

    Actually it's been awhile since I've spent time hanging out in a pool hall, but I do have positive feelings about them. The whole experience is very sensual—the sounds, the smells. They are easy to romanticize. Think of all the songs and movies and stories inspired by pool halls. There's a feeling of camaraderie, of belonging. And there's a tinge of seediness and adventure that I like—it's not as wholesome as bowling, for example. Ivy likes all that, too. For her it's a connection to her father, a refuge from a home where she feels misunderstood and unappreciated. It's too bad she happened to meet Gil there, but I think she would have met him or someone like him no matter what. She was looking.

8. Which part of the novel did you enjoy writing the most?

    I enjoy the part of the writing process when I'm learning about the characters. I have a sense that they already exist somewhere, and I just have to be quiet and let them talk to me, interact with each other, and show me what to write about them. Of course, I rewrite and rewrite and rewrite after that initial discovery. For me writing is a refreshing escape from real life. I come back to my daily responsibilities refreshed, as if I've been away on a visit.

9. Who are some of your favorite writers and how have they influenced you?

    The authors I love most to read are Tobias Wolff, Alice Munro, Grace Paley, and Alistair Macleod. I've read most of their work aloud with my husband. I love the way they write about relationships. I love their careful use of just the right words. Their dialogue is real, rich, and varied. They write about the ordinary in extraordinary ways. Though they are far better writers than I'll ever be, they inspire me by showing me what great writing is.

10. You're also the author of the novels *Bread and Salt* and *Roses Take Practice*. What themes do they explore? And what are you working on now?

I think a lot of my work touches on people's necessity to create emotionally safe spaces for each other in which healing and growing can happen. Sometimes the people who do this for each other aren't the most obvious pairings. I write about how people who want to be there for each other often don't know how and the pain that causes. I'm interested in the damage done when people aren't appreciated for who they are.

I keep writing about seventeen-year-old girls. That stage of life in which separation and attachment issues loom large fascinates me. Wylie in *Roses Take Practice* and Ivy in *Digging to Indochina* are both desperate to find a way out of their family situations and their town. The sisters in *Bread and Salt* are forced away from home by circumstance.

All three books carry the message "Life is tough, but worth it, at least for moments here and there."

I'm in a strange phase of my writing life. These three novels seemed to always be there waiting to be written. I've spent the last fifteen years working on them, sure I had something to say, those stories to tell, and I just had to do the writing. I've had *Bread and Salt* in my head since I was ten years old! I was intimidated about writing a historical novel so I wrote the other two first, to show myself I could do it.

Right now I have lots of ideas and even a few interesting characters beginning to whisper in my ear, but none is compelling to me the way the characters in these novels were. I'm interested in issues of race and racism and social justice, and whatever I write next will, in some way, explore those topics. I'm considering writing some nonfiction—articles or personal essays about my teaching experiences.

About the Author

Connie Biewald has been passionate about writing since she was five years old. She is a teacher, a librarian, and a Growth Education resource person at the Fayerweather Street School in Cambridge, Massachusetts. In her Growth Ed role, Connie works with children, parents, and other teachers to explore the essential topics of human development, self-esteem, the use and misuse of power, altruism and community service, sexuality, and the appreciation and understanding of differences. This work is strongly reflected in her writing.

Connie has two other novels, *Bread and Salt* and *Roses take Practice*, also published by iUniverse. She is the recipient of a Massachusetts Cultural Council artist grant and a PEN New England Discovery Award. Connie is the mother of two teenage sons and is a wicked pool player herself.

978-1-58348-546-0
1-58348-546-5

Printed in the United States
56485LVS00002B/295-312